THIRTEEN STORIES OF HORROR

Volume 1

Edited by

Nick Steverson & Marisa Wolf

Three Ravens Publishing
Chickamauga, GA USA

Thirteen Stories of Horror: Volume 1
Is a collective work of contributing authors and Published by Three Ravens Publishing
threeravenspublishing@gmail.com
P O Box 851, Chickamauga, Ga 30707
https://www.threeravenspublishing.com

Table of Contents

From the Apartment Manager:

"Welcome, welcome! Please, come in, come in, don't be shy. It's a dreadful night out there, wouldn't you say? Much better inside. So happy you took an interest in renting one of the floors in our fine establishment. We so rarely have any vacancies. Quite lucky, you are. It seems as though once they move in, our residents just stay forever."

"Well, enough of my rambling on and on. I'm sure you're eager to see your final resting place. Come, come, follow me and I'll show you the way. We'll take it one story at a time, for each one has its own unique quality, almost a life of its own."

Unclean Hands by Dave Butler

Hiram looked left, right, and across the street. The Fulton home sat on a two-acre lot at the edge of town, its neighbors all on similarly-sized lots. The nearest homes were yellow dots in the dark night, and Grand Junction was a swarm of such dots, farther away.

The police car parked in front of the Fultons' home was an ominous sign of what Bishop Parker had warned Hiram might lie within, but the neighbors seemed blissfully unaware.

Lightning flashed out in the desert, and Hiram felt a fleck of moisture on one cheek.

He climbed the brick steps of the bungalow, feet heavy and slow. All the lights inside were on, suffusing yellow illumination into the warm August night through every gauze-curtained window. The curtains were thick enough to hide the details of furniture and occupants from casual inspection.

On the porch, Hiram detected the smell of blood.

Blood and worse. The stenches of death were low and humiliating. Mankind was made in the image of God, male and female, but when mankind broke down, he smelled like a sewer.

It being Sunday, Hiram was not wearing his customary overalls. He'd driven to Grand Junction to place a well and deal with the pinkeye in a small rancher's herd, but he'd known he'd be here over the weekend, so he'd brought Sunday clothes. He was dressed in those clothes now, with a button-up shirt, a skinny black knit tie, and pleated wool trousers. He wore his Redwing Harvesters, having forgotten to bring a pair of Sunday shoes with him, and his fedora rode comfortably on his head.

Because he didn't have on his overalls with their large pockets, he'd left his pistol under the seat in the car. He did have his bloodstone in his pocket, which should warn him of falsehoods. When a person lied in Hiram's presence, he felt a sensation in his thigh like a strong pinch.

Hiram rapped on the door with a single knuckle. It opened to reveal the sagging, jowly face of a man in a tweed sport coat. Despite the heaviness of his face and frame and the general air of fatigue about him, his hair was thick and red, and his skin was unlined. He nodded at Hiram, eyes bleary. "You the war hero? Woolley?"

Hiram took off his hat and shook his head slowly. A dry desert breeze ruffled his thinning hair. "There was nothing heroic about the war or my part in it.

Unclean hands all around. Are you Detective Rogers? Bishop Parker thought you might be able to use some help. He said . . . he thought I might be useful."

"What Mr. Parker described to me was nonsense on stilts." Behind the detective, Hiram saw goldenrod-colored carpet, green plush chairs, and a low, glass table.

"People exaggerate," Hiram said. "And they misunderstand. But I think Bishop Parker thought perhaps I could help you understand the victims a little better. Maybe that would assist you in finding the killer."

"I'm from here," Rogers said. "I know enough about you Mormons to know Mr. Fulton was some kind of cardinal or something."

"He was a patriarch."

"Maybe that's why Parker wants you along. Something extra special I don't know about the other victims?" Rogers asked. "Jack and Martha Green, small farmers? Bill Dunsley, bricklayer?"

Hiram shrugged. "Maybe there was more to them than that. Most people have depths you wouldn't suspect on a casual meeting."

"Parker described dowsing rods and written hexes." Rogers harrumphed. "He said you came out here to fix sick cattle with your charms. You gonna use your magic powers to solve the murders?"

"I don't have magic powers," Hiram said. That was true, though it was at least half an evasion. Hiram had his Grandma Hettie's lore, he knew how things worked. "But someone's going around Grand Junction, killing Mormons. Maybe I can at least help you understand Mormons a little better."

Rogers stepped to one side, and Hiram drifted into the house, settling his hat back onto his head. The smell of blood and feces grew stronger. In the center of the room, lying on the goldenrod carpet like an oversized slug, lay a turd the size and shape of a sweet potato.

"For starters, then," Rogers said, pointing at the potato. "Is that a Mormon thing? Your people shit on the floor?"

Hiram sighed. How much should he explain?

He pivoted slowly as he pondered. A small kitchen adjoined the parlor, with a cellar door beside a cramped pantry. A short hallway punctuated by three doors ran past the kitchen into the back of the house.

"Where are the victims?" he asked.

"In the bedroom at the end of the hall," Rogers said. His face twitched slightly. "You don't want to see them. The killer tied them up facing each other and cut them to pieces slowly."

The detective was right; Hiram had no interest in seeing the crime scene. He'd look anyway, in a minute.

"Older folks?" Hiram asked.

"Seventies." The detective jammed his hands into his trousers pockets and looked at the carpet. "You're not from here."

"Utah," Hiram offered.

The detective nodded at the feces on the floor. "I think that's got to belong to the killer. I think it tells us he's just a complete nut job. Or, maybe, he was on the way out, felt nature running its course, and wasn't quite sure where the toilet was. So he just committed to the deed in the moment."

"Unfortunately, no," Hiram said slowly. "That tells us something entirely different. It tells us that the killer knows some . . . call it arcane lore. And maybe it tells us that he doesn't care if we know he knows. Maybe he's taunting us."

"Arcane lore." Rogers grunted. "Dowsing rods. You think the killer is a wizard."

"It's an old bit of burglar's craft," Hiram said. "Like a hand of glory, but cheaper."

"What's a hand of glory?"

"The hand of a hanged felon, pickled and turned into a candle. Its light makes burglars undetectable. It's an invisibility spell, if you want to think of it like that."

Rogers shook his head. "And crapping on the floor?"

"It's a charm that stops the burglar from being caught."

Rogers raised an eyebrow.

"A person who commits a crime in someone else's house," Hiram explained. "A burglar. If he leaves . . . feces . . . behind, he can't be caught."

"Because he's invisible?"

"He just . . . can't be caught," Hiram said. "It's a charm and it will act to defeat investigation."

Rogers grunted. "We should just give up, then. The man took a shit, so he wins?"

"His charm will act to protect him." Hiram nodded slowly. "How exactly that will play out, we'll see. But we should bear in mind that his hex may cause us to miss things or may make our charms malfunction."

"Nuts," Rogers said. "And also disgusting."

"Some charms leave you with unclean hands," Hiram murmured.

Rogers grunted. "Like you said, unclean hands all around."

Hiram shrugged.

"And you do all these things?" Rogers asked. "Pickled finger-candles, defecating on the carpet?"

"I'm not a burglar, Detective."

Rogers guffawed. "But you know . . . spells."

"I know how a few things work," Hiram admitted. "I know how to dowse a well. I know how to cure cattle of a murrain. But I don't know thieves' charms, or murderers' charms. I don't know how to hurt people with my craft. Grandma . . . the woman who taught me wasn't the sort to use curse dolls or black fasts."

Rogers nodded, chuckling.

"May I look around?" Hiram asked.

"Careful where you step," Rogers said. "I can't swear our perpetrator hasn't left other burglar charms waiting for us."

Hiram forced himself to go to the bedroom first. The victims were still posed where they had been murdered; kneeling opposite the bed from each other, hands tied together across the middle. They were white-haired and wrinkled, a couple whose bodies had already been defeated by time. Their mouths were gagged, and their flesh had been whittled away, one little piece at a time. Gore soaked the comforter, the carpet, the side table, the walls. Blood was spattered on the ceiling.

Hiram fought back the urge to vomit, then sat on a white-painted wooden chair in the corner and contemplated his options. Until there was a suspect, none of the usual divination tools would be useful. An Eye of Abraham required that the suspect be brought into the presence of the written charm, which would cause his eyes to water. If the murderer came into the presence of his victim, the wounds would open and bleed again, but that again would require Hiram to identify the murderer first. Sieve and shears and clay balls and other techniques needed a list of suspects for the divining tool to choose from.

And any of these might be thwarted by the criminal's defensive charm.

But the bodies of Jack and Martha Green and Bill Dunsley had been mutilated, too. Their bishop, Bishop Parker, had asked Hiram to look into the murders, and Rogers's superiors had agreed, out of respect to the bishop, to let Hiram tag along.

As long as he didn't get in the way.

One wall of the bedroom held a painting of a mountain landscape, two streams cutting across a meadow beneath gray cliffs. Another held Indian Paintbrush neatly pressed between sheets of glass.

Who would want to kill such a couple, and why?

But the Greens had been equally harmless, an innocuous old couple who kept goats and chickens and rented out their pastures to their neighbors who owned horses. They'd stopped going to church a couple of decades earlier, but no one had any grievance against them.

And Bill Dunsley was beloved by his neighbors for all the free work he'd done for them over the years. Half of them remembered him from when he'd been bishop, as a younger man.

Hiram stood, and then the sight of the side table arrested him. Blood spattered across the dark-stained wood, but the spatter ended crisply at a straight line. A straight line intersecting another straight line, that together suggested a rectangular object had been lying on the side table when the blood had been sprayed across the top of it.

What rectangular object was that, and where had it gone?

He searched the bedroom, looking for a book-sized and -shaped object, and found none. He saw nothing else that gave him any sense of who the killer might have been.

In the hallway, he met Rogers again, who followed him as he explored the rest of the house. The bathroom was neatly-tiled and clean, reinforcing Hiram's view that the turd on the parlor floor was an act of magical craft.

The remaining doorway in the hall opened into a study. A wide desk sat beneath floor-to-ceiling bookcases. The bookcases were full of ledgers and document boxes, and a single ledger lay on the desk, beside a sharp letter-opener, a little blade only three inches long.

Hiram picked up the ledger on the desk; it was too large to be the rectangular object he was looking for and wasn't marked with blood at all.

"What is this?" Rogers squinted at the bookcases. "Some kind of record being kept here? I thought he was a glazier, but these look like the shelves of an accountant or . . . something. Is this about the cardinal thing?"

"Brother Fulton was the Stake Patriarch," Hiram said.

"So he kept records?"

"You know your Bible, Detective?"

"Vaguely," Rogers said. "Let's assume yes, and when I stop understanding what you tell me, I'll push for detail."

"At the end of the Book of Genesis," Hiram said, "Jacob blesses his sons."

"I don't remember that part specifically."

"Zebulun shall dwell at the haven of the sea," Hiram recited, "and he shall be for an haven of ships; and his border shall be unto Zidon."

"You memorize the whole Bible?" Rogers asked. "Or just the exciting bits about being 'an haven for ships'?"

"Large chunks of it," Hiram admitted. "Jacob's other blessings tend to be longer, that's just a short one for an example."

"Thanks for sparing me."

"The blessings are little personal prophecies. They tell each of his sons about their descendants' future. For instance, that Judah would be the royal tribe. Joseph's descendants would be scattered far and wide, that sort of thing. Jacob, as patriarch of his family, gave a special blessing to all his sons. Customized prophecy, each son got his own personal bit of scripture."

"I get it," Rogers said. "This is all ringing a vague bell. Maybe I heard of this sort of thing as a kid. But so what?"

"In Mormon tradition, a father can still do the same thing for his children. But also, a stake . . . think of that like a diocese . . . will have a man whose calling is to be the patriarch. So young people can go to him, and he gives them their own personal bit of scripture. A little prophecy for them to help through life. It's called a 'patriarchal blessing.' In fact, one of the things it does is give a person a tribe of Israel to . . . belong to."

"Jesus," Rogers said. "You Mormons."

"Yeah," Hiram said.

Rogers waved an arm at the bookshelves. "So all this is prophecies?"

"So to speak," Hiram agreed. "Personal prophecies, customized guidance. Each one not of special interest to anyone other than the person it's directed to, mind you."

Rogers took a box down from the shelf, opened it, and raised the top document to reading distance. "'You are of the lineage of Ephraim,'" he read. "'You will labor at the work of Ephraim. You will fear the Lord your God all your days.' Good grief, how is this of interest even to that one person?"

Hiram shrugged. "Everyone craves identity. And direction."

"Is nobody worried that this kind of thing takes away their free will?" Rogers asked. "Or pushes them in a certain direction?"

"You mean, if you get a patriarchal blessing that tells you to become a carpenter, does that sort of force you to become one?"

"Something like that," Rogers muttered.

Hiram considered. "I guess free will's a problem for everyone, whether you get a patriarchal blessing or not. People don't stop going to psychics, or getting their horoscopes read, out of fear of losing their free will."

"You get a blessing when you were a young man?" Rogers looked sidelong at Hiram.

Hiram nodded.

"What did it tell you?" Did Rogers look envious?

Hiram shook his head. "Personal things. Things of interest to no one else but me."

The patriarch of his own stake, old Brother Call, had told him that he'd have a gift for understanding how God's creation worked and how to get things done. That he would see things that others could never see. Grandma Hettie had sat in the cramped living room in Pleasant Grove to listen to the blessing while Brother Call gripped Hiram's skull tightly with both hands.

That very night, she'd begun to teach Hiram her craft.

Rogers put the box back. "So young people came to Patriarch Fulton, and he'd give 'em a little blessing, what, about a page and a half long, and type it up. And it looks like he kept copies."

Hiram nodded.

"That's a lot of blessings," Rogers said. "This guy's been in office too long."

"He wasn't a politician," Hiram demurred. "Some jobs, you find the guy who has the gift for it, and you leave him there to do good as long as he can."

Rogers shrugged.

"He probably gave copies of the blessings to the young people, too. Scripture's no good if you can't refer back to it."

"You ever get weird blessings?" Rogers asked.

"I guess a lot of them are pretty similar," Hiram said. "I suppose because people's lives are pretty similar, and most of us need basically the same advice everyone else needs. But once in a while, yea, you see something unusual."

"I remember now," Rogers said. "As a kid, I heard a story."

"About patriarchal blessings?"

Rogers nodded. "I know a fellow who said his cousin had just had a blessing. I don't remember that he told me the name of it, but I think it's got to be one of these."

"Probably," Hiram conceded. "Though we do other kinds of blessings, too."

"You Mormons."

"Yeah."

"But the cousin's simple, see? An idiot. And in the blessing, he gets told that Satan was cast out of Heaven by four angels, and this kid is one of those angels. And Satan really wants revenge on this kid, so now the kid's come down to Earth, to protect him, the Lord made him simple-minded."

Hiram nodded, trying to ignore the sickly smell of blood.

"Not clear how being simple-minded protects anyone, of course."

"Maybe it stops him from being tempted," Hiram said. "Takes away the burden of choice. The simple-minded are like children; they don't really have sin like the rest of us do."

"Yeah, maybe." Rogers grunted. "Free ride to Heaven for idiots. You ever hear of any weird blessings like that?"

"Not quite like that, no."

Rogers turned to look around the office. "If these boxes were full of bearer bonds or bank account details, then I'd say you probably found a motive for the murders." He shook his head. "But this stuff . . ."

Hiram flipped through the pages of the ledger. It was an appointment book, with preprinted dates for the year 1925, and appointments noted at the bank, the barber, and other businesses. Sundays were dense with church meeting times, and many afternoon and evening appointments were simply annotated as full names with an asterisk beside them. Sometimes the meetings were memorialized with a family name and a note on the identity of the relevant child: Thueson girl or youngest Everett son.

Probably appointments made by people who wanted to come to the patriarch for a blessing.

He closed the ledger and it felt wrong. Loose.

Holding the leather book up, still closed, he looked at the top of its pages. He saw a tiny gap, an irregularity.

Opening the volume again, he rifled through, looking for the gap. He found it easily.

Today's page, and the pages for the three previous days, were missing. They'd been torn from the volume, leaving just paper stubble in the spine of the book.

"What are you seeing?" Rogers asked.

"Today's page has been torn out," Hiram said. "Odd."

"Not odd at all," Rogers told him, "if the killer had an appointment with Mr. Fulton, and wanted to hide that fact."

"Pretty dark to think that Fulton had an appointment in his calendar, and it turned out to be with his murderer."

Rogers raised his hands. "Just a hypothesis."

"Why not take the whole book?"

Rogers shrugged. "Maybe it seemed less conspicuous just to take the pages. More likely to escape notice."

The suggestion bothered Hiram, but he couldn't quite think why. He turned his attention more closely to the shelves. The ledgers were desk book calendars, and the document boxes had dates written on their spines in neat ink lettering. They were in order, so Hiram easily found the current box.

It contained typed blessing transcripts, also in chronological order. In addition to the words of the blessing, each document had a year and a sequential number typed at the bottom of the last page, forming a kind of chain of serial numbers: 1925-009, 1925-010, and so on. At the top of the blessing, the name of the person receiving the blessing was typed, along with the names of other people in attendance: parents, generally. The most recent blessing was a week old.

"What are you thinking, Woolley?" Rogers asked.

"I don't know," Hiram admitted. "So far, I'm just thinking."

Long moments passed in silence.

"I need to look at the bodies," Hiram said. "At their hands."

"I thought you were here to tell me the weird Mormon stuff," Rogers told him.

"I'm just looking," Hiram said. "With you."

Rogers followed Hiram back into the bedroom. Again Hiram gagged and managed not to throw up. Kneeling beside the corpses, Hiram examined their fingers. "Feel this if you want to, but Brother Fulton has calluses on the first two fingers and thumb of his right hand."

"What does that mean?"

"You're the police detective."

"That doesn't make me Sherlock Holmes!" Rogers snapped. Then he sighed. "You're going to tell me he got those calluses from writing with a pen."

"I think so." Hiram probed at Sister Fulton's fingertips again. "But her fingers are all callused, and her thumbs on their outside edges."

Rogers frowned. "Thumbs on the outside edges? What's that supposed to mean?"

Hiram stood. "I think it means that Sister Fulton typed up the blessings."

"I didn't see a typewriter in the office," Rogers objected.

"We keep looking."

There was no typewriter in the kitchen or in the small, recessed pantry. There was no rectangular object, either. Could the rectangular object be the typewriter? Hiram didn't think typewriters were that small, but what did he know?

The cellar door opened onto wooden stairs descending steeply toward a cement floor one story below. Hiram found the light switch against the wall and descended, a few steps ahead of Rogers.

"You grow up here in Grand Junction, then?" he asked the detective.

"Foster homes," Rogers said. "In Grand Junction, yes."

"Was it hard?" Hiram asked. "Was being an orphan the kind of experience that made you want to . . . take care of other people? Is that why you became a policeman?"

"I didn't say I was an orphan," Rogers said. "I said I was in foster homes."

Hiram nodded. "I lost my own father young. And mother. I was raised by my grandma."

"I didn't have a grandma," Rogers said. "And who the hell knows why I became a cop. I just did."

Hiram turned around and peered into the shadows in the corners of the basement. He saw a washing machine, a pile of coal, and a small desk, almost directly under an electric bulb, that bore a typewriter.

"'Underwood,'" he read.

"That is a typewriter," Rogers said. "A common model, as far as I can tell. So did they do it down here, then?"

"The murders?"

"The blessings. He gave the blessings, and she typed as he went." Rogers kicked at the concrete floor. "Only I don't know how much the ambiance would have suited."

"It wouldn't have been down here." Hiram closed his eyes and imagined. "Probably in the parlor. The young person would have sat on a chair, maybe a wooden chair from the kitchen. And Brother Fulton would have put his hands on the young person's head."

"You Mormons can't get enough of that laying on of hands."

"We're not the only ones. Did your foster parents not take you to any church?"

Rogers nodded. "They took me to church. It didn't stick."

"A blessing is kind of a solemn moment. Like a prayer. And the person asking for the blessing is a guest. So you'd do it in a nice part of the house. Sister Fulton listened, I guess. And then came down here and typed it up after."

"Maybe she wrote them beforehand," Rogers suggested. "And he just read them."

"That's not how it works," Hiram said. "You say what you feel inspired to say in the moment."

"So you just make it up."

"If you're saying you don't believe in inspiration, then sure, the person giving the blessing is just making it up. Grabbing words out of thin air, I suppose."

Rogers was quiet for a moment. "You feel like yours was accurate?" he eventually asked. "Your . . . patriarchal blessing?"

"I do," Hiram admitted.

"Because it was the same as everyone else's?" Rogers asked. "Or because it really told you things about your . . . life?"

Hiram hesitated. "My patriarchal blessing isn't the same as everyone else's."

Rogers cleared his throat. "So what's this all got to do with anything?"

"I'm just here to answer questions," Hiram said. "And look around. But I guess I'd say, why on Earth would anyone want to kill Brother and Sister Fulton?"

"Wasn't for money," Rogers said. "I can't imagine it was for power."

"Oh, it could have been for power," Hiram said.

Rogers snorted. "Mr. Fulton didn't have a kingdom to usurp, is what I mean."

"No," Hiram said. "But he had spiritual gifts. And the line between a spiritual gift and . . . and what you might call 'magic' . . . well, there is no line. The right kind of evil, the right kind of monster, might have wanted to kill Brother Fulton for power."

"If you believe in spiritual gifts."

"You don't have to believe Fulton had the gift of prophecy," Hiram pointed out. "Others did believe it. And the killer might have believed it."

Rogers harrumphed and looked away.

"Sexual jealousy seems out," Hiram added. "Revenge? Why else would anyone commit murder?"

"We're back around to the nutball theory," Rogers said. "Maybe the droppings on the carpet aren't evidence of a magical act, after all. Maybe we're dealing with a pure mental case here."

"Maybe."

But there was at least one more reason why a person might commit a murder, a reason Hiram had seen motivate more than one crime in his thirty-five years. A person might murder to protect a secret.

"What are you thinking, Woolley?"

"There was a rectangular object on the bedside table during the murders," Hiram said. "You can tell by the pattern of the blood spattering. But it's gone. Have you seen it?"

Rogers shrugged. "You think the killer took that? Along with the diary pages?"

"Maybe." Hiram considered. "I wonder if we've really searched everywhere in the house."

Rogers turned about. "Nothing much to search down here."

Hiram searched the basement anyway. He expected it to be a pure act of showmanship, but he patted about inside the barrel of the washing machine. He examined the undersides of the steps. Rogers played along in good humor, looking underneath the desk and beneath the typewriter.

"I checked under the bed," Rogers said.

"Did you reach under the mattress?" Hiram asked.

"I'll search now." Rogers shook his head. "Feels like a waste."

"We're looking for something like a book or a notebook," Hiram said. "It will probably be spattered with blood, at least a little. I'll check Fulton's office again."

They climbed the stairs. Hiram listened to the sound of Rogers grunting and poking about under the mattress as he opened Brother Fulton's document boxes and began searching them.

He flipped quickly through the boxes, starting with the oldest. He was operating on a guess, or at best a thin inference, but if he was right, it would be easy to find what he was looking for. He flipped through the blessings looking at back pages only, counting the serial numbers to find the one he expected to be missing.

There it was: 1907-32 was gone. Seventeen and a half years ago, probably.

Hiram put the box back. He was scanning the ledgers, looking for 1907, when he heard Rogers behind him.

"Find anything?"

"Not yet," Hiram said. "Still checking these boxes. You?"

"Bingo."

Hiram turned. Rogers stood grinning in the doorway, holding a steno notepad. Its edges were curled and worn, and its cover was smeared with blood.

"Where'd you find that?" Hiram asked.

"Under the mattress, like you said."

Hiram's bloodstone lay inert. The bloodstone was said to do many things, including stanch the flow of blood and summon rain, but the thing Hiram relied on it for was that the stone detected and warned its bearer of lies. Was it confirming to him now that Rogers was telling the truth?

Hiram wished again that he was wearing overalls and carrying his pistol.

"Let's look at that," he said.

They flipped the pages together. Each page was full, but the writing was odd. Hiram saw curls and swirls and V-shapes and spirals made with pencil. None of it resembled English.

"Arabic?" he asked. "Or . . . Sanskrit?"

"It's your Book of Mormon text," Rogers said. "Haven't you seen it? Looks just like this."

Hiram frowned. Was it possible that Brother Fulton's spiritual gifts had extended beyond his calling as patriarch? Had he been attempting some sort of translation project, Joseph-like?

Rogers laughed. "Naw, I'm pulling your leg. That's Gregg shorthand. Secretaries use it to take dictation, because it's a crazy-fast way to write."

"Can you read it?"

"No, but this has to be Mrs. Fulton's notebook, doesn't it? She sat in the room with her husband and took the whole thing down in shorthand. Then later she went downstairs and typed it up."

"The criminal didn't take it because he didn't want to be caught holding it," Hiram said, telling something very close to a lie. "But he wanted to hide it, so he shoved it under the mattress."

"You think the identity of the killer is in here?" Rogers asked.

Hiram wanted to backpedal away from the potential lie. "We need to take a look at any blessings recorded over the last three days. Let's see if they tell us anything about why the Fultons might have been murdered."

"Like what would that be?" Rogers pressed.

Hiram shrugged. "Something about the identity or direction of the person receiving the blessing, I suppose. But maybe that's not it at all. Maybe the person came and quarreled with Brother Fulton about something unrelated. Maybe the killer isn't worried about what the blessing said."

But he thought the killer did care.

"Huh." Rogers blinked. "Well, I have to thank Bishop Parker for sending you over, after all. You're building me up a nice little theory of the murder."

"Let me finish checking these boxes," Hiram said. "Maybe you can go look in the sofa and in the kitchen cupboards."

"What am I looking for?" Rogers frowned. "Oh . . . the calendar pages."

Hiram nodded.

As he heard Rogers's footsteps receding toward the kitchen, he grabbed the 1907 appointment book and started from the front, counting meetings marked with asterisks. He was looking for the thirty-second.

The thirty-second entry in the year 1907 read Green, foster son.

Someone had stolen the patriarchal blessing of the Greens' foster son. Hiram's breath caught in his throat.

"What are you looking at there?" Rogers asked from behind him.

Hiram shut the appointment book and turned around. The jowly police detective stood in the door, pointing a pistol at Hiram. In his other hand, he held a knife. It was a fighting dagger, with a long triangular blade. The knuckles of his hands were scabbed and hairy, the skin jaundiced.

"You killed Brother Fulton because of the blessing he gave you when you were young," Hiram said. "That's insane."

"That would depend on what the blessing said," Rogers shot back. "Wouldn't it?"

"Whatever it was, it also made you kill your foster parents. The Greens. Harmless, decent people."

"You don't know whether they were decent," Rogers said.

"Is that what you're going to tell me?" Hiram asked. "That you were beaten? That the Greens didn't treat you right? They starved you, made you work too hard?"

"No," Rogers admitted. "They were good people."

"But you're not." Hiram looked into the shadowy pits of Rogers's eyes. "There's something wrong with you. Something the Greens knew about. Something Brother Fulton knew. Something that made you kill them."

Rogers grinned, his teeth long and yellow in the lamplight. "You're forgetting old Bishop Dunsley."

"You have the pages from Brother Fulton's diary," Hiram said, "but they don't matter. That was a trick. You came here to take the written copy of the blessing Brother Fulton gave you in 1907."

"That's all I wanted from the Greens, too," Rogers said. "The copy they'd tucked away in their little lock box. But they resisted me."

Hiram edged away from Rogers, putting the desk between himself and the police detective. He tried not to look at the letter opener lying on the desk.

"You're not the simple one," Hiram said. "No free ride back to Heaven for you."

Rogers's mouth twisted into a scornful sneer. "No Heaven at all. Not for me."

"Sins can be forgiven," Hiram told him. "Almost all of them."

"What about you, Woolley? Did your patriarchal blessing tell you that you were of the lineage of Ephraim?"

Hiram nodded. "That's common enough."

Rogers tightened his grip on the knife, bringing its tip up to point toward Hiram. "Mine said, 'You are not a descendant of Israel. You are a son of Belial.' Have you ever heard such a blessing, Woolley?"

Hiram shook his head, eyes fixed on the knife, gleaming yellow.

"Neither had the Greens, my foster parents. I tried to listen to the words of the blessing, but they were hard to hear, because . . . Sister Green, my foster mother, started crying."

"In 1907," Hiram said.

"And the blessing was very short."

Hiram nodded.

"Fulton went on. 'You have sinned gravely, having murdered the parents who were the flesh of your flesh and the bone of your bone.'"

Rogers stopped. He breathed heavily, as if he was climbing a steep hill.

"And that was true," Hiram said.

Rogers nodded. "That was true. I killed my father on purpose, because . . . he was a bad man. My mother wasn't a bad woman, but she attacked me, to defend my father. I didn't mean to . . . but she died."

Hiram realized he was leaning back against the bookshelves. He tried to straighten himself up and couldn't. His back bent as if beneath a load.

"What else?" he croaked.

"The blessing said, 'You may repent and be saved by the power and grace of the atonement of our Lord, but you will not do so. You are a son of Belial, and you will do the work of Belial in your lifetime. Though it will avail you nothing, you will murder your foster parents, Brother and Sister Green, and you will be damned to Hell.'"

"You memorized it," Hiram murmured.

"It was striking," Rogers said. "I read it again and again. When I slept, I saw the words as if they were tattooed onto the undersides of my eyelids."

"Dunsley?" Hiram leaned onto his knuckles on the desk, sucking in warm air.

"They told him," Rogers said. "As I recall, they said they 'counselled with' him. They needed advice, I guess, about what to do about their damned foster son. Their foster son who was prophesied to kill them."

"You should have run away," Hiram said.

"I did." Rogers grunted.

"Fled to the desert," Hiram said. "Become a monk. Lived like a hermit. Never come back."

"I became a police officer." Rogers stepped toward the desk, and Hiram forced himself not to back away. "I served the community. I protected people. I stopped crime."

Was his face becoming longer, or was it a trick of the yellow light?

Thunder rolled outside the window.

"The Greens knew?"

"They knew." Rogers's voice was flat. "I didn't hide. I . . . was repenting. I was doing what was right."

A wave of fatigue washed over Hiram. What kind of police officer had Rogers been, really? Had his guilt driven him to sacrifice himself? Had his history of violence manifested itself in recurring fits of anger and injury?

"They said they would hold on to the blessing," Rogers said. "No one would ever know, but the blessing couldn't be destroyed. The blessing was God's word on the subject."

"You went back to take it from them," Hiram suggested.

"I'm up for promotion," Rogers said. "And some questions are being asked about my . . . parents' deaths. Awkward questions. Questions that could end my career, that could stop me from . . . helping people. And I was afraid that the blessing would come to light."

"Did you just kill the Greens out of hand?" Hiram felt sick.

"I broke into their house." Rogers's face was elongated and off-color, like a caricature drawn with a pen on a banana. "It was easy, the locks and windows are the same as they were all those years ago. I was just going to take my patriarchal blessing, nothing else."

"They resisted," Hiram said.

"They called me to repentance." Dark tears, red like blood, streamed down Rogers's heavy cheeks. "They wanted to save me."

"You killed them."

"I made my blessing come true," Rogers said. "I proved the prophecy of it."

Hiram's heart ached. "Then Bishop Dunsley."

"Because he knew," Rogers said.

"And then the Fultons."

"How could they not remember?" Rogers asked. "And even if they had somehow forgotten the boy with the murderous blessing, it was typed up in their archive, and had to be destroyed."

"You defecated on the floor," Hiram said.

"I knew I'd need it when I heard Parker was sending you over." Rogers grinned. "I had a teacher, too."

"And the theater?" Hiram asked. "The slicing of flesh, all the blood? Was that all just to throw off pursuit? Just to convince your superiors in the police that the murderer was a random insane person, with no rational motive for killing these people?"

Rogers stared at Hiram's necktie. He shuddered, flared his nostrils, and managed to get his breathing under control. Finally, he smiled. "Oh, no," he said. "I did those things because . . . because they were satisfying. Because I am, in fact, a son of Belial."

Hiram snatched the letter opener from the desktop and stepped back. He narrowly avoided getting filleted as Rogers lunged forward to slash across the desk, trying to gut him.

Could Hiram even defeat the detective? Was Hiram already himself beaten by the man's burglar charm?

The detective lunged with the knife again. Firing shots would attract attention, maybe. Hiram sidestepped and grabbed for Rogers's neck. He got a fistful of thick, red hair and, with that handle, he managed to throw the man sideways and away from him. He slashed with the letter opener but missed, and then the hair tore from the detective's scalp.

Rogers tumbled to the floor and Hiram was left with a wad of hair in his grasp. He ducked back into the hall, pulling the door shut behind him. If he could get out to his car fast enough, he could escape the scene. Maybe he could convince other policemen that Rogers was the killer, but if not, he could at least flee.

Or grab his pistol from the car.

He heard glass shattering in the office.

Which could only mean that Rogers had leaped out the window into the front yard.

Hiram slipped around the corner of the hall into the parlor, just in time to see Rogers charging up the steps. Lightning flashed behind him and rain gusted in through the open doorway. Hiram dropped the objects in his hands and hurled himself against the door, slamming against it just as the bigger man struck the other side. They collided like bucks locking horns. Rogers slipped to one knee, Hiram roared, and he managed to push the door shut, losing his hat in the process.

He locked the bolt and chain.

Rogers hurled himself against the door a second time, making the whole wall tremble beneath his weight.

Hiram spun about on his knees, looking for a rear exit from the bungalow and seeing only windows. He rushed to cross the parlor to throw a window up, and gunfire erupted in the front yard.

The front windows shattered, glass raining to the yellow carpet. Hiram dove to the ground to get out of the line of fire.

He found himself lying on the carpet beside the turd.

Rogers's turd.

His gorge rose and he almost vomited, but, at the same moment, he had a thought.

"I'm coming in there after you, Woolley!" Rogers bellowed from the front yard. Hiram heard the brassy rattle of pistol shells being shaken out onto the front walk.

What would Rogers say to the other policemen? It wouldn't matter to Hiram, if Hiram was dead.

On all fours, Hiram scrambled about the room. He found Rogers's clump of red hair, even redder at the roots where Hiram had drawn blood by yanking the hair from the detective's scalp. He found the letter opener.

Fighting back the urge to vomit, he picked up the turd, and ducked back into the hallway.

"Last chance, Woolley!" Rogers roared. "Open now or I kick down the door!"

Hiram pulled a heavy face, arms, and legs from the turd. With his pinky, he stabbed eyes and a mouth into the crude head, and then two little nostrils. He'd never made a curse doll, and Grandma Hettie had certainly never taught him to do so. What words could he say that would possibly give effect to this dark, foul charm?

Unclean hands, indeed.

He jammed the wad of red hair down onto the turd-born curse doll's head. This little monster was not in God's image. Was Rogers even in God's image? But the words of Genesis 2 might do.

"And the Lord God formed man of the dust of the ground," he said, "and breathed into his nostrils the breath of life; and man became a living soul."

Fighting back the urge to vomit, he leaned over his monstrous creation and blew onto its face.

Rogers fired again, and bullets came through the front door. They shattered a lamp and a window at the back of the parlor, and then Hiram took the letter opener firmly into his grip.

He heard Rogers kick the door, and then he heard the door bang open.

Hiram stabbed deep into one of the turd-doll's legs.

Rogers screamed and fell.

Hiram stabbed the doll in the other leg, and Rogers screamed again.

Hiram leaped around the corner of the hallway and into the parlor. Rogers lay bellowing face down on the floor, the knife and the pistol both on the carpet beside him. Hiram kicked away the weapons.

"I'll tell them it was you," Rogers gasped. The detective rolled over on his back, staring up at Hiram with narrowed eyes. His legs trembled.

"No one will believe you," Hiram said. He dropped the curse doll back onto the carpet, then wiped his hands on the goldenrod fibers. Keeping one eye on the detective, he stepped to the kitchen sink and washed his hands. Finally losing control of his stomach, he spat thin bile down the drain.

"Then kill me. Spare me the humiliation, at least."

"There's a limit to how dirty I'll get my hands." Hiram kicked the detective's knife back within his grasp. "If you want to do something, you'll have to do it yourself."

"You're a cruel man!" Rogers bellowed.

Hiram ignored him. He picked up his hat and straightened his thin tie. Turning his back on the snarling detective, he walked through the ruined door into the warm night. Rain poured down on him, and lightning flashed in the distance.

But there was no shouting, no posse, no hand-cranked police siren in the distance.

Had Rogers' charm concealed all his secrets, including his battle with Hiram?

Hiram lifted his hat to let the water flow over him; it felt good to be clean. He listened to the sound of Rogers's death throes on the goldenrod carpet, and then he headed for his car.

"The tour of our first story is complete. You don't want to stay? The smell, is it…Hm. I will say, this floor could lead to a blessing for your own young ones. No? More it is. Let us move on to the stairs, up to the second story."

* * * * *

They Called Him Jack
by Matt Novotny

7 August 1888
Whitechapel

They say the first kill is the hardest.

He waited, straining to hear over the pounding of his heart, the knife held beneath his coat in a white-knuckled grip. There was a flash of yellow as she passed beneath the streetlamp, the shawl as dirty and ragged as the woman wearing it. At first, he thought it was only his imagination, an illusion of the fog, but in the next pool of light, he saw it again.

"Find the yellow shawl," they'd told him.

In a place like this, how many can there be?

He followed cautiously from across the street, certain he was obvious, that everyone was staring, watching him. Watching her. When he could not hide, he strode purposefully, wearing the armor of his station. In this place, with the hope of wealth that those like him brought into the mazes and alleys, it was a measure of invisibility nearly as complete as the darkness.

She and others like her were called "unfortunates" in polite society—and for the most part they were people he had empathy for in a second-hand kind of way. Through reading the paper or when he gave his annual contribution to the poor to demonstrate the illusion of generosity to his peers.

She was brazen, stopping for a word here or a jibe there with the other patrons of the night. One exchange carried on the damp air, her voice shrill and taunting.

"Is that what you think now, Clancy Davis? I'll give you a piece of my mind, that's what, and save your pennies for the missus!"

"Now, Martha, don't you be on like that! A piece was what the pennies were for!"

She reached a quieter section of the road and nervously glanced about while he faded into the deep shadow of a doorway and nearly fell over the unconscious drunk who'd taken shelter there. The man snored loudly, and the woman stopped, staring at his hiding place.

What if I'm seen? He swallowed, breathed deeply, strengthened his resolve. *If I'm caught, there will be no one else to...* He wrenched his mind away from completing the thought.

It was a chill night for summer, with a weak drizzle drifting from a sky half cloud and half coal smoke. The grit and filth of the city covered him with an oily residue that no amount of scrubbing would free him from. He scanned his surroundings with narrowed eyes. Despite the chill, he was grateful for the rain.

At least it washes away the stench and keeps people's eyes on the ground.

Martha peered into the gloom then hurried away. The heels of her boots clicked on the wet cobblestones, sending echoes that bounced off the walls and closed shop fronts. There were no dosses, no alehouses here. He followed until they reached a deserted stretch of street where she stopped beneath the next lamp. She saw him then, straightening to display her charms, eyes widening when he showed silver gleaming against his palm. She tilted her head at the shadows before entering the alley. Her fingers trailed the brick beneath a worn sign that read 'Buck's Row' before she crooked her finger, motioning for him to join her in the shadows.

21 December 1887
Six months earlier.

Doctor Thomas Bond smiled at his new bride as their carriage bounced and rumbled over the city cobblestones. They stopped for a moment for another carriage to clear the way.

"My dear Cybil, you've made me a very happy man!"

"I feel the same way, dearest," she said, hugging his arm.

The doctor's man, acting as coachman, heard the exchange in the relative quiet and snickered to himself. "In course she made the old goat 'appy. She's 'aff 'is age!"

Cybil heard the man grouse and blushed prettily, covering her mouth to stifle a laugh as she and Thomas exchanged a look.

He grinned at her before banging on the roof of the carriage with his cane.

"What's that now, Edward? What's that? Mind the road!"

"Which I is watchin' it now, sir, ain't I?" Edward replied.

It's true though. Thomas thought as he watched her looking out the windows at the bright, snow-dusted streets. *She is young. I'd never expected to marry again now my children have grown and gone. Except for Rose, and they do get along well.*

Cybil was a younger daughter of Lord Dashwood by his own second marriage and carried all the dark beauty of her mother's ancestry. Because of her mixed parentage, she was branded "not quite the thing" in the upper tiers of London society. Considered unsuitable as a wife of the aristocracy, the peerage never openly criticized the daughter of the former ambassador to Egypt, delivering their barbs with all the subtlety of a knife in the dark.

Despite Bond having no official standing, Dashwood felt the addition of a renowned surgeon to his circle would be a benefit. In accepting the offer, Bond gained access to a social stratum one couldn't reach without an invitation in addition to a young and beautiful wife. Perhaps he could aspire even so high as a knighthood.

There was a jolt as the carriage staggered into motion again, and a harder one as they lurched back to a halt. The sudden scream of a horse overwhelmed the usual noises of the street and Edward's curses alike. Cybil covered her ears, trying to block out the animal's pain.

"Edward!" Bond demanded. "What's going on?" The carriage shook as Edward climbed down and poked his head through the window.

"A cab a'ead broke a wheel an' flipped on 'is 'orse, sir. If they can't free 'im they'll 'ave to put 'im down."

"Thomas!" Cybil said. "Make it stop!"

"Was anyone hurt?" Bond asked.

"No sir, just the 'orse."

"Thomas?" Cybil asked. "Surely they can't allow the poor thing to suffer?"

"Go around." Bond said.

Edward shook his head. "Can't. Street's blocked and cabs' is built up be'ind. It'll be hours afore it's cleared."

The horse let out another scream, and the shouts gave testament that the owners were failing to calm the animal.

"Thomas, please," Cybil begged.

"All right." Bond collected his bag. "Stay here." Cybil nodded, tears in her eyes.

"Keep her safe," he told Edward. "I'll return shortly."

Bond approached the accident and the crowd that had formed around it. He saw a big grey half under the shattered remains of the hansom cab. The crowd had attempted to clear the wreck, but the animal kicked at any who got too near. The driver knelt beside the horse, trying to calm it.

"I hadn't expected to find a hunter here," Bond said, admiring the horse. "Are you the owner?"

The man nodded. "Aye, you've the right of it. A face like a duchess and a bottom like a cook! She's a good horse, my Daisy. Retired from her hunting days but too proud for pasture." He stroked the horse's neck. "You know hunters, then?"

"I ride with the Badminton hounds."

"I know them well. My father was a houndsman there."

Daisy struggled for a moment, let out another scream and snorted.

"Shhhh," the driver soothed. He looked at Bond with tears in his eyes. "It won't be long now sir, I've sent for the knackers."

"An unjust end for so fine a beast," Bond said. "I can ease her way, if you'll allow."

The man gave Bond a puzzled look.

"I'm a surgeon." Bond explained. "A small incision, barely felt, and Daisy can pass peacefully from this world."

"I'd not wish to impose upon a gentleman…"

"A small gesture of thanks for the many hours of pleasure those like her have given me."

"Then I'd consider it a mercy."

Bond withdrew a scalpel from his kit, then knelt next to Daisy. He lay his hand on her neck and she shivered at the unfamiliar touch, but calmed at the murmured words of the driver. With a sharp stab, Bond opened the great vein in Daisy's throat, covering the flood with his hand to avoid soiling his clothing. In a few moments, she gave a final, great sigh.

Bond stood, wiped the scalpel then his hand on a handkerchief before replacing the instrument in his bag.

"Bless you, sir." the driver said, standing. "What do I—"

"Nothing," Bond said, handing the man a coin, more than he knew the knackers would pay. "Save to take her home."

Bond came back as Edward was helping Cybil out of the carriage. "Where are we, Edward?"

The driver handed her down gently, an incongruous look of happiness on the enormous man's face.

He looks at Rose the same way.

"The Strand, sir. A block over is 'Olywell and bookseller's row. A bit north and Aldwych Street would bring us back across."

"Thomas? Can't we walk?"

"It will be cold."

"I don't mind as long as you're with me."

"All right," Bond decided. "Edward, stay here. We'll go around and hire a cab to take us home. Bring the carriage once they've cleared the street."

"As you say, sir."

"Good, that's settled," Bond said, offering his arm to Cybil. "Shall we be off, then?"

"Thomas, look!" Cybil said, drawing him toward a shop front. The battered shingle above the door read WARE'S CURIOSITIES. Cybil's eyes sparkled as she pulled him toward the grungy window and pointed excitedly to a French porcelain doll nestled amongst piles of books, small furniture, and other bric-à-brac.

"Isn't she exquisite? Oh, we *must* go in!"

"Of course."

A bell jangled on its spring as the door opened, mingling the brisk air of the winter day with the atmosphere inside. The place was warm, if not inviting. Redolent of dust, paper, and ink above a hint of herbs and resins that spoke more of an apothecary than a bookseller, a mélange that struggled to cover the faint undertone of rot. The sullen glow of coal laid up in the grate and weathered Turkish carpets utterly failed to provide any sense of cheer.

"Hello? Is anyone here?" Cybil called.

Bond glanced at cluttered displays seemingly put together at random. African masks adorned the same wall as groupings of Persian knives, while small, grotesque statuary of a peculiar greenish stone held court with feathered and sea-shelled fetishes from the south Pacific. Toward the back was a row of shelves hosting indistinct forms in what were obviously large specimen jars.

"Welcome to my cabinet of curiosities," said a sonorous voice. "Here you will find the rare, the strange, and the forbidden. Theron Ware at your service." The man limped from a back room. He was short and thick-lipped, with a shaggy fringe of salt-and-pepper hair around his otherwise bald head. "What's your pleasure?"

"We've come to…" Cybil started. "That is, I'd like to see the doll in the window."

Ware fairly glowed. "Ah! A lady of discernment and taste! One moment and I'll fetch her for you."

As he stumped toward the window display, Bond noticed the man had a clubbed foot. Ware caught his gaze.

"It sometimes pains me with the cold, but I'm accustomed to it."

Ware retrieved the doll, Bond set his bag down and thumbed through a few pages of an illuminated tome that lay open on a lectern of mahogany and brass carved with gargoyles. The pages were of vellum and written with a reddish ink. The illustrations were both erotic and disturbing.

Forbidden indeed. Any one of these illustrations would run afoul of the obscenity laws. He turned another page. *The writing appears to be Latin, but the margin notes are—is that Greek? No. Something else.*

He stopped when he realized the "ink" was most likely blood. Despite the sometimes grimness of his own profession, Bond removed his hand in distaste.

"Now," Ware said, bringing the doll and her chair to a nearby table, "she's very old and fragile, but our treasure here isn't a mere doll." He produced a silver key, placed it in Cybil's hand, and pointed to a keyhole. "Made by the infamous LeMarchand himself. She's an *automata.* No more than a half dozen turns if you please, and you will see what she can do."

Cybil inserted the key and turned it gingerly. Once she was done, she looked to Ware.

"Press here." He showed her a small switch concealed in the chair's base.

When she pressed it, music played, and the doll moved her head from side to side.

"Just a music box," Bond said.

"Wait," Ware replied.

The music continued, chimes in a minor key. The doll stared straight ahead, then stood and raised her arms. With the whisper of hidden bellows, her voice sprang forth, wild and sweet, cascading in gentle harmony.

"Oh, she sings!" Cybil looked enchanted. "I've never heard anything like it."

"She does indeed," Ware said.

Bond saw the rapt look on Cybil's face as she listened to the automata sing. He drew the shop keeper aside. "What's your asking price?"

Ware smiled, a glint of avarice shining in his eyes.

"Before we discuss price, would you care to browse my other stock? There are many other unique items. Perhaps the grimoire you were examining? The Codex of Aozoth was once a prized exhibit of the Hellfire Club. There are many collectors who would envy such a possession."

"No, thank you," Bond said, reaching into his coat. "Now, about the doll."

"Allow me a last chance to tempt you," Ware said. "Unless I miss my guess, you are a physician?"

"How did he know?" Cybil asked, coming up and taking Bond by the arm.

"I'd say he noticed my bag," Bond said, amused.

"Just so," Ware agreed. "I've recently acquired something from one of my contacts in Damascus, perfect for a man in your position." He reached beneath the counter and brought out a leather-bound box. At first Bond thought it was another book, but Ware opened it to reveal a gleaming array of knives, scalpels, and other implements.

"Oh! What is it?" Cybil asked.

"A surgeon's field kit," Bond said. "An extensive one. May I?"

"Of course! I would value your opinion. My source assured me these were made for the royal physician to Queen Isabella II before his unfortunate demise."

Bond carefully examined the kit. The tools were fitted with ebony handles and the folded and polished steel gleamed, even in the reddish light of the coal fire.

"Fine work," Bond said admiringly. "Though I don't recognize some of the implements. What is this?" He pointed to a glyph stamped in the steel.

"Only a maker's mark—no doubt from the royal craftsman."

Bond replaced the tools. "I will consider, then. Give me a price for each."

Ware opened what Bond suspected was his accounts book, and after some calculations, passed him a piece of paper. Bond raised an eyebrow at the prices. Both were expensive, as he'd expected, but the surgical kit was easily twice what he'd pay if he commissioned a similar set from Herrod's.

"We'll take the doll." Bond said.

"No interest in the instruments?"

"They are exquisitely made, to be sure, but not at that price. They are, after all, only tools."

Cybil slipped the paper from his hand. "We'll take them."

"Cybil, I—"

"Now then, Mr. Bond," she said teasingly, "you obviously want them, and I happen to owe you a wedding gift." She put a finger to his lips. "And I have my own money. So, unless you want me to buy both, you'll let me get them for you."

Bond's gaze softened as he looked into her eyes. Her youth belied a strength of will, whether from her parentage or circumstance he didn't know, but it made him admire her all the more.

"Very well," he said. "We will take these now. And I'll leave you with the address the doll is to be delivered to. I trust you will make the arrangements?"

"Of course, Doctor." Ware smiled. "It will be my pleasure."

15 August 1888
London

"Thank you for joining us, Doctor," Inspector Abberline said.

"I must confess I was surprised at the request," Bond said, setting his bag on a nearby table. "But I'll be happy to provide whatever aid I can."

"What can you tell us about the state of the victim?" The inspector turned away from the body and nodded to the coroner. "Show him."

"I've already told you what—" the coroner began.

"You have, Baxter," Abberline said. "Now we will hear another opinion."

"Look and be damned then," Baxter said. He pulled back the sheet covering the woman. "I'll not look at that fucking mess again, and I don't understand why—"

"Watch your mouth, you!" the sergeant barked.

"Stand down, Sergeant Thicke," the inspector said, "No need to compound his rudeness with more of the same."

"Yes sir."

Abberline faced the coroner squarely. "Why, Baxter? Why is because Commissioner Sir Charles Warren has asked for outside expertise, which Dr. Bond has graciously agreed to provide. Why is because the commissioner feels it will help our case. And why is because we work for him and will do as we are fucking told! Does that cover why for you, or shall I repeat myself?"

Baxter had the grace to look embarrassed. "Your pardon, Inspector, I meant no offense. But as the doctor will see…" The coroner lifted a cloth soaked in vinegar to his nose and turned away from the corpse, fighting down his gorge though he'd already seen the body.

Bond lifted the sheet but paled slightly at the state of the body. He distracted himself by reading through the file the inspector had given him and comparing Baxter's notes to the corpse. The woman had been slashed to ribbons.

"Martha Tabram," he read aloud. "Thirty-nine stab wounds. Cause of death, exsanguination. Her lungs and kidneys are…" He stared at the coroner. "Missing."

"Removed postmortem," Baxter said.

Bond stooped to inspect the corpse more closely. "You there, Sergeant… Thicke, is it? Would you bring that lamp behind you? Thank you."

Thicke held up the lamp, clamped his mouth shut, and broke into a heavy sweat. He looked away as the Doctor prodded the body cavity with a probe.

"No, Mr. Baxter. I think not."

"What?" Baxter asked sharply.

"The majority of the stab wounds appear to have happened *after* the organ removal, not before. The general lack of bloodiness, particularly the final cut to the throat, indicates she had already bled profusely before those were made." He locked gazes with the inspector. "Whoever did this removed the organs while she was alive. First the kidneys, then the lungs. The cause of death was suffocation."

"God in heaven," Thicke said. "What sort of monster could—"

"It has to be a medical man," Baxter said. "A student at the hospital or—"

Bond shook his head. "Certainly not. The young men at the university are from fine families. None of my students would take part in this... this... abomination! These incisions are ragged and clumsy, not the work of a skilled man. You may be looking for a butcher or perhaps a knacker-man. Possibly a street gang trying to make a statement. The angle of the wounds suggests the killer is likely right-handed."

"Thank you, Doctor," Abberline said. "I hope we can call upon your expertise again?"

"Of course, Inspector. Whatever I can do to help."

"Jesus," Thicke swore. "If one of the gangs has started killing bang-tails, the papers will have a field day."

"Given the state of Whitechapel, it will be surprising if anyone notices," Abberline said. "However, due to the brutality of the crime and the nature of the victim, I must insist that the details of this case"—he looked pointedly at Baxter—"and any speculation, are not to leave this room."

31 August 1888

She struggled frantically as the knife pierced her, groaning against the gloved hand pressed over her mouth. She fought with all her strength to free the scream it held back, to call someone, anyone, who would hear, who would save her. The woman clawed at him, ragged nails tore at the fabric of his coat and dug into the flesh beneath. He tightened his grip as she tried to bite, watching the light of hope drain from her eyes.

Blue eyes. Like *her* eyes.

"Even if they hear," he whispered, his words sharper than the blade, "they won't come."

She shuddered with a momentary weakness, knowing it was true.

He forced her against the filthy brick of the alley wall. The smell of damp stone, old sweat, and perfume was nearly overpowering. Their struggle was hidden by the very shadows she had invited him to. He relaxed his grip, just enough for her to take half a breath. No more.

Power over life and death was one he often wielded, but never like this. He couldn't think on that now—they wouldn't allow it.

He twisted the blade. Her stillborn scream changed to a helpless mewl, the sound of a kitten crushed beneath a carriage wheel.

"What you feel is the drug on my glove taking effect."

From the mouth of the alleyway came a shout of drunken laughter and the echo of footsteps as a couple entered from the main street. He shifted the woman so they both could watch the new arrivals and pulled her even further into the darkness.

"It's a curious powder obtained from the Caribbean," he whispered. His voice took on the cadence of a lecturer. "It paralyzes the voluntary muscles entirely, but there is no loss of perception or feeling. I'm sorry, but you must feel it all. There's nothing I can do to ease your suffering."

They would be angry if they knew. I'm not supposed to drug them.

They waited while the other pair finished their business. Once, she managed a tiny sound, the merest whisper of the terror in her mind. Almost lifted a hand, reaching toward them. Anything to be noticed.

I will have to carry additional doses from now on.

He took a swallow from his flask, the absinthe easing a mouth and throat gone dry, fighting terrors of his own, but there was time. His first wound had been for pain and fear rather than injury. Tears streaked the woman's cheeks as she watched the others leave. Once they were gone, he lowered her to the cobblestones. Her mouth spasmed as she gasped like a fish out of water and tried to scream. After a moment, he cut away her dress, an artist preparing his canvas before beginning to paint.

Around her he inscribed a circle in coal powder with symbols he copied from the book, then said the words they had given him to say. He paused, staring into the other shadows, listening to the drip of water, the distant mutter of the city that found him through the fog. The rain would wash the writing away, along with most of the blood.

A low groan escaped her. She moved.

Impossible!

He panicked and stabbed savagely. Fresh pain flared in her eyes. They stared at him, accusing, but because of the drug she was unable to close them. She would see everything until the night came. He raised the knife again, then remembered and struggled to regain control.

I can't fail them. Not again.

He checked her carefully. Her breathing was barely perceptible, but her pulse still hammered in her veins.

I have to hurry now.

He severed the tendons in her arms and legs with deft cuts.

Now, if the drug fails, she won't be able to escape.

He took a new instrument from his case and lightly caressed her face with it.

With another pull at his flask, he set himself to his last task. When he was done, he carefully placed her eyes in a jar filled with the solution they had given him, then cleaned and stored his equipment. The other organs he put in an old sack he would discard for the stray dogs on butcher street. He raised the jar, peered through the cloudy liquid in the dim light, and remembered the question he had seen in the depths of those eyes. The only question that mattered, and one he had no power to answer.

Why?

With a last slow look to make sure no one had seen him, he hurried away into the dark.

21 June 1888

It was six months to the day when they took them.

Bond entered the foyer with a jaunty step. It had been a day of triumphs and marvels, and he was in the mood to celebrate. He had expected their butler, Giles, to greet him in his usual fashion, with Cybil close behind once she heard his arrival.

Everyone must be busy with the preparations.

Soon they would be on the way to their summer cottage by Lake Geneva, and the fresh air would refresh and revive them before returning to the city. The servants not on furlough had gone a week since to restore the place to good order and Rose and her governess had left yesterday. He and Cybil would coach down to Canterbury and Folkstone before taking a steamer across to Calais.

"Cybil? I'm home!" he called. He removed his hat and jacket before he realized that other than the labored ticking of their grandfather clock, the house was silent.

Maybe they're upstairs. "Giles? Cybil?"

With a sense of alarm, he grabbed his cane, first checking the parlor and drawing rooms and then the upstairs bedrooms. With each empty room, his sense of dread increased until it overpowered his reserve. He ran through the rest of the house shouting, trying to find any sense of life, but there was nothing.

Perhaps she's been called away? Some emergency? But where is Giles? Where is the cook?

It was on his second trip through the dining room that he saw it, plain as day, on the table.

The Book, and next to it two letters. He snatched the one in Cybil's hand up, snapped the seal, tore the letter from the envelope.

My Dearest Thomas,

They have only given me brief moments to write this. They have Rose in their keeping, and now me. Rose is frightened but unhurt. She was brought so that I would tell you she is alive. I do not know what has become of Agatha, but they took away Giles and Mrs. Marshberry.

They have left instructions for you. They will not tell me what they want, but they laughed when I asked them if they wanted money and said that if you do as they demand we will be reunited. I've also been told to tell you not to go to the police, and that if you did so, you should never see us again.

Please give them what they want. I know in my heart that it is something terrible, but I cannot bear the thought of not returning to you.

Until we are safe in your arms again.

All my love,

Cybil

Bond felt a rush of rage. He'd heard of things like this happening, of course, but for them to take both his daughter and his wife, not to mention the governess, butler, and cook, was simply monstrous. He would have given his fortune for any of them. Bond was not a man without considerable influence, notwithstanding his connection to Lord Dashwood. Whoever was behind the kidnapping was playing a very dangerous game indeed.

He stared at the book for a moment.

Ware. If he has harmed either of them, there will not be enough left for them to hang.

He reached for the second letter with shaking hands. He cracked the seal and unfolded it.

Cybil said they didn't want money. What then?

He read it, then again, and then a third time, shaking his head as if by sheer repetition he could erase from his mind what he saw there.

They are mad and without hope of cure or redemption. And they have Cybil and Rose!

Fragments of the letter echoed in his mind.

They needed a surgeon.

We know you would buy their safety if you could. Fight for them, perhaps even die for them, but what you will do—is kill for them.

Tears streamed down his face at what they asked of him. Demanded of him.

We will show you the way. Wait and we will send word.

He did not have the strength.

You are chosen.

It was a ritual they claimed was old when the stars first rose over Memphis and men called it Men-nefer. As the Pharaohs had once had their organs placed in canopic jars to preserve them for the afterlife, to save his family, he must likewise collect offerings.

Read the Sacred text.

Against his will, he reached for the book. What had Ware called it? The Codex of Aozoth?

Five must die.

He unlocked the hasps. Inside, they had marked the passages they wanted him to know.

And a god will rise.

1 October 1888

"Mister Baxter, this theory of yours is completely unacceptable! You have not a shred of supportable evidence except for the removal of various organs. For all we know, the killer may be a chef or a poulterer!"

Bond turned away from the table. He'd been awakened by a rough pounding on his door and found Sergeant Thicke waiting for him with a carriage and orders to take him to the coroner's office at once. The previous night had not one, but two murders, and his expertise was once again requested by the Department.

"Forgive me, Sergeant. My family and servants have already decamped to our holiday lodgings, so I'm somewhat at loose ends. I've delayed only because of urgent business at the hospital." He explained to the waiting Thicke as he gathered his things.

It was a small lie, but the only way he could conceal what had happened. These last months had been a torture of uncertainty and loneliness, with only brief notes from Cybil or terse, infrequent missives from her captors to let him know that she and Rose were alive.

Now he made show of examining the bodies beneath the watchful gaze of Inspector Abberline while Baxter reeked and wrung his hands. The coroner's face grew more florid by the moment until he thought the man would spare him the argument by dying of apoplexy. Bond drew the sheet up over the woman's face as he struggled to breathe. The first victim had been his and seeing her in the cold light of day was more raw than what had happened beneath the gas lamps. The second woman was the victim of another, killed with a brutality that shocked even him.

"You said—" Baxter began angrily, pointing at Bond, then lowered his voice at a look from Inspector Abberline.

"You said that the incisions were ragged and unskilled. These are not!"

Baxter's face was flushed and the smell of cheap gin that came from the man was nearly overpowering.

"Yes, I've studied the reports you sent over, which is why I'm here."

"Then—"

"And on examination," Bond said, holding up a placating hand, "the killer's technique appears to have improved, but they are still far shy of the mark. That doesn't mean you can accuse—"

"Why not?" Baxter asked. "Leave no stone unturned. Anything to stop"—he gestured wildly at the bodies—"this."

Bond held up a handful of files.

"Martha Tabram, date of death 7 August. I believe we dealt with her circumstance on my last visit. Unless you would like to review the photographs?"

"I—" Baxter began, then shook his head.

"Mary Nichols, 31 August. Seven stab wounds. Throat cut, eyes and liver removed." Bond slapped the two files on a side table before holding up the next.

"Anne Chapman, sometimes called Dark Annie. 8 September. Throat cut, tongue removed." The file joined the first. Bond held up two more, one for each of the bodies they had been examining.

"Elizabeth Stride, 30 September. Throat cut, Womb removed." He held up the last file. "And Catherine Eddows, also 30 September. Multiple slashes to the face and neck. As with the first victim you had me examine, the kidneys were taken. Postmortem, Miss Eddows was fully disemboweled."

"The kidneys are the giveaway," Baxter protested. "You have to know something about—"

"Very well," Bond said. "Inspector Abberline, have you interviewed Mr. Baxter in connection with the murders?"

"How dare you!" Baxter exploded.

"Leave no stone unturned. Your words, sir! Do you see how you react to the mere suggestion you be questioned?"

"That isn't—"

"And yet you have all the requisite skills. For that matter, so do I."

"As do the young gentlemen—"

"Who are the sons of some of the wealthiest and most influential families in England," Abberline broke in. "Including the son of the magistrate! No, Baxter, we'll hear no more of it. I'm quite convinced that were there a likely suspect among his students that the doctor would recognize it."

"Be assured gentlemen, I will do anything within my power to see this ended. Now, if there is nothing more?"

"Nothing, Doctor, except to thank you again for your time," Abberline said.

1 November 1888

"Ware! Open up! Damn you, Ware!"

Bond rapped on the door with his cane and stared at the shop with loathing. It had been nearly a year since he had come to the place. If anything, Ware's shop had reached an even deeper state of decay and disrepair. It clung to the row of shopfronts like an abscessed tooth that festered below the surface, spreading pain and corruption to the clean flesh around it for want of a dentist.

When he had recognized the book, he had thought to confront Ware at once, but the second letter had made it clear he was to have no contact. Ware was not to be touched, but after Bond's latest task, this was where he was told to come.

"Break it down," he told Edward.

He had been a comfort to Thomas these past months. Unavoidably, he had taken the coachman into his confidence, relying on the big man's nearly slavish devotion to Rose and Cybil. He had no doubt that, given the chance, Edward would remove any threat he might face by tearing it limb from limb.

"Right!" Edward said. He moved forward just as the door creaked open. Ware had already turned and was making a stumping retreat across the room.

"Come in, Doctor, and close the door behind you."

Bond entered behind Edward, bag in hand. He watched Ware make his way behind the counter. In the time since he'd last seen him, Ware seemed to have shrunken in on himself. The pepper had gone from his hair, and in addition to the limp, he was now stooped. He leaned heavily on the counter, poured from a bottle into a single glass, and tossed off the contents in a single swallow. His voice, once deep and melodic, emerged hoarse and creaking from his chest with all the charm of a gallows-rope. The shop was no better, with mostly empty shelves and pale patches of floor where the carpets once had lain.

"Do what you've come to do and go."

"Where are they?" Bond demanded.

"I don't know. Even if I did, I wouldn't tell you."

Edward fairly leapt on the man, holding Ware up by the greasy lapels of his suit.

"Which is sumthin' we'll be seein' about now, ain't it?"

Ware looked at Edward with a flash of fear, which quickly faded to indifference. It was a look Bond knew from the terminal wards. A look of the broken and the dying, but there was a hint of craftiness at the end.

"If you kill me, you've no hope. None at all."

"Put him down, Edward," Bond said. "All right, Ware, explain your part in all this."

Ware licked dry lips and reached again for the bottle before Edward knocked his hand away. "First, what have you brought me?"

Bond set his bag on the counter and opened it, then carefully removed the contents.

"There—tongue, eyes, lungs, womb. That's everything."

Ware moved the sealed jars to a cabinet behind the counter.

"Almost everything," Ware said. "Five must die."

"I've done what they asked," Bond said bitterly. "And more than five have died."

"There's no turning back from what we've done. Did you think you were the only one?" Ware asked.

"No. I've seen the work of the others."

"It's why you were chosen."

"Why were you chosen?"

"Because I had the book!" Ware said. "Because I'd read it and understood the ritual. Once I tried to sell the cursed thing, they knew I would know what was happening when they… When you…" Ware reached for the bottle again. "It's my fault. All of it! If I hadn't found it, I—"

"Ware… Who are they?"

"You've read the book, the same as I have. You know who they are."

"The Hand of Aozoth. I know what they are, not who."

Ware shook his head. "I don't want to know, and neither should you. All I know is that they're everywhere." He poured another drink. "Finish your task, Doctor. Maybe they will give you back what you've lost."

"How do I know they're even alive?"

"The letters—"

"Could have been written at the start."

Ware knocked back the drink. "They said you'd say that." He nodded to a door in the back. "In there."

"What is it?" Bond asked.

"Hope."

9 November 1888

The clatter of the carriage steps unfolding echoed in the alleyway. The day had struggled with an iron-grey sky, and as it surrendered to the night Bond stepped from the carriage into the wisps and eddies of fog drifting along the streets. It seemed to him Whitechapel had breathed a grateful sigh as winter finally set in. Like the city, he had paused, waiting for the vigilance of the constabulary and the masses to relax, and for the Hand to command his next and final errand.

"You know where to go?"

"Which I know the way off Dorset Street," Edward said.

Bond nodded and reached up to lay a hand on the coachman's arm. Despite the cold, Edward was pale and sweating.

"It's the last, Edward. Once it's finished, they will be safe, and we will all go very far from here."

"Which I…" Edward trailed off, nodding in return before raising the steps and chucking the horse into motion. Bond watched him go.

Also like the city, as day followed day with no word or resolution, the darkness had come ever closer, so that he felt that every breath was drawn only that he might eventually scream.

At least tonight there is no question, no hunting through the streets as a hound to my victim's fox. It's been arranged and all I need do is make my way to the doss house to finish the deed. This is the last. The heart I must retrieve is too precious for them to allow it to be left to chance.

Bond walked into the rising fog, keeping to the shadows more from habit than necessity. He felt the envelope in his pocket but knew the address by heart.

Ware had been right. They gave him hope in that small room, faint though it was before they withdrew it.

Cybil had been waiting.

She sprang into his arms at once, clinging to him while she wept into his coat. He stroked her hair and held her as if he could protect her from all the dangers of the world, as if he had not already failed in his duty as her husband. He kissed her hands as they parted. She was pale and thin, with hollow cheeks and dark circles beneath her eyes, but she smiled up at him.

"Thomas, my darling! I didn't know if I would ever see you again."

"Nor I you. Is Rose…" He searched the room with his gaze.

Cybil shook her head. "They kept her below, in case…" She paused. "Rose has been very brave. She misses you and sends her love." She gripped his hands. "They don't hurt us. We take care of each other." Then she hurled herself into his embrace once more. "Oh, Thomas, I can't imagine how you've worried! What do they want? When can we come home?"

"What have they told you?"

"Only that you are doing important work, and they will free us when you're done."

Bond closed his eyes, fighting tears. It was a small mercy that she didn't know what a monster he had become.

A masked figure stepped through a door at the back of the room. His robe was the color of old blood, belted with a rough rope that ended in an iron weight.

"It's time," said a man's voice, somehow familiar.

Bond pulled Cybil behind him. "No! Edward! Edward! Come at once."

This ends now. Cybil can help us find Rose and we can escape. Flee to America or somewhere else far away.

Edward burst through the door, but the figure leveled a pistol at the pair. Bond saw the big Webley revolver and knew that if he fired it would kill them both.

"Wait!" Edward froze.

"That was foolish, Doctor." Mask held out a gloved hand. "Come, Mrs. Bond. Your daughter is waiting."

Cybil released Thomas, stopping only to kiss him fiercely. "We'll be all right. Hurry back to us." She walked past the man to where another waited.

"Ware has your instructions." Mask said, then backed through the door. Bond heard the bolt shoot home with a *crack*.

"What's this then?" A voice from beneath a shadowed archway pulled him out of his reverie and back into the street. "A fine, fine gentleman here to visit the likes of ol' Sykes."

Bond tried to step aside, but the man moved to block him.

"Get out of my way," Bond ordered.

"Don't be rude now gov'ner. It's dangerous to be alone here after the lamps is lit. You're lucky I found you. Why, without Sykes here to keep you safe, there's no tellin' wot might 'appen."

Sykes lunged forward, placing a hand the size of a small plate against Bond's chest.

"A coarse there's a cost for that kind of protection. Why don' we start with what's in that bag? Who knows, without Sykes 'ere, you might even meet ol' Jack!"

Sykes never saw the knife. His eyes went round, and he made a gasping, choking start. Blood fell from his lips as Bond pushed him back into the shadows that had spawned him. He wiped the blade on Sykes's coat and leaned close.

"Or you might."

Bond continued on his way, working through the maze until he reached his destination.

"Thirteen Miller Court," he said, and rang the bell. The woman who answered had a weary kind of beauty. One that could still be glimpsed, like the glow of bronze beneath a tarnished facade on a sunny day.

"Yes?"

"I've come to see Mary. I beg your pardon if I've arrived late."

She stepped back and opened the door to let him pass, already dressed for the boudoir. "Your man paid for the night, luv. We have all the time we need."

"Yes," he said, setting his bag on the stand next to the bed. He turned to her as she locked the door, looking for a last moment of innocence from her in a life that had been anything but, then raised a gloved hand and blew a bit of powder into her face. He watched as she stiffened and fell to the floor. He lifted her onto the bed and began setting out his instruments.

"Where should we begin?"

21 December 1888

The bell on Ware's door rang with the same cheer as a grave-bell on a windy day.

Did the breeze tugging the strings create a melody, Bond wondered, *adding life and music for those who lay below, or did someone wake in the cold, silent dark, gasping out their last while their salvation relied on fevered tugs of a fraying thread without knowing if anyone was there to hear? How many times had that thread broken? How many times had someone never tied it to a bell at all?*

A throb came from the pouch concealed by his coat, a strident pulse that filled him with dread as it had since the first impossible beat. He'd fought the urge to show Edward, or one of his colleagues at the hospital. Anyone who could verify that his last act had not removed his sanity along with what little was left of his humanity, but the burden was to be his alone until it was delivered. Traded for

Cybil and Rose and the dream of a simple, normal life he would once have scoffed at.

When Bond received the summons, he almost didn't believe it.

It's nearly over. Nearly finished, and they won't be able to keep us from leaving this time.

He took comfort in the reassuring weight of the Enfield service revolver in his coat pocket.

"Show yourselves!"

Incense smoke drifted lazily in the air, rising from a charcoal brazier. The scent of the room along with its unusual heat, made Bond faint and nauseous.

"Come in, Doctor." Ware came from the back room wearing one of the old blood-colored robes. His mask was attached to the rope belt by a thong passed through one eye. Another cultist moved past Bond and secured the door.

"Show me the heart," Ware said.

Bond stared. "What? You're one of them?"

"I told you, we are everywhere. We all started as something else, Doctor. You started as a physician. A surgeon and a healer. Today you are a killer. I began as a huckster that P.T. Barnam would be proud of. Now the treasures I sell will bring a new age to the world."

"New age!" Bond spat. "An age of carnage. An age of slaughter."

"An age of magic," Ware countered. "Deny it if you can."

"What magic?"

"You know."

"You can see it when you bring me Cybil and Rose and not a moment before!"

"Come now, Doctor, make no demands over which you have no control. We are at the end. Fulfill your bargain. It is the night of greatest darkness, and the time of waiting is past. If you did not obtain the heart, we shall have to secure one." Ware displayed a nasty smile. "From another source."

Another man, robed and masked, entered from the back room.

"We are beginning," he announced.

"It's now or never, Doctor," Ware said.

Bond lifted the pouch over his head and gently reached inside to remove the heart. He placed it on the counter. When he took it from the girl, holding it in his hand and severing the veins and arteries, he felt her life end. After, he had wrapped it carefully in linen strips inscribed with passages from the book and performed the ritual, same as he had with the others. It was when he picked it up to place it in his bag that it began beating again.

Ware looked in awe at the beating organ on the counter.

Bond had hoped to be with Cybil and Rose before trying to escape, but with the odds stacking against him, he had to force Ware to release them. He drew his Enfield and shoved it into Ware's face.

"Don't move! You have what you wanted. Bring them here now or so he—"

Bond felt a sharp pain as he was struck in the back of the head and the Enfield bucked in his hand. He felt himself fall. Blackness closed in and his vision faded to a single point. He recognized the voice just before it took him entirely.

"Thank you for joining us, Doctor."

"Abberline?"

"He could have killed me!" Ware swore.

"Yes, I suppose he could have," Abberline said. "But he is wanted below."

"Bring him then!"

Bond faded in and out until someone struck him with a ringing slap.

"Get up, you, unless you want to be dragged."

Bond staggered to his feet, guessing from the voice and the presence of Inspector Abberline that the other man was Sergeant Thicke. Ware gave him a look of seething hatred, holding the bloody wound on the side of his head, while Abberline reverently placed the heart back into its pouch before passing it to the shopkeeper. Ware wore the pouch as Bond had, then snatched up the doctor's bag before hurrying from the room.

"Abberline, please," Bond said. "I don't care what you are doing. I've done everything you've asked. Kept your part of the bargain."

"After you." Thicke prodded him forward, gesturing with his pistol.

Abberline led them through the room where he last saw Cybil and past the arched door where he had lost her again. Beyond was a landing with stairs of ancient brick and crumbling mortar that descended into the sewers and tunnels that lay beneath the city. From a row of wall hooks, Abberline took a lanthorn that sprang to life with a sickly greenish flame and held the echoing blackness at bay with a wan circle of wavering light.

They followed him down until, turning off into a side gallery, they abandoned the brick tunnels for passages of nitrous-dripping stone and an evil-smelling lichen that gave off a pale phosphorescence.

Despite his coat, Bond shivered at the cold. Eventually, they reached a pair of ancient bronze doors so covered in corrosion that he couldn't discern the bas-reliefs carved into their surface.

As soon as Abberline opened the doors, the rise and fall of a droning chant washed over them, all the more horrific because Bond recognized it at once. It was the song of the automata.

They entered a cavern where columns of dripping stone carved into nightmare visions joined heaven and earth. The singing came from cultists who filled the galleries that lined the irregular room. Five celebrants holding shallow basins surrounded a stone altar while a sixth used Bond's ebony handled blade to draw glowing sigils in the air.

"NOooooooooooo!" Bond dropped to his knees, screaming at what he saw. Even in the dim light he recognized the knife, and there was an organ resting in each basin. Except they were too small. They belonged to a child.

His child.

They had removed them from Rose and replaced them with the ones he had provided.

The priestess set the knife next to Rose's body, removed her mask, and turned to Bond.

"Don't mourn, darling," Cybil said. "We can still be together, like it was before. Tonight, death itself will die as Aozoth rises! Rose will need her father."

The celebrant holding Rose's heart removed his mask.

Not Dashwood too.

"They will say you are the father of the twentieth century,"

I have to take her body from this place.

Bond nodded, reaching out. "Help me up."

They have my gun and my knives, and I'm no match for Thicke, but they haven't taken everything.

As Thicke helped him rise, Bond took a dose of powder from his pocket and tore it open as he staggered. He blew it into the sergeant's face, pulling the gun from Thicke's grasp as he fell.

"Let me tell you about Death!"

Bond shot Abberline before the man could draw his big Webley, then fired randomly into the cavern, scattering the cultists in all directions.

There must be other entrances.

When the Enfield clicked empty, he took Abberline's pistol and emptied that as well.

"Help me, Thomas!" Cybil begged. Sometime during his rage, she had been shot. The robe's color concealed the blood, but a wet stain was spreading across her robe.

He stared at her a moment before walking numbly to where Rose lay. He gathered her small body to him, rocking back and forth as he sobbed into her hair. He felt her heartbeat against his chest.

"Goodbye, Daddy."

An icy shock went through him as she buried the knife to the hilt in his chest, but she clung to him as he tried to pull away. At his end, he saw hell in her eyes.

His name was Thomas Bond, but the world called him Jack.

The second story of our building is a true classic. I love the European-inspired architecture. Fun for the whole family. A truly promising future awaits…but yes, of course, you can see the next floor as well.

* * * * *

Buyers' Remorse by Melissa Olthoff and Nick Steverson

Corey Greer turned his sedan down the road and smiled as his new home came into view. The two-story house was over a century old and didn't have central air, but he'd gotten such an amazing deal on it he couldn't complain. The cynical part of his brain pointed out the old prison cemetery located on the back corner of the property might have something to do with the suspiciously low price. It wasn't his problem if other buyers were too chickenshit to overlook some old, rotting corpses. *Their loss, my gain.*

A shiny black Mercedes was parked out front. A familiar young woman casually leaned against it with her arms crossed and a bright, professional smile on her face. She waved as Corey pulled into the driveway.

"Ms. Freedman?" he said with a nervous smile as he stepped out of his car. "Corey Greer. It's nice to meet you in person."

"You too," she replied as she walked up the driveway and firmly shook his hand. "And just call me Lyz."

Her bright green eyes, smooth caramel skin and coiled ebony locks had him grasping for words. But it was the light freckling across her nose and cheekbones and the kind look in her eyes that really took him over the edge into love at first sight.

"H-hi, Lyz." He cleared his throat. "I mean, hi. It's a pleasure."

Lyz's smile widened, and she swept her open palm toward the house. "Are you ready to see your new home?"

Corey couldn't have stopped his grin if he'd tried. "Yes, ma'am."

The scarred hardwood floor provided the cushion for Corey's face when he fell off the couch a few weeks later. He flopped over onto his back with a groan and checked his watch. It was only a quarter to nine.

"So much for sleeping late on my day off," he grumbled as he rolled to his feet. While he thoroughly enjoyed his new job at the veterinarian clinic, last night had been a late one, and he'd passed out on the couch before he could make it to his bed. "Might as well get to work."

After a hasty breakfast of eggs, slightly stale toast, and cheap coffee, Corey dragged himself to his room and got dressed. He didn't bother with a shower. Lyz had told him the previous owners left all sorts of junk behind, and he'd designated today as attic clean-out day. By the afternoon, he was certain he'd be covered in dust and cobwebs.

Corey trudged upstairs to the attic door, gripped the iron handle, and shoved it open with a shrill *creak* of ancient hinges in desperate need of grease. He had to duck to pass through, but the pitched ceiling within was more than tall enough for him to stand upright. Golden motes of dust floated in the air, illuminated in the rays of sunlight through the windows. He immediately began to sweat and cursed the lack of central air, but once he got the windows opened and set up an old metal fan he found in a corner, it was bearable.

Corey stared at the sheer amount of crap packed into the narrow room. "This… might take a while."

He spent the day digging through the discarded treasures of complete strangers. By the end of it, he had piles of boxes sorted for trash and for keeps, a reasonably clear section to walk, and best of all, he was finally able to get to the large, sheet-covered object that had taunted him from the dusty back corner of the attic. Curiosity had nearly driven him mad, but there had been too much junk in the way to reach it until now. The sheet itself was covered in weird symbols that seemed to be complete gibberish. He stepped closer to examine it when something crunched under his shoe.

Hastily, he took a step back and looked down at the line of white crystalline powder that ran in a circle around the base of the sheet-covered object. Well, it *had* been a circle—now the substance was scattered around the floor thanks to his clumsy feet.

Corey knelt down and examined the powder. "Salt?

Some of the salt grains had gathered in the deep scratches on the floor, outlining them in white. They matched the symbols drawn on the sheet. His brow furrowed as he stood and looked around the attic. Now that he knew what to look for, he could see there were symbols scratched into the floorboards, baseboards, and all along the walls.

"What the hell?"

Timidly, he touched one and his finger came back covered in black. He rubbed his fingers together and his nose caught a scent that reminded him of old campfires, as if whoever drew the weird symbols had used the end of a burnt stick.

Probably someone's pain in the ass goth kid. He snickered. *Or one of the past owners was looney as shit.*

Impatient to see what lay beneath, he grabbed the sheet, yanked it off, and promptly jumped back with a startled shout. "*Holy shit!*"

Eyes wide, he stepped closer to examine his new treasure.

"No fucking way…" Corey breathed as a slow grin spread across his face. "This is absolutely going in my fucking living room."

Deputy Frankie Quinn crouched on her heels, grateful she'd chosen to wear her trusty combat boots. A cool breeze, heavy with the musky-sweet scent of decay, rustled the trees and swept a few fallen leaves across the young man's—boy, really—face. He wouldn't mind, but she carefully plucked them off anyway.

One came away sticky with blood.

Rage and sorrow twisted up inside her, and she silently vowed to find whoever had cut his young life so short.

"What a waste," Dr. Eric Krattman said quietly.

Slightly older than her middling thirties, she'd seen far too much of the medical examiner in the past few months. He pushed sandy brown hair out of his face and snapped on a pair of gloves as he crouched on the other side of the body. "This kid should be living up his senior year of high school, not rotting on the ground."

Quinn's jaw clenched. "What're we looking at, Dr. Krattman?"

"The work of someone who's watched one too many slasher movies," he said with a little too much cheerfulness. His hands told an entirely different story as he treated the body with care and compassion. Gently, he peeled aside the torn shirt, revealing a deep gash carved across the young man's chest. "See how this curves?"

Quinn's eyes narrowed as she noted how it grew shallow toward one end. "Left-handed?"

"If the killer used what I think he did, yes." The ME smoothly stood and strode the ten paces to the cherry red Mustang GT parked at the edge of Crow's Point. She followed and winced at the deep gouges torn through the metal of the driver and passenger side doors. The damage was more jagged than the wound on the young man's chest, but it was obvious the same weapon had been used on both. Eric's cheerful expression hardened as he traced a gloved finger along one of the deeper gouges. "I think it was a hook."

Quinn suppressed a shudder at the amount of force it must have taken to gouge the metal so badly. "Where's the second vic?"

"This way."

She followed him away from the popular make-out spot and down one of the well-maintained trails. They didn't have to go far.

The girl was lying on the ground as if she'd decided to take a nap in the middle of the trail. No blood, no trauma. If it weren't for the terrified expression stamped onto her face and her disheveled blonde hair, she would look peaceful. A bouquet of white lilies had been left in her hands, and several more lilies were braided into a necklace and placed around her neck.

The ME knelt at her side and gently shifted the flowers aside. Deep purple bruises ringed her throat.

Quinn eyed the size of the bruises and compared them to Eric's hands. "Left-handed and male."

He nodded. "In all likelihood."

The beginning of autumn tended to be dry, and this year was no exception. The trail was solid hard-packed dirt and held no footprints. Quinn inspected the area anyway, hoping for something, *anything* the killer might have dropped in his pursuit of the girl. *Nothing. Damn it.*

"First all those teenagers drowning in the quarry last month, now this." Eric stood up and stripped off his gloves. His eyes met hers somberly with just a hint of sharpness lurking in their grey depths. "Maybe my Grandad's stories are true. Maybe this place *is* cursed."

Quinn snorted. "There's no such thing as curses. Just evil people doing evil things." The breeze kicked up again, and she impatiently shoved a strand of blue-streaked brunette hair behind her ear. "And dumb teenagers doing dumb things. Every year we tell them it's too dangerous to swim in the quarry. Every year they ignore us. This year they just… paid the price."

Eric frowned at her. "Hell, that used to be us, remember? And there was the witness report about something pulling them under—"

"I talked to that kid, too," Quinn said with a shake of her head. "He was drunk and traumatized from watching all his friends drown. With the amount of alcohol in his system, I wouldn't have been shocked if he claimed the Loch Ness Monster did it."

The crunch of gravel under tires and a short blast from a siren alerted them to the ambulance's arrival. Eric looked back down at the girl. "I'll get these two back to the morgue and let you know what else I find."

A sigh ripped its way from somewhere deep in Quinn's battered soul. "And I'll go inform the families."

"You sure you don't want me to handle that, Frankie?"

Her shoulders stiffened at that familiar drawl. Apparently, the ambulance hadn't been the only vehicle that pulled into the gravel lot. With a sigh, she turned to face her arch nemesis, her rival, her biggest headache, and general all-around pain-in-the-ass rolled into one annoyingly handsome package. Her fellow deputy, Trent Miller.

The former all-pro quarterback turned law enforcement darling gave her a shiny smile. "I mean it, Frankie. I don't mind."

"I've got it," she said shortly and stalked past him. She forced her jaw to unclench and called back, "But I appreciate the offer."

She snorted softly as she walked back to her truck. *He can smile all he wants, he just wants to muscle in on my case. As usual.*

Later that day, Quinn drove past the old John Ketch house in her deputy sheriff's truck. Outside, she saw a young man industriously ripping out old boards from the porch steps. Fresh lumber with the tags still attached leaned up against the house. *Glad someone finally bought the old place. It needs some fixing up.*

The man looked up and gave her a friendly wave and smile. She waved back and made a mental note to stop by sometime soon to introduce herself—as a representative of local law enforcement, of course. If the mood struck her right, she might throw out some flirty vibes because that smile had been damned cute. But not right now.

Right now, she needed ice cream and quality time with her dog. It had been a long day and she needed to decompress.

Slowly, as if crawling his way up from a deep pit, Corey woke up shivering and stiff as a board. The last thing he remembered was falling asleep in his new favorite chair after another late night at the vet clinic.

"Damn it. Furnace must've gone out. I did *not* need this," he mumbled as he forced aching muscles to work. It took more effort than he'd ever admit to, but at last he was able to sit up. He scrubbed his face and groaned, both about his muscle aches and the possible expense of an emergency furnace repair, when a sharp gust of wind snapped his eyes open.

He wasn't stiff as a board, he was *sitting* on boards. His back porch to be exact.

"Well… I guess that means my furnace isn't out." He chuckled and used the porch rail to haul himself to his feet. "Man, I haven't sleepwalked this badly since I was a kid."

The cold morning breeze rippled through the long grass of his still untamed backyard, colorful oak leaves dancing in the air. Unbidden, his gaze was drawn to the large oak tree on the southwest corner and the graves sheltered beneath its wide boughs. He'd walked out there exactly once and felt... cold. Which was ridiculous, because it had been the middle of summer. He wondered if he'd feel cold if he walked out there now.

He took exactly two steps toward the back steps before a gust of wind shocked him further awake. He shook his head and pulled open the back door. *Clearly, I need coffee.*

After making a pot of cheap coffee barely one step above the gas station brew, he stumbled into his living room with a full mug warming his hands. He wrapped his favorite green blanket around his shoulders and sat in what must be the world's coolest living room chair. Idly, his fingers traced the fingernail marks gouged into the armrests as he cautiously sipped at his steaming coffee.

He'd almost fallen back asleep when his phone *dinged* with a new message. He exchanged the mug for his phone, hoping it was his hot realtor again. She'd messaged him occasionally in the past few months, just checking up on him, but he had yet to work up the courage—or the funds—to ask her out. Unfortunately, instead of seeing *Lyz Freedman* on his display, it was his bank, oh so helpfully informing him that his balance was too low for his next auto draft insurance payment.

He let out a bitter laugh and dropped his phone back on the side table. *Guess I still don't have the funds.*

The hot deputy with the blue-streaked hair popped into his mind. She'd driven past a few weeks ago, and he'd seen her around town a few times since. Frankie seemed more down to earth than Lyz, less fancy in her worn combat boots and beat-up old truck. He might have better luck asking her out. *I mean, she did smile and wave at me.*

His mood perked up before it plummeted again. It didn't matter how fancy a chick was or wasn't if his bank account was still in the negative. He'd have to pick up some extra shifts at the vet clinic. Maybe find a part-time job to cover the unexpected costs of new, or in his case very *old,* home ownership. At the rate he was going, he'd never have the cash to ask anyone out.

Nice guys might finish last, but at least they get to finish. Us broke guys never even get to start...

13

Quinn blinked the flash of the camera from her eyes. She wished the scene before her would disappear along with it, but the horror remained.

"Ever seen anything like this?" the crime scene photographer asked.

Quinn shook her head and fought back a gag. "No."

She pressed a handkerchief over her nose and mouth in a futile attempt to block out the overwhelming coppery scent of blood and gore. Even with the cloth, she could taste it on the back of her tongue. Longingly, she thought of the crisp, *clean* air outside that bloody hotel room, but stiffened her spine. This was her case, and she had a job to do.

Still, Quinn cringed with each step she took into the motel room. The blood in the carpet was so thick in places it pooled around the sanitary booties wrapped around her boots. If her worst nightmare had been multiplied by a thousand, then doubled again, it wouldn't compare to the carnage before her.

A man—she only knew it was a man because his genitals had been pinned in the center of a 'pin the tail on the donkey' poster taped to the wall—had been butchered and dismantled as if he were livestock. In an effort to avoid staring at the mess smeared all over the cheap mattress, she shifted her gaze to the nightstand… and immediately wished she hadn't.

"Punch bowl."

Quinn turned towards the sound of Dr. Eric Krattman's voice. "*What?*"

"It's a punch bowl," the ME clarified. He pointed at it with his silver pen. "You see? The killer stretched the stomach out into a bowl and filled it with the victim's blood. The eyes are floating in there somewhere." He grimaced and pointed to the coffee table. "The top of the skull was sawed off and used as a drinking bowl."

Quinn forced her stomach into submission. "That's… that's terrible."

Drawn by a mix of duty and horrified fascination, she tried to take a step closer to the nightstand only for Eric to block her way with an outstretched arm.

"That's not the worst of it," he said as blood dripped down from the ceiling, where cheerful pink and purple streamers had been strung in colorful loops glittering with confetti and sparkly tinsel. "Take a closer look, but don't step any closer or you'll get splattered." He jerked his head toward the crime scene photographer. "Just like Gerry did."

She frowned up at the ceiling and didn't bother to stifle her gasp. Those weren't party streamers. They were the man's intestines, looped back and forth between the window and the bed. Her sharp eyes caught tiny splotches of pink and purple on the cracked and faded ceiling.

"Spray paint?" Her eyes widened. "The killer *spray painted* them?"

"Real sick fuck," Gerry muttered as he held up his camera. "I've got what I need, I'm out."

With that, the skinny photographer darted out the door. Seconds later, the sound of someone vomiting out everything they'd ever eaten reached them. *At least he waited until he'd cleared the crime scene.*

She swallowed hard as saliva pooled in her mouth and resisted the urge to go join him. "What else you got?"

"There's a bucket over there with the kidneys, gall bladder, and appendix floating in yet more blood," the ME continued in a flat tone. "The kind of bucket people around here use for bobbing for apples." His smile was odd. "'Tis the season, and all that, right?"

"Please tell me this was all done post-mortem," she said faintly.

Something swayed in her peripheral vision, and she snapped her head around, one hand dropping to her sidearm. She really wished it was something she could shoot, but she wasn't that lucky. Tied to the victim's ribcage, which had been propped in the armchair in the corner of the room, was a set of lungs floating in the air. Multi-colored plastic rings littered the floor as if the killer had been playing ring toss with the victim's ribs.

"How..." Her voice failed her.

"I still haven't figured that out," Eric admitted as he peered up at the lungs. "How in the devil the killer managed to keep enough helium in them baffles me. I mean, look at how distended they are." A thread of excitement wove through his voice as he pointed out the neat stitching. "They're filled to the breaking point, but somehow, he sutured them so tight the gas hasn't leaked yet. That takes skill."

Quinn tore her horrified gaze off the perversion of a balloon and scowled at him through her handkerchief. "What the hell is wrong with you, Eric? It *baffles* you? It takes *skill?* You sound like you almost admire the sick fuck who ripped apart and *played* with this poor man!"

"Deputy Quinn..." Eric gave her a strained smile that didn't reach his eyes. "Frankie, this is the job, remember? I perform autopsies and deal with corpses for a living. If I let it affect me, if I don't at least *try* to shield myself from the horror, I'll break." He waved a hand at the foot of the bed where the man's legs stood upright in slippers. "It's not callousness, and it's not admiration—it's armor. I make jokes, and I focus on the how. That's my job. Your job is the why and the who."

"Damn it." Quinn drew in a slow breath and then gagged at the stench. "You're right. Sorry, Eric."

"Don't sweat it." Eric's jaw tightened as he gazed at the blood-soaked scene. "Admittedly, this is a little beyond our normal."

Anger, both at herself and at the killer, rose up in Quinn's chest, but she shoved it back down. Emotions, justified or not, weren't going to help her process the crime scene. She needed to focus on the facts and look for evidence, not waste time being appalled for someone she could only get justice for... not save.

She closed her eyes and counted to ten while taking steady, controlled breaths through the useless handkerchief. When she felt her calm return, she opened her eyes again.

"Have you found anything that might help us find the killer?"

"Possibly," Eric said and carefully navigated the macabre hotel room to the tiny attached bathroom.

He stood to one side so she could walk in. The old tub was filled to the brim with crimson water. Blood spattered rubber ducks, toy boats, and a doll's head with the eyes gouged out bobbed on the surface. She grimaced at the wet towel hanging on the lone hook on the wall before the mirror snagged all of her attention.

A message in the victim's blood was scrawled on the mirror in dripping letters: THE CARNIVAL OF CARNAGE IS BACK IN TOWN. WHO BETTER TO HOST THE PARTY THAN YOUR FAVORITE CLOWN? WE'LL DANCE AND SING TO THE MELODY OF YOUR SCREAM. STEP ON UP, DON'T BE SHY, IT'S THE FUNNEST WAY TO DIE!

Quinn stared. "*What in the actual fuck?*"

"It reads like a calling card," Eric said quietly.

Quinn reread the words, committing them to memory, before she turned to face her ME, a man she'd known for years. "What do you mean?"

His gaze slid to the side. "It just… reminds me of something I've heard before."

"More of your grandfather's crazy bedtime stories?"

"Probably." Eric turned back to the victim on the bed. "There were many."

"And I thought my childhood was fucked up," Quinn muttered before she gave herself a mental shake and focused. Carefully, she tucked away her handkerchief, snapped on a pair of gloves, and collected a few stray hairs from the side of the tub. In all likelihood, it was the victim's hair, but there was always a chance the killer had gotten sloppy with bath time. She also bagged up the towel.

She ventured out of the bathroom and back to Eric who was examining the remains of the torso on the bed. "When would you put the time of death?"

"Impossible to say until I can conduct a more thorough investigation at the morgue." Eric sighed. "Based on what I can see, I'm confident this scene is at least forty-eight hours old."

Quinn nodded and headed toward the exit. "Keep me appraised. I need to go speak with the manager again and canvas the other guests. This room wasn't rented out, but maybe someone noticed something."

Eric tossed her a casual salute. "You got it, deputy. And good luck."

It was not, in fact, her lucky day. The greasy little manager was less than helpful, and none of the current patrons had seen or heard anything. She slid her aviators down over her eyes and tipped her face back to the deep blue autumn sky. As she fought for some semblance of calm, another truck with County Sheriff emblazoned on the side pulled into the narrow parking lot and parked next to her.

Deputy Miller hopped out and slid his Ray Bans down so he could peer over the top like a preppy douchebag. "Heard you caught a nasty one. Want me to take a look, see what you might've missed?"

She stared at him for a moment before she snorted. "You know what? Knock yourself out, Miller."

Quinn stalked to her truck and flung her notepad onto the passenger seat in a fit of frustrated rage. People were dying in her town left and right and she was helpless to do anything about it. Eric was only partially right. Solving the why and the who was certainly part of her job, but the most important part was to protect and serve her community.

And she felt like she was doing a pretty shit job with the whole *protect* part of it right then.

In the next instant, Miller rushed out of the hotel room and vomited all over the pavement. She smirked. It was nice of her nemesis to make her day better.

"Deputy Quinn, fancy meeting you here," the vet tech said cheerfully as he fielded off her dog's excited jumps.

"Just Frankie is fine. I'm off the clock," she replied distractedly as she attempted to calm Cosmo down. Unlike normal dogs, her big derpy goofball *loved* going to the vet.

"Okay, Just Frankie. I'm Corey." The vet tech knelt and scratched her big mutt behind his floppy ears. "And you must be Cosmo. Who's the bestest boy?"

Quinn stared down into his faded blue eyes and abruptly placed his face. "You're the guy who bought the old John Ketch house!"

"If I got a nickel every time I've heard that in the past few months, I wouldn't be working on my day off," he said with a rueful grin. "Then again, if I wasn't working today, I wouldn't have gotten to meet you."

Quinn laughed. "Are you talking to me or my dog?"

His grin turned just a touch wicked. "Definitely you, Just Frankie."

13

Quinn sat in the dusty, dim records room deep in the bowels of the precinct, seriously regretting her life choices. Her back ached from hunching over the old files, her eyes burned from the lack of adequate light, and she'd sneezed so many times her nose was raw from the cheap tissues. Unfortunately, the older files had never been digitized, and there were far too many boxes to drag upstairs to her desk.

She leaned back in her chair, amazed and more than a little disturbed at the sheer number of files. "Maybe there's something to those crazy stories after all."

Eric's grandfather, Chris Branson, had once been the country sheriff, but everyone knew the job had cracked him decades ago. He'd been forced into an early retirement and had spent every day since camped out on his front porch trying to drink himself to death.

With a sigh, Quinn skimmed through the current case file spread out on the desk, but it was just a cut-and-dry domestic disturbance turned fatal. She slapped the file closed and let out another explosive sneeze.

Despite the wildly varied MOs, she was convinced they were dealing with a single killer, or perhaps two perps working together. Whoever it was, they knew what they were doing, leaving very little for forensics to work with. If she couldn't find something to connect all the recent murders down here, maybe she'd have to go pay Branson a visit. Of course, the way her luck was running, this would be the day he finally managed to drown his damn liver.

Repressing the urge to throw the dusty, *useless* report across the room, she tucked it back in the box and pulled out the next file. The quiet had become oppressive hours ago, so she'd taken to reading aloud to fill the silence… and to drown out the occasional *squeak* from the mice skittering around in the shadows.

"Henry Freedman, black male, early forties, prominent local horse trainer convicted of the rape and murder of a young woman. Summarily executed on September 13, 1901." She flipped the single sheet of paper over and scowled. "That's it? That's all there is on this one? Did they not even bother with proper investigations back then?" She sighed and gently put the folder away. "Don't know why I'm shocked with how things were in those days, but damn. No due process at all."

Quinn dropped the next file when her radio squawked. "*All units, Dispatch, code 10-62 at 836 Main.*"

Before she could grab it from the far side of the table, her nemesis responded. "*Copy, Dispatch. Deputy Miller enroute.*"

"Damn it, Miller." She shoved back from the table and haphazardly gathered her things. "*I'm* on call. You're such a fucking glory hound." She clicked the transmit button on her radio. "Deputy Quinn enroute."

This latest crime scene wasn't on the outskirts like Crow's Peak or the ratty motel. The killer had struck in the very heart of their town. Quinn's hands tightened on the steering wheel as she turned into the historic district where the streets were fitted red bricks and the lovingly maintained buildings were older than the oldest living resident. Desperately, she hoped that *this time* the killer had fucked up.

Miller's truck was slanted across two parking spots midway down Main Street, while Eric's ME van was tucked up neatly next to Hershel's Bakery. As she pulled in next to him, she sucked in a sharp breath of surprise. There was an SUV on the other side of the van. An SUV with Country Sheriff emblazoned on the side.

"Rutledge dragged himself away from the desk for this one? Shit…"

Quickly, she got out of the car, strode through the small crowd on the sidewalk, and ducked under the yellow crime scene tape. The frosted glass door covered with cute cupcakes and sprinkles was firmly shut. With a deep breath to steel herself, she yanked the door open.

Miller whirled around and intercepted her before she got more than one step into the bakery. "Maybe you should sit this one out, Frankie."

She snorted, twisted her arm out of his grasp, and strode around him. A large part of her immediately wished she'd listened to her nemesis. The rest of her told that part to suck it up and be a professional. So what if blood was splattered so thickly over the bakery's display case there was no telling what was inside? After the still as yet unsolved clown case, she could handle a little gore.

Sheriff Tom Rutledge stood to one side of the display case, thick arms crossed and balding head perspiring slightly despite the frigid temperature of the room. Absently, she noted the absence of working HVAC, but most of her focus went to the young woman laid out on the counter, where the ME was conducting his exam. He shifted to the side to pull something out of his kit, and Quinn got her first real look at the victim.

She had time to see the number fifty carved into flesh before the chief deliberately blocked her view. It didn't matter. She'd seen the victim's face, seen the horror permanently stamped into delicate features.

"Becca," she gasped.

Miller laid a comforting hand on her shoulder, but she shrugged him off, unable to stand being touched in that moment. His usual cockiness was absent as he murmured, "I'm sorry, Frankie."

Honestly, she would've preferred it if her nemesis were his usual douchebag self. She tightened her jaw, pulling hard on years of training to maintain her composure. She'd drifted apart from her high school best friend over the years, but they'd still talked, still gossiped over coffee, still gone out for the occasional margarita at Crazy Pete's Cantina.

They were supposed to go out next week so Quinn could dish—or vent—about her upcoming date with Corey.

Rutledge wiped his forehead with the back of his hand. She tried not to notice how badly it shook. He'd been out of the field for a long time, preferring to deal with the political side of the job rather than get his hands dirty. "Frankie, go home. Take the day off."

Rage drowned out her sorrow and shock. "*No!* I need to—"

"You need to *go home*, Deputy Quinn," he said, voice hardening. "Your relationship with the victim means you're off this case."

"Go home and take care of yourself right now, Quinn. We've got Becca. Don't worry. She's in good hands," Miller added in what was probably supposed to be a conciliatory tone but just came across as condescending. "Take a few days off. You can come back fresh and get back to work on your other cases. I'll even help you."

"I don't need—" Quinn bit back the harsh words clamoring to escape. As much as she wanted to lash out at Deputy Douchebag, he really didn't deserve it this time. Her eyes burned with the effort of holding back tears, but she couldn't stop herself from trying to see Becca one last time.

When Rutledge used his considerable bulk to prevent it, she turned on her heel and stormed out before she said something that might get her fired. She kept her professional mask firmly in place as she worked her way past the gawkers, kept a lid on her distress as she got back in her truck, kept herself *under control* until she was safely away from the crime scene and anyone who might see. Finally, hands shaking, she pulled behind the local grocery store and gave in to the wrenching sobs that tried to tear her apart.

The storm of tears eventually passed and left her with slow-burning rage. She could handle rage.

"Like hell I'm going home," she growled out. Hastily, she wiped her eyes dry, splashed water from her bottle onto her face even though she knew her eyes would be bloodshot for some time yet and got her ass in gear. "Time to go see the old sheriff."

Dust trails filled the air behind Quinn's truck as she rolled down the seemingly endless dirt drive. Not for the first time she thought about how it took longer to navigate Sheriff Branson's driveway than it did the main highway. After another two meandering curves and one massive pothole that rattled her teeth, the old ranch house *finally* came into view.

As always, the old man sat on his front porch in a rocking chair older than he was, with a shotgun propped up next to him and an old-fashioned revolver on his hip.

"Afternoon, Sheriff," she called out as she shut the truck door.

"You a long way from town, Quinn." Branson leaned forward and spat a stream of brown tobacco juice into the grass. The half empty mason jar of moonshine on the table next to his rocking chair explained his bloodshot eyes. Half a dozen empty ones in a crate behind him told a longer story.

"Yeah, well…" Her hands curled up into fists. "I could use some time away."

He nodded and gave her a knowing look. "Heard about your friend. Good girl, that one. Shame. She had a lot of life ahead of her."

Quinn paused halfway up the porch steps. "You heard about that already?"

Branson chuckled. "Young lady, I might be a retired drunk, but I'm a retired drunk who still hears things. Your phone don't stop ringing after 30 years as sheriff just because you retire." He hesitated and his gruff voice gentled. "I'm sorry about your friend, Frankie."

Quinn hugged herself and looked to the side. "I've consoled countless people when they lost someone. Said all the things we're trained to say. Now that it's me, I'm not sure how some of those people didn't punch me in the face." She turned back to the old man, her eyes hot. "I don't want comfort, Branson. I want answers."

Branson flicked a lazy hand at the empty chair. "Have a sit, Quinn. Take a nip if you think it'll help." He picked up the jar, took a pull that would've landed Quinn on her ass, and held it out to her with a raised eyebrow. When she shook her head, he shrugged and took another, longer pull. "Doesn't seem to help me none, but I figure one of these days I'll drink enough all my problems'll finally disappear."

Quinn dropped into the old rocking chair. "You shouldn't talk like that, Sheriff. And you *sure as hell* shouldn't drink like that."

Branson just grunted in response.

Quinn rocked the chair with the toe of one boot, leaned back, and let the quiet of the countryside sooth her battered spirit. Squirrels rustled through the trees, crows cawed in the distance, and leaves danced in the breeze across the untamed grass fields.

As much as she wished otherwise, reality wouldn't leave her to enjoy the peace for long. The memory of Becca's mutilated body flashed in her mind, and the coppery stink of the crime scene flooded her nose, briefly eclipsing the crisp, clean air. Her jaw clenched. She wasn't here to hide, she was here for answers.

"I can see why you never come to town anymore," she murmured as she tried to think of a way to ease into asking about the town's history without bombarding the old man with questions. "It's beautiful out here."

"Cut the shit, Quinn," the old sheriff grumbled and turned bloodshot eyes on her. "You came out here to pick my brain about something." He shook his head. "Just spit it out. Blunt. That's what you're good at."

"Still an asshole, I see."

He gave her a wide grin. "But now I'm an asshole who doesn't have to be polite." He shrugged and took another sip from the jar. "And I can drink the good stuff without hiding it."

"Your liver hates you." Quinn rolled her eyes before she did as ordered and spat it out. "It's all these murders. All of them have some sort of calling card or signature and they all feel familiar to me. It's like—it's like I've seen them before, but I haven't, you know?" She let out a frustrated sigh and gave serious thought to taking a drink from the jar. "I know it sounds like I'm grasping for straws, but I swear there's something linking all these murders together. There's no way they're all isolated incidents."

Branson didn't immediately respond. Instead, he rocked slowly back and forth, the old wood creaking in a steady rhythm. His eyes were hard as he stared out into the distance.

At last, he said, "You been down into the old records yet?"

"Yes, sir, but I didn't find anything." She paused. "Not a damn thing that made sense, anyways. There's… there's a lot down in that record room. More than a small town should ever have."

Branson kept rocking and didn't answer her implied question. "What makes you think they're all connected?"

"Call it a gut feeling, because I sure as fuck don't have any evidence. Outside of a stupid amount of batshit crazy murders stretching out over the *entire history* of our damn town!"

Again, he didn't take the bait, didn't even acknowledge it was there.

"Feelings don't solve cases, Quinn." He folded his hand over his belly, still not looking at her. "If they're connected, there'll be a pattern. Something that links them all together. Your gut's trying to tell you something, girl." He turned and locked eyes with her. "Maybe you should listen to it."

"I'm trying, damn it!"

"Serial killers have a ritual they stick to," he replied patiently, seemingly unaffected by her frustration. "Sometimes it's a method of killing, sometimes it's a cycle. Like the moon."

"The moon." A derisive snort escaped Quinn. "You think I didn't check to see if the cases were connected to the full moon? At least that would make sense——"

"I didn't say the full moon."

Realization rocked her. "You—you *knew…*"

He just stared at her with that professional cop face, the one that gave nothing away.

Quinn shot to her feet as determination burned through her. "I've got to get back to the records room. If the lunar cycle fits the new killings, I can link it all together and catch the killer."

Branson bowed his head as his shoulder sagged. "It won't work, girl. I done tried. I tried until it drove me mad." He glanced sidelong at her, his gaze conflicted. "The cop in me wants you to leave no stone unturned and to catch the son of a bitch. But the old man in me wants to tell you to let it go. To keep your distance so you don't end up like me—an old drunk slowly drinking himself into an early grave on his front porch."

The resignation on his face said he knew exactly what she would do. Quinn could no more keep her distance than she could hide on this porch. She'd sworn an oath to the people of this town, and she'd do her damnedest to uphold it. As she stared down at the old, defeated man, her hands twitched. She wanted nothing more than to drag him down to the station to help her, but she knew it wouldn't work.

The old sheriff had given up long ago.

Yelling at him would do nothing but waste her time. And the clock was ticking down to the next murder.

"I have to try, Branson."

With that, she rushed to her truck and started the long drive back to the station.

Eric stepped out the front door and onto the porch. "She's a determined one, huh, Grandpa. Why didn't you tell her?"

"She wasn't ready." Branson sighed as his grandson sat down in the chair Quinn had just vacated. "As it is, she'll just drive herself mad. Maybe I should've kept my mouth shut." He grunted and gave Eric a sad look. "Probably shouldn't have told you about all those cases when you were a boy either."

"I don't know about that," Eric said and took a slow sip from the mason jar. "They've come in handy over the years."

"Holy shit." Quinn's fingers tightened on the last of the folders spread out over the table. Her shoulders ached, and her eyes burned from pouring over all the old case files for the last three days, but it was worth it. "It fits."

Branson was right. It wasn't the full moon. It was the *dark of the moon*. Unlike the full moon, the dark of the moon lasted anywhere from 1.5 to 3.5 days depending on the month. Thank fuck for the Farmers' Almanac. Not only had she been able to correlate the older case files with the lunar cycle, she'd been able to look up when the next one would hit.

She had time. Not a lot, but enough to keep investigating. She could stop the next killing. She had to. She just had to make sure Deputy Douchebag and Sheriff Gutless didn't get in her way.

Her phone beeped with a reminder, and she cursed as she noted the time. Her fingers tapped an indecisive beat against the table. She was tempted to cancel, to keep working, but… burning herself out wouldn't do anyone any favors.

An eager smile replaced the frown. She had time. Time to solve the murders, *and* time to get ready for her first date in… forever.

Two months later

Corey fussed with his hair for the millionth time. He wasn't sure what to expect tonight. In fact, he was determined to expect nothing. He didn't want to mess up his third date with Frankie by being a pushy bastard. But *damn*, he really hoped they'd make it back to his place after dinner.

It seemed like they'd been cursed. After a great first date, they'd been trying to sync up their schedules, but had only managed one other date in the past two months. Frankie was understandably busy with the recent string of murders, and he'd had to cancel a few times as well due to several emergency surgeries at the vet clinic.

He resisted the urge to check his phone again. Frankie's last text had said she was running behind and that she'd meet him at the bowling alley before dinner.

"She'll be there." He let out a slow breath and checked his hair one last time in the mirror. "It's going to be a great night. I can feel it."

He jogged down the steps and into the front hall, searching for his jacket. When he didn't find it on the hook next to the door, he ducked into the living room and found it slung across the back of his favorite seat. As he strode across the room, he caught a glimpse of the sun just before it slipped below the horizon. He snatched his jacket off the old chair and smiled.

It was time to go.

Quinn glanced at her phone, nerves thrumming through her, ramping up her tension. *Almost time…*

Beep! Beep! Beep!

With a snarl, she silenced her alarm. This month, the dark of the moon lasted just over three days. If the killer stuck to his pattern, he could strike at any time. And if the past months had taught her anything about the perp, it was that he *would* strike. It was the how, and where, and *why* that eluded her.

Quinn grimaced at her phone, one finger hovering over the screen. She should text Corey and cancel their date. But… she'd already cancelled on him twice in the last two months, and since she didn't know where to look for the killer, or even know what his target would be this month, she had nowhere better to be. Besides, their date was in the center of town, so she'd be centrally located if she got a call.

As an additional compromise, she dressed in practical clothes, the kind that would work for a casual date or chasing down a deranged psychopath. She wrinkled her nose at her mirror. A little makeup might help, along with the cute necklace Corey had won for her at the harvest festival last month.

Finally satisfied with her appearance, she slid into her truck, her belly fluttering with dueling nerves. "Oh man, I'm so late."

Impatient as she was, she was careful to drive at the speed limit, especially with the light drizzle that was bound to turn the roads to shit if it got any colder. She just hoped Corey forgave her for being obnoxiously late again.

As Quinn pulled into the bowling alley, her radio squawked. "*All units, Dispatch, possible B&E at 1004 Orchard.*"

"Copy, Dispatch. Deputy Miller enroute."

Her hand tightened on the radio. Miller was on call tonight, but he wouldn't listen to her about the killer. He didn't think it was the same sick fuck. He had a batshit crazy theory that their sleepy town had been targeted by some sort of dark net social media challenge for murderers. As if that made a lick of sense.

She clicked the transmit button on her radio. "Deputy Quinn enroute."

"I've got this Quinn, it's just another break-in at the cider mill. Probably just a couple of teenagers trying to snitch some of John Bailey's latest batch of hard cider."

"Damn it, Miller. Wait for me."

"Not a chance. Go enjoy your date."

Why did everyone in this stupid town have such a fascination with her dating life? What little there was of it. She sighed as she flicked on her emergency lights and pulled out of the parking lot, tires squealing on the damp pavement. "Sorry, Corey."

Her date would have to wait. She had a killer to catch.

The drive to Bailey's took forever. Not even halfway there, the temperature took a nosedive, and the persistent drizzle began to ice over the roads. She pried one hand off the wheel long enough to radio Miller.

"Miller, Quinn. I'm ten out. What's your status?"

He didn't respond.

"Shit."

Quinn drove faster. The weatherworn sign for Bailey's Apple Orchard and Cider Mill flashed by on her left, and she slowed for the turn. Despite her care, she slid off the road midway through. Her knuckles turned white as she fought to stabilize her truck. The vehicle rocked as she finally came to a stop, a gnarled old apple tree inches from her driver's side door.

"Miller, I'm here. Talk to me."

Nothing.

"Dispatch, Deputy Quinn, I've got a possible officer down, requesting backup."

Static. She strained her ears and thought she heard the honeyed southern tones of their night dispatcher, but whatever she'd said in reply was lost to the static.

"Damn it!" She slammed her radio down and picked up her cell phone to call it in. She stared blankly. "No signal? I'm not *that* far out of town."

Her heart pounded in her chest. She was out of time. She could feel it.

Quinn strapped on her service pistol, made sure her backup piece was in place, and grabbed her flashlight before sliding over and climbing out the passenger door. Rather than use the icy drive, she jogged through the trees, heading straight for the rustic cider mill. Miller's truck was haphazardly parked near the entrance.

The rest of the parking lot stood empty but for an old tractor that hadn't moved in years. Teenagers wouldn't have hiked out here. Not on a night like tonight. Caution urged her to try her phone one last time. It wouldn't even turn on.

Cursing Miller out in her head, she ghosted past his empty truck to the cider mill.

The gift shop attached to the mill took seconds to clear. No light shone from within, but her eyes had adjusted to the darkness well enough to peer through the wide, picturesque window. The shelves full of overpriced knickknacks, local honey, and apple butter were all built into the walls, leaving an open space with nowhere for anyone to hide.

That only left the mill itself, a long, two-story building fashioned like a barn with high windows. Pressing her back against the wall to the right of the main entrance, she let out a slow breath and *listened*. She caught the faint hiss of the rain, the creak of the old apple trees as they groaned beneath the growing weight of ice on fragile limbs—no. That wasn't the groan of the trees. That moaning, pain-filled sound came from *within* the building.

Abandoning caution, Quinn pushed the door open and sidestepped, gun and flashlight carried in the Harries stance as she swept the room. Crates and machinery filled the massive space. This was no show room, it was the production facility for the best damn cider in the county—and it was impossible to clear the room from the door.

The overpowering sweet scent of apples undercut with the sour tang of fermentation and rot slapped her in the face as she slowly paced inside. Another groan drifted on the air, filled with so much pain that it almost sounded inhuman. She quickened her steps even as her eyes constantly moved, searching for threats, searching for Miller.

She found him in the center of the room. Tied to a chair and beaten within an inch of his life. If it weren't for his deputy uniform, she wouldn't have recognized him. Even his hair was the wrong color, completely soaked with blood as it was. Red dripped from his mouth, his nose, his fingers. Nausea twisted her gut when she saw the odd shape of his torso. The clinical part of her catalogued his numerous injuries and noted the broken ribs would make it dangerous to move him.

The rest of her wasn't sure how he was still breathing.

"Easy, Miller. I've got you," she breathed out as she reached for her knife to cut him free.

His eyes opened, bare slits, hazy with agony. His jaw worked and fresh blood trickled from his mouth. "*Run.*"

Her flashlight flickered and died.

At a rough chuckle, Quinn spun around, eyes straining to see in the stygian darkness. A hollow *thump* drew her gaze toward the back of the room, where a large shadow leaned against a stack of crates. The shadow moved, and another hollow *thump* echoed through the cavernous space.

"'ello, Pig." The shadow straightened up. "And 'ere I thought I'd only get to kill one piggie tonight."

She snapped her gun up. "Don't move, asshole."

"You mean like this?" He laughed and sidestepped. "What are you gonna do, little piggie?"

Quinn stroked the trigger, the sharp *crack* of her sidearm echoing in her ears… along with the amused laughter of the madman she no longer had eyes on.

His coarse voice crooned out of the dark. "You know what they called me in the papers? The Cockney Cop Killer. But that's too fancy for the likes of me."

Quinn drew in a steadying breath, aimed at a deeper shadow, and squeezed off another shot.

"I always preferred Pigsticker," he continued in a conversational tone after the echo of her shot faded. "'Course, that name fit better when I used a knife. Decided that was too quick after one of you pigs nearly got the best of me." Another chuckle, another hollow *thump*. "I beat him to death with his own nightstick."

A desperate rattling cough pulled her attention to her fellow deputy. She had to finish this now. Miller wouldn't make it otherwise.

Quinn strained her ears, but the madman had fallen silent and all she could hear was the pounding of her heart. Desperately, she spun in a slow circle, trying to spot him in the shadows. Movement flickered in the corner of her eye. Before she could turn, a wooden baton slammed down on her arm.

The *crack* of her wrist breaking competed with the stabbing agony that shot up to her elbow. Her fingers spasmed, and her gun tumbled away as a heavy weight slammed into her side. All her breath exploded from her lungs in a single, painful rush as she hit the smooth concrete floor, but she didn't forget her training. She brought her arms up to protect her face and thrust her hips upward, trying to throw her attacker off-balance.

His weight didn't budge. He just laughed and knocked away her arms before catching her necklace in one hand. His other arm was held against his chest as if it were injured, but it didn't seem to slow him down.

Snarling in rage, she slammed her good fist into her attacker's side beneath his ribcage. Once. Twice. Horribly quick, he shifted his position like a champion wrestler and pinned both her arms with his knees.

"That tickled, piggie." The hand tangled in her necklace abruptly twisted it tight, cutting off her air. His white teeth flashed in a grin as he leaned closer to her face. "I promise this will hurt."

No matter how she struggled, she couldn't get free. Her heartbeat thundered in her ears. Gray sparkles danced at the edges of her vision as it narrowed and dimmed.

She felt his hot breath wash over her cheek again. "Don't worry, love. I won't let you die. Not for a long time."

Quinn gritted her teeth and smashed her forehead into his. Pain erupted in her head, but his weight *finally* shifted, and she flung him off to the side. The necklace tightened, cool metal digging into her skin, and then it snapped. She sucked in a gasping breath and twisted, her good hand reaching down to her waistband.

The madman roared and slammed his nightstick into her ribs. She curled up as fire burned into her side. He laughed and drew his arm back to hit her again. Her hand wrapped around her backup gun, and she rolled away as the nightstick descended again. Not fast enough. She screamed and fought back the urge to clutch her knee. It wasn't important right now.

Still screaming, Quinn rolled onto her back, ripped her gun from the concealed holster, and emptied the magazine. She was too close to miss. He bellowed and tumbled to the floor.

Shaking from adrenaline, she rolled to her feet. Sharp pain stabbed into her throbbing knee, but it held her weight, and she backed away from the downed madman. Her broken wrist wouldn't cooperate, so she tucked her empty gun under her arm and awkwardly swapped out the magazine. Cautiously, she approached her attacker, gun trained on his center mass, though the dark stain soaking his chest and spreading out from beneath him told her she'd hit him at least once.

His chest rose, breath rattling. "Stupid… pig."

Her flashlight blinked back on, the brilliant beam cutting across her fallen attacker. His eyes seemed to flash green, almost like the reflection of a wild animal, and the flashlight flickered wildly as a green corona flared around him like spectral flames.

Before she could suck in a shocked gasp, the flames died. The light steadied. No more green, only the harsh white of the pitiless flashlight illuminating a face she'd grown to care for. A face set in a snarl of agony and hatred. Between one blink and the next, his eyes turned the familiar blue of faded jeans.

And his expression shifted to confusion.

"Frankie… w-what—why?" His hand pressed against his chest, fingers instantly soaked in deep red. Panic twisted his expression, and tears filled his eyes as he stared up at her. "Help m-me."

"Corey," she wheezed, her abused throat burning as she forced the words out. "Corey, what, *no.*"

He let out a gurgling sigh. The light in his eyes faded away, and they stared sightlessly, *accusingly* at her. Her gun lowered, disbelief and shock leaving her frozen in place. She took a shaky step towards him.

Behind her, static blasted from a radio. Her eyes widened and she spun around. Her fellow deputy had his radio clipped to his belt. The static cleared, and the steady voice of their dispatcher came through loud and clear. *"Backup inbound. Deputy Quinn, Deputy Miller, what is your status?"*

"Miller!" She limped to his side, but her nemesis had stopped breathing. His eyes stared sightlessly as his head drooped. "No, no, no."

Hands shaking, she cut him free, eased him to the floor, and began CPR. Her broken wrist screamed, but she didn't stop. Not even when his heart refused to beat. Not even when his lungs refused to draw breath. Not even when emergency lights flashed outside, the familiar blue and red washing over her in a comforting wave.

She didn't stop.

Winter was nearly over, and the sunlight held some warmth. Quinn's wrist cast had finally been removed earlier that day. For whatever reason, instead of heading home to her dog, she found herself driving out to Branson's place. She'd been doing better lately but getting the cast off had stirred up all the memories of that awful night, and her battered soul needed a little peace.

Branson didn't bat an eye when she pulled up. He just jerked his chin at the empty rocking chair, sipped at his moonshine, and waited for her to speak. It didn't take her long before every detail spilled out of her, even the ones she hadn't told anyone else about for fear of losing her badge.

"I just… I don't understand." She slowly shook her head. "Corey… *Damn it,* Branson. You fed me crumbs last time, but I *know* you know more than you told me. Tell me the truth. I need to understand!"

He didn't look at her. "You ain't ready for the truth."

"She is."

Quinn snapped her head up. "Eric?"

The county medical examiner quietly walked out onto the porch, his winter jacket unzipped and his sandy brown hair rumpled. "Tell her, Grandpa."

A deep sigh rocked the old man's body, but his shoulders rolled back, and he looked at her with something close to pity on his face. "You killed the Pigsticker, right? That's what Corey called himself? Deep voice, English accent, held his left arm like it was twisted up, crippled?"

Unsettled, Quinn nodded.

"I killed him, too. Some twenty years ago. Or at least I killed poor Herbert." Quinn drew back, but the old man's eyes hardened on hers, his words coming faster now. "The Count, the one who carved up your friend? Last time the number was 49. Poor Bob's final words as he lay bleeding out on the floor were 'I wish I could've gotten just one more.' I grew up with Bob, we played poker every Saturday—that wasn't his voice. I got the Florist thirty-three years ago when I was a wet-behind-the-ears deputy. The Clown? Killed that sick fuck *twice*."

Quinn's head spun, and she gripped the armrests, digging her nails into the soft wood. "What are you saying?"

"The killers in this place don't stay dead, Frankie." Branson shook his head slowly, despair and helpless rage stamped into his features. "No matter how many times we kill them, they come back." His fist slammed into the armrest, and he glared at her through bloodshot eyes. "The faces change, but the killers don't. I can't explain it, can't prove it, can't make anybody *believe me*." The rage drained away and left a defeated old man behind. "All I could do was gun down men I *knew* were innocent, until I couldn't take it anymore."

She shoved herself to her feet and shook her head. "No. You're crazy. Corey was the killer. It's over."

"It's not over," Eric said, reaching out to grab her arm. "They'll be back. Every last one of those fuckers were sentenced to the electric chair, confirmed dead, but they *keep coming back*."

She stilled. "I went through every file in that damn record room, including the ones from the old prison. There was nothing there that matched those killings."

Branson reached behind his chair and pulled out a stack of worn folders. Carefully, he set them on the table next to the full jar of 'shine. "That's because there was nothing there to find."

"*Why*? Why would you pull the records?"

Branson smiled, but there was nothing of humor in the ghastly expression. "To try to keep those who followed me from tumbling down the rabbit hole."

Quinn snarled and ripped her arm away from Eric. "You kept us in the dark!"

"No," Eric said quietly. "We were protecting you. Protecting all of you."

"Tell that to Miller." Grief and guilt nearly flattened her, but she glared at the two men. "Oh wait. You can't."

"Frankie, we're sorry about—"

"Don't." She backed off the porch, one hand hovering near her concealed carry gun. "Just stay the fuck away from me."

As she stomped to her truck, shaking in rage, she heard Eric curse. "Frankie, wait! Let us explain. There's more to it!"

"I don't have time for your ghost stories," she snarled back as she slid into the driver's seat.

Before she slammed the door shut, she saw Branson turn to his grandson with a sad expression. "Told you she wasn't ready."

Lyz draped the sheet over the old electric chair and smoothed out the wrinkles. Getting it back up to the attic had taken a bit of creativity. She'd never had anyone actually use it as living room furniture before.

From her purse, she withdrew a charred piece of oak and carefully stenciled the proper symbols. Symbols to purify, to protect, to contain. Symbols to attract, to bind, to warn... though nobody ever heeded the warning. It was a delicate balance, one her family had never quite managed to achieve. The blood on their hands was so thick it was black, blood that now liberally coated her own soul.

Her hand tightened around the sliver of wood, but she was careful not to snap it. It was literally irreplaceable. The wood had once been part of her great great grandfather's horse barn, retrieved from the ashes after it had been burned to the ground by angry townsmen. It was a small, sad piece of her family history... and so much more.

A shiver ran through Lyz as the temperature dropped.

Behind her, a familiar voice whispered, "It won't be long before he finally comes back to us."

The small hairs on the back of her neck rose at that refined, elegant, *beloved* voice, an atavistic reaction she'd never been able to suppress. Lyz blew out a slow breath and gently placed the charred piece of oak back in her purse before she turned around.

A woman in her early twenties stood in the shadows, white gloved hands clasped in front of her and a kind smile on her face. She was classically beautiful, with hair the color of the sun and skin as pale as alabaster. Her navy-blue dress with white polka dots, cinched around her waist by a matching cloth belt tied into an intricate bow, had been the height of fashion. Her shoes, black leather shined to perfection, added two inches to her diminutive height and still the top of her head barely reached Lyz's shoulder.

"I hope so, Grandmother Elizabeth."

Elizabeth gracefully walked toward her. As she passed by the small attic window, the sunlight made the gold in her hair shine. She reached out with a delicate hand and placed it against Lyz's cheek.

She didn't feel it, as much as she wished she could. Not right now, not unless the circumstances were exactly right. Tears burned in her eyes.

"I do so wish I could hold you, child," Elizabeth crooned.

"So do I." A single tear trailed down her cheek as she glanced back at the covered chair. "Mother says the others might just be too strong for him to beat."

"Hush, child," Elizabeth said in a soothing tone. "Your granddaddy is the strongest man I ever knew. Wasn't a horse he couldn't train or a problem he couldn't solve. He'll come around when the circumstances are right. These things have to be done properly after all." Her blue eyes scanned the symbols on the sheet. "You're getting better." She looked down at herself. "I'm not even see-through this time."

Lyz dropped her gaze to the floor in shame. "But I still can't feel you."

"None of that, Lysander Annabelle Freedman." She planted one hand on her hip and shook a finger in her face as a stern note hardened her voice. "You've done far better than your mother, your grandmother, or any of your aunts could. You stand tall and proud."

Lyz cleared her throat and wiped the tears from her eyes. "Yes, ma'am. I'm sorry. I just— it's just… I don't want to disappoint you."

The smile returned to Elizabeth's face. "I couldn't be *more* proud of you, child. Didn't you hear me just now?"

"Yes, ma'am." Lyz looked back over her shoulder at the shrouded piece of dark history. "But what if the chair's hold is too strong?"

"Honey, not even death was strong enough to steal my Henry from this plane of existence. Do you really think that chunk of wood is strong enough to hold him back from me? He knows what he's doing. You just have to trust his judgement— like I always have."

"Of course I trust him, Grandmother. It's just…"

Elizabeth's expression turned to that of concern, and she took a step forward. "What is it, child? You look like you're about to have nervous breakdown."

Lyz cleared her throat and fought back the tears. "It's hard to watch what happens to these people. I mean, look at poor Corey. He was so strong. He was able to host seven spirits. Seven of the most powerful and evil spirits chained this chair. That's more than anyone else I've sold this house to." Her eyes dropped to the floor and her voice softened. "And he was a nice boy. He didn't deserve what happened to him."

The crunch of gravel under tires caught both their attention. Lyz rushed to the window to see a truck parked in front of her real estate sign.

"Best put your sales face on, dear. We can pick up this conversation at a more appropriate time."

"Yes, Grandmother." Lyz ran a hand down her sport coat and cleared her throat. She exited the attic, shut the door behind her, and calmly walked down the stairs. Once out the front door she put on her biggest "I'm so happy to see you" smile and approached the idling truck.

The truck's door opened, and a tall African American man stepped out. He wore a trucker style ball cap, a button-down flannel shirt, faded blue jeans, and worn square-toed work boots. His lean yet muscular physique spoke of hard labor rather than a gym, and the calluses on his palm rasped against hers as they shook.

"Ms. Freedman, I assume?" he said with a warm smile. "Henry Jones. It's good to meet you."

"You too," Lyz replied. "And just call me Lyz. Are you ready to see the house?"

Henry shook his head. "I saw the inside online." He pointed toward the back of the house. "What I want to see is out there."

With that, he set off for the backyard. Lyz struggled to keep up with his long, excited strides. She only caught up when Henry came to an abrupt stop, gazing out over the open field with his hands on his hips and a pleased expression stamped on his face.

"This here'll do fine," he said.

Lyz kept her sales smile firmly in place. "Fine for what?"

"For the training."

She had no idea what he was talking about. "Training? What do you mean?"

Henry looked down at her and chuckled softly. "Sorry. Sometimes I forget context is key in conversations." He fished a business card from his shirt pocket and handed it to her.

"Jones Breeding and Training," Lyz read aloud. There were two black stallions on either side of the card reared up on their hind legs. "You work with horses?"

"When they work with me," Henry answered. "Breed them, raise them, train them, but most importantly, love and respect them." He nodded toward the wide stretch of open field. "This is twice the land I have now and half the price I paid. The house is just a bonus." He pointed at the large oak. "I can put the stables there and off to the center three training rings. I only have room for one at my current place."

"Oh, he is perfect…" Elizabeth said from the porch. She stared at Henry with a look Lyz had never seen on her great great grandmother's face before. Hope. It was hope.

Henry glanced over his shoulder with a slight frown. "Did you say something?"

He couldn't see Elizabeth. Nobody outside of the family could. Lyz forced her smile to widen. "Oh, I was just saying this place seems perfect for you."

Thunder rumbled in the distance, stealing Henry's attention away. He gazed out over the fields and tilted his face up toward the sky. "Looks like a storm's rolling in."

"All units, Dispatch, code 10-62 at 4567 Hamilton Way."
"Dispatch, Deputy Quinn… enroute."

"Generations of the same family have occupied this floor. The story is steeped in their history, and they often have the lowest electric bills of any of our residents. They're truly lovely people, as most horse-lovers are…All right, up to the fourth story."

* * * * *

Hungry by Kevin Ikenberry

Mike Patton stopped mid-stride in the kitchen and scratched his upper thigh. Through the jeans there was little relief, and as a hot, biting pain blossomed he thought, *What bit me?* As he unbuckled his belt and fumbled with the bottom of his Pittsburgh Steelers t-shirt, the heat rose a thousand degrees. Sliding his jeans down, Mike expected to find a spider, or something else, clinging to the skin. There was nothing there, nor in the pants leg. The site itself looked more like a fresh mosquito bite and despite how bad it felt, there was no hint of redness. Mike ran a finger over the hot, swollen area for a long moment.

"Something got me good." Bent over, arms down the legs of his jeans, he was the picture of immodesty as his wife walked out of the laundry room.

"What are you doing?" Lisa laughed and lightly smacked his underwear-clad ass.

"I think something bit me." Mike straightened and pointed to the site. "See?"

"Doesn't look so bad." Lisa poured a glass of water from the sink. "What was it?"

"No idea. Felt like an ant bite." Mike pulled up his pants and buckled them. He grew up in Georgia, and spending untold hours outdoors in the miserable, humid summers acquiring similar bites, made him sure of the cause. "We still have that allergy stuff?"

"You mean calamine lotion?" Lisa's shoulder-length black hair caught the sun against the kitchen window. Her petite Asian features were flawless. "Up in the cupboard above the dishwasher. You find an ant or anything?"

"Nothing on my leg or in my jeans. Where's that lotion?" Mike sighed as he found it, behind an opened box of adhesive bandages, and set the bottle on the counter. "I'll put some on when I get back."

"Is it itching?" Lisa asked. "Are you still going to the store?"

"No, it's not itching yet. It will, though." Mike ran a hand through his longish black hair as he grabbed a list of groceries from the table. "We still need this stuff for dinner tomorrow, right?"

"Well, yeah."

"Then I'm going to the store." Mike grabbed the keys. "Anything else?"

"Just be safe." Lisa smiled and blew a kiss. She always said the same thing, and it never failed to make him smile. The smile froze as he stepped into the garage. Pain shot upward towards his abdomen. Disoriented, with a shaky hand on the hood of Lisa's white sedan, he struggled to breathe.

His tongue felt thick and pasty. Breath hitched and rasped in uneasy rhythms. Cold sweat ran down his spine even as the heat flourished all over his body.

What the hell? Mike leaned forward and placed his forehead against the cold metal as his vision began a violent spin. Hands trembling, he reached for and missed the passenger side mirror.

Lisa! The words would not come. Pain exploded and the room spun faster. *Lisa!*

Again, there were no words. Instead, his stomach chose to empty itself. Vomit splattered the concrete floor. Focus dimmed as his eyesight started to fail. The retches kept coming, louder and more violent with each passing second.

Lisa!

Finally an incoherent noise left his mouth, followed by wracking coughs. The blackness at the edge of his sight grew larger, more inviting. The pain and the heat never relented, instead growing worse with every passing second. Lisa seemed so far away, and so scared, as she screamed his name.

It will be okay. It will —

Peter Weir searched the hardware store for an outdoor children's gate in vain. The infernal thing was not in hardware, nor in home projects, or decks, or anywhere near the other gates and doors. A uniformed sales associate walked towards him and smiled. Maybe, just maybe, she would know where to find a gate. The perfect gift for his sister's family, and he couldn't find the damned thing anywhere. Peter shook his head as his smartphone rang. He glanced at the screen and frowned. The on-call service.

"Doctor Weir," he answered.

"Peter, this is Mike Adamson at Saint Thomas. I have a male patient in the ER, twenty-nine, normally fantastic health, with what looks like a necrotizing fasciitis on his upper right thigh. He's running a very high temperature, and his blood pressure is erratic. Can you come and take a look?"

Peter spun on his heel and walked toward the front of the store, mind racing at all the possible causes. The obvious came first. "Something bite him?"

"He's in and out of consciousness right now. His wife said he complained that it felt like an ant bite. I've got our attending surgeon here, Doctor Ben White. He's not convinced it isn't a rattlesnake bite."

In the middle of winter? Weir shook his head and chuckled. "Keep that old codger away from that leg until I get there. Have you ordered a full CBC?" The complete blood count test would provide as much information about the patient's internal conditions as possible. Time and information were the biggest weapons Weir had at his disposal.

"Just now. How fast can you be here?"

"Ten minutes. Just down the street." He ended the call and moved faster, around couples with their children and shopping carts full of projects. Outside, he jogged to his car. Necrotizing fasciitis - skin-eating diseases - were very random and misunderstood. Most of the time, there was at least some shred of a cause. Something was not right. He searched the contacts section of his phone and tapped the number marked Peak Infectious Disease Specialists, his office.

"Brenda, Doctor Weir. I'm headed to Saint Thomas for a consult. ER thinks they might have a NF. Let Doctor Shelby know, will you?"

"Will do." Brenda's midwestern accent reminded Weir of an actress whose name he could never seem to remember.

"Thanks," he said and ended the call. The drive to Saint Thomas took five minutes, much less than it felt. He hustled through the emergency room's physician entrance, stepped into a staff bathroom, and scrubbed down. With a stethoscope hung around the neck of his dress shirt and fully disinfected hands, he walked into the common area and caught Mike Adamson's eyes.

"Mike," Peter said. "Where's our guy?"

"Room Five." Mike said. "CBC came back. White blood cell count is off the chart and his infection markers are crazy."

"Is he septic?" Peter asked. "Or SIRS?" Systemic Inflammatory Response Syndrome was the whole body's reaction to a serious known infection.

"That's where you come in, smart guy. I don't think he's septic yet, but he's close." Adamson shrugged. They'd been residents together for several years and knew each other better than most of the rest of the staff.

"Any kidney function?" Weir asked.

"Minimal. He's severely dehydrated, too. We've hung two liters of fluid already and started him on a morphine drip."

Peter nodded. "Where's White?"

"On his way." Adamson said and handed a couple of sheets of paper to him. Medical history. Half of it was still blank, and the implication was clear. Go in, ask a lot of questions, and figure out what in the hell was happening. "Go talk to him. I'll be right there."

Lisa Patton held her husband's hot, limp hand and tried to appear composed. Doctor number three entered the room and offered her a quick smile. This one looked at Mike with care in his eyes unlike the cold fish surgeon and the clueless ER doctor. Mike lay sleeping on the bed, his skin bright pink except for his sallow gray face. Hitching ragged breaths gave the only sign he was alive.

The doctor looked at the readouts of the various machines around Mike's head before he looked at her again. She stood and shook his out-stretched hand as he smiled. "Peter Weir. You're Lisa?"

Lisa nodded. "Yes."

"When did this start?" Weir motioned for her to sit back down, and she did before her quivering knees gave out.

Lisa looked at her watch. "An hour and a half, maybe. Mike was going to the store, and I heard something in the garage after I thought he'd gone. He was laying in the floor surrounded by vomit. I couldn't get him up…." Her voice broke and tears filled her eyes. "His-his eyes were rolled back in his head, and he twitched a lot until I…got him around."

Weir squinted. "How did you get him around?"

"I slapped him." Lisa shrugged. "Hard as I could."

The doctor chuckled. "It was enough to get him here, right?"

Lisa found herself smiling through her tears. "Guess so."

"Let's take a look here." Weir pulled back the blanket over Mike's legs and gasped. "Holy shit."

On Mike's upper thigh, a red, black, and purple smear covered more than six inches of space like two globs of butter slowly melting together. Black at the center and radiating outward, they were far enough apart to have not been caused by a venomous bite. The marks did appear to be spreading by gravity, which venom tended to do.

He looked over Mike to meet her eyes, his cheeks hot with embarrassment. "Sorry about that. I've never seen something this bad. Was there anything here before a couple of hours ago?"

"No, he said it felt like an ant bite." Lisa shrugged. "Looked like a mosquito bite when he showed me."

Weir pulled on a set of examination gloves. "Well, I can tell you that this isn't presenting like anything I'm familiar with. Don't let that scare you. Sometimes things react differently in different folks." Gloves on, he began to touch and probe around the site. The angry, red skin was hard to the touch. Mike stirred and moaned but did not wake. "The skin is firm in some places and pocked with fluid sacs in others."

"Does that mean anything?"

"Yes and no. This is cellulitis, inflammation of the skin. Odds are it's going to get worse before it gets better. These black areas are the areas I'm worried about."

Lisa watched him working, trying to feel beneath Mike's skin with his fingers. "What is it? I mean what's causing the cellulitis?"

"Doesn't look like a full blown necrotizing fasciitis. That's a good thing, but it's too early to tell. There's some blackness here that could be it, but I doubt it. I can't feel how deep this swelling goes." Weir stepped back and removed the gloves. "Has he been awake since you came in?"

"A little bit. Just said he was hungry and went back to sleep."

"His vitals are improving, but I really doubt he'll want to eat anything for a while." Weir's eyes dropped to her legs for a moment. The streaks of yellow vomit obvious across her pants. "If you want to go home and clean up…"

Lisa's face flushed. "You're going to admit him?"

Weir nodded. "Straight to Critical Care. He's pretty sick."

"I'll stay until he's in a room." Lisa nodded.

"Would you like me to find you some scrubs?" Weir asked. "Or something to drink?"

Lisa shook her head. Her eyes back on Mike's slackened face. "I don't want to leave him."

Weir didn't say anything else and left the room. Tears ran down Lisa's cheeks as she looked over Mike's yellow face and bright red body. What had they done to deserve this? Her mind whirled with a million unanswered questions. Watching Mike breathe, every other care in the world seemed so far away.

Darkness.

Mike fluttered to consciousness in the dark without startling. The soft whirr of machinery and the faint tinge of antiseptic said "hospital."

What the hell happened?

He remembered lying on the cold, oil-stained garage floor. The hint of oil in the smell of the dust and grime. Opening his eyes took a moment longer than expected. He clicked his tongue against the roof of his mouth and found no purchase. Mike looked for something to drink but saw nothing within reach. A pump whirred and clicked. An intravenous line ran into his right elbow and a sensor covered his index finger. Raising his arm felt normal, if detached a bit. His left arm only held a blood pressure cuff. The cuff inflated and tightened around his upper arm. Looking to either side as far as his head would turn, a monitor was nowhere to be seen. A remote control rested against his thigh, but he didn't reach for it. Something in the darkness felt good around him. The peacefulness resonating and centering in its goodness. He was alive. He was -

Hungry.

Mike blinked. Was he hungry? His stomach felt a million miles away and lined with lead. A drink of water, yes. Food? Aches trailed throughout his body. Every movement, even the curling of his fingers, seemed to happen in slow motion and as if he watched someone else. Turning his head took a herculean effort that left him dizzy and nauseous.

Hungry.

In the low light, he could see the blanket over his right leg was much larger than over his left. What had happened?

Infection. He remembered through the haze of the day. Where was Lisa?

A wall clock came into focus. Half past two in the morning. Lisa was home, in their bed, alone and terrified. Mike thought about calling her but decided against it. A call from the hospital, this time of night, would send her into a panic. He wished to be home, with her curled up next to him like a cat in the sun. Better to let her sleep. She would be back in the morning, just in time for-

Hungry.

His right leg twitched at the word. The sound of it came as if another person stood in the room. Mike felt the chills building, a stony detached feeling in his knuckles came first followed by uncontrollable shivering. Every breath took effort. Gooseflesh pimpled under the flimsy hospital gown. He grabbed the thin blanket and pulled it up with trembling arms. The movement let him feel a catheter placed in the most uncomfortable spot imaginable to a man. Sensors snagged and pulled in his chest hair, heavy and annoying.

What in the hell is wrong?

The television remote control clattered to the floor. Looking at the oversized white plastic controller, he thought for a moment before pressing the call button on the bed rail. A nurse appeared at the door less than ten seconds later.

"You're awake?" Silhouetted against the light in the hallway, Mike could only tell it was a surprised woman with short hair.

Mike nodded and tried to smile. Given how he felt, it probably looked like a grimace. "Can I get some water?"

"Sure," the nurse said and disappeared. The door swung slowly closed and gave him a lingering view of the hallway. The typical carpeting and paint scheme of a normal place seemed distant. Like he would never get back there. He was still looking at the door when it opened again, and the nurse walked silently across the

tile floor. The line between the tile and the carpeting of the hallway stood out like a physical barrier.

"How sick am I?" Mike asked as she fumbled a straw into his mouth. The sip was too short to do more than wet the tongue.

The nurse, a pretty younger woman with brown hair and kind eyes and frowned at the same time. "The doctors will be doing rounds soon. You're in the ICU, and that means that you're pretty sick. How are you feeling?"

Hungry.

Mike shook his head. Not real. "Tired and cold."

"The chills?"

Mike nodded once, suddenly very tired. "Yeah."

The nurse looked above his head, to the monitors he could not see. "You're running a pretty high fever."

"How bad?"

"One hundred and four point six. I can't get you any more blankets." Again the frown that tried to be a pitiful smile. "My name is Cammy, by the way. I'll be back to check on you in a few minutes."

"Nice to meet you," His eyelids heavy, Mike heard her tell him that if he needed anything to push the call button. She was already moving out the door as Mike felt sleep coming to overtake him. He took a deep breath.

Hungry.

Stop it. Mike thought. *I'm not hungry.*

Hungry.

A tremor started in his right leg. Within seconds, his leg bounced again and again into the mattress. The bed groaned and shook from side to side as the voice growled again.

Hungry.

Shaking violently, Mike's eyes snapped open. His leg throbbed and his crotch burned. Fingers of ice slid up his spine and down his arms. The conflict of feelings overloaded him. Eyes on the remote, he could not manage to lift his hand. Words would not come, and there was not enough breath in his lungs to scream.

Don't panic. The alarms will sound. They'll come running. Every medical drama he'd ever seen told him so, and he tried to believe it.

Hungry!

The voice roared again and again. The tremors increased, the bed shook from side to side. On their own, his arms moved toward the hem of the blanket. With a sweep, he threw the blanket off and felt a scream die on his lips. From his swollen testicles to his ankles, his right leg was a ghastly purple and red. Quivering black blisters the size of his fist covered the flesh in all directions. They shook and sloshed with the tremors. White pus leaked from smaller blisters between the monsters. His leg continued to shake. A blister in the center of his thigh ruptured as he watched. Clear, viscous liquid drained in all directions. Two inches long, filled with yellow fat and blood, the abscess began to pulsate. It contorted and moved as if mouthing the words.

Hungry.

The up and down tremors gained direction, pulling him toward the edge of the bed. His leg moved uncontrollably toward the door as it opened. Cammy shrieked and dropped the laptop computer in her hands. Plastic shattered and spread across the floor.

"Help," Mike screamed. "Please help me!"

Cammy stumbled backward into the hallway, a hand over her panicked face. A flurry of frenzied activity started in the corridor as he stared at his leg. Fresh pain exploded, bringing tears to his eyes and great heaving screams from his lungs. He could hear people asking what to do. He tried to cover his legs with the blanket and his leg lashed up towards his arm. Mike flinched away. *What the?*

Hungry.

Thigh thrashing and pulling, Mike struggled to focus. The world seemed farther away. Everything distant, blurry, and muted. He grabbed the remote and mashed the emergency call button. As he did, his leg settled to the bed as if nothing had happened. The lights snapped on, voices called out to him, but there was nothing he could do. Moving was impossible. Nothing responded. A warning klaxon began to sound.

"CODE BLUE. INTENSIVE CARE ROOM TWO ONE ONE SIX. CODE BLUE. INTENSIVE CARE ROOM TWO ONE ONE SIX."

Cold hands pressed onto his chest and arms. Something slapped down over his mouth and nose. Cold, dry air made him cough and sputter as the darkness came. An instant of intense pain blanked every other sensation out. The voice rose from a whisper to a scream.

Hungry.

His leg began to move, and he could not stop it.

"Get away!" He screamed into the oxygen mask. No one heard him.

Hungry.

The open wound closed and smacked together like thick, wet lips. The leg lashed up towards the unsuspecting nurses with an open maw and incomprehensible teeth. The heat in his thigh exploded and the voice shrieked in delighted rage. His thrashing body burst free of the hands restraining it. Light became darkness as the world faded away.

This can't be happening.

Lisa?

The voice roared at her name. A wet ripping noise filled Mike's ear, and he began to scream.

Hungry!

The room smelled of blood even through the stiff plastic contamination suit. The metallic taste filled Peter's mouth as he pushed through the plastic vestibule into Mike Patton's room. The precautions were an afterthought now. As if they alone could hold in the danger. The body lay there, gray and cold. The blood spatters across the floor, walls, and ceiling caught Peter's eye. A stream slashed across the fluorescent light fixtures. A dark crimson stain surrounded Mike's lower body, soaking through all of the sheets and pooling on the floor. There was so much blood. Peter pulled back the soaked sheet across the body and blinked.

What?

Mike's leg was completely detached at the hip bone, severed in a ragged way with strips of flesh hanging from the meat around the cold gray femur. The nurses said that his leg ripped itself off. The wounds pulsed and contorted as they tried to save him. Nothing could be done as he thrashed and snarled at them. They said the wounds snapped at them like teeth. His leg flipped and thrashed at them while Mike died screaming over and over again.

"Hungry," the nurses reported. "Hungry."

When his leg detached and severed the femoral artery, he bled out quickly. The staff left the room in shock. The infectious disease protocols, to seal off the room and restrict access, did not bring calm or reassurance to the staff. The ones crying on the picnic tables outside and smoking cigarette after cigarette with shaking hands would never be the same. He'd seen them as he ran into the hospital. Their eyes followed him, full of blame for what had happened. It was too late to save Mike Patton. Only the Centers for Disease Control, and their critical response team, would be allowed to collect and sample the corpse. The hallways were busy. Nurses and staff with strained faces hustled the beds of the very sick to other parts of the hospital. No one would be allowed to stay in the wing until the investigations were completed. Rumor and gossip could scare the fragile patients into more serious issues.

Peter focused his attention on Mike's face. Nothing from medical school could have prepared him for this scene. The room was something from a deranged slasher flick. There was no way that any of it was real. He wondered when the staff would pop out from behind the curtains and yell "Gotcha!" However, the longer he stood silent and confused, the less likely it was. Blood and tissue lay everywhere. A medical explanation escaped him.

How could this happen? He glanced at Mike's face, calm and serene in the carnage. His right leg lay a good two feet from the severed thigh, the foot overhanging the end of the bed. The abdominal cavity, and the ropes of intestines, were clearly visible in the tear.

What in the hell-

The leg twitched and Peter jumped backwards.

Jesus!

Peter ran from the room without another thought. Running down the hallway, his heart trip-hammering, Peter ducked into the washroom and scrubbed his hands.

It was a long time before he felt clean.

Lisa raced into the hospital. After she'd run her second red light, an El Paso County Sheriff's deputy on a motorcycle pulled her over. As the man dismounted his bike, Lisa rolled down the window. The cold air stabbed at her flushed cheeks and threatened to freeze the tears running down her face.

"I'm sorry! I have to get to the hospital!"

The officer paused. "What hospital?"

"Please! My husband is crashing! They called me!"

"What hospital, miss?"

Lisa screamed. "Saint Thomas! Please!"

For a moment, she thought he was going to arrest her. The officer pointed at her. "Turn on your hazard lights and stay right behind me!"

Within seconds, they tore down the freeway at high speeds. At the main entrance to the hospital, the officer asked for her keys, but Lisa was already running toward the door. A few people turned to gawk as she pounded the elevator call buttons over and over again. She gave up and sobbed loudly as she ran up the stairs to the second floor. As she burst into the Intensive Care Unit, Doctor Weir stepped out from behind a console and caught her by the arm. "Lisa?"

She stopped and saw everything in his eyes. "Mike?"

Weir paused. "I'm sorry, Lisa."

Her knees began to shake. As she sank to the floor, Weir caught her and put an arm around her shoulders. He was talking to her, something about trying everything to save him. The infection was too much for his body to handle.

None of it really mattered.

Lisa sobbed into her hands. The cold feel of her wedding band against the hot tears on her cheeks brought fresh sobs. What was she supposed to do now? They had so many plans. They were so young.

"Why?" She sobbed into Peter Weir's neck as he held her.

Oh, Mike.

"We're going to Hawaii next week." Lisa sobbed. "This can't be happening. Oh God, please no! Please, bring him back!"

A million thoughts raced as she cried. So many things they wanted to do. Dreams they shared and wished to come true reduced to nothing in the blink of an eye without a cause. *Why him? Why now? I can't even tell him I'm late.*

Eight months later, and two floors up from the Intensive Care Unit, Lisa gave birth to a perfectly healthy boy. She named him Michael Anthony Patton, Junior. Visitors from the hospital staff on Mike's case came by through the day after delivery one-by-one. The nurses and their tears, the doctors and their clinical look at the baby to cover their own efforts not to cry. Lisa could not tell if they were scared, or if their visits were more from morbid curiosity. The birthing room was a mixture of sadness and joy, much like the last year had been.

After lunch, when all of the grandparents decided to give Lisa some peace, she lay back against the bed and watched Michael sleeping. He would be ready to eat again soon. He certainly relished it. There was a soft knock at the door.

"Come in."

Peter Weir walked in the room looking much the same as he had the first time they met. He did not say anything as he approached her and sat on the edge of her bed. Lisa leaned forward and wrapped her arms around his shoulders and fresh tears came. His hands were on her back, smoothing her hair as she cried silently. There would never be another Mike, but this good man would come close.

"Are you okay?" He asked without pulling away.

"Yes," Lisa managed to say. "It's so hard."

"It is hard." Weir said. He took a breath. "You're the strongest woman I know."

Lisa sobbed once and squeezed him tightly until Michael stirred. The soft peal made her smile. Her little boy was healthy, and the nurses said the way he took to eating was better than any baby they'd ever seen.

"Time to eat," Lisa said with a laugh.

Peter let her go. He stroked her face as they pulled apart. "When you're ready-"

"Yes." Lisa smiled through her tears. "Yes, Peter."

Weir smiled and blushed. "Okay."

Michael squealed louder. Lisa tilted her head towards the clear plastic bassinet. Two little fists punched the air and wobbled. "Hungry little guy. Eats every two hours like clockwork."

Peter wanted to say something, but the feeling of *deja vu* stopped him. He looked at the healthy pink baby as Lisa scooped him up in her arms and offered her breast to him. She looked up at Peter, but he was still watching the baby and wondering why something he'd seen for years bothered him

The baby's legs twitched as he ate, making Lisa giggle.

Peter could only stare.

Author's Note:

"Hungry" is based upon actual events. On February 16, 2014, what happened to Mike in the kitchen of his home actually happened to me. While my situation differed greatly from Mike's, within about eighteen hours I was admitted to the Critical Care Unit of a local hospital with a fever in excess of 105 degrees, minimal kidney function, and teetering on the edge of septic shock. Over the course of the next several days, my medical team raced to get ahead of the necrotizing fasciitis in my right thigh. They saved my leg, and ultimately, my life with their care. I originally wrote this story in 2014 several months into my recovery and, in tribute, the doctor in the story shares the first name of my doctor. Thank you for everything, Pete.

"Shall we pause for a snack? I know it can be so tiring, climbing all these stairs. Do you need a doctor? No? We have quite a few in the building…Well if you're sure you're fit to continue, upward we go."

* * * * *

Wraith by Marie Whittaker

In 2027 Sleepy Eye, Minnesota, few things were a commodity, but salt was at the top of the list.

It had all started with a seemingly harmless crack in a sidewalk down in the Tenderloin District of San Francisco. That crack was a little deeper than most thought. It was a fissure that ran deep below the city into the volatile earth. What the world mistakenly thought was some kind of methane gas escaping was actually the beginning of The End. Patient Zero was an undeserving homeless woman who'd been asleep in a big cardboard box. She'd taken the blast of dark mist straight in the face, tried to run, and hit the ground like a sack of we sand.

Enter Wraith One.

The following weeks went by like cinema as I watched my species perish to near extinction. I was only fourteen when people started dropping like bricks and rising like kites, oily black in the shadows like the shades they were.

And then the world crumbled in on itself. The world fell. Three years had gone by like molasses in Minnesota pond water since then.

People died fast, and wraiths appeared from the piles of bodies, sheets of black death clawing their way out of an oil spill. I'd watched a few of them being born, if I could call it that. Spawned was more like it. They were predators who hunted humans.

First, there was the buzzing, humming sound to let a victim know they would soon be dead. Then there was the dark mist that sprayed from the wraith's face hole. It was sort of like a spider paralyzing its prey. The human would go down hard, and the wraith would go to lunch, devouring the person's soul and fluids as their body died, shriveling into nothing more than a leathery husk that drifted on the wind, skittering down deserted streets like crumpled, yellow newspaper. From that husk, after the wraith finished its meal, would emerge a new wraith, what was left of the person who had been killed.

Most times.

Other times, the wraith would eat the human, and no new wraith would spawn from the mess. I still didn't know why. Was it that the human was sick with something? Would some disease like cancer stop a new wraith from being born?

And it wasn't just a physical or biological thing. Wraiths were supernatural. Nothing natural or pure could exist and gut the world the way they did. Wraiths were oozing, cloaked evil in a physical form. Deadly and ravenous.

The dominant predator at the top of the food chain.

Three years later, the world was full of starving wraiths. I was a commodity for them just like protein powder was for me. The root cellar in Sleepy Eye at my family home was my safe haven. Three years is a long time for a young woman to exist inside a hole in the ground with no contact with the outside world. Skin hunger began to drive me insane. Humans are social creatures by nature. I wanted someone to talk to. To touch. It wasn't a sexual thing by any means. I was lonely and wanted to find my tribe.

I wanted a hug and a back rub and a reassuring pat on the shoulder. All the things I got from my dad and my friends at school before the fall. Thinking about my dad hurt really bad at first, before my heart hardened.

As close as I could figure, it was my seventeenth birthday. My dad named me June "Bug" Dempsey on June thirteenth, about seven hours after my mom died. "June" had fallen away quickly, thank God, and "Bug" stuck around. These days, I scarcely remembered my last name.

To celebrate my birthday, I crafted a plan to leave the root cellar and Sleepy Eye, Minnesota, to see who was left. Maybe I'd make it to the west coast someday. I figured I might as well check out the Golden Gate Bridge and Ground Zero at the same time.

Who knew Dad's Mossberg pistol-grip 20 gauge, loaded with rock salt, would be my salvation? Like me, Dad didn't like to kill anything. It had been summer, and the coyotes wouldn't leave the hen house alone, so he used rock salt to make believers out of them. The shotgun remained loaded and leaning next to the door as we worked in the shop. Dad was teaching me welding, which was the next step in my survival education. I loved working with him. We were partners. I looked just like him, with black hair and pale skin, ice blue eyes that came from my grandmother. I wanted to be an underwater welder when I grew up. They got to travel to the ocean, and made bank at the same time, but we'd learned about the wraiths a few days before. Dad had known back then, three years ago, that they were coming for us. He taught me how to use that shotgun for self-defense. Wraiths were coming for everyone that drew breath.

We were both at the workbench, and I welded while he coached me. We were nearly done. I finished the bead and was really happy with the job I'd done. I looked up at my Dad, and that's when I saw the dark mist blast him in the face. He dropped at my feet, and I instinctively skittered back against the shop wall by the door. I couldn't see well through the welding helmet, so I lifted it up just in time to see my first wraith as it murdered my father. I didn't know what to do, frantically looking for a way to help my dad as he clawed at the floor to get away. My fingertip brushed the barrel of the shotgun where it leaned behind me.

I palmed the grip with my left and pumped up a shell with my right, then put a hole through the wraith right at what would have been a human's chest. The thing shrieked as it was blown backward off my dad, where it plastered itself against the shop wall like a greasy poster. The hole in its chest grew as rock salt ate through it, gradually disintegrating the entire thing. It took four excruciatingly long seconds of listening to it scream before it faded to black dust.

It took longer than that for my dad to die. I turned and dropped to the floor beside him. His body seized over and over again. The wraith had begun draining him before I shot it. Dad's face was withered. His eyes were flat in the sockets, like they were cardboard cutouts. His hands were bones with thin hide stretched over them. One rested on my forearm as he stopped moving. I didn't know it at the time, but I had stopped a new wraith from spawning from the remains of my father.

That lesson became branded in my brain like an item in my own personal survival guide. Bullet Point Number One.

After that day, I raided the house, barn, tool shed, and shop, loading everything I found useful into the root cellar and went into survival mode. Shotgun shells were easy to reload with rounds of chunky salt and crimp closed again. Dad had taught me that, how to weld, vegetable gardening, and basic self-defense since I was little. In middle school, we turned our attention to rebuilding a 289 gas motor into a recycled biofuel engine for my science fair project. I'd taken first place with that engine. To celebrate, Dad and I dropped the motor into a modified dune buggy frame and tore around the back forty like it was a racetrack.

They were the good days.

I observed wraiths as they took over my world and recorded their activity in my journals. I shot the ones that came to the farm, at first trying standard scattershot, but learning quickly that didn't kill them. It had to be rock salt for some reason. I enjoyed hunting them, but it still squicked me out to hear them scream at death. The sound was something like a mix between a coyote howling and rusty metal grating against uneven asphalt.

They skimmed the place a lot. I hunted them. I hid silently until I could get back to the root cellar if I got scared, but I learned all about them. Wraiths were faint hearted, giving up quickly. They had the heart of a mushroom and the attention span of a peanut. They didn't bother animals. I'd set our stock loose after dad died. The chickens stuck around for a few months and so did two of the horses. The rest were lost to the wide open. Wraiths didn't look twice at anything breathing besides humans.

I wasn't so full of myself to think that other people, somewhere out there, hadn't survived, too. I wondered about them.

If there were any survivors who hadn't considered holing up at the salt mines in Utah, I would have been surprised. I caught onto the fact that salt kills wraiths just a little too late to save anyone else from what authorities thought was a medical pandemic before the fall. It wasn't. They weren't zombies. I'd seen clean through a wraith before. Depending on the lighting, they were transparent. Besides, why would anyone listen to a fourteen-year-old kid talking about a shotgun full of rock salt?

If only people had stopped trying to retain their normal way of life and listened to the warnings of others, I wouldn't have been as lonely. People simply disregarded the news of mass death back when the Internet still worked. It was mind boggling. My aunt Janice would have said they "poo-pooed" the warnings. Though other people had suffered—and that meant every bit of depth the word could harbor—from denial during that first week, heeding the warnings had never been a problem for me and Dad. From the first time a video of a wraith spawning hit YouTube, I was a believer. While others claimed it was an Internet hoax and attempted to hold onto life as they preferred, the smart ones, like my dad and me, hunkered down at home and tried to prepare. Our mistake was thinking our rural map dot would shield us somewhat. That video circled the globe in about four minutes. It circled my mind almost daily.

One should never poo-poo a wraith.

It had taken under a week for things like the Internet to go down. Power and running water went after that. People dropped from other things like heat strokes in the south if they survived the wraiths. My root cellar didn't freeze or overheat. It got chilly, but it stayed livable in both winter and summer.

I hadn't seen a wraith in over a month. My plan was to make it from home to Salt Lake City, Utah, as I searched for other survivors. Dad's old Ford had a paper atlas tucked into the glove box. There weren't many people left as far as I knew. Maybe a couple hundred hidden away in clusters across the States? Smoke pillars occasionally drifted into the sky, which I decided were like neon fast food signs to wraiths. Only someone who was suicidal would start a fire. They were beacons that wraiths followed to their next meal.

My buggy was loaded with everything I could strap to it, including the filter mechanism I'd created for producing fuel for my science project. Dried apples from the orchard and some root vegetables from the greenhouse kept me healthy and kept for a long time without getting gross. I filled tanks from the water well and took as much as I dared carry. I left the farm, armed and mobile, after sunup.

I did my best not to look inside cars as I wove through piles of ruin on the highway. That was an easy mistake to make, as I'd learned during my first outing a couple years back. Some people refused to let themselves be killed and eaten, and I'd happened on a family in a car that took the matter into their own hands. One of the parents had used a handgun to save them all from what seemed inevitable at the time.

I wouldn't make that mistake again. I skirted Sleepy Eye and was onto the freeway in minutes.

But my mind was tormented as I glanced behind me at Sleepy Eye. It grew smaller, deserted buildings stood bastion at the edge of my current reality and the only safety I knew. Seeing the city without people kept my world fairly small. I stopped at well-lit, deserted convenience stores when I felt it was safe. It was all so eerie. So quiet. I moved on quickly, dodging husks of human remains blowing along the ground like tumbleweeds. The tiny ones broke my heart. Wraiths didn't discriminate based on age.

My mind was churned, always thinking about survival. Millions of people died in just a few months, and they left plenty of supplies around. The stores were deserted, but in some cases, there was a good bunch of stuff left on the shelves if the place hadn't been looted. I'd take a glass half full over a half empty one any day. I'd need to find a sporting goods store soon for a new pair of boots and some more shotgun shells to reload with salt.

After the sting of leaving home faded, I found that the open road was invigorating. After a while, dodging abandoned vehicles became as routine as staying between the lines on the road. The buggy had a squatty windshield, but no roof. I wore the goggles we'd bought after we painted the buggy fire-orange.

Another year of survival was under my belt, and I celebrated with a chocolate protein shake while kicking my feet back and forth over the edge of a bridge in Sioux Falls, watching birds fly toward the horizon. It was peaceful. I was glad to be out of the buggy and taking a break from the noise of the motor. Fog churned and consumed foothills, and the air held the sweet smell of rain. It was gorgeous to witness. I checked the long bridge both ways. Nothing seemed to be creeping up on me, so I laid back on the warm concrete with my arms stretched out to either side as the fog threatened the sun.

That's when I felt an odd vibration beneath my hands. It was subtle and had a slow rhythm. I held my breath and then shot to my feet with the Mossberg gripped in one hand. The vibration was footfalls, and they came from my right, which, sadly, was the closest way off the damned bridge.

A figure, just far enough away so I couldn't tell if it was male or female, neared as I heard the slapping of their feet on the pavement. They would be on me in less than a minute.

"Help!" It was a man, and he was running for his life. Two wraiths streaked above the road behind him, shades moving in for the kill. It didn't appear as though they'd tried to mist him yet, which was weird. Still, this guy was as good as dead. I leveled my shotgun right at his head as the first of the wraiths overtook him. I lowered the weapon, thinking better of wasting a shot and drawing their attention. It was too late to save him from the misery of being eaten. Both wraiths misted him, and he went down, clawing at asphalt. The closest of the wraiths jumped him and began feeding, tearing at his chest and abdomen.

The other wraith attacked it. I was shocked; I'd never seen one turn on another. But it made sense. They were starving. Luckily, they continued to tear at one another with their claws and were so engrossed in the fight they didn't notice me. They were a tumble of black smoke. They screamed, a predatory sound that resonated bone deep since I was a prey animal on that bridge. I had heard it before. It reminded me of coyotes calling in the plains out back of the house back in Minnesota. Also like the coyotes, the smaller of the two wraiths tumbled free of the larger one and slunk away. That's when the buffet started for real.

I began backing away, feeling for the buggy as I went, as quietly as I could while the thing ate. I needed to put space between us. What was one hungry wraith would soon be two unless the dead guy was sick or whatever, and a wraith couldn't spawn from his remains.

That's when the other wraith returned and attacked the wraith that was feeding. It was fascinating to watch them fight. It was even more enthralling to watch the winner actually devour the loser.

That's how I learned that wraiths would eat one another. I wondered if that made the winners any different? Maybe stronger or smarter or something? I didn't hang around to find out.

Finally, my hand brushed metal. I spun and tossed the shotgun into the passenger bucket seat and dove behind the wheel. I was certain my dune buggy could outrun anything that decided to follow me. Nothing did.

My heart was stung, and my spirits sank. The only other person I'd seen in years, and he was gone. Maybe staying out of big cities was a better idea than driving through them. I gritted my teeth and kept driving, wondering if a new wraith had spawned back there.

The wraith that would have turned my dad had almost gotten me too. I thought that wraith had, at one time, been one of the neighbors who owned the farm up the lane from us. The Buchanans, I think it was. It had been one of the biggest wraiths I'd seen to this day, and the dad over there had been a giant of a man. The bigger the human, the bigger the wraith that took its place. This fact was documented in my journal and underlined. And circled a few times.

The hours on the road were exhausting. I hadn't checked the map in a while, but the road beckoned me ahead, so I kept going. There were mountains in the distance when the sun set, so I knew I was headed west. That's what mattered. I hated to do it, but I had to get some sleep so I could stay sharp. The next off ramp came into view, and I left the freeway. I turned down an alley in Nowhere Town, USA, behind a row of old brick buildings and stopped with the nose of the buggy under a fire escape. I grabbed my gear and hustled up the metal ladder all the way to the top. The moon was bright, so I had a decent vantage, watching from safety as a cluster of shades came apart from the shadows below.

They'd likely been tracking me since I pulled off the freeway. I counted five. They were all over my buggy, nudging at it and creeping beneath the chassis. Their buzzing made the hair at the back of my neck pull tight. I hated that they defiled something I would be touching in the morning. One by one, they tired of searching and drifted off to look for someone else to eat. I moved in near silence as I rolled out my sleeping bag and chewed on a dinner of out-of-date beef jerky.

Although the creatures were fast and shuffle-hovered along the ground on all fours, sort of like a cross between the Grim Reaper and an oily iguana, they were dumb as a box of hammers and about as aware of their surroundings as a rutting bull elk. When they were locked onto a meal, they gave less than two shits about what was going on around them. The buzzing hum they made was the worst. Enough of them in the same space sounded like a heard of freshly hatched katydids. My ears were always tuned in to that sound.

Sleeping under the stars was something I enjoyed when we'd gone camping back when I was a kid. It took a while to fall asleep, but eventually I got some rest.

I woke with buzzing in my ears. My mind was lost in a hypnogogic state, and I wrestled with grogginess as my eyes focused, wondering if I was only dreaming. I hadn't moved; I was still lying flat on my back. I gripped the Mossberg's pistol-grip but didn't move as I listened.

The buzzing was close, but I couldn't tell which direction it came from. I turned my head, looking in all directions, but the rooftop was empty, except for me and my makeshift camp. I rolled onto my belly and crawled toward the ladder, inching my way just enough so I could look down. The buzzing was louder. I pushed forward with my toes and looked down the ladder and straight into the face of a wraith that had somehow climbed almost to the top of the fire escape, just a few feet from my face.

I'd never been so close to one. It had eyes, two of them, and they were a sick shade of yellow in oozing sockets beneath the cover of the thing's cowl-like appendage that hung over the head. An oversized maw gaped below the eyes.

It shrieked, and I jerked backward, but it reached so fast that its claws caught in a few thick strands of my hair that had fallen over my shoulder and hung down. It yanked hard, rapping my face against the tarpaper rooftop. The pain was unreal as I gathered my hair at my scalp and tried to free myself from the wraith's grasp. More buzzing erupted. It felt like the weight of the thing dangled by my hair, which began to snap. A huff of dark mist shot upward past the edge of the building, coating my hand. The skin there erupted in white hot pain as if I'd shoved my hand into a bank of hot coals.

I got one knee under me and then came to my feet. At some point, either the wraith let go, or my hair tore free, but I got away. I lunged for the shotgun and flattened onto my belly, made a tripod with my forearms, and waited for the thing to come into view.

It didn't make me wait long, buzzing ferociously. One arm quested over the top, claws grasping the edge of the roof. I drew steady breaths. The wraith fearlessly heaved itself upward, hovering inches above the surface. As it turned toward me, I put a bead on the head and blew the top off, sending black dust into the air, three stories off the ground.

More buzzing erupted from the ground. I stole a glance at the next wraith, which was a good way down the ladder. I hung over the side of the building and shot the next one off the fire escape, wondering how I could have been naive enough to think they wouldn't be able to climb up to get me? The buzzing stopped.

Mental note: wraiths can shuffle-hover their way up ladders.

The grip of my left hand grew weak enough that I nearly dropped the shotgun. I went to my sleeping bag and sat, cradling my arm in my lap.

The sky was lavender to my right. Stars fought for the last moments of darkness to my left. My wrist and hand burned badly, and I trembled so hard that the slick fabric of the sleeping bag hummed from the vibration. I adjusted my seat until I sat in silence, feeling the first of many tears begin to fall. I stayed that way as the sun broke the flat horizon in the east. Only then did I look at my withered hand.

My left wrist had taken the brunt of the blast. There wasn't any blood, but the flesh of my forearm and the top of my hand had pulled back somehow, kind of like atrophy. The fingers were drawn into a loose fist. I could move my thumb somewhat. I was thankful for at least some remaining use of my left hand.

I withdrew a canteen and extended my arm, dousing it with cool water from the well back home. The thought of Sleepy Eye was enough to start the tears up again.

I scrubbed tears from my face angrily, for the first time doubting my decision to leave home.

Maybe my quest was foolish. Perhaps I would get myself killed.

But what was the alternative? To live and die by myself, locked away below ground in a root cellar?

That was no life. I could always go back home. I wouldn't always have the means to quest on.

I'd been driving for nearly two days. I'd bandaged my wrist so tightly that the wrap acted as a splint. The pain faded into a dull throb that was almost something I could ignore.

The road narrowed. I drove until the mountains held clear detail and then kept driving through some of the most beautiful forests I'd ever seen. There was still snow on the ground in some places. The air smelled crisp—so clean it almost made it seem like a place where there could never be something deathly hunting my species. But I knew they were out there. The wraiths owned all the places, even those of such beauty.

I stopped in the road and checked the map. True to my fears, I was off course. I'd dropped south, driven past Denver, and was near the small town of Redmond, Utah. Salt Lake City was just north. I figured I might as well check it out, so I headed into town.

Redmond was quaint and surrounded by deserted farm buildings and forest. I drove by a small lake where there were too many deer and Canadian geese to count. It was a place that would have been nice to live in before the fall.

I killed the motor and sat still, listening and checking my surroundings. My bladder was screaming at me. I got out with my shotgun and walked to the rear wheel, reaching for the button of my jeans. I handled my business quickly, vigilantly searching for the multitude of wraiths that I knew had to be out there.

It was odd that I hadn't seen more of them in the hours and days since I left home. They must have been starving to death a little faster than anticipated but—

Something that was fast enough to move in a blur darted to the other side of the buggy. I was so startled, I dropped the shotgun, and it smacked against the asphalt and skidded a few feet away. I dove for it and came to my feet, realizing there'd been no dark mist. No buzzing. I sprinted to the other side of the buggy and leveled the gun at a man who crouched there.

A startled, twentyish, Asian guy glanced up at me as I readied to shoot him in the face.

"What the hell?" I yelled. The taste of coppery blood coated my tongue from where I'd bit the inside of my cheek in the shuffle to recover the shotgun and protect myself.

He put his hands up defensively. "Shhhh," he hissed.

"You attack me and then shush me?" The sound of my own gravelly voice was a shock. "That's some nerve, buddy." I cleared my throat.

Psst. I glanced to my right at the sound, and I saw a young, black woman crouching next to a burnt out car. She tried waving me over.

I wasn't budging. I hadn't seen another person up close for too long. I would not simply lower my weapon and get friendly.

The guy next to me started whispering. "I'm sorry I scared you. I was afraid you'd scream or something if I just walked up to you."

"I'm no screamer," I whisper shouted back at him.

"Put the gun down, please?" he asked.

I backed off, keeping them both in my line of sight. The girl stood up, showing me her palms.

"I'm Baxter," the guy said as he came to his feet. "That's Sarah."

"What do you guys want?" They didn't seem much like the Welcome Wagon type.

The girl's eyes darted to my buggy. I looked between them and took a step toward my ride. "I will absolutely put a hole in whichever of you two tries to steal from me." They didn't need to know the shells I had loaded were full of salt. If I shot one of them, it would hurt badly enough to change both their minds.

"Hold on," said Sarah. She took a step toward me. I turned the barrel her way, extending the arm-length weapon with deadly control. She stopped fast. Maybe she wasn't a complete dolt. "We're doing the Lady's work. We aren't going to steal anything from you."

My eyebrows shot up. I looked at Baxter. "So, the Lady told you to run up on me?" This lady and I needed to have a few words.

"I saw the gun and panicked," he said. "Sorry."

"The Lady welcomes all," Sarah interjected. She looked at my bandaged wrist. "You're hurt."

"Keen powers of observation." I was still shaken from nearly having my ass kicked by the two wraiths on the rooftop. I wasn't going to get back to sleep after that. I was exhausted, in pain, and honestly, feeling very grumpy.

I lowered the shotgun. "Back off." I stepped toward the driver's seat, and Baxter stepped back to give me plenty of room.

Sarah's face was incredulous. "You're leaving?"

I nodded, taking my seat. They just stared at me. "Look," I sat up, gripping the roll bar. "You'll be fine. Rock salt kills them." I plopped back down, settling the gun next to me.

"No kidding," Sarah said. I sensed a lot of sarcasm.

"The purge will pass," said Baxter. "It is written." His expression told me he was being genuine with me.

"Purge? Written where? You mean this apocalypse was forecasted somewhere?"

They looked at one another. "The Bible maybe?" said Sarah.

I stopped in the process of starting the buggy. I was no Sunday schooler, but I had gone to church with my dad when I was a kid. There had been forty days and forty nights. They were plagues. There had been no lessons on a "purge" that I recalled. And then there was this thing with the "Lady" they mentioned. They watched me like they were ready for me to call them out. I did.

"I studied the Bible. This sounds a lot like horse shit."

"It is newly found scripture. And you might try some respect." Sarah crossed her arms. "Maybe it's better that you leave."

When the decision was mine, it felt fine to leave. Now that it was someone else's suggestion, not so much. I shrugged it off and started the buggy.

Baxter stepped into my path. "Please, wait."

"Ugh," I groaned, letting my head fall back against the headrest. I stopped the motor.

"Come with us. We'll show you the way. You can meet Lot. Then you'll understand."

"Lot?" He wasn't helping their case.

"The very man. He can teach you. Then, if you still want to go, I won't step in." He smiled.

I considered it. I'd left the safety of my home to find people. I found two, and they knew where there were more. I had a weapon and transportation. I'd watch my own back and stick close to the exit.

"Lead the way."

Baxter ran around the side of the buggy and jumped in.

I looked at him. He smiled.

"That way," he pointed forward, to the road ahead.

"I'll get the others. See you soon." Sarah didn't even look at me. *Whatever.*

I started the buggy. "Don't try anything dumb. I will toss you out and back over you for good measure."

"Are you always this violent?" He looked around the cockpit. One hand came up as he began to reach toward the console.

"Don't even."

Baxter dropped his hand. "Understood."

"How far is it?"

"Five minutes north of here."

I started down the road.

Five minutes went by like lightning. Baxter guided me to a left turn off the road to the tallest chain-link gates I'd ever seen. The fence continued out of sight along the road in both directions. He got out to open it, waited for me to pull through, then closed it up again behind me. He got back into the seat and instructed me to continue along a dirt road to the north.

We meandered through hills of white gravel. Huge, yellow haul trucks lined a flat lot to our right. We rolled right up to the entrance to an actual cave that was big enough to drive one of those trucks into. I hit the brakes.

"Is this the only way in?"

"I'm not sure. Why? I mean, it's huge in there. I think there's another entrance like this one."

I narrowed my eyes at Baxter, looking for the truth in his answer. He babbled. That wasn't a good sign.

"So, if just one wraith gets in here with us, we're done. With no way out. And you're okay with going in there, knowing that?"

"It's a salt mine. Relax. The Lady provides."

Baxter was an interesting person. His heart was in his words. He truly believed the Lady would protect him inside the cave. The one thing the cave had going for it was that, unless Baxter was lying, there was salt inside. Somehow, Baxter and company had managed to survive.

I wanted to meet those people. On some level, their knowing I existed made me real. I went on a leap of faith and continued into the yawning darkness inside the cave.

Baxter wasn't lying when he said the cave was huge. Echoes of light stretched farther than I could see. I stopped the buggy next to a line of golf carts in the first small room we came to, which was simply a widened part of the road. We got out just as Sarah pulled up beside us, driving one of the carts. They'd apparently mastered biofuels and rigged up generators to run on biofuel as well as the carts. Another female and two men got out of the cart with her. That was the first time I noticed they all wore white shirts and dark blue pants.

Baxter and I followed them along a trail around a curve once I gathered my bag and weapon.

"You won't need that here," Baxter whispered.

"It's comforting." I didn't take my eyes off the others as we tromped along, our shoes crackling on white rocks.

What they led me to was an amazing community of people living in underground wooden sheds. Beside some of them stood rounded greenhouses that were lit up inside. We passed groups of others who smiled at me as we walked on.

At the end of the large cavern was a building that was a little larger than the sheds. It was coated in textured white paint. A giant cross stood on top. The door stood open. The six of us walked in.

A slight man in overalls sat behind a desk at the end of the room. We walked down the middle, through rows of pews. He wore wire-framed glasses below a set of caterpillar eyebrows. When he looked up, a smile spread wide across his face. I guessed him to be about fifty years old. Not an old man, but he was distinguished and grey.

Sarah and the others sat in a pew to the right, and Baxter scooted into one opposite. I sat on the end beside him. The guy at the desk put his head back down and continued writing. The room was quiet and awkward. I nudged Baxter.

He looked at me.

I gave him a look that said, "What's going on?"

He held up a finger and nodded with a small smile.

I sat back, allowing myself to rest. It seemed like I'd been on edge for my whole life. Time ran on. I considered getting up and leaving.

Finally, the guy set down his pen and closed the book he'd been writing in. He left the desk, came toward us, and sat down on the altar. His feet were bare and dirty.

"Baxter, who do we have here?" He spoke well, but his voice was high and a little nasally.

"This is, um…" Baxter looked at me. "What is your name, anyway?"

"June Bug Dempsey. It's nice to meet everyone."

"Excellent, Miss Dempsey. The Lady welcomes you." The man turned to the back wall and gestured toward a white statue of a woman who had her hands thrown up protectively around her face. It was hardly flattering. Sodom and Gomorrah came to mind.

"My name is Lot."

"People call me Bug. Called me, I mean," I stammered. *Lot? Really?*

"What happened to your arm?" He inclined his head toward my bandaged wrist.

"A wraith sprayed me. I've learned to fight faster. To hit them before they can hit me."

"Ah. Is it bad?"

"No. It's small. Could've been worse."

"Good. And where are you from?" he asked.

"Sleepy Eye, Minnesota."

His eyebrows shot up. "How did you survive there?"

"I went underground. Stayed in the root cellar and learned to fight them." It sounded like tough talk, but it was really how I'd made it through.

"What brings you west?"

"I was looking for other survivors," I said. My voice sounded young. Childlike. I wasn't sure I liked it. "I got a little lost on the freeway on my way to Salt Lake City."

"Yes, but why Utah?"

"Salt." I didn't much care for the third degree. I fidgeted in my seat.

"And where did you encounter this wraith that sprayed you?" he pried.

"A couple hundred miles back." I looked at Baxter.

"You should see her vehicle," Baxter interjected. "It's very…rugged."

"You have a vehicle?" Lot perked up.

"I haven't been walking all this way." I took a deep breath. "Look, it's been a long couple of days, and I'm not feeling great. I'm still messed up after nearly being killed recently and I'm afraid I don't have the patience for all the questions."

"Of course," he said. "I didn't mean to make you uncomfortable, Bug."

I relaxed slightly. "Thanks." I looked over at Sarah and the others. "What were you guys doing out in town earlier?"

"We patrol for two things. One is to find other survivors like yourself, and the other is to track wraith activity as our footprint grows," answered Lot.

"Footprint?" I asked.

"Our safety zone. We've been steadily pushing back, gaining ground," he responded.

"So, you think there are no wraiths in town?"

"Almost. Redmond is nearly clean. The wraiths are much like alligators. They're all appetite with no reason."

"I used to think so, too."

"What do you mean by that?" asked Sarah. She stared across the aisle at me without a smile.

"I mean, I'd never seen a wraith climb a ladder before last night. Before, they just hovered along the ground, eating anyone who didn't see them coming first."

She huffed. "Wraiths don't climb anything. They can't. They don't have the brain to do anything like that. They forget what they're doing in about thirty seconds and move on. She's lying."

"Screw you," I said, incredulously. "What reason do I have to lie?" I sat back again, keeping my eye on her.

"So, if they climb so well, how do our fences keep them out?" Sarah's tone was accusing. Maybe she thought I was trying to impress Lot with my claims.

"I don't know. I don't have all the answers. Maybe it's because they're beginning to evolve."

Lot burst into an abrupt belch of laughter. He recovered quickly. "Oh child, they cannot evolve. Wraiths are simply a non-sentient purge, brought down on men who lack faith. They're incapable of reason."

"And women lacking faith," added Sarah, looking right at me.

"And women," agreed Lot. "The chosen shall endure until the purge dies out. It is written."

"By whom? She said it was in the Bible," I said, gesturing to Sarah. "It isn't."

"The Lady provides, Bug. Don't forget. She is loving to all her children and has saved scripture for us when we need it most."

"You can't simply rewrite the Bible." I hoped I didn't offend too badly, but it needed to be said.

"I am Scribe to the Lady Edith," said Lot. "We commune daily, and she provides her gospel. Her prophecy is righteous word. She is our provider and protector. Her wrath will be mighty."

I stared. I was a little crushed. The first people I found were a bunch of religious nuts, holed up on top of a huge stockpile of the only ammunition I knew to work against wraiths, which I'd confirmed were evolving. They were starving and eating each other. It appeared they grew smarter as a result. I carved out time to make a new entry in my journal, adding this fun fact to a growing list of the ways my world was new and screwed.

"Lot" had everyone believing the Lady, or Edith, was a deity. In the Bible, Edith was Lot's wife, and she'd been turned to salt for not listening. He'd best hope she carried a big stick when she showed up to protect them.

I reached for my bag. "It's been nice meeting you all. I'm going to continue on to Salt Lake City like I planned." I looked at Baxter. "Thanks for the kindness." I wanted to shake him though, rather than just tell him goodbye. If he placed his faith in reformed religion with a belief that they'd be protected from wraiths, rather than realizing wraiths had the resources to take them all down, he was in big trouble. I slung my bag over my shoulder and picked up my shotgun, then stepped into the aisle.

"So sad to see you go," said Sarah.

I didn't bother responding.

"The Lady beckons her scribe," said Lot. He stepped up toward his desk, ready to write more into the Bible. "Sarah, Baxter, why don't you and the others walk

Bug to her vehicle and show her to the gate?" asked Lot. "And best wishes to you, child."

"Thanks, but I know the way out." I started walking.

"I insist." Lot wasn't smiling anymore.

"Fine." I kept walking.

Baxter caught up to me. "No convincing you to stay, huh?"

"Not a chance," I said. Then I dropped my voice. "Wraiths are evolving. Do you understand? You're not as safe as he'd have you believe."

"But the Lady…" he started but drifted off. He sighed loudly. "I understand. You're not familiar with Her ways."

"All I'm saying is, if a wraith can make it up a three-story fire escape to come after me, a wraith can climb a fence to get to you."

"We have weapons and plenty of salt. I mean, if one of them really did find a way in."

"It only takes one. They'd multiply too fast. One could wipe you out in a half hour."

We'd made it back to the lot where my buggy was parked next to Sarah's golf cart. The four of them talked among themselves as they got in. Baxter took the passenger seat in my buggy as I got settled.

The laughter and talking stopped abruptly. It was weird and eerily quiet. I looked up and saw why.

A wraith hovered in front of the golf cart, and another climbed from beneath it. They'd obviously held onto the undercarriage, stowing away to be brought in when Sarah returned.

So much for non-sentience.

"No," Baxter said.

Everything after that happened fast but appeared to be in slow motion. The wraith howled, leaned inside the cart, and misted the two young men in the back. Sarah screamed and dove out of the cart. The girl in the passenger seat wrestled with the door handle and kicked it open. She tried to run, but the wraith at the front of the cart blew mist and jumped on top of her. She screamed and clawed at the ground, but the shade was on her, consuming and goring her body with its claws.

I was horrified. There'd been no warning. No buzzing. I started the buggy as Sarah sprinted into the cavern, yelling for Lot. Baxter opened the door to get out but stopped short when the wraith who'd misted the two in the back of the cart slammed both clawed arms down on the hood of my buggy.

"Get down!" I yelled, just as the thing blew a thick cloud of mist straight at both of us. The cloud of deathly fog swirled against the short windshield and dissipated.

We knocked heads, trying to get out of the way quickly. The other girl stopped screaming, finally sucked dry. I put the buggy in gear and hit the gas without looking up. The nubby wheels thump-thumped over the wraith and lurched, roaring ahead a few feet until we smashed into the granite wall.

My good hand was already wrapped around the stock of the Mossberg as I bailed out. "Baxter!"

He didn't reply, and I didn't have time to check on him. I had five rounds ready, one good hand, and two wraiths bearing down on me. I dusted the first and shook a new round into the chamber, leveling the barrel at the second wraith, which blew my mind by skittering away.

"Baxter! Now's a good time to get the hell out of the buggy!" I yelled, running after the wraith. Baxter sat up as I sprinted past, head lolling a bit, but he focused on me quickly. I planted my feet and took aim, but I couldn't fire.

Lot, Sarah, and about ten other people were running straight into the path of the wraith. When they saw it coming at them, they stopped. Sarah screamed. Again.

"Get down!" I yelled, keeping the wraith in my sights. It veered toward Sarah, likely because she was so loud.

I was so scared. Not for my own safety. Not really for the safety of the people clawing over one another to run away. I was terrified of missing the one shot I had at dusting that wraith. A miss meant the end of a colony of survivors. I didn't know how many people were holed up in the cave, but it had been three years. That likely meant kids. Babies.

I steadied and tucked my hair behind an ear, hearing my dad's voice telling me to breathe out. "Don't squeeze the trigger until you're ready," he'd said.

I was ready. The shot echoed in the cavern, and the wraith disintegrated in a burst of black powder. Lot helped Sarah up from where she'd fallen on her stomach when she tried to run.

"I see you," he called.

I didn't know what he meant by that, but I didn't have time to ponder all the crazy. I had to get back to the buggy where I'd left Baxter, punch drunk and trying to get out. I turned and sprinted the few feet around the curved path.

I skidded to a stop. Baxter was out of the buggy, kneeling over the shriveled husk of the girl who'd been killed. He was in danger of being in range when the new wraith spawned. His face was warped with terror and grief.

"Get back, Baxter! The remains are a gate to below ground. Another one's coming!"

It was far too late. Baxter yelped and backpedaled on all fours as oily claws burst upward, barely missing him. The rest of the shade rose up, a vertical cloud of death, ready to claim lives.

"Hey!" I yelled. "Over here!" I waved my free arm to get the thing's attention. The head turned slowly as it zeroed in on me.

My chest was tight with fear. I seated a new round of salt, ready for death to try again.

But it didn't come at me. The wraith turned to the golf cart, lowered to the ground, and slithered into the back seat where two fresh meals waited. It went to work digesting, and I ran toward the cart.

Lot ran to Baxter and helped him up. I couldn't hear what they were saying, but out of the corner of my eye, I saw Baxter run into the cavern. That made me happy. I liked Baxter and wanted him safe.

Three shots remained. I took aim and stopped, realizing the salt would blast to bits against the metal cart unless I found an unobstructed line of fire. Rock salt was a killer, but it was also weak material that wouldn't pierce much. I hated to do it, but I ran straight at the wraith.

It finished with the first body, sucking it dry quickly, and hovered against the ceiling of the cart instead of coming to get me. I picked up a handful of gravel from the ground and whipped it at the cart, trying to antagonize the beast, and ran up to the windshield. It held ground, safely behind metal and glass. If I didn't get to it quickly, I'd have two wraiths to deal with instead of one, which was much less manageable.

So, I opened the door.

A thick beam of dark mist shot from inside the cart. The shade was waiting for me, ready to blast me into a state of paralysis so it could go to lunch. I dropped to the ground, small rocks digging into my kneecaps and then my thighs and belly. I rolled to my side under the open door and shoved the gun upward into the darkness circling there and fired with a hell of a lot of hope that I'd hit the wraith. Thankfully, a cloud of black dust huffed out of the cart, and everything went silent. I hid my face from the remains as they drifted to the ground.

I rolled onto my bottom and sat crisscross apple sauce with a loaded shotgun in my lap for about three minutes. I sensed people behind me, heard whispers, but I kept my attention trained on the back seat of that golf cart.

First came the buzzing, then the head and claws exploded from the dried-out human remains. I dusted the new wraith before it could get out of the cart. Everything was so silent. No one spoke. I didn't get up, just rested the Mossberg in my lap and shook my hand out to stop the sting from the recoil. My mind whirled, but I was so damned tired.

So, this is life.

Lot's voice brought me back to the moment. "You see, the Lady Edith, she has come, just as prophesied," he said. "She comes from the darkness and brings the sun with her! She who was lost and led astray is found! She, our Lady, our provider, our warrior goddess and protector! The prophecy is fulfilled!"

I'd come from the safety of my root cellar, far to the east. I'd gotten lost on the freeway but found purpose. I'd honed my skills at turning wraiths to dust and managed to save a bunch of people. It was my life, and I'd live it. I turned to see him standing with his back to me. Light from the artificially generated bulbs mounted to the cavern ceiling filtered through his sparse hair. Clusters of people, too many to count, grouped together behind him.

He twisted, gesturing right at me. "She has come!" he declared. "From the darkness and into the light!"

The crowd repeated his words, vigorously shouting and raising their hands. "She has come! Our Lady Edith is risen! We are saved!"

My jaw dropped, but my heart swelled. A sector of what addled humanity remained on the planet had faith in me. They were no replacement for my dad or the friends I'd once had, but it beat being alone. A sob broke free from my chest.

I was June Bug Dempsey from Sleepy Eye, Minnesota.

And, although they all had bats flapping in their belfries, and would require a test of my trust, I'd found my tribe.

"Finding the right place to live often feels like the end of the world, I know. I understand, my friend, I do. But the tight-knit community of our residential family here will truly make it worth your trouble. You too will be a believer. Back to the stairs."

* * * * *

Dark of Night

by Christopher Woods

"**D**aniel Keller?"

I slowly set down the empty shot glass that had held rye whiskey a moment earlier and turned with my right hand near the gun at my side. "Depends who's asking."

"Lieutenant Jacobs. Captain wants to see you, sir."

"What does Captain Renner need me for? I don't work for you anymore."

"He didn't say, sir."

"What if I don't *want* to go see Captain Renner?"

"I reckon that's what the squad outside is for, sir."

I chuckled. "Then I guess we need to go see Captain Renner."

"That would probably be better, sir."

Fort Seward wasn't very far, so I left my horse tied to the hitching post in front of the saloon and accompanied the lieutenant and his squad back to the fort. I didn't plan to be long, or I would've put him in the stables.

Everyone was quiet as we walked toward the fort. I guess they were as curious as I was as to why the captain had sent for me, anyway. I was just a tracker, and I didn't do that anymore.

I was led straight to Renner's office. He stood from behind his desk as I walked in.

"You can go, Jacobs."

"Sir." The lieutenant walked back out the door.

"I know you said you were done with this, Danny," Renner said as he motioned toward the chair. "But this is really important."

"It's always important," I said.

"This is a little different. We've gotten some reports lately about some strange things going on up north."

"That's Sioux territory."

"That's part of why I need you. You're the only tracker I know who could track Sioux if needed."

"I told your predecessor I don't do that anymore." I sat in the chair he had indicated.

"I'm familiar, and I'm familiar with why. I can guarantee this has nothing in common with what happened before. I don't need you to track down Indians.

What I need you to do is confirm that it was Indians who attacked the Wilkins Ranch."

"The Wilkins were attacked?" I looked at the captain in confusion. "Wilkins has a good relationship with the Sioux."

"That's what worries me. I need you to go there and tell me whether it was the Sioux or not. I can send Jacobs and his squad with you. He's a good kid, young, but he's got a good head on his shoulders. He's nothing like Lieutenant Devereaux."

"He's alive, so there's one thing he doesn't have in common with Devereaux." I stood up. "I'll check the ranch for you, but I'm not tracking down any Sioux. Not for you or anyone else."

"I'm not asking you to, Danny. I just need to know if it was Sioux that did it."

"Then I'll be on my way."

"I'll tell Jacobs to get his men ready."

"I'll meet them at the ranch."

"Well, Roy, it looks like we have our work cut out for us," I said as a patted the big, gray gelding's shoulder. "I know I swore I wouldn't do this again."

Roy snorted.

"I should've just told him no. But I know Wilkins and he's got two kids. If someone hit his place…" I let the statement drift off.

Jenny and Tate were the Wilkins' two kids. The last time I was at the ranch was in '72, close to two years ago. That would put Jenny about twelve and Tate ten years old. Jack and Annie had a pretty good sized herd of cattle and I figured the kids helped run them.

I pulled Roy up as I saw vultures circling in the distance.

"That doesn't look good at all," I muttered. "That's a lot of buzzards."

The buzzards were circling due north, but the Wilkins Ranch was northwest.

"I'm thinking we probably ought to check that out before we go to the ranch," I said.

Roy snorted.

"You don't think so?"

He snorted again.

"Well, what do you know? You're a horse."

It was a long day's ride to the Wilkins Ranch and by making this detour, it would add another half a day.

"Actually, you're probably right." I patted Roy's neck. "But that sure is a lot of buzzards."

I followed a dip in the ground, headed north. It paid to stay as low as possible, even in flat lands like these. The last thing I needed to do was come across a war party. And the Sioux didn't like white men that much, especially after what Devereaux had done.

They had me tracking a "war party" last year. I told him from the moment I started tracking that they weren't a war party. Devereaux refused to listen. When we caught up to them, Devereaux attacked and killed the Sioux. There were four old men, two women, and four kids.

I refused to track for the cavalry after that. I went back to Seward and reported it to the captain before I rode out. Devereaux was discharged soon after.

Six months later I ran into him in Fargo. There was an ugly argument that ended in gun fire. I wasn't fond of shooting people, but I was a fair hand at it. Devereaux was mean and he enjoyed hurting people. He went too far with the Sioux, yet he blamed me for what befell him. I guess it's human nature to find someone else to blame for your own shortcomings. It happens often enough and will probably keep happening as long as people are being people.

I smelled it a long time before we got to it.

"The Sioux didn't do that," I muttered as I looked across the flatlands littered with the corpses of buffalo. "I'm not sure what would do that."

I rode through the hulking beasts. At first, I thought it could've been a poisoned water source until I got close to the first body. There were long cuts all the way from the front to the back on the first cow.

There was a total of twelve buffalo, each with similar cuts. They been dead for a couple of days. The last one I came to was missing large chunks of meat.

The ground was torn all to hell around the buffaloes and it was hard to get an idea of what actually happened to each of them. The tracks I could find were just confusing. The track was longer than a bear. And oddly shaped. I had never seen anything like it.

Worse, it looked like one creature had done all this.

"I think we need to get to the ranch," I said and gently kicked Roy's sides. "Giddup!"

We rode west at a gallop with my hand resting near my Colt. Roy could keep this pace up for a while. I hoped it was enough. I wasn't sure I wanted to be sleeping out here on the plain tonight.

I could see the light of their campfire long before I got there. Jacobs and his men were camped just outside of the Wilkins' ranch.

"That's at least one good mark for him," I muttered. "He's not traipsing all over the ranch grounds messing up the tracks. But they probably already did that."

Roy snorted. The big gray gelding was tired. We had covered a lot of ground to get to the ranch.

"I know buddy." I patted his sweat-soaked neck. "I've been working you pretty hard."

"That you Keller?" A familiar voice came from the darkness.

"Yeah, it's me, Frank."

"Figured it was. No one else would be out riding around tonight."

"Nobody with any sense, Frank. Something feels off out here."

"I thought it was just me," he said. "I've been feeling something ever since the sun went down."

"There something going on out here," I said. "Something bad."

"We knew that already," he replied. "When you see the ranch in the morning, you'll know what I'm talking about."

"Reckon I'll go on in to camp and get Roy settled in." I patted the horse's wet neck again. "He's done a bit of work today."

"Go ahead, Danny. Don't worry, I'll be keeping watch."

I started to ride toward the camp.

"And Danny?"

"Yup?"

"Jacobs ain't nothing like Devereaux. Kid's got a good head on his shoulders. He may be a little green, but he's got sand."

"Good to know, Frank."

As I got closer to the firelight, I could see the men. They were closer to the fire than I would've expected, and it may have been because they were feeling the same thing I was. Obviously, Frank was feeling something.

Whatever it was, it had come with the darkness. It was like the night was heavy or something. I had spent some time with a tribe of Cherokee Indians a few years back. They had a strong connection with nature and there was a lot to admire in them.

Buffalo Rider, one of the Cherokee I had met, had told me about nights like this. He had described the exact feeling that I was having and called it the night of the long knives. He said it was a night to keep your weapons close at hand because the Wendigo walked the lands.

I always figured it for a folktale, but whatever had killed those buffalo was big and strong. I'd never seen tracks like that before.

Jacobs nodded as I rode Roy into the light and past them where the other horses were tethered. I stripped the saddle from his back and laid it upside down so the bottom could dry out. I tied him with the other horses and gave his tired muscles a rub down. Today had been a hard one for the old fella.

I heard someone walking toward me and turned to find Jacobs.

"Cap said you could track a snake across a flat rock, Keller."

"I'm a fair hand at it, but I don't know if I'm that good."

"I hope you can make heads or tails out of this. I really hope this isn't the Sioux."

"Me too, Lieutenant." I placed the brush I had been rubbing Roy down with beside my saddle to let it dry as well. "We damn sure don't need them all riled up. I can't imagine them coming after the Wilkins. He had a pretty good relationship with 'em. But who really knows?"

"I don't know much about the Sioux," Jacob said. "So far, I haven't been able to figure out how any of the Indians think. But I'm new."

"The Sioux are warriors and hunters," I said. "Much like all of the tribes. They don't think like we do. We build communities and towns and think of things on a permanent basis. We build a town and it's usually still there years later. I wouldn't be surprised if some of these towns are still around in another two hundred years. A Sioux village probably won't be there a year later, they move with the herds. Frankly I'm surprised their village up north of here is still there."

"Last I heard it still was," he said.

"I guess they're just trying to keep an eye on us."

"Maybe," he said. "Could be because the buffalo are still around. They're a little west of us."

"They've been over here recently. I found a bunch of 'em slaughtered over east of here. That's why I'm late gettin' here. Something killed a little over ten of 'em. I couldn't tell exactly what it was, but it looked like it was only one attacker. I've never seen anything like it— and I've seen a lot of things."

"Something killed ten buffalo?"

"Twelve."

"Jesus."

"Left 'em all layin' there," I said. "Except one. One of 'em was chewed on. I would've thought wild dogs or wolves, but the only tracks I found were from something I ain't never seen before."

"Like what?"

"Well, if I knew what it was, then I wouldn't be saying I ain't never seen it before."

He chuckled. "You have a point."

"I guess we can go by on the way back to town so you guys can see it for yourselves."

"That might be a good idea. I'm going to try to get some sleep. Even though I doubt it will come. Something is really off tonight."

"Cherokee would claim the Wendigo roams the night."

"Wendigo?"

"Great big man-eating monster."

"Now *that's* gonna make me sleep better."

"Glad I could help, Lieutenant."

"Asshole."

I grinned. I couldn't help but like Jacobs. He was so unlike Devereaux, who had been an arrogant fool. Jacobs seemed much better. I guess over the next few days, he would either prove me right, or show me my judgement of a man's character was off.

I laid my bedroll not too far from where Roy was picketed with the other horses. With the heavy feeling of the night, sleep was hard to come by. Sometime early in the morning that heavy feeling dissipated and I was able to get a few hours. I'd never felt anything like this.

"Guess that goes with seein' tracks of somethin' I've never seen before," I muttered as I rolled my bedroll back up.

I smelled coffee and joined Jacobs as he re-stoked the fire with a coffee pot hanging beside the big stew pot.

"You're up early for a Lieutenant."

"I couldn't sleep much last night. I finally gave up and took a guard spot this morning. Everybody bunked close to the fire, I'm not even sure how you slept out in the dark."

"Roy'll let me know if somethin's wrong. I always keep him close. It would probably do you well to camp closer to your horses. They were restless until that weird feelin' ended."

"Sergeant Bell told me the same thing," he said. "I told him we'd do that from here out."

"Frank's been out here long time, Lieutenant. It would pay to listen to him."

"Captain told me that when he put me in charge of this platoon."

"The new Captain seems to have a good head on his shoulders."

"You say that like you're surprised," he said. "You don't have a very high opinion of officers, do you?"

"The fact that you listen to Frank helps. There are good officers and bad officers. Try to be one of the good ones."

"I do my best."

"That's all you can do." I filled my cup with coffee. "Soon as I finish this, I'm going to go make a pass through and see what I can find. If you don't mind, keep your boys here till I get back."

"You don't want anyone with you?"

"Better off if I'm in there by myself. I need a clear picture of the tracks."

"Alright."

I finished my coffee and walked out of the camp, leaving Roy tethered with the other horses. I did a full circle around the ranch finding where the other soldiers had shown up before and entered. I also found where the rider who had initially reported the incident came and went.

I stopped as I saw a familiar track. Whatever had killed the buffalo had been here. It was the same weird print, wide as a bear track, but a lot longer. The odd thing was that I found no tracks leaving.

Staying to the side, I followed the strange tracks toward the ranch house. Whatever it was, it went to the barn first and I could already smell what I would find in there. I needed to look though, so I pulled my bandanna over my face and stepped inside.

I scowled as the stalls came within view. Blood had puddled in front of them. It had run out of the stalls. I stepped past the first puddle and looked over the railing. There wasn't a lot left of the horse. A pretty good portion of it looked to of been eaten much like the last buffalo I saw out on the plains.

Shaking my head, I moved to the next stall. It had killed this horse just for the hell of it, it seemed. Whatever this was, it liked to kill. And whatever this was, it wasn't Sioux.

I already knew what to expect in the next stall, but I had to look anyway. My eye twitched as I took in the bloody scene. This horse had put up much more of a fight and the side of the stall had several broken boards. Whatever was doing this had attacked this particular horse with much more fury than the others. My guess was the stallion fought back and hurt whatever it was enough to piss it off.

I hated to give it that name but what Buffalo Rider had described to me seemed accurate. The Wendigo had ripped this horse apart.

By this point it had been coated in blood, leaving an ominous trail out of the back of the barn.

I followed the tracks as they approached the house with a sense of dread. The horse had enraged it, and I was afraid its fury hadn't dissipated before it reached the house.

It was fairly obvious that the noise from the barn had woken Jack and Annie. There were spent bullet casings at the door. Jack had gotten off at least three shots with his Winchester before it reached him. His body lay in the far corner of the room almost torn in half.

When Wilkins had built this ranch house, he had made a really high ceiling in his living room. He built a chandelier out of antlers. This is where I found Annie. She had been impaled on the antlers and left there. The best I could tell she had been alive when it left her impaled on the antlers. Her hands were torn and bloodied where she had tried to pull herself off of them.

"Bastard!" I cursed.

The sense of dread increased as I followed the bloodied trail to the stairs. It went straight to the kids' room. To my surprise there was no sign of the kids' blood in their room, nor any sign of the kids.

The Wendigo had left stains on their beds as he took them. But he didn't kill them. His bloodied tracks led toward the window and ended about a foot inside where a scorch mark circled the room. It marked the floor, both walls, and the ceiling.

"What the hell?"

The window was unbroken, and the wall unmarked past the scorch mark. It didn't make any sense. All sign of the Wendigo ended in that room.

"You're telling me this is some mystical monster?"

"I'm tellin' you a story I was told some years ago. Now I'm lookin' at that story play out right here in the Dakotas. I've never seen anything like what I'm seein' here. I can say for certain it wasn't a Sioux war party."

"What the hell am I supposed to tell the men?" Jacobs asked. "Do you actually think Sergeant Bell is going to accept a *Wendigo*?"

"You might be surprised what your men accept." I pointed back at the ranch house. "Take them inside and show them what's there."

"You can explain the tracks?"

"I will." I looked back at the ranch. "But I'll warn you, Lieutenant, it's ugly."

"What was described to me by the Captain sounded pretty bad."

"Then gather the men and meet me south of the barn."

The men were quiet as they followed me along and I pointed out the weird footprints.

"I've seen these prints one time before," I said. "A ways east, I found twelve buffalo slaughtered. The only tracks I could find were these."

"Just one man?"

I looked back at a young soldier. "Jenson, is it?"

He nodded.

"I ain't never seen a man leave a track like that." I squatted down and pointed toward the front edge of one of the tracks. "See these little grooves? These are some sort of claw."

"Someone couldn't make a fake boot?"

"That's a damn good question and it was the first one that I asked myself until I saw some of those tracks where it jumped at one of the buffalo. The claws extended to gain traction like a cat. There are a few of those up here that show the same thing. I'll show you when we get to them."

"This some sort of animal?" Frank asked with a slightly worried look.

"That's what we need to figure out," I said.

They followed as we entered the barn.

"Smells like dead for days," one of the men said.

I nodded and opened the first stall.

"Jesus," Jenson said.

I pointed at the tracks where the beast had extended its claws. "This is what I was talkin' about."

A young red headed soldier gagged as he saw the horse.

"You might not want to look at the third one," I said and led them to the second. "This one, it killed for fun. Neck's broke and it's been cut up after. Not as much blood from the wounds. It was dead for most of that." We moved to the third stall. "Now this one hurt it, I think."

The redhead backed out of the stall and retched.

"Told you," I muttered.

"One man didn't do that," Frank said.

"Agreed."

They were all quiet until we stepped into the living room of the ranch house.

There were several soldiers that gagged as they backed back out of the room.

"We have to get her down from there, Lieutenant," Frank said.

"Agreed, Sergeant. But this needed to be seen."

"One person couldn't have done that either." Frank pointed at Annie's body.

"I can't argue that. But there's one set of prints."

"The kids?" he asked.

Someone groaned.

"They're gone but I need you to look at the room before we do anything."

The bedroom was crowded as we all examined the burn ring along the outer edge of the room.

"Now let's get Jack and Annie out of here and bury them," Jacobs said.

"Damn right, sir."

I was looking at their pale faces as we finished burying Annie and Jack.

"There's nothin' more we can do for Jack and Annie," I said. "But I gotta wonder what it wanted with the kids."

"Way I see it," Jacobs said as he squatted beside the fire and took the coffee pot off of the hanger. "We have a couple of choices here. Now this is a long way out of our experience but if it took the kids, they may be alive. Do we go back to the fort and give a report like this, or do we hunt this son of a bitch down and kill it? We might get to save those kids in the process."

He looked around at the men as he stood back up. "I know I can order you to do what I want to do but this ain't some Sioux raiders. If what we can see is accurate, this is some kind of damned monster. What I want to do is mount up and see if we can find this bastard and fill it with enough lead to sink it six feet in the ground, but I hesitate to order you men to follow me."

"Reckon you don't have to order it, sir," Frank said. "You go after this thing, and I'll be riding with you."

I nodded. "Agreed. This thing needs killin'."

One by one each of the men nodded. Some of them were pale as sheets when they did, but not a single one chose not to hunt this thing down.

"There ain't no tracks leavin' the ranch but there was back where those buffalo were killed," I said. "I'd say we can start there and see if we can track it. We find it, we do what Jacobs said and fill it with lead."

"Then we're ready," Jacobs said.

"We have about enough time to reach the spot before dark. Then we can start trackin' this thing down."

We reached the buffalo about an hour before dark and I led them around and showed them the tracks left behind. Bloody tracks headed north.

"I say we ride another hour and get some distance between this and camp. I don't reckon I want to smell this all night." I mounted and Jacobs nodded, a grim look on his face.

There was no doubt about this being the same thing that was at the Wilkins' place. No one spoke as we rode north.

I watched the ground, so I didn't lose the trail. I kept raising my gaze to the surroundings until I saw Frank. He was constantly running his eyes from side to side looking ahead of us.

He caught me looking and nodded. "You're alright, Keller. Just keep tracking it."

Knowing I could keep my focus on the trail helped and our pace quickened.

The sun was low in the west when I pulled up near a copse of trees. The troop stopped as I rode into the copse to find a spring with a small stream feeding a pond.

"Fresh water," I said as I rode out. "This is as good a place as any to camp."

Most of the men were still quiet as they set up camp. The night fell with a heaviness that wore on all of us. Something was wrong out in the darkness, and we could all feel it. The night stretched on for hours and hours without much in the way of sleep.

It seemed like the feeling of wrongness moved around and the horses were as restless as the men. The sense of dread lifted with the rise of the sun. It was the damndest thing I had ever seen. It was like a veil had lifted as the night fell away.

"Still sure of this, Lieutenant?" I asked.

He nodded. "Something has to be done, Danny."

"Yep."

"Do you have any idea what the hell is going on?"

"Buffalo Rider claimed it was the Wendigo that caused that feelin' of dread. They called it the Night of Long Knives."

"I could sure do without that every night."

"Me too."

We rode north again following the trail left behind by the Wendigo. It wasn't as easy to follow as it had been when the trail had blood left over from the kills. But I had a sick feeling about where this trail seemed to be heading. The Sioux had a village in this direction, and I was a little worried about our own skins if we ran into a war party. We didn't have a lot of friction between them and us but there was always the chance it could blow up pretty quickly.

They were talking a lot about a new commander named Custer who thought he could bring the Sioux to heel. I didn't envy the troops when that fight came. I wasn't sure if this Custer had any idea how many Sioux there really were out here. I was afraid they would underestimate Sitting Bull and Crazy Horse.

"We're gettin' a little far into Sioux territory," I said as Jacobs rode up beside me.

"I was going to tell you the same." He pointed ahead. "Not too far up there is a village."

"I'm gonna have to move ahead of you fellas," I said. "I need you to stop here for a bit. If this thing stays on this tack, it went straight for the village."

"I can give you a couple hours if you need it."

"That would be the safest thing to do. Let me scout it out before we just ride in there."

Jacobs pulled his watch from his pocket. "If you're not back by two, we're riding in."

I nodded and nudged Roy's ribs and rode forward at a slow canter. It was an easy pace for the horse and he covered ground fairly quickly. I rode with my Henry across my lap and my right hand near the action.

I smelled smoke before I came within sight of the village. There wasn't much left burning, but the majority of the teepees were gone or still smoldering. I wasn't sure what the Wendigo got from burning the tents, or even if it was the one who did it.

Its tracks had come straight here after the slaughter of the buffalo.

I dismounted, looped the reins over a sapling, and made my way into the remains of the village on foot with my rifle in hand. As I made my way through the village, I found signs of blood where Indians had been killed but there were no bodies.

It was eerie walking through where so many had obviously died and there was no sign of them. There were patches of blood near every teepee, and I figured there were more inside the charred remains of the tents. The smell of burnt leather filled the air. I glanced at my watch to see it was two o'clock.

"They can come on ahead anyway," I muttered.

Something moved that I caught with the corner of my eye, and I span around with my Henry raised. I was staring into dark brown eyes across a raised rifle pointed at me.

She was about five and a half feet tall with raven black hair. Her buckskins were torn and bloody.

I took a risk and lowered my rifle, hoping she would do the same. I didn't plan to hurt the woman. If she had lived through this, she was probably in bad enough shape.

"Not here to hurt anyone," I said in Cherokee, the only Indian language I had any passing knowledge of.

Her eyes widened at the familiar language and the rifle dropped a little.

She started speaking fast and I tapped my ear. "Slow."

She pointed around at the camp. "Wendigo."

I nodded. "We are hunting it."

She looked around with an eyebrow raised. Some expressions are the same everywhere I go.

"They come soon."

She nodded.

"Is there anyone else here?"

She shook her head.

"Is there anywhere you can go?"

She shrugged and motioned around at the destroyed village.

"Do you want to come with us?"

She snarled toward the destroyed village, patted the rifle stock, and nodded.

I grinned. She had spirit, without a doubt. It looked like she wanted to join the hunt.

I motioned toward Roy. "You'll have to ride with me."

She scowled but followed me to the horse. I mounted, and she jumped up behind me. We rode back south to meet the soldiers.

"You go off for a couple of hours and come back with a girl?"

I laughed at Frank who rode a good way out in front of his men. "Reckon she's the only one left in the village."

"The whole village?"

"Yep. Looks like it was here after the buffalo. I'm pretty certain it hit the ranch first, then the buffalo, then here. I didn't see any sign of the kids, though. It left to the north."

"Is it the same one?" he asked as we rode toward the rest of the men.

"God, I hope so. I don't even want to think about more than one of the damn things. Same size footprint so I think it's the same one. What I can't figure is what it did with all the bodies. They were all gone at the village."

The girl behind me spoke, "Wendigo threw them all in the hole."

Apparently, she knew some English as she had followed the conversation. Her answer was in Cherokee, though.

"The hole?"

"Hole in world."

"I didn't see a hole anywhere."

"Wendigo closed hole after throwing all inside. All but me."

"What's she sayin', Danny?"

"She said it threw all the bodies in a hole in the world that it closed afterwards."

"Never mind," he said. "I don't think I want to know what she said anymore. I'm going to act like I didn't ask."

"Is it any stranger than us out here hunting a damned Wendigo?"

He sighed. "Probably not, but I'm sure missing the fort about now."

"Me too."

"Meh… too," the woman said in halting English.

Frank snorted.

Jacobs rode up and I felt the woman tense up. Her rifle started to raise, and I pushed it back down, looking back over my shoulder at her. She was staring at the rank insignia on his uniform.

I felt a point against my ribs.

"Child Killer," she growled in my ear.

I held the rifle down. "Not Child Killer. Different person. Child Killer is dead."

The knife wiggled. "He is dead?"

"I killed him."

She let out a long breath and the point of the knife left my ribs. She was still tense but at least my kidney was safe for the moment.

"What was that?" Jacobs asked.

"She saw your rank and thought you were your predecessor."

"Devereaux," he spat the name out in disgust.

"Lucky she didn't shoot you, Lieutenant." Frank chuckled.

"Tell her I am nothing like that bastard."

"I did," I said.

"I'd love to find him and give him what he really deserves."

The knife point was back at my side.

"You said you killed him," she growled in my ear.

I answered in Cherokee. "I did. They don't know about it."

"If you lie to me, I will kill you, Pathfinder."

"I wouldn't lie about somethin' like that."

The knife pulled back again.

"What's she saying?" Jacobs asked with his hand near his pistol.

"She has issue with Devereaux. Can't say I blame her."

Frank looked at the girl. "Devereaux's dead."

Jacobs looked at Frank with a raised eyebrow. "Dead, you say?"

"He picked a fight with the wrong man in Fargo six months ago," Frank said staring pointedly at me. "This fella was more than just an old man and some kids, so it was too much for him."

I kept my face impassive. "Couldn't have happened to a better fella."

"Agreed," Jacobs said. "Can't say I'm disappointed to hear it. He should have been hung after what he did."

"It was suitable," Frank said, looking at the girl behind me. "This way, he lost everything before he lost his life."

"This is good," she said softly. "You will still pay for your part when the time comes, Pathfinder."

"I expect so," I said.

"What did she say?" Jacobs asked.

"She's satisfied with the outcome, Lieutenant."

"Good. The man was a disgrace to the uniform."

I knew I would have to pay for my part but now I knew the Sioux agreed with that as well. Which meant I might pay for it earlier than I expected if I stayed in the Dakotas.

"That's if the Wendigo doesn't get me first," I muttered.

"You are already spoken for, Pathfinder. Wendigo is not the one who comes for you. Red War Dog has sworn a blood oath."

"I'm guessin' he wasn't in the village."

"Red War Dog rides with Crazy Horse."

"Guess I'll just have to wait," I said in Cherokee, then switched to English. "We need to circle the village and see where its trail goes or if it does a disappearing act like it did at the ranch."

"Lead the way, Pathfinder," Frank said.

"You understood that?"

"I know a little Cherokee," he said, as his horse settled in beside mine riding back toward the village. "You know that wasn't your fault, don't you?"

"I led him there."

"I spoke to some of the men who were there. You tried to stop it."

"I should have shot him then."

"In front of a platoon of soldiers? They'd have shot you."

"He couldn't have ordered that family killed."

"Does no good to take that on yourself," he said.

I shrugged.

He shook his head, and we rode on in silence.

I stopped just north of the village where bloody footprints led away into the grassland.

"Looks like it's still heading north."

"Comes from forest," the girl said.

"Forest?"

She pointed north. "Spirit Guide says the Wendigo is born in the forest."

"Not many forests here," I said. "But there's one to the north."

Frank looked over at the girl. "Can't discount old stories. Most myths come from real things."

She pointed toward the village ruins. "Wendigo is real."

"Did you see it?" I asked.

"Only a little. It was black as night. Very big. I didn't see much more. Horse ran over me and I was knocked out. I woke up to see it throw bodies in hole. I snuck away."

"Big? How big?" Frank pointed at a soldier that was almost six and a half feet tall. "Big like Armstrong?"

"Bigger."

"Shit. What the hell is this thing?"

"Bad news," I said. "That's for sure."

"It took out a whole village full of Sioux, Danny." Frank looked over his shoulder at the woman behind me. "Were the warriors still in the village?"

"Some of them," she answered.

"Damn." He shook his head.

He pulled up and dropped to ride beside Jacobs. I had a sneaky suspicion what they were talking about. I glanced back to see Jacobs nod before he nudged his horse's sides to ride up beside me.

"We're going to turn east," he said. "Sergeant Bell brought up a valid point. If this thing took out a whole Sioux village, we need to report back to the Fort and get more men. Are you seeing any sign of the kids?"

"Not so far."

He let out a long breath. "Then I'm afraid this is probably our best bet."

I sighed. "You're probably right."

"We'll need to camp tonight. We can't risk the horses riding in the dark."

I nodded and began looking for signs of water.

I felt a tap on my shoulder.

"Water," the girl said pointing east.

She knew quite a bit of English, but she only spoke Cherokee. She understood most of the conversations we had.

We rode almost an hour before we found the waterhole she spoke of, and the sun was getting low in the west.

There was a palpable sense of relief from the men after we turned east and to tell the truth, I was feeling it myself. Anything that could take out a whole village of Sioux made me very nervous.

Just after the sun went down that strange feeling of wrongness once again filled the night. It was stronger than the night before and sleep was still hard to come by.

"Newton, Givens, and Black… First watch." Frank pointed at the three men. "Everyone else try to get some sleep."

"Good luck with that," Corporal Newton muttered.

It took several hours, but I finally dropped off to sleep. Not sleeping the night before probably had a part to play in that.

I jerked awake, mid-motion grabbing the Henry. I wasn't sure what woke me until I heard another scream in the darkness. It was long and cut off at the end.

"Sentries! Sound off!"

"Here!" Givens stepped in out of the darkness.

"Here!" Corporal Newton yelled.

There wasn't a third voice.

"Shit!" Frank cursed.

"Where's Ferguson?" Another voice came from behind me. "Where's Dale?"

I vaguely remembered a tall brown haired private. I quickly glanced through the faces. He wasn't there either. His bedroll still rested where he had laid it out.

"Formation! Jenson and Randall, get the horses inside the circle! Everyone else, rifles up!" Frank kept his rifle aimed out into the darkness in the direction of the scream.

I glanced to my right to find the Indian woman standing right beside me with her rifle raised as well.

"Wendigo is very fast," she said.

Something sailed out of the darkness over our heads to land inside the circle. I was afraid to take my eyes off the darkness to look at what it was.

"Jesus Christ! Is that a head?"

"It's fucking Dale!"

"Shit!" I cursed.

Something moved and I caught a glimpse of the firelight reflecting off a dark shiny surface. It was moving toward the left flank at an incredible speed. I didn't even get a chance to get off a shot. Neither did Corporal Tanner before he was already dragged back into the darkness.

He fired his rifle once and I caught a glimpse of black skin in the light of the shot. I was afraid to fire because I might hit Tanner. A moment later I wished I had as Tanner began to scream.

My eyes narrowed and I stepped back.

"Keller?" Frank asked.

I picked up a burning brand from the fire.

"What the hell are you doing?"

"Going to give us some light," I said and threw the burning log out into the dry prairie.

I had to fight every instinct to do it. One of the most horrible things I'd ever seen was a wildfire. But I was pretty certain that what we needed right now was something horrible. I reached down and picked up another and slung it in a different direction along with three more in other directions.

It only took moments for the dry grass to ignite.

The wide-eyed horses hadn't reacted as much to the Wendigo as the fire. I saw movement again and stepped back to the line. Fire reflected off of something black and I opened fire.

I was still unsure about the speed of this thing, so I didn't know how much to lead the target. The woman had said it was fast, so I led it by quite a bit.

There was a roar that sent chills down my spine. I may or may not have hit it, but I was fairly certain I pissed it off. It shot out of the darkness again straight for our lines. Armstrong, the large private, attempted to grab it as it got within arm's reach. It stopped for a moment and grabbed Armstrong by the neck. I heard a crack just before I pulled the trigger on my Henry.

The Wendigo was close to 8 feet tall with black skin that may have had scales. Its huge hands ended in razor-sharp claws. I had never seen anything like it.

Moments after I shot, the soldiers opened fire as well. The Wendigo rocked backward. I levered another shell into the Henry and fired again over and over.

It flailed around where Armstrong had been standing and claws caught both Jenson and Randall, nearly cutting them in half.

My Henry clicked as the last shell was ejected. I dropped it and palmed my six shooter, stepping forward toward the creature. It roared once more looking directly at me and I put three shots right into its mouth. It finally stumbled. It seemed it was more vulnerable inside the creature's mouth.

It roared again with blood spraying from its mouth, and I put the other three shots right behind the first. It jumped and slammed into me knocking me down. A huge weight landed on top of me as it twitched in its death throes.

The weight made it hard to breathe but it eased as Frank and Jacobs dragged it off of me.

I was covered in the creature's blood but by some miracle it hadn't cut me with its claws. I thought it might've been dead just after it jumped.

As I sat up, I noticed the feeling of wrongness was still in the air.

There were multiple roars out in the darkness.

"Fuck me."

The horses went crazy, nearly running us down as they bolted.

"Wrong way, you stupid bastards!" Frank held his hands out. "There running straight for the monsters."

The flames were getting larger as they spread outward, and I could see it reflected in a *lot* of eyes. Horses' screams echoed through the night.

"Dammit, Roy," I muttered.

There were only seven of us left and we closed in close to the campfire with rifles raised.

It started to lighten, and I thought we might see daytime. But it seemed to be coming from the south, and it was still close to midnight…

I span around and my mouth dropped open. There was a man running across the plains toward us… And he was on fire. As he got closer, I realized he was moving faster than anything I had ever seen, and the flames weren't burning him. I thought maybe they were coming from him.

"Here they come!" Frank yelled.

I turned back toward the glowing eyes, shoving cartridges into my pistol as fast as I could.

"Looks like Red War Dog is shit out of luck."

The woman motioned toward the Wendigo. "Red War Dog would have to work very hard, anyway, Pathfinder."

She sounded impressed.

The dark creatures charged, and the camp lit up like daylight as the burning man leapt over us.

"What the hell is that?" Frank dropped to one knee with his rifle raised.

"Don't shoot him!" I yelled. "I think he might be on our side!"

It became quite obvious he was on our side when the night lit up and he was wading into what looked like an army of creatures that looked almost exactly like the one we had shot. He had drawn a pair of swords that glowed with the same fire that covered his body.

Bullets barely fazed the creature that lay dead behind us, yet these swords cut through them like butter.

I heard something behind me, dropped, and turned with my six-gun out. A woman stood there with her own pair of glowing swords. She dropped one into a sheath, reached out as fast as a snake, and snatched the pistol from my hand.

"Wouldn't want you to shoot someone," she said with a grin. "You good?"

I nodded and she handed me the pistol back.

She pointed at two men. "Kharl, Allen, take your squads and join our illustrious leader before he kills them all. My squad will stand guard."

I thought Armstrong was a big guy but this fellow, Kharl, was enormous. The swords in his hands looked like daggers.

He and four others charged toward the right flank while the other man took four others and ran toward the left faster than any man should be able to run.

The woman turned back toward me. "I'm sorry, my husband can get a little carried away. Kel tends to charge out into the middle of things."

She nodded her head toward the burning man in the center of the Army.

"Who the hell are you people?" Jacobs asked. "And what the hell are those things?"

"Those, my friend, are demons. We fight them whenever we find them."

She held out her hand to grasp his. "I'm Rhayne, Rhayne Rourke."

"Lieutenant Ivan Jacobs, US Cavalry."

"Well met, Lieutenant. I'm sorry we didn't make it sooner." She motioned toward where Armstrong lay. "We can only run so fast."

The Cherokee woman stepped forward. "Adawehi."

"Not exactly angels…" Rhayne paused.

"Hinhan."

"Ah, forgive if I translate badly but that's night flight?"

"Nightwing," I said. "And you didn't really answer the question. Who the hell are you people?"

"We are the last line of defense between them and you. We are the Soulguard."

"Lots of pets have disappeared from this floor. I'm sure it's not the neighbors complaining — they're all so well behaved and almost never wander in the nighttime. Those noises are something else entirely. No worries, no worries, nothing that will touch you. Did you have children, did you say? There is a level of protection on this story…but we should continue the tour."

* * * * *

Three Graves Later

by H.Y. Gregor

Faint green light pulsed in the arctic night sky. Bill Henderson stared up at the aurora in awe. Even after months at sea, weeks sailing through the ice-strewn northwest passages, the sight still amazed him. Darkness cloaked the sky earlier and earlier each night as summer faded into autumn.

The crew said the sun would stop rising at all soon enough.

Bill's fingers twitched as he visualized how he'd bring the brilliant sky to life with charcoals when he got back to his bunk in the *Adiona*. Not for the first time, he rued leaving his pastels back in England. After packing everything on the list issued by the ship's quartermaster, there had been precious little space left for personal items.

Bill had sacrificed a pair of socks to make room for the charcoal pencils now safeguarded with his personal effects.

Adding colors would have to wait until his return to England. For now, he'd make do with black and white. Bill locked the vivid memories away in his mind until he could share them with the world.

Cartographers had already done their part to map the arctic—even if all they'd done was squabble amongst themselves and argue about projections and distance measurements. The cartographer said the ice floes shifted. Apparently, it made accurate mapping nearly impossible.

Bill didn't care. He wasn't a navigator; he was an artist. Maps were all well and good, but what the world needed was pictures of the marvelous frozen desert that surrounded him. The alien wonders of a land totally untouched by man.

Bill would be the one to give it to them.

"Bill! You ain't getting paid to stand with your mouth open like a damn fool. Get over here." Isaac Scott, captain of the *Adiona*, waved at Bill from across the ship's ice-slicked deck.

Bill's mother would have called Captain Scott "a man of presence" if she ever had cause to meet him. Though far from a nobleman, he carried himself with the calm assurance of a man who could walk through the frenzy of a battle without blinking—and he had. Before setting his sights on arctic exploration, Scott had battled men at sea.

Scott claimed there was little difference between the two posts. Men—even men at war, men with orders to kill—were capable of choice. Capable of mercy.

The cold would kill you just as easily as any enemy—and spare you no empathy or prayers in doing so.

Bill joined his captain at the rail, trudging with caution. Everything was slick with ice; the decks, the windows, even *Adiona's* rigging dripped with icicles long as a man was tall. The rope ladder with its sturdy wooden rungs draped over the side of the ship, waiting for their descent onto the craggy ice below.

In a few days a sledge crew from *Adiona* would deliver the equipment they'd brought to resupply the base camp. All Bill and Captain Scott had to do was follow the cairns already erected and mark the safest path for the sledge team to travel. It was a journey of two days, maybe three, if the advance team's marks were lost to snow drifts. Simple as an expedition this dangerous ever was.

Bill's head still spun when he thought about the trek ahead. At seventeen years of age, on his first arctic expedition, *he* was embarking on this trip with Captain Scott.

Night fell in the arctic unlike anything Bill had ever seen. Ungodly early. Hellishly cold. Worse and more disorienting by far was the alien surroundings—snow-capped ice floes and frozen tundra as far as the eye could see.

There were no sputtering gas lamps here, and no cloying pollution choking out the lights. No whinnies of horses or drunken vagrants stumbling down cobblestone streets.

No—everything out here looked the same. No signs marking city streets, no fountains or statues that pinpointed your exact location in a labyrinthine city like London. Instead, there was unending white in every direction, and the unyielding north's frozen sea. Bill's calf muscles screamed in protest as they trudged up yet another ridge.

There was beauty in it still. His teeth chattered as he squinted out at the sea of ice and snow before him. *Charcoals will serve me well in this.* Maybe he would even leave a few sketches in black and white to contrast the unearthly wonder of the northern lights.

Bill glanced at his captain. He had to be approaching fifty, but the man was a fount of boundless energy. Bill huffed.

The cold didn't stop him from sweating. At first it was a curiosity—the contrast of the wind biting at his face and the heat his body still generated from the exertion.

His breath creating icy mist that hovered in front of his face like an oncoming storm front.

Then the sweat soaked through the layers of wool he wore like armor against the cold. Now the night wind brought the black-hearted bitch of winter. Everything Bill wore beneath his oil-slicked overcoat—from his heavy long johns to his even heavier sweaters—froze.

"Captain?" Bill finally shouted into the wind. He rubbed his hands together, praying for some warmth to return to his frozen fingers. Two days marching had given him sympathy for the dogs who would soon make this same journey.

You were saving your fingers, you charcoal loving fool, he reminded himself. *Who needs all their toes? God gave you ten.*

"Sir, are we very close?" Bill stumbled forward and grabbed Captain Scott's elbow when the man didn't reply.

Scott came to a halt and pointed ahead. A faint yellow light glowed on the horizon. The advance camp, nestled against a cliff face.

"Thank God!" Bill breathed. A memory of warmth crept into his toes.

The camp was empty.

Lanterns hung on poles outside the largest of the tents—lit but fading. *Someone* had been here recently. Somebody had to light the lamps.

"I'm going to circle the camp," Captain Scott practically shouted above the wind. "Go through the tents and meet me back here."

Bill's heart leapt into his throat. The last thing he wanted was to be alone in this forsaken place. What if they couldn't find anyone from the advance crew?

A blacker thought by far entered his mind, unbidden. *What if you do find them?* The thought sent a shiver down Bill's spine that had nothing to do with the cold.

The tents stood defiant against the arctic winds. Bill went through them methodically, doing his best to pay attention to details to answer questions Captain Scott would surely ask. *They've just gone out. They'll be back any moment.* He stumbled over a pair of boots and his arms cartwheeled. The motion over-corrected his balance and he crashed to his knees.

Wincing, Bill eased into a sitting position and rubbed his knee. He glared at the offending boots with their peeling soles and frayed laces. There was a hole in one toe—doubtless why they'd been cast aside by their owner. *Wherever he is.*

He glanced around the tent's confines. Canvas cots with bedrolls, supplies, and chests of personal possessions lay out in wait. Nothing out of the ordinary at all.

They'll be back at any moment, he reassured himself.

He inspected each tent. Night crept on without any sight of the men they were supposed to meet. Food stores lined one side of a tent clearly meant to be a mess or gathering hall of sorts. The hair on the back of Bill's neck rose. Everywhere there was the sense of absence—of abandonment so complete it made graveyards seem lively.

Any moment.

Bill sat just inside the entry to the largest of the tents, sheltered from the wind but still easily enough spotted by Captain Scott whenever the man returned—he should have long since returned. His ears strained for approaching footsteps. He jumped when they finally crunched across the snow, breaking the quiet of the otherwise ghostly camp.

"Come with me." Captain Scott stomped past Bill without even looking at him.

Bill scrambled to his feet, grateful for the distraction. He snatched a fresh gas lamp before hurrying to catch up to his captain. They approached an outbuilding of sorts built into the cliffs at the back of the camp. To call it a shed would have been generous—Bill's grandad wouldn't even have deemed it a fit hovel for his hogs.

Captain Scott veered toward the haphazard structure. The wood had been piled up against the cliffside. It looked like one gust of sturdy wind would knock the whole thing over.

"Captain?"

"The explanation." Captain Scott didn't elaborate. He walked a half-circle around the structure, finally coming to a halt where it met the icy rock face.

"Put that down and give me a hand," Scott said.

Bill put the lantern down, pushing aside his misgivings. At least he wasn't alone anymore—and he welcomed the distraction. Being away from the main encampment was a mercy.

Scott pried at the largest of the boards. When it didn't move, he pointed at the piece just above it. The slats were interlocked, almost woven together, and one of the smaller boards had effectively wedged the larger into place.

"Give that a push," Scott ordered. Bill complied, applying pressure to the indicated board with first one, then two hands. The sturdiness of the building took him by surprise. This was more than just a heap of scrap. He gritted his teeth and shoved with all his strength, wishing he wasn't shaking so badly from the cold.

Just when he was convinced the board wasn't going to budge, it gave completely. The sudden lack of resistance sent him crashing to his knees for the second time. His trousers caught on the wood and tore through the outer layer.

Fresh blood seeped through the fabric of his long johns.

Bill winced as he pushed himself back to his feet. The whimsy of traveling unexplored territory was gone, replaced by a nightmare. Still, he'd been careful not to complain—not even once. To have Captain Scott mock him now would be humiliating.

Once the first planks were removed, the structure fell apart quickly. A gaping hole opened up behind what Bill now realized was a makeshift door. He almost forgot his misery as the last of the wood fell away, revealing the entry to a cavern.

"You think they're in here, sir?" Relief flooded through Bill like a swallow of good whiskey. It would be warmer in the caves, and any quarters the crew set up inside would be sheltered from the elements.

Bill grabbed the lantern from the ground, eager to move forward to the safety he was sure lurked just beyond the cavern's threshold.

But Captain Scott didn't move. His eyes were shadowed and hawk-like over the layers of scarves wrapped around his mouth and nose. A furrow creased his brow. The intensity gave Bill pause.

A soft wind filled the silence, and the night air seemed to breathe around them. Bill chewed on his lower lip. His gaze flickered between his captain's face and the looming tunnel. The wind picked up, more roar than whisper now. Bill tried to wiggle his toes—felt nothing. His teeth chattered.

"Captain?" Bill's voice quavered. "Sh-should we go in-inside?" *Please let us go inside.*

"Something's not right here, lad."

"You said this was the explanation," Bill argued. It was obvious. Why had Captain Scott suddenly changed his mind? The crew must have moved their operations inside for some reason.

Something haunting flickered in Scott's eyes. The expression, brief though it had been, gave Bill chills that had nothing to do with the cold. *Think it through.* He swept his gaze back over the camp.

If the advance crew had moved inside—wouldn't they have taken their equipment with them? At least some of it?

Maybe they'd carried more supplies than Bill had guessed. But even the food was still in the tents. That didn't make any sense. There were supposed to be great white bears this far north. Surely, they wouldn't leave food out to draw unwanted attention.

Bill looked back at the mouth of the cave and the planks of wood strewn on the ground around them.

"Someone locked up this tunnel from the outside, didn't they, sir?" Bill whispered.

Scott nodded. "I think so."

"S-so—where are the others who—who…" Bill cast his mind around for answers, but he couldn't even form a proper question. The camp was empty.

Where had *everyone gone?*

A torrential wind caught up the hem of his overcoat and drove needle-sharp crystals of ice into Bill's face. He squeezed his eyes tight and blundered toward the shelter promised by the tunnel. His shoulder crashed into Captain Scott, and the two men lurched into the passage.

Isaac Scott didn't believe in ghosts, but that didn't stop them from haunting him. The gas lamp's warm glow shuddered in time with the cabin boy's shivers. They'd uncovered an opening that seemed to lead deep into the cliff.

The tunnel's very existence set his teeth on edge. This was his third arctic expedition, and he'd never seen anything of its like. Ice cracked, floes shifted, and natural caverns opened up from time to time. But this was *stone*. Scott ran a hand over the rough walls. There wasn't any evidence of tools or human industry that he could see to suggest men had carved this opening. As far as he could tell, it was natural.

Scott glanced at the gangly youth carrying the lamp. His crew had started out a skeleton, having opted to carry equipment and dogs over men. *Adiona's* sailors were tired, its first mate dead, and their old cartographer so stiff with rheumatism it was a miracle he'd agreed to the journey at all.

Bill was young, strong, and eager to prove himself. He was quick to follow orders, even if his eyes occasionally harbored a glazed look that Scott associated with artists and fools. Bringing the lad along had been the most obvious course. Now Scott wondered whether he'd made a mistake.

He didn't know Bill's mother, but that wouldn't stop her from coming after him if the lad didn't make it back to England.

Bill Henderson might someday be a ghost.

So many of the men Scott had led into battle haunted him. That the specters were in his mind gave him little comfort. Scott rubbed his hands up and down his arms in a futile attempt to warm himself. At least they were out of the wind now.

But what in God's name is going on?

A whispered rumor came to the forefront of his thoughts. Legends of vengeful spirits. Men who worshiped dark gods and undertook even darker practices.

It was no secret what had happened to the Halsted Expedition the year before. Storms had ravaged their sails, ice damaged their hull beyond repair. Food stores ran short in the cold black of the arctic winter. Then the crew mutinied, and the new leader started picking off the weak and unpopular.

And ate them.

When rescue finally came from Hudson Bay, they hadn't found men. They'd found animals—savage men gone more than half-mad with starvation and the Arctic hysteria that every sailor dreaded.

Men with souls and minds twisted so irreparably that they tried to murder the crew on the USS *Resolve* sent to save them.

The evidence recovered by the *Resolve* was proof enough that the tale of the Halsted Expedition wasn't just truth, but nightmare. A black mark on the history of nautical exploration, of navy men, of England's reputation.

What was worse—*Resolve* had never found the entire crew. Not even their remains. An impossible number of men had simply vanished into the boundless arctic ether.

Their comrades had been in no condition to share the story of the missing men—not after the sailors on *Resolve* had been forced to put them down.

Scott shook himself. Warring with the trepidation clinging to his thoughts, he forced his mind to the task at hand. There was food in the tents, even if it wasn't much. Warm blankets, probably spare clothes. The tents would offer some shelter—but not nearly as much as the tunnel.

This damned unnatural tunnel.

Time to be decisive. Scott wasn't a man to hesitate in the face of danger. In truth, there wasn't any proof of danger.

So why was every alarm bell in his mind going off?

"Let's see where this takes us." He pressed forward without waiting for an answer from the cabin boy.

The passage narrowed as they explored further. Soon, Scott could reach out and touch both sides with his hands. The tunnel doubled back on itself in a hard switchback.

A soft scuffling sound filled the air.

Scott stopped dead, and poor Bill nearly crashed right into him. The cabin boy veered away and bounced off the cavern wall. Scott grabbed the lad's elbow to steady him. Bill's panicked expression confirmed that Scott wasn't imagining the sound.

Scott held a finger up to his lips to indicate the need for quiet. A ridiculous gesture, he realized belatedly. He was merely holding a mitten in front of his face, but Bill seemed to get the message. Scott mimed lowering the lantern to the ground. Another ridiculous notion—if someone waited around the corner, they'd surely already seen the light.

The scuffling fell until Scott could barely hear it—a mere whisper of whatever had made him stop cold just moments before. He lowered the swath of scarves from his face, caught Bill's eye, and mouthed, *"Stay here."*

Scott rounded the switchback, stepping cautiously as he moved away from the lamplight. He raised his hands in front of him. Moments later they bumped against a rough surface, the material scraping against his mittens. Scott had barely moved five paces from the corner, and his eyes adjusted to the light. A rough wooden door blocked the way.

He squinted. Well, a door of *sorts*. The planks had been lashed together haphazardly, and the whole thing leaned against the wall more than anything. The odd sound redoubled, a rhythmic scraping punctuated by another, more piteous sound.

Whimpering.

Scott steeled himself and pushed the makeshift door aside, taking care to make as little noise as possible. The noise died. Scott's heart pounded a rapid tattoo in his chest, so loud he was sure it could be heard beyond the threshold. He strained his eyes but couldn't penetrate the dark beyond.

Nothing. He padded back to Bill and took up the light.

"What is it?" Bill's eyes were wide as deck lamps.

"Not sure." Scott shook his head. "Might just be…"

Might just be what? A wounded animal—behind a door? A wounded man, maybe, but how…?

Too many questions. The only way to get answers was forward.

If the sores on his wrists were anything to judge, the sailor had been tied up for some time. Bill's stomach churned at the sight of the man on the ground. He was hogtied like a beast, forced into a ball with his wrists and ankles bound so tightly the cords had cut through his skin.

But the worst was his eyes. Half-open, his pupils rolling around like a madman's. Never still. Never focused.

Never *human.*

Captain Scott leaned over the man, muttering quietly to him. The stranger flinched away from him like a wild animal. Bill half expected him to snap his teeth and try to bite the captain.

"Sir, maybe we should…"

Run? Bill bit back the words.

The man twitched and rocked, the motions tugging at his bindings. The cords cut deeper and deeper into his skin. Blood slicked his wrists.

Bill swallowed his revulsion and forced himself to look at the man's hands. They weren't just dark with blood but blackened by frostbite. He'd never use those hands again.

"Hold him still," Scott ordered.

"Hold—? Yes, Captain." Bill dropped to his knees and carefully positioned the lamp outside of easy reach. The last thing they needed was the man's thrashing to knock over their only source of light. *You wanted to go into the cave, remember?* Bill grimaced as he took hold of the man's shoulders and pressed firmly down on them. *It would be warm. Sheltered from the elements. Safe.*

He didn't know what was going on, but he'd never felt further from safe in his life.

The sailor's disjointed twitching continued as Bill put more pressure on him, willing him to be still. It was like he didn't know Bill or Captain Scott were there at all. The man's eyes rolled into the back of his head. Half-lidded, all Bill could see was a sliver of milky white beneath fluttering eyelids.

He looked away.

Captain Scott took off his fur mittens, then his woolen ones, then his leather gloves, shedding layer by layer like a snake until his hands were bare to the cold. He drew the long knife he kept strapped to his belt. Lamplight flickered off the dull iron. Bill winced when Scott pressed the tip of the blade to the cords between the man's hands and feet.

At least they let him keep his boots. The thought floated to the forefront of Bill's mind. He frowned. *They who?*

The others. There had to be others. Somebody had built the structure walling off the tunnel, had put up the rough door and…

And tied this man and left him for dead.

The sailor grunted as the first cord snapped. The rest followed in quick succession. The man convulsed, then kicked his newly freed legs. Bill gritted his teeth and pushed down harder on the stranger's shoulders. His skin was stone-cold beneath the thin shirt.

"Easy there, man," Captain Scott said. "We're here to help." The knife sliced through the cords binding the man's wrists together in one quick motion. Bill dropped his hands away as soon as his captain lowered the knife.

Scott started tugging at the buttons of his oilskin coat, then pulled it off. "Bill, you have a flask?" Bill nodded numbly. "Give him a drink. Just a little."

Bill reached for his pack, fumbled the straps, and realized he'd have to take off his own mittens to release the buckles. He huffed a sigh and peeled the snug woolen mitts off. His mother had made those for him.

Bill dug through his pack and pulled out his whiskey, unstoppering the cap before he handed it over. Captain Scott leaned over the stranger with his fingers pressed against the man's wrist. Taking his pulse.

Bill moved to crouch by the man's head. He was perfectly still now. Eyes fully closed. Lips blue. He looked half-dead to Bill already.

What a waste of good whiskey.

Still, Bill touched the flask's opening to the corner of the man's lips. A thin line of deep amber liquid trickled into his mouth. Orders were orders.

The man's eyes snapped open. They were wild, at least half-mad. He bolted to a sitting position, shoving Captain Scott's coat away from him like it had burned him. His chest rose and fell with shallow, panicked breaths.

Then he started to scream.

Scott's heart sank in his chest at the injured man's wailing. He knew its like all too well. Heard it countless times—not in the arctic, but on warmer seas. It was despair made noise. The senseless, agonizing sound of a man broken—a man waiting to die.

The sailor seemed to run out of breath all at once. The tunnel's unyielding dark swallowed the screaming until only rapid breaths remained. A grimace split the man's face. He pushed himself to his feet—and ran.

Away, further into the strange network of tunnels they'd stumbled upon. The hair on the back of Scott's neck stood on end. The man's retreating form vanished into the darkness.

Perhaps it was a good thing… Scott's mind strayed to the camp outside, fully equipped. He and Bill could stay there safely tonight, then return to the *Adiona* for more men—the physician. Help.

"We've got to go get him." Bill's hoarse whisper took Scott by surprise. The captain turned to take in his cabin boy—he wasn't even sure how old the lad was. Sixteen? Seventeen? Surely not much older. It was Bill's first arctic expedition. His first time at sea at all, as far as Scott knew. Inexperienced, true, but as exuberant as a youth could be.

Captain Scott, naval hero and survivor of two arctic expeditions, wanted to retreat to the safety of the camp—to bar up the tunnel and the dying man inside it. He wanted to *run*.

And Bill Henderson—barely a man—wanted to delve deeper into the strange tunnel's depths.

"Have you ever heard of the Halsted Expedition?" Scott didn't know what madness drove him to asking the question. Bill's head cocked to one side, and he opened his mouth to answer—then frowned and closed it. His cheeks and nose were bright red with cold, but what color there was beneath drained from his face.

He has, Scott thought. *He doesn't want to admit it, but he has.*

He couldn't blame the boy. Scott didn't want to dwell on it either—though it was likely he knew more details than Bill.

The Halsted Expedition had wrecked not far from their current coordinates. Two days' walk, maybe three. Scott stood and held his hand out to help Bill to his feet.

"There aren't many who agree on what happened to that crew." Scott's voice fell to a whisper of its own accord. "But we know what the ones still alive were like when the rescue teams made it through the ice."

Bill's lip quivered.

"You're right, of course. We've got to go after him. I couldn't live with myself if I didn't try," Scott continued. A weighted pause filled the air. He fixed Bill with a scrutinizing frown. "But you don't have to come with me, lad. You can wait in the camp. If I'm not back by—"

"No!" Terror slid across Bill's face. "No, please. I'll c-come with you. Please."

"You needn't," Scott said slowly. "If I don't come back, somebody needs to alert the ship."

"I couldn't find the ship by myself, sir." Bill fixed his gaze on his boots. Scott realized it was probably true—the boy wasn't a navigator. He wasn't even a proper sailor, not yet.

Lord, give me strength. I do not want this boy to become a ghost.

Scott took a deep breath. The thought was selfish, and he knew it. There was little guarantee the others wouldn't return to the camp while Scott was there—no telling what might happen to the lad if he was found there alone. *If the Halsted Expedition was here…*

And a darker truth was painted in Bill's defensive hunch. If Scott left him and didn't return, the boy would start being haunted by ghosts of his own.

"All right then. Get the lamp and keep the light steady."

The tunnel maintained a straight path into the earth, and soon they heard the injured sailor's ragged breathing in the darkness ahead of them. Bill's own heart pounded so loudly he was certain Captain Scott could hear it—they could probably hear it all the way back on the *Adiona*.

The path opened up into a small cavern of sorts. The circle of Bill's light barely extended a meter in front of them. There was no sight of their quarry—only wheezing breaths and woeful moans that echoed in the chamber like some forbidding symphony. *Go back*, his groans begged. *Go back and spare yourselves.*

Bill fought back a shudder. *The Halsted crew mutinied against their captain.* He glanced sidelong at Scott. Despite the cold, the man had left off his right glove. He clutched the handle of his knife with bone-white fingers.

"Ho, there!"

Bill jumped at Captain Scott's sudden call. He scrubbed a hand over his eyes, trying to clear them of the stubborn ice crystals clinging to his lashes. Crates and barrels scattered haphazardly on the ground around them, some broken open. Supplies and gear had been strewn about, apparently without regard for their contents. Hard tack biscuits and untouched tins of food piled up at random.

"*Ahoy.*" A hoarse voice cut through the darkness. Bill took an involuntary step back and stumbled into something. He yelped and turned, brandishing the lamp like a weapon.

He'd backed into the rough-hewn cavern wall. The lamplight trembled. *Fool. There's nothing to fear.*

Isn't there?

The small voice crept out from a dark corner of Bill's mind. Scott had asked him about the Halsted Expedition. Everyone *knew* what had happened to that crew. Mutiny and murder had been the least of it.

Ragged breathing punctuated the silence. Bill glanced sidelong at Captain Scott. The man was still, standing tall. Resolute and fearless.

I can be fearless, too.

Bill turned in a slow circle, squinting at the corners of the cave that he could see. He had no idea what he hoped to find—but he had several good ideas of what he hoped he didn't. He paused as the light fell on a pile of ruined cargo. The barrels had been smashed almost beyond recognition, save for the circular iron staves that were scattered amongst the wreckage. Stark white stood out among the aged wood and rusted iron and caught Bill's eye. He took a small step forward and winced at the sound of his boots scuffing against stone.

Silence.

Bill took another step forward, still peering at the piled goods. He toed the slats of wood and scattered foodstuffs to shift the mess—and stopped cold. *Bones.*

Buttery warm light flickered on their milky white surfaces—long and short, curved and straight. Bill's knees quivered, then started to shake uncontrollably as he peered closer. He'd seen skeletons before, at museums. Displays of animals and humans as testaments of the work modern science had done to learn about anatomy and biology.

He fell to a crouch to scrutinize the finding. What had they possibly been able to hunt up here? Seals, he supposed, or the great white bears he'd heard so much about. None of the bones were large enough to have originated from a bear, surely. Their white surfaces were broken by small divots in circular patterns, the bones cracked in some places under an unknown pressure.

Long, straight bones. Shorter, curved ones that looked eerily familiar. Fragments that might have been from an animal's tail or—

Or fingers.

"I am Isaac Scott, captain of the HMS *Adiona*." Bill's heart threatened to leap out of his chest at Scott's pronouncement. The captain's words echoed in the chamber.

Bill whirled—anything to look away from those skeletal remains, the remnants of God-only-knew… *Not men. Dear God, don't let them be human.* His light flickered on two white pinpricks in the distance. He froze.

A pair of eyes glittered out from the darkness.

"We seek the crew of the *Atreus*," Scott continued.

Bill stepped closer to his captain. Close enough to support him if something happened—*if what happens?*—if not quite cowering behind him.

Not quite.

"We met a man near the entrance here. He was unwell." Scott lifted his knife slightly, angling it between them and the man lurking outside the circle of light.

"He is gone." The words were stretched, halting—almost as though it had been a long time since he'd last spoken. Or as though he'd forgotten how.

Footsteps scuffed on the stone, but the eyes didn't move. Bill turned toward the sound just as something heavy cracked into the base of his skull.

They'd bound Scott's wrists as tightly as the poor sod they'd encountered in the tunnels. They'd taken his gloves, though he wasn't sure whether his fingers prickled more from the cold or lack of blood flow. They'd left his feet unbound but taken his boots.

He'd been discarded on a wide ledge of sorts. His captors sat below, perhaps twenty meters away, encircling a fire pit. Close enough to tease its warmth—cruel enough to deny him its embrace.

The four men below spoke in hushed tones, their whispers a susurrus echoing faintly in the cavern. Firelight flickered across gaunt faces. Three were bundled against the cold, the fourth in shirtsleeves. The latter crouched and held his hands to his mouth, gnawing away at something Scott couldn't quite see.

He didn't want to see. Then the sailor's hands fell away. Crimson smeared his lips and chin.

Scott turned his gaze immediately.

He and Bill had been unceremoniously dumped against a pile of crates with HMS *Atreus* stamped across them in dull letters. It was the advance crew they sought— but not as Scott hoped to find them. Not anymore.

The *Atreus* had fallen afoul of the Halsted expedition's black madness.

Beside him, Bill shifted against a crate. His legs twitched, his bare feet scattering the nearest bones—starkly white. Stripped of all flesh by ravenous mouths.

The lad hadn't opened his eyes yet. Blood crusted one knee and his scarf near the corner of his mouth. Scott nudged the boy with his shoulder, and Bill's eyes fluttered open.

"Reverend?" Bill's eyes slid across Scott's face, completely void of focus or understanding. "Reverend Keyes?"

A knot clenched in Scott's throat. "It's Scott, lad. Captain Isaac Scott."

Confusion clouded Bill's eyes. He looked younger than ever. Before Scott could say more, a heart-rending scream wrenched through the air.

Two more men stepped into the firelight, dragging a third behind them. All three were stripped to the waist, each rib bone visible in their emaciated chests. The third man crashed to the ground, still screaming. Thrashing.

Scott strained at the ropes binding him, but knew it was futile. Even if he could get free, there was no hope. They were outnumbered and lost besides. They couldn't escape, let alone save this man from—

Something gripped Scott's arm. He jerked away from the tight grasp, heart pounding in his chest so loud he knew his captors would hear them. A shrill ringing sound filled his ears. He couldn't keep his eyes off the bound man.

"Captain." Bill's eyes shone fiercely now. His fingers scrabbled against Scott's arm. "Captain we've got to get out of here."

One of the animals masquerading as a man lifted a knife. He spoke, the words lost to Scott, and the eyes of every living thing in the cavern were fixed on him. A blast of frigid wind swept through the darkness. Embers kicked up into the air, flying in all directions and threatening to kill the fire completely.

A snuffling sound rose into the air. It seemed to come from everywhere and nowhere, rising into a crescendo of guttural hunger that lifted the hair on the back of Scott's neck. The fire burned so low Scott lost sight of the prisoner and his would-be killer but flickered back to life as quickly as it had died.

Scott found himself grabbing Bill's hand and squeezing it tightly.

The madman—the animal—knelt in front of the bound prisoner. His knife flickered in the light of the fire. The sight was transfixing. Almost beautiful. Scott's gaze fixed on the blade against his will.

Scott's scream joined those of the man on the ground when the knife pierced his abdomen. The rabid snarls of undying hunger filled the air. As one, the men around the fire shifted.

Chaos descended like a pack of rabid wolves.

O God, the Father of heaven: have mercy upon us miserable sinners.

O God, the Son, Redeemer of the world: have mercy upon us miserable sinners.

O God, the Holy Ghost, proceeding from the Father and the Son: have mercy upon us miserable sinners.

Bill heard the prayer as clearly as ever. How many times had he been forced to recite it? For a moment, he was transported back to his family's small church: the rough pews, his brother's hand-me-down shoes pinching his toes. The reverend's resounding basso filling the air.

O holy, blessed, and glorious Trinity, three persons, and one God: have mercy upon us miserable sinners.

There was no God.

There were only sinners. Horrors. Darkness.

The prisoner didn't die quickly. The savage's hands tore into his flesh as soon as the first knife scored his torso. They fell onto him like scavengers, hands and mouths stained dark with blood. All the while that unnatural snarling, growling presence raking the inside of Bill's mind with its inhuman hatred.

Bill's stomach roiled worse than any seasickness.

He pressed his face into the crook of his elbow. While this could block out the awful sight, there was no escape from the noise. The men below grunted and snarled along with that monstrous *thing*, and Bill knew that the captive's screams would live on in his memory eternal.

Bill curled up against Captain Scott like a child clutching his mother. *O God—*

But there was no God.

Captain Scott pounded his fist against Bill's shoulder. He jumped and stared blankly at the object that Scott held out to him. It was a shattered fragment of bone. Scott cursed and grabbed Bill's wrists, then started sawing away at the ropes binding him.

Sensation swept back into Bill's wrists in a flood of pins and needles when the ropes fell away. He hissed and pulled back from Scott, fighting off curses. The men below them were still intent on their meal, but they couldn't risk drawing any attention.

Scott held shaking fingers to his lips and gestured for Bill to follow. They crept away from the light. Bill bit down on his lip to keep from crying out as the cold bit into his bare feet. Soon enough, they'd be numb, and he wouldn't feel the pinpricks of pain. Scott stayed close to the wall until they reached a gaping passageway hewn into the stone. He turned into it without pause.

Bill hesitated. How could they know they were going in the right direction? A shout rose from the pack of men by the fire. Bill glanced over his shoulder—couldn't help it. Two of the scavengers had fallen into a brawl. Blood smeared their faces, their coats. The captive's carcass lay just beyond them. They'd cracked open his ribs like a pig for the slaughter, and—

Captain Scott seized Bill by his collar and yanked him into the tunnel.

Isaac Scott didn't believe in ghosts, but he was at great risk of becoming one. He half-carried, half-dragged his cabin boy down the passage they'd found. The inhuman shrieks and snarls echoed behind them.

There had been a great many ghosts of late.

They may have stumbled down the passage for minutes or hours when the light glimmered around a switchback. He crept up to the turn cautiously. Death may wait around the corner, but at least it would be a reprieve from the harrowing scene they'd left behind. He swallowed against the bile rising in his throat and stepped into the light.

An oil lamp sputtered quietly atop a stack of crates stamped with HMS *Atreus*. A man slumped against the wall. His eyes startled open as Scott approached.

"No!" The man reached toward his belt with a shaking hand. Scott spotted the pistol just in time. In a fit of near-madness, he threw himself at the man and wrenched the gun from the stranger's hand.

"You're not?" the man asked.

"Not…?" Scott prompted, but the man didn't reply. Scott took a steadying breath. The gun's weight was a grounding presence in his grip.

"We're not with *them*," Scott said.

"*Halsted.*" The man's eyes bulged. His skin was sallow, face gaunt from hunger and, Scott suspected, lack of sunlight. Was it possible the madness had somehow spared this man? He glanced around. This wasn't exactly a hiding spot.

"Not *Halsted*," Scott confirmed.

"*Atreus?*"

"No. *Adiona*. We just got here. What is this place?" Scott asked.

"B-b-lack gods," the man's gaze slid away. "Old place. Found it. Found *Halsted*. F-found…" he shuddered and wrapped his arms around his chest like a child seeking comfort.

Scott's mind rejected the prospect of ancient gods as vehemently as it did the existence of ghosts. The ravenous growls from the cavern came back to him; human teeth marks in human bones; men lost to their baser natures. He shuddered.

They'd found the doomed *Halsted* expedition's lost crew—or a specter of it. How many men would have crewed that ship? How many could have survived that first winter?

Scott didn't know, but he *did* know that the *Atreus* carried almost one hundred fifty men. Either the caverns were so labyrinthine they'd devoured evidence of so many men, or *devoured* was far too accurate a word.

This evil could be nothing more than man, but Scott wasn't sure it was an alternative he preferred. *Ancient gods or baser evils of the flesh.* Who could say which was worse?

"Captain?"

Scott turned toward Bill. The boy pointed to an open crate with a shaking hand. It was full of bound clusters of dynamite.

He hadn't expected to find hope down this passage, but he welcomed it with open arms when it came. Not escape— *not yet, we'll find it*—but some small measure of hope.

"You know how to get out of here?" Scott turned his attention to the man on the floor. The stranger's lip trembled, but he nodded. "What's your name?"

"Tom."

"Let's go then, Tom. Let's go home. Bill, grab as much of that as you can carry." Scott jerked his head toward the dynamite before leaning down to offer Tom a hand up.

Scott's years in the navy had taught him that steady confidence could be just as catching as panic, and so it was now. Tom hesitated only a moment before accepting his help. Bill packed several sticks of dynamite into his trouser pockets and clutched another bunch to his chest.

Hope. If Tom could get them out, Scott could collapse the tunnel. *And we'll end this hellhole for good.*

Bill's mind raced as they followed the muddled Tom through a warren of seemingly unending passages. The darkness pressed in against him from all sides, threatening to suffocate. They would run out of light eventually. And then out of hope.

Tom stopped at a split in the passage. He had a manic glint in his eye, and he muttered under his breath. He seemed to weigh his options carefully before finally branching left. Bill hung back and tugged at Scott's sleeve.

"Captain," Bill said softly, "I think…"

"I know, lad." Scott's words were barely audible. His gaze was fixed on Tom's back. "But he's harmless enough. I've got the gun, and you've got the dynamite— and we've got no choice."

Scott moved on. Bill clenched his teeth against the protest building within him. *We can't trust him.* But Scott was right. What choice did they have?

The passage opened up not long after. Reddish light burned ahead, its source just out of sight. Bill didn't need to see it, though. The coppery tang of blood filled the air—mingled with other, far less pleasant scents of offal.

Tom had brought them right back where they'd come from.

Bill caught Scott's eye. The captain nodded, and they turned as one to flee back down the passage.

"*Nooo!*" Tom's wail chased them down the tunnel.

Blood pounded in Bill's ears. Tom was on their heels, his breathing wild and erratic.

"They'll spare me if you come," he gasped. "Must—spare me."

A new passage opened off to the right, this so narrow that Bill knew they hadn't passed through it before. They pushed into the passage. Ahead of him, Captain Scott had to hunch his shoulders. Bill's elbows brushed against either side of the rough-hewn walls. The part of his mind not reeling in panic wondered, not for the first time, who had built this labyrinth.

Who… or what.

The passage opened abruptly. Bill's bare feet slipped on a shelf of ice. Captain Scott caught his collar, saving him from landing arse-first. Beyond lay a glassy expanse of ice.

Bill grabbed Scott's forearm and took a ragged breath. He didn't look at his feet. *God gave you ten toes. You don't need them all.*

The numbness was a mercy.

"They'll spare me. *Me.*" Tom growled, more beast than man. He was closing in.

Bill's lungs burned with exertion. For a moment, he couldn't summon the energy to worry about Tom. He'd never been so tired—so terrified—in his life.

The sounds of the dying captive's screams came back to him in full force. *They murdered him, just like that.*

Captain Scott said something, but Bill's ears rang with memories of the bestial festival of blood they'd so narrowly escaped. *They didn't just kill him. They* ate *him.*

Scott spoke again, this time tugging something out of Bill's hand. He'd completely forgotten about the dynamite he'd been carrying. There was more in his pocket. He took it out and silently handed it over to his captain. Scott moved to the tunnel's entrance and tossed the sticks inside, holding one back. He raised the lantern.

"Run. Now." Scott's jaw set with grim determination.

"You'll trap us." Bill's heart dropped into his stomach as he realized what Scott was doing.

"There will be another way out," Scott argued. His eyes were cold and dead. He didn't believe it.

"You can't—"

Something flickered at the corner of Bill's vision. He turned in time to catch the manic glitter in Tom's eyes as the man lunged out of the passage. He threw himself at Captain Scott.

Scott lifted his hands in defense, dropping the lantern. Bill's heart lurched. He grabbed the light before it could tumble over. Tom smashed a rock over Captain Scott's head. Blood trickled from the wound.

They cut him up and ate him while he was still screaming. Bill knew what the captain had meant to do. He'd seen the fate that Scott meant to spare them from.

They were going to die either way.

Before he realized what he was doing, Bill fumbled for the last stick of dynamite. Scott and Tom fell back to the tunnel opening—gunmetal glinted in the low lantern light.

Tom sank his teeth into Scott's shoulder. *Adiona's* captain screamed just as a piercing wind whipped down the tunnel. Howls and grunting followed the wind— snarling savagery of men made beasts and ancient things best left alone in their black holes.

Scott slipped and the two men tumbled to the ground, Tom's teeth still locked on the captain's flesh like an attack dog taking down its target.

Bill held the wick of the dynamite to the lantern. There was no time for prayer, and there was no God anyway. He tossed the stick into the passage where Scott had laid the others, then grabbed Scott's ankle and tried to drag him down the slope.

The world exploded.

Bill slipped and landed hard on the ice as the catastrophic *boom* shook the cavern. His ears rang from the force of the blast. He lost his grip on Scott's foot. A chunk of rock the size of his fist cracked into the base of his skull, sending him crashing to the ground. Stars exploded in his vision.

Bill stared at the lantern's feeble glow—so much like the candles in church. A thick layer of sediment covered him, and dust lay heavy in the air. By some grace— perhaps the last he would ever know—the light hadn't tumbled or gone out.

Silence.

Bill put a hand to the back of his head and looked up. Captain Scott lay prone just an arm's length away. Face turned upward. Eyes glassy and staring.

Bill rolled onto his stomach and vomited. The contents of his last meal spewed across the ice, the liquids freezing almost immediately. He shook and wretched until his stomach heaved, empty and shrunken.

Dead.

They were all dead.

Soft weeping permeated the silence. Bill jumped at the sound, sending a wave of pain and nausea sweeping through his skull. A figure hunched in the darkness just beyond Scott's body. It muttered incomprehensibly, a constant flow of words that had no meaning.

"Tom?" Bill thought that was his name. He wiped a hand against his watering eyes—the ringing in his ears was ceaseless. He could barely hear his own voice.

"Spared." Tom reached for Scott's body. Horror clamped over Bill's heart like a fist, squeezing it cruelly. He didn't have the strength to fight Tom off. He couldn't watch the horror that was about to occur. He lacked the strength to move.

Then Tom grabbed the gun and put the barrel in his mouth.

The gunshot was strangely quiet after the explosion moments before. The mass of gore and fragments of skull that blasted from Tom's head was nothing to what Bill had already witnessed that day. This was something he understood.

Growling, gravelly and full of menace, filled the cavern.

Bill crawled forward, ignoring the throbbing in his head. He pried the gun from Tom's hand. Lifted it to his own mouth. Pulled the trigger.

Click.

Click. Click. Click.

The bastard only ever had one bullet.

Bill threw the gun as forcefully as he could. Scraping and crunching sounds emanated from the other side of the collapsed tunnel. They were coming for him—for all of them.

Easy prey.

Every clatter of the pickax striking the ice drove another spear of dread into Bill's mind.

Scrape, crunch.

The sounds of his frantic digging echoed around the subterranean chamber. It was never enough to block out the animal howls in the blocked tunnel behind him. It had been a mercy to find the pickax, but a shovel would have been better.

Lift, swing, crunch.

He ignored the prickling pain in his head and neck. He had too many injuries to count, now, and nowhere to hide from them. It was only a matter of time before they broke through the rubble. They had a whole crate of dynamite—he'd seen it.

They had superior numbers. They had blind rage and savage strength and explosives. *And black gods and blacker hungers.*

What did Bill have? A stolen gas lamp. A rusty pickaxe.

And, of course, the bodies. He'd dragged them out onto the ice with him, and now their vacant eyes watched him dig.

Bill's ragged breath misted in the air through the scarf tied around his nose and mouth. The scarf couldn't keep off the chill. A hundred layers weren't enough to war with the frigid air.

A halo of pale yellow light flickered as the gas lamp sputtered. Bill's only light in the entire godforsaken arctic—nearly out of fuel.

The last light he'd ever see.

That wouldn't matter for much longer.

Specters danced in the encroaching shadows. He drove the pickax's spike into the ice with all his strength, the blow jarring his numb hands. Chips of the lake's hellish surface flew into the air. Sparkled like fireflies.

Another thing he'd never see again. *Don't think about that.* The air burned his lungs and throat. *God, even breathing hurts here.*

Scrape, swing, crunch.

The ice gave beneath the blow. It should have been a relief, but white-hot rage filled him. He glared down at the inky black depths of the lake through three inches of damnable ice.

The shrieking in the tunnel rose to a crescendo. *They know I broke through.* That in his last act of defiance, he would deprive them of the thing they wanted most. But he was running out of time. Bill kept a careful grip on the mining tool as he widened the breach in the ice.

The vicars loved to tell their parishioners about the fiery torments of hell. Reverend Keyes would die of shock if he knew how wrong he was. Bill could tell them all the truth, now.

Hell wasn't a furnace. It was an icebound tomb.

Swing, thud.

Bill rammed the pickax down into the ice again. It gave all at once, and he yelped as the ax's head slipped beneath the surface and into the water below. He snatched the handle back before the whole thing could vanish into a watery tomb.

Silence, sudden and complete, slipped through the subterranean chamber like a plague. Unseen, but no less deadly for it. *They're gone*, he thought. And then, *"They'll come back with the dynamite."*

His knees started to shake. Bill sat down, scooting back from the two holes he'd now broken open into the ice—no more than two mirror-like black circles stark against the white ice.

Like the devil's eyes glaring up at him from the icy depths of hell.

Bill wrapped his arms around the pickax. He wasn't sure when he started rocking, or when he started praying. The Lord's Prayer slipped from his lips, long-remembered from childhood when his mother taught him to pray at his bedside. He pressed his forehead against the haft of the mining tool and rocked back and forth with the prayer's familiar cadence.

"You just remember God while you're on that ship, Billy." Mother pinched his cheeks. Her eyes crinkled with her forced smile, sending tears streaking down the sides of her face. "Blessed are the pure in heart, for they shall see God."

That was always her favorite beatitude. Bill took his mother's hands in his and squeezed them. The last shrill whistle to board the Adiona *split the air.*

"Our Father, who art in heaven…" she began.

"Mum," Bill whispered. Heat rose in his cheeks.

His mother squeezed his hands with a strength he'd thought beyond her years. Never one to be rushed, she murmured the whole prayer before releasing him.

"Go with God, Billy. Go with God and come home to us."

"And lead us not into temptation; but deliver us from evil…" Bill choked back a sob.

Reverend Keyes said evil was in all kinds of normal things—normal temptations, like gluttony, or looking down a woman's blouse when you thought she couldn't see.

Bill knew better now. The devils were here—lurking in the collapsed tunnel behind him, waiting to drag him down into the frozen lake, eager to lead men into evil deeds.

Well, he *thought* they were men. Surely they had been, once.

"For thine is the kingdom, the power and the glory, for ever and ever…"

Renewed shrieks rose from beyond the cave-in. The hair on the back of Bill's neck stood up, and he braced himself for what would surely come next.

He wasn't disappointed. A resounding *boom* tore through the air.

"...for ever and ever, amen."

13

The pickax shattered through the ice for the third and final time. Ice-cold sweat slicked Bill's hands. Tremors wracked his body. He tightened his hold on the tool and smashed it into the ice, widening the circle.

It was important to care for the dead. Their bodies had to be interred with faith, on holy ground, to save their souls. *Swing, crunch.*

A chunk of ice bigger than Billy's head broke away from the rest. The pickax slipped in his grasp. Fell from fingers so numb he could no longer feel the tool in his hands.

Slipped into the water's coal-black depths.

A sob caught in Bill's throat. The hole wasn't big enough for a body. Not yet.

He fell to his knees and started clawing away at the ice with blackened fingertips.

13

Bill would be damned if he let those *creatures* get their way.

Three graves.

Go with God and come home to us.

A small part of Bill's mind whispered that he really only needed one opening. One watery grave. He meant to do the thing proper, though. One man still lived, and the living needed comfort. Closure.

The sound of tumbling rocks clattered above him. It was over. They'd broken through.

Bill grabbed Tom by the shoulders. He barely registered the man's fractured skull or the fragments of mottled gray brains that dragged behind him on the ice. Bill pushed the man's feet together and pushed them into the hole in the ice. One final shove, and the lake's depths swallowed the body like a living thing.

Tom didn't deserve to be spared a brutal fate, but Billy couldn't stomach the idea of another person being consumed like they were no more than animal flesh.

One man still lived. The living needed comfort.

Boom.

Bill turned to Captain Scott, fighting tears now. They burned in his eyes, then froze on his lashes. *It's my fault he's dead.*

We're all dead.

"I'm sorry, sir." Bill slid his captain's body into the second grave, well away from Tom's. A blink, and the body vanished.

Inexplicably, Bill's mind strayed to the charcoals in his bunk. A bitter laugh stabbed his throat. Once, there had been beauty everywhere— free for the taking as long as you looked for it.

There was no beauty in this death. No art to be salvaged from the ice. *God, I wanted to come here. I asked for this.*

Maniacal laughter rippled across the cavern. They were inside.

Bill reached into his pocket for the last item he had of any value. He was beyond shaking, now, too cold to feel the metal bite into his skin. His numb fingers fumbled with the flask's lid.

One last drink.

The things that were no longer men howled with rage as they pounded down the slope toward the lake. Bill turned away and lifted the flask to his lips. Searing heat blossomed in his chest for the first time since leaving the *Adiona*. He may be a dead man, but at least he'd go out warm.

The things that were no longer men howled with rage as they pounded down the slope toward the lake. He turned away and drained the flask. Searing heat blossomed in his chest for the first time since leaving the *Adiona*. For a breath, he forgot the nightmares.

Bill dropped the flask from charcoal-black fingertips—fingers that would never sketch a masterpiece.

Smoke lingered on his tongue as he stepped into the third grave.

God have mercy on my soul.

"The thermostat does seem to stick at the lower end on this story. Should you choose this floor, perhaps invest in extra blankets, or a space heater. Explosives are not recommended, but of course whatever you need to survive comfortably. Let's have a drink before continuing upstairs."

* * * * *

Hyarkeen's Challenge

by Rob Howell

Taria halted as she neared the wrought iron fence enclosing the hill. A tombstone had haunted her nightmares, and beyond the fence were more tombstones than she could've dreamed possible. They rose up the hill to fade into the mist settling around the hill's peak. Some still stood upright, but most canted one way or another. A few had fallen over.

They littered the hill like so much trash.

A dark green, almost black, moss covered it all and it smelled old, musty, and spoiled.

She stared at the stones for several minutes and then walked around to the entrance. Intricately carved, the gate's workmanship was achingly, painfully beautiful. The words "Hyarkeen's Challenge" curved along the iron crosspiece. Precise, sharp representations of twisted, grotesque creatures adorned its uprights.

One caught her eye because it wasn't a creature. Not a gargoyle, demon, or troll. She bent down to look at it.

It was a woman. As she peered at it, it seemed to shift, losing its perfect precision. Then it stopped, perfect again.

And it was her.

With chilled heart, she looked past the gate to the tombstones, searching for the stone that had summoned her, but it eluded her sight.

She stared behind her at the past. She wanted to go there, but that wasn't possible. She turned back to the gate. Ultimately, she knew she must enter the gate. And Hyarkeen's game.

The gate opened smoothly, evenly, without a creak. Without a hand pushing it open. The road beyond the gate beckoned, leading up to the peak of this hill.

She took a deep breath and stepped over the threshold.

Behind the gate, lying on its side, cracked as if broken by time and covered with moss, was the stone she'd come to see. The moss covered everything except the words: "Sir Richard Killaire, another who failed without honor." The mocking words hammered the iron-gray of her despair into the red-steel of anger.

She snarled, "I will not let this be."

Only the echoes of her rage answered her, at least at first. Then the hint of laughter underneath.

The other player in this game.

She growled and strode up the hill looking for that opponent. However, every time she looked down to her right was *that* stone with *that* epitaph. It didn't seem to move, just was always there.

Always there, unlike her husband now. A husband who had taken this challenge to save all he held dear, but instead...

Finally, she reached the crest of the hill. A man sat languidly behind a stone table, watching her with much interest. He looked a dandy, with a plumed hat at a rakish angle, a hint of eyeblack, and manicured fingernails. His tunic was of particolored silk trimmed with embroidery of gold thread. The embroidery's pattern gave her a headache.

She said, "I must play. I shall wish for my—"

"I know you will play, Lady Taria Killaire. The stakes, those I need not know, you may choose your prize if you win." He stood and grinned, showing bright white teeth. "Remember, though, this is *my* game, and mine it shall always remain."

Suddenly the world disappeared, and she stared at the existence of failure, glimpsing her agonized husband, and recognized the eternity of horror that awaited her.

"That's only if I lose," she snarled.

Then there was only Hyarkeen, his gaudy colors standing out even more against the gray nothingness of failure. His smile dripped sarcasm. "Indeed. Only if you lose. For after all, *many* souls have defeated me in *my* game."

"I know no one has ever defeated you. Yet, they all had a chance. As do I."

"That is also true." He swept off his plumed hat and disappeared, leaving merely the laughter she now realized had surrounded her since she got here. "Let the game begin."

All that remained was a door in the gray nothingness. Oaken, banded with iron, and pitted with age, the hinges connected to the grayness, as if it was a wall of stone.

She calmed herself and opened the door. Beyond lay a smooth, grassy lawn. On either side were stands filled with jeering courtiers in rich velvets and silks, jewels sparkling on each hand and at each of their breasts. Hyarkeen stood on his hands juggling balls of fire with his feet.

The watchers turned their jeers toward her. Their glee held vengeance, as if Taria had wronged them all, though she recognized none of the faces.

She stepped forward—

The ground disappeared, the faces gone, not even the gray. Just nothingness.

And falling.

Reflexively, she screamed. However, as the seconds and minutes passed, her voice gave out, the screams fading.

And still she fell.

She thought of Richard before the battle where he'd won their manor, bestowed by a grateful king. He'd had his father's armor and weapons, none of which fit well, but he'd kissed her with joy. "This is our chance, my love, and I'll not fail you."

He hadn't failed her... then. She hissed, "And I'll not fail you now." She accepted her fate and relaxed, ready to strike the bottom and, at the very least, have an end to all.

She continued to fall.

Hours, perhaps days, seemed to pass. Still she fell, and her determination turned to grim anger, then hate. Finally, the blackness ebbed, and she could see to a point. She saw stone and as the light grew, she realized she wasn't falling and probably hadn't been falling for some time.

Ropes bigger around than her waist held her in place. A sticky yellow-green tar-like substance dripped from the ropes down into unseen slime pit.

A drop splashed on her mouth and neck. She couldn't do more than spit it out and ignore the taste of... blood, death, and ancient hate.

Bile rose, and she stopped thinking about the taste to focus on keeping her stomach down.

Clapping and cheering rang out behind her. She twisted her head around and there were the gleeful courtiers again. Some now wore the visage of best-forgotten nightmares. She saw now that the same gold-thread embroidery that decorated Hyarkeen's tunic decorated theirs as well, though only around the cuffs.

The embroidery made her head hurt again, pushed on by the mocking laughter.

Then their eyes turned away from her. They leaned forward, pointing at her left. She turned her head to see a colorful hunched shape running smoothly along the ropes.

The shape stepped above her, legs straddling her body. It was a spider, bloated and smelling of old blood, holding its stinger poised to strike.

She pulled her eyes away from the stinger and studied the creature's face. It was Hyarkeen's, and on his head the plumed cap remained. At the same jaunty angle.

He gave her a white-toothed grin and said, "Congratulations, milady, you are skilled. Sometimes the best way to fight is to not fight at all. Few learn this lesson, and so they perish in the first match, giving all they are to nothing. I caution thee, however, the first match is ever the easiest, and lest you win all three, the game is mine."

A drop of poison slid out of the side of his mouth to drop on her cheek. It carved a painful curve as it slid along her flesh, thence to drop away.

Hyarkeen smiled. "But you must forgive me, I am forgetting my manners. Allow me to introduce Kariak."

At that, another hideous spider stepped into view on the web.

"Is she not beautiful?" He paused, gazing at the loathsome creature. "Long have we remained together, she and I. Family we are, and many precious children have we had."

At that, she realized hundreds of smaller spiders surrounded her. They all patiently stared at her with ebon eyes, clearly hungering for their portion of the feast.

"Kariak and our latest offspring shall be your challenge. Your task is to survive." He began to leave but turned back for a moment. "Oh, and of course we're all extremely venomous."

Hyarkeen's laughter followed him as he scurried up the web.

She found herself standing upon a strand, released from the web's hold, and working desperately to keep her balance. She could hardly walk, as the slime along the strands both clung to her feet and also made the silk as slippery as a frozen river.

The little spiders skittered toward her, then stopped when Kariak clicked her mandibles. They milled in clear frustration.

Then Kariak took a step.

Taria moved back, tottering on the web.

Kariak took another.

She eased back again.

Kariak rushed forward and Taria tried to run but slipped within moment from the treacherous footing.

She fell just a few feet, landing on her back in the web. The little spiders converged on her.

The courtiers' laughter returned, merrily scourging her.

She twisted to her left, but her right arm had fallen around the web and the slime wouldn't let her move. She then tried to go right, but again, the slime held her fast. As she struggled, her head fell back, and the slime grabbed her hair.

A spider reached her foot and bit her ankle. She could feel the venom in its bite begin to soak into her system. The second pierced her calf, then another her thigh, and another her breast. All the hundreds swarmed about her, sinking their fangs into whatever part of her they could find. Each bite was miniscule, but the poison spread, paralyzing her arms and legs.

She thought of Richard, of his hands, calloused from training yet always soft on her arms. Of *his* bite. Of his love.

Those memories spread about her, much as the venom did. She remembered every place he'd touched her with those hard hands scarred by war. The venom took away all sense of feeling, leaving only icy, numb memories of her loss.

"No!" She snarled. "I've lost *nothing*. I *had* that love, something these demons will never know, and I will die with that glory!"

She reached for the poison, eagerly drawing the venom of each bite into her, seeking to capture every bit of the killing essence within her to enhance that feeling before she died. Spider after spider gave all they had.

One slipped off her, sliding into the abyss.

Another fell, and then more, each dying as she sucked all their poison into her body, seeking, yearning, hoping for the glory of Richard's sandpaper-like touch.

Concerned, Kariak approached as the last of her children fell away. The giant spider pounced angrily on the woman, driving her stinger into Taria's chest, piercing her again and again in the monster's rage. Kariak's venom was far stronger than her offspring's and the woman accepted it too, now aching to join Richard in the hell Hyarkeen had sent him.

Kariak fell as her children had, giving so much of her death that her life passed with it. The spider landed on her back, eight legs askew, wrapped in her own web.

The woman remained, urging the venom throughout her.

But the spiders were dead, and no more venom filled her veins. As the poison ebbed, so did her memory of Richard's breath on her neck. Desperately, she sought for every drop, pushing the poison through her to hold that memory before she died.

Then all the poison was gone, and with it, the heartbeat that had intertwined with hers.

I live, she thought. And wept.

The laughter stopped. The courtiers muttered among themselves.

Hyarkeen skittered back over her, stinger poised again. The stinger twitched as Hyarkeen gazed at Kariak's fallen body.

The courtiers tittered, but their laughter was hesitant, unsure.

The spider in fool's motley spoke, his voice calm and composed. "Congratulations, for you have won again, and wounded me as well."

A deafening silence descended upon the spider's arena.

The white-tooth grin returned. "Still, it's been so long since I've had the chance to play the next game. It's my favorite."

The laughter returned, courtiers jeering more than ever.

"Shall we go back to the entry hall?" he continued.

And the gray nothingness surrounded them, just her and Hyarkeen in his human form. He peered at her.

"What?" she asked. She twisted around to see what was wrong. The slime, at least, had disappeared. In fact, she was as clean as if she'd had a bath. Refreshed. Energized.

Exactly as he wants me, she thought with terror.

"Yes…" He tapped his chin. He was suddenly at her back, his breath hot on her neck, an oily perversion of Richard's love. "Oh, my, indeed so."

She whipped around, but he was no longer there. Nor was she in the gray nothingness, but instead, a large black and red checkered room. She stood on a red square next to one wall. In the row ahead of her stood a line of warriors, each wearing armor and carrying spears but facing away.

All eight of them turned to face her, nearly defeating her right then. Each had Richard's face. The faces were haggard, bruised, dirty. Scarred. Their armor was torn and rent, stained with blood, mud, and worse. Their eyes held the desperate look of warriors knowing the final charge was coming and they could not stop the foe.

Soon, over their dead bodies, all they held dear would be torn down.

They turned back, grimly raising their weapons.

She glanced to her right. There was a priest in rich, thick red robes. For a moment, she felt relief, and opened her mouth to ask for a blessing. The priest shook his head, and he too had the same horrified, exhausted face of her husband. The holy symbol he wore reminded her of Hyarkeen's gold embroidery. One glance made her head hurt and she turned away.

To her left was a woman in a long, lush crimson silk gown wearing a tiara with dozens of rubies. The face was the same, though. Her husband, dried blood streaking his cheek.

She looked down the row, and all were her husband as well, including, somehow, the stone castles at each end.

Across the board were more figures, Hyarkeen's pieces. Imps pranced merrily, eagerly anticipating the game. Demons sharpened the barbs on their tails as they laughed at her. Two large dragons immersed themselves in their flames, feeding on the fire.

Above it all she could hear Hyarkeen's laughter. He waved from across the board as if they were long lost friends. Then he straightened and became a king in his domain.

"You are all that matters here," he called. "Your husband is, as he has always been, of no moment, but should you fall, you will fail. Fitting that you are the important one here, as you are far stronger than he. You recognize the bishops, knights, and rooks. The ones to the front, well, they are pawns, but then aren't you all."

And the laughter soared as the monsters advanced. Her pawns stepped to face them.

Both sides moved in steps that seemed predesigned. Soon, however, she began to catch the feel of the game, and started controlling the movements herself.

Still, the pace was extremely fast. The monsters blurred as they moved, and her pieces raced to defend her.

Suddenly, one of the demons leapt at a pawn and ripped it apart; shaking the meat out from the armor as it merrily ate him. Her husband's face turned towards her in agony right before the demon threw his head into its mouth and crunched down.

Then another pawn got eaten, along with a knight and a third pawn, each death more grotesque than before. All ended with Richard's face twisted in horror. Hyarkeen capered at each death, but even when he somersaulted, he landed with his plumed hat at the same jaunty angle.

She achieved victories of her own, but the death of a dragon or demon held no joy for her.

Soon, many of both sides' pieces were gone. She was left only her husband the queen and a few of him as pawns. Worse, she saw the upcoming pattern, horrified to see that her queen, who'd been her greatest defender in this battle, was doomed.

She didn't know what to do. The monsters advanced implacably toward her defenses, and this was not her game. This was Hyarkeen's game, and she still did not grasp all of the rules.

And she was sick of his rules, his game.

"I will not let this be," she snarled and moved herself directly at the dragon preparing to immolate her love.

"You cannot do that, it is not allowed," said Hyarkeen.

"Nevertheless, I shall."

"Then you shall die."

"It is what I came to do. It is the boon I came to beg from you."

And suddenly the game was over, she and Hyarkeen stood next to the stone table on the hill. Still, the tombstone mocked her, but blessedly, the laughter had faded.

"Then you have won, my lady, for death is all I ever give," he said. "What shall your prize be?"

"I choose…"

Before she could claim her prize, images of possible choices flooded her mind. Limitless wealth and beautiful homes. Untold power, and incredible skills. Music soaring, and finally of love.

Richard's love.

You must choose quickly." Hyarkeen grinned.

"I choose…"

Still the images came, more and more vividly, pressing her, haranguing her, each with their need to be chosen. Intertwined with them now were memories.

There was Richard when they first courted. So young he'd been, and she'd been younger still. He'd recited a poem that first time, one he hadn't quite memorized, and he'd stumbled over the words. The freshly minted knight, blooded but once at the time, had blushed in shame.

He was so lovely. So honest. I couldn't help but smile.

Then he smiled back, and I was lost.

Unbidden came the understanding that with death, Richard's love would pass from the world without memory.

At that understanding, Hyarkeen's grin widened. "Choose, or the opportunity shall pass forever."

"I choose…"

Images of their wedding day surrounded her. The joy in both families at the rarest of creatures, a wedding of both politics and love. The king had blessed that union, and fortune had followed.

"Mere moments away, milady," urged Hyarkeen, the mocking look back in his eyes. "Choose."

The courtiers appeared and jeered as she struggled. Another memory hammered into her.

There was Richard as he'd been that last time. Proud and brave, thinking Hyarkeen held the chance to save what was left after the king who'd sponsored them died, leaving only his feckless son. A son jealous of his father's love for Richard.

They'd both known it was a vain hope, but Hyarkeen's Challenge had seemed the best choice. For his love, he'd faced hell. For her love, she'd brought hell to its knees.

All that gone…

"Come, come, my lady," said Hyarkeen with his jaunty hat and impossibly white teeth. "I haven't all day, and your husband's soul awaits you in death. Choose now!"

"I choose… life," Taria said finally, brokenly

And he laughed and laughed and laughed.

"Do you like a game night with friends? This floor has some of our most social residents, always challenging each other to a friendly competition. No high stakes here, it's not as though your soul is on the line... Ah, very well. Come, come, there is more to see."

* * * * *

Undergrowth by Kacey Ezell
and Marisa Wolf

"**O**kay, Dad. I love you. I gotta go." Jaylin leaned forward to kiss her dad's stubbled cheek and inhaled deeply. As always, the woodsy scent of his soap enveloped her, making her feel safe and protected, even if only for this one moment.

"Okay, Jayjay," Jay Brendle said, patting her back. "You be good, and study hard. I'm real proud of you."

Jaylin swallowed hard against the familiar lump of grief. "Thanks, Dad," she said, letting go and standing up. She smiled into his dark eyes. "I'll see you Sunday, okay? We'll watch the game together."

"I've got a game Sunday?"

"No, Dad. You retired a while ago. But the boys are playing on Sunday, so I'll come back, and we'll watch the game, all right?"

"Oh… okay. Sounds good, Jayjay!"

"Love you, Dad."

"Love you too!"

Tahani, Jay's primary nurse, stepped forward and offered Jaylin a hug of her own. Jaylin wrapped her arms hard around the woman's slender shoulders.

"He's getting worse," Jaylin breathed, closing her eyes against the tears that threatened.

"Today is rough," Tahani said, her voice calm and collected as always. "He'll be better on Sunday. Good luck with your house!"

"Thanks," Jaylin said, stepping back. "I'll text you when I get to Grantsbury."

"Sounds good. Take care of her, Zzumo!"

Jaylin looked down at her best friend and partner. Zzumo lay next to the door with his head on his front paws, his eyes locked on Jaylin.

"C'mon, Zzumo."

Zzumo pushed himself up to his feet and stretched before walking to her side, signaling that he was ready to go. Jaylin blew one more kiss in her dad's direction, waved to Tahani, and stepped out through the screen door of her dad's cottage.

"At least it's a pretty neighborhood," Jaylin murmured to Zzumo as they crossed the well-manicured lawn. Spreading shade trees dotted the grounds between the cottages and several late-summer blooming shrubs showcased a colorful riot of flowers as they approached the main building of the Rolling Hills Retirement Home and Memory Care Facility.

Since it was such a lovely spring day, Jaylin opted not to cut through the main building. Instead, she took the flagstone path that wound through the campus and would lead her directly to the underground parking garage.

"This is a good place for him, Zzumo," Jaylin said, as if he'd voiced the anxiety currently swirling in her head. "Dad gets great care here. Tahani's been with him for years, and she said this center is the best."

Zzumo angled closer to her as they walked; not quite leaning, but close enough that Jaylin dropped her hand and pet the top of his triangular head. Even for a Belgian Malinois, Zzumo was a big dog. He weighed in at just under 75 pounds of pure muscle, and his shoulder bumped Jaylin at mid-thigh as he reassured her that, as always, he was right there with her.

"Thanks, bud," she said softly, stroking Zzumo's ears. "You're right. This is where he needs to be, and he does better if we're not hovering over him. He said it himself, he wants us to go and have a life somewhere, not sit around and watch him deteriorate."

Jaylin's voice caught on the last word, and she cleared her throat to regain her composure. Zzumo raised his head, pushing up into her hand.

"It just sucks." Her therapist had recommended she talk to Zzumo this way when the two of them were going through rehab together after Afghanistan. "Dad was always the strongest man in my life. Even though he had a brutal schedule during football season, I knew he always put me first. And now, here I am, moving him into a retirement home. Feels like I'm betraying him."

Zzumo whined, so softly Jaylin barely heard it. She blinked several times to clear the annoying moisture out of her eyes and let herself smile.

"No, I know. You're right. This is what Dad wanted. And I'm grateful that his career gives us the option of getting him this level of care… but still…"

Jaylin stopped and scrubbed her hands over her face, running her fingers back through her short, natural curls. Zzumo halted beside her, ever vigilant against threats both internal and external. Jaylin inhaled a deep lungful of air and blew it out in an explosive sigh.

"Okay," she said, dropping her hands to her sides. Zzumo nosed under her left hand, and she stroked his velvety ears. "Enough. This is the play. We've got this, right bud?"

She looked down at her partner's face, noting the fine tracery of scarring along the left side of his head from the shrapnel wounds he'd sustained. That had been years ago, and his coat hadn't fully grown back over those lines. But that was okay. Jaylin had her own scars. Together, the two of them still made a damn fine team.

"Yeah," she said, bending down to stroke his face in both of her hands and tug playfully on the skin behind his collar. He leaned forward, butting his head against her chest as she scratched his neck in the spot he liked best. "We've got this. New adventure. First and ten, right? After all we've been through, how hard can remodeling an old house be?"

Jaylin Brendle patted Zzumo one more time before dropping a kiss between his ears. Then she stood up, rolled her shoulders back, and lifted her chin. She was the daughter of Jay Brendle, the best all-pro defensive end to ever play for the Pittsburgh Steelers. She was Zzumo's handler and partner. She was a survivor.

She could handle creating a new life in a small Georgia town.

Grantsbury had quaint down to a tee. Gingerbread Victorians down oak-shaded avenues, quirky shops built into old cottages, a rambling creek that peeked through the vegetation along half the major roads.

"No flooding though." Jaylin tapped her fingers on the steering wheel and glanced in the rear view mirror. Zzumo swiveled an ear toward her, his eyes unblinking on the cyclists idly making their way through the trailing vines along the side of the road. "One less bill to pay, not having to worry about flood insurance."

Zzumo huffed in response, which summed up both of their general attitude toward insurance. She smiled and slowed as the speed limit dropped, indicating they were about to pass through town or approach a speed trap – she made a noise rather like Zzumo's when it proved to be both – and on a whim pulled into an open parking spot a few car lengths beyond the police cruiser.

There were several adorable businesses along the street, and she hadn't had the time or opportunity to check any of them out during her house hunting. Given she had at least two hours before the moving company would arrive, doing a little reconnaissance and securing a snack seemed more appealing than lingering inside an empty house.

Jaylin was completely ready to tackle the project she'd signed herself up for. But some food first wouldn't hurt.

A brief glance ensured the road remained clear. She slid out of the car and swung around to unfasten Zzumo and slip on his vest. He could unclip himself and finagle the car door open, though she preferred to save such things for necessary events. A muscle in her shoulder twitched and she checked her peripheral, but nothing had changed. Small group of pedestrians a block ahead, blocking the sidewalk and chatting. Cop car a block behind. Empty street.

Zzumo hopped out on her signal, and his ears immediately swiveled, tension beyond his usual 'on the job' alertness. Jaylin leaned her head to the side, stretching her neck, then shifted to the other direction until a vertebrae clicked back into position.

The air was still, warmer than she'd prefer for May, but not out of the ordinary. Unlike a city, the town had no sour smell of too much humanity (or too much of their bodily fluids), and instead–

The air was still. Her thoughts juddered, cramming the words back to the forefront. *Why…?*

She tilted her chin, took in the flowering trees lining the sidewalk. Each of their crowns swayed softly, in a breeze that didn't reach the ground. It shouldn't bother her, now that she'd reconciled the disconnect of motion and feeling – probably something to do with the shape of the buildings, the alley ways, molecular flow and altitude.

It didn't help, so she put the oddity in a box. Not a pressing concern, a breeze that didn't touch the sidewalk. All the more reason to get her and Zzumo into air conditioning, or at least under an effective ceiling fan.

Arrowroot Cafe and Pastries, the name scripted beautifully across the window a door up, boasted a white and blue striped awning and a set of unoccupied wrought iron chairs and tables set in a gated patio. Perfect in case it was the type of establishment hesitant to let Zzumo in without complaint.

She locked the car and turned toward the cafe, motion halting her again before she reached for the glass door.

The cop had left his patrol car and strolled down the sidewalk with body language that screamed 'casual.' Her heart beat faster for a moment, then calmed, and Zzumo kept an ear in that direction, but his nose pointed at the door in front of them.

Cops had to eat, too. Jaylin held her breath for a count of three – nerves about the house, a new town, the fact she hadn't heard from her realtor, nothing of importance – and stepped into the store.

"Welcome!" A disembodied voice, female and cheery, floated from somewhere behind the red-topped counter. "Sit wherever you like. I'll bring water for the dog and a menu for you in a sec."

"Yes ma'am." Jaylin did not crane to find the source of the voice, and reminded herself anyone working would have seen her and Zzumo coming through the wall of giant window. She slid into a cushioned seat against the wall, and Zzumo settled next to her, his gaze fixed on the counter, nose twitching.

After a moment, a figure straightened behind the cash register, resolving into a smiling woman with perfect curls and a lacy-edged red apron. Before she could say anything, the door swung open again, and the officer walked in, hand lifted in a wave.

"And here I thought I'd have a quiet afternoon. Sit on down, Ethan." She craned her head to the side and called back to a curtained off room. "Customers, Benny, get a move on."

A man, ostensibly Benny, shoved the curtain aside with a pair of menus, balancing a water bowl and two glasses in his other arm. He dragged his left leg a bit as he walked, but no pain or tension showed in his beaming expression.

"Take your time," the woman said, aimed at Jaylin. "And keep in mind pastries are half-off in the afternoon. Which is why Ethan is in here, I imagine."

"I'm getting lunch too, Ms. Nina." The cop's voice was low, a hint of a drawl that would have made Jaylin sit up and take notice if she weren't holding herself still for first impressions in her new town. "Can't live on pastries alone."

"Not what you said last week." She grunted, but a dimple appeared as she failed at entirely hiding her smile. "Sit, no one likes it when you hover in uniform."

The man angled toward Jaylin, his smile slight but warm. "Would you or your partner here mind if I take the table next to you? I usually prefer the corner, but don't want it to feel crowded to you, given all the empty tables."

His consideration relaxed her shoulders, and she rested a hand on the back of Zzumo's neck. "It's a free country," she replied, tilting her head to make it a friendlier response.

"Ethan," he said, offering his right hand as he pulled out the chair with his left.

"Sheriff," she said, reaching across her body and taking the offered handshake — and squeezing just enough to let him know she knew the art of this subtle male ritual. "I'm Jaylin, and this is Zzumo."

"His vest says service dog, but he's watching the cafe as much as he's watching you. If I didn't know better, I'd say he was a K-9 officer."

Jaylin blinked at Sheriff Ethan's oh-so-casual insight and felt her lips stretching into a smile.

"Close," she said. "Retired military working dog. Retrained, but old habits, etc."

"Huh. Yeah, for people, too. Where did y'all serve?"

"Turkey, Japan, Africa, Afghanistan. All over."

"Army?"

"Air Force."

"Well, thanks for your service," he said with a wink, and lifted the hem of his short uniform sleeve to show off a US Marine Corps tattoo on a nicely defined shoulder.

Jaylin smirked. "Thank you for yours, Sheriff."

"You're most welcome."

"Ethan Malone, you let this nice young lady relax, you hear? She doesn't need an interrogation with her lunch!" Ms. Nina swatted playfully at the sheriff before turning to Jaylin. "Don't pay him any mind, miss. What'll you have?"

Jaylin ordered a cobb salad and a lemonade, and tried not to be obvious about continuing to check out the cute sheriff. He ordered his sandwich and chips with that same laid-back, easy drawl and playful demeanor she'd noticed before. When he finished ordering, he smiled up at Nina with a megawatt grin that had the older woman blushing red to the roots of her perfect curls.

Damn, southern boy knows how to turn on the charm, too.

Zzumo let out a snort and turned to stare at Jaylin, almost as if he were asking if she were serious. She hid her own tiny blush by bending down to scratch behind his ears.

"So what brings you both to Grantsbury, Jaylin and Zzumo?" Ethan asked once Nina headed back to the counter. "Unless you'd prefer to maintain your air of mystery."

"I thought Ms. Nina said no interrogations." Jaylin raised an eyebrow at him, only to have Ethan counter with that devastating smile.

Oh, Lord. And he has dimples.

"I gave you an out," Ethan pointed out. "Tourist season isn't quite over yet, but I'm not getting that vibe from you two."

"Perceptive," Jaylin said.

"Yeah, well, it's my job. So?"

Jaylin relented. "We're moving here," she said. "I bought a house in town a couple of blocks away. We're meeting the moving company after lunch."

"Oh!" Ethan snapped his fingers and grinned again. "*You're* the lady who bought the old Parker place! Good for you! Beautiful building, it will be good to see her fixed up again."

"That's the plan," Jaylin said, and then smiled at Benny as he silently delivered her order.

"Thanks," she said. Benny nodded back, and then moved to disappear behind the curtain again.

"Well, welcome to Grantsbury," Ethan said, sitting back in his chair as if to give her space to start her lunch. "Let me know if you need anything, all right?"

"Thanks, Sheriff," she said, picking up her fork.

"And call me Ethan," he said. "Everyone does…most everyone, anyway."

He said this last bit quietly, while his eyes tracked to the cafe door. A sudden tension flashed through his expression so quickly Jaylin wondered if she'd imagined it. His sunny grin disappeared as well, replaced by a mild smile beneath serious "cop eyes".

Beneath the table, Zzumo shifted, drawing closer to her and squaring up to the door as it opened.

"OOOH!"

The woman was tall, thin, and had sandy blonde hair in two braids that draped over her shoulders. She wore a pair of denim short overalls over a tank top, and Birkenstock-style sandals. A man with dark hair and a thin layer of stubble followed her in. He, too, wore denim overalls, but his were full length. Jaylin just had time to wonder if the overalls was some kind of "matchy-matchy power couple" attempt before the woman barreled through the tables towards them.

"Oh my gawd! I love your dog! Hi precious baby, look how sweet you are! Oh my goodness, you need some pets!" Her voice rose through the octaves with every step and word, and Jaylin found herself leaning back as she reached down to grab the handle on the back of Zzumo's vest.

"Please stop right there," Jaylin said, careful to keep her tone calm as she raised her free hand, palm out, in an attempt to stop the woman. Under the table, Zzumo lay still, but she could feel a low growl rumbling through his body where it pressed against her legs.

"Oh, but I just want to pet your adorable little guy!"

"Zzumo is working right now, it's not a good time to pet him. You're making him nervous. Would you mind backing up a ways?"

"But–"

"Missy, back up," Ethan said, his voice kind, but carrying a steely undertone of authority. "You heard her. The dog is working, and he's clearly wearing a vest identifying him as a service dog."

Missy looked at Ethan, her eyes going wide and glossy with tears as she put out her lip. Jaylin mentally revised the woman's age downward by about ten years.

Or maybe that's just her maturity level...

Jaylin watched as Ethan gestured to the dark-haired man. He sneered in response, which made Jaylin's eyebrows shoot up, but he stepped forward to grab Missy's shoulders and guide her toward a table by the counter. He murmured something in Missy's ear as they walked, and she sniffled and giggled.

"Wow," Jaylin said softly.

"Yeah… sorry about that. Missy and Doug Archer. They own the local plant nursery. Missy's… a fan of animals."

"So am I," Jaylin said, unable–or maybe just unwilling–to keep the judgment out of her voice. "That's why I wouldn't let her agitate Zzumo. He'd have taken her hand clean off."

"Maybe you should have," Ethan said, and then ducked his head. "Sorry, that wasn't kind. I shouldn't have said that."

"Don't like her?"

"Not anymore," Ethan shrugged, and gave Jaylin a rueful grin. "That's the problem."

"Old flame?"

"Something like that. High school hook up. Ancient history…for me."

"That explains Doug's attitude." Jaylin stroked Zzumo's ears, then sat back up and wiped her hands on her napkin before picking up her fork again.

"Yeah, he doesn't like me much. But they're not bad people…for vegans."

"You don't like vegans?"

"I don't like vegans who insist on being smug about the fact that they're vegans."

He said this last with a grin and Jaylin snorted softly. Sure enough, as soon as they were seated, Missy ordered for the both of them. This involved a process during which she grilled Ms. Nina about what animal-based products might be on her chosen dish–a protein bowl of some kind–and requesting all kinds of complicated substitutions. Jaylin had seen several clearly labeled vegan options on the menu… apparently these weren't good enough for Missy and Doug.

To Ms. Nina's credit, she took the order cheerfully enough, and only rolled her eyes once she'd turned back to face Ethan and Jaylin. Jaylin pressed her lips together to avoid laughing out loud and ducked her head to focus on her salad.

Small town indeed, she thought. *Everyone's in everyone else's business. This is going to be interesting, Zzumo.*

Beneath the table, Zzumo let out a sigh, and Jaylin had to fight not to start laughing again.

Moving truck just passed the office. Pretty sure it's yours - I'll meet them there!!!

The cheery text from her realtor contained ten emojis Jaylin couldn't entirely decipher, but they all seemed positive.

She put the white bakery bag that Ms. Nina had pressed into her hands in the passenger seat and fastened Zzumo in the back of the car. As she moved, she forced herself to keep only her peripheral on Sheriff Ethan as he stood on the corner talking to an older couple. The gentleman kept one hand on the woman's back, his other slashing the air with some restrained tension, but it wasn't her business. Ethan didn't need her backup, she didn't know any of these people, and she had to get to her house and meet the movers.

Suzanne "just call me Suzie, darling, everyone does" Menard, her realtor and entree to the town, was a friend of a family friend and passionate about her clients in a way Jaylin had mostly adjusted to.

"Shouldn't be surprised she'll be there before us or our stuff," Jaylin murmured, glancing in the rear view mirror to get one more drink of the handsome cop – and check for oncoming traffic, of course. There wasn't any, just the trio engaged in intense conversation at the end of the block.

The drive to her new home was short and uninterrupted by other cars or streetlights, though the stop signs at every corner would take some getting used to. The gorgeous old trees lining the sidewalks were still filling out their leaves, making the bright blue moving truck in a driveway – her driveway – easy to spot.

Suzie's black luxury SUV took up the pullout next to it, but there was room for her to maneuver and park without blocking anyone in. The faster she could get all this taken care of and luxuriate in the feeling of being on their own in a new space, the better.

Jaylin took a breath, muttered a reminder for patience that was meant more for her than Zzumo, and straightened her shoulders. Suzie was a lot, but she meant well, and the movers were professionals. She had this.

"Jaylin Brendle, as I live and breathe. Officially welcome to the neighborhood, darling. I just had the boys start unloading toward the back, I couldn't bring myself to open those big double doors without you here." Suzie strode forward, her heels miraculously uncaught by the grass, and brandished a set of keys that she magically tucked away in time to hug Jaylin without stabbing her.

"Got the locks changed just this morning, and here's your new keys," Suzie sailed onward, tucking her arm into Jaylin's on the other side from Zzumo, and moving them forward in a gesture so graceful Jaylin resolved to replay it later. "Now I can stay and walk you through anything you need, help direct the movers, or get right on out of your way. Your preference."

It had been a while since Jaylin had been around her mother's family, but that side was full up with put-together southern women with sparkling personalities and ferocious wills, and she hadn't lost the knack of rolling with the action. Zzumo kept pace, his ears angled toward the movers, and Jaylin smiled.

"You mentioned the sellers left some unusual items, Ms. Suzie. Why don't we get the movers taken care of, and you can walk me through that?"

"Perfect, darling. Perfect. I know just where we should start!"

"You've been so helpful, Ms. Suzie." Jaylin kept her eyes focused politely on the older woman in front of her, not roaming about the slightly overgrown grounds that belonged officially to her. "I really appreciate it."

"Nonsense." The realtor straightened proudly and patted Jaylin's elbow. "Your daddy did big things for the Steelers, but we remember when he put off the draft a year and brought home a national championship." Her smile fairly glowed across her face. "Go Dawgs." Suzie stepped back and gestured broadly at the space around them. "Now you go get settled, and I'll call to see how you're doing soon."

Jaylin waved as her realtor backed her SUV out of the driveway and turned in the direction of her own house all of two blocks away. "I'm sure we'll see her again before long, but what do you say we go pick a room to get started in?"

Zzumo waved his tail and pivoted, glancing back at her when she didn't immediately follow.

With a huff of a laugh, she stepped after him, her gaze possessive on the rich green of the old craftsman home that was now, truly, hers. It could use some sprucing up, a gut job on the kitchen, and a thorough cleansing of the attic, but overall: perfect.

Especially once she successfully tackled the forest of boxes left behind.

Later that night, Jaylin put the last book into place on its shelf and straightened. Her back let out a satisfying series of pops, and Zzumo lifted his head off his paws with a little whine.

"Okay, bud, I know. I should have made dinner an hour ago, but I just wanted to get that wall of boxes handled."

She looked around the living room with a deep sigh, but she couldn't suppress the feeling of contentment as she took in the now-full built-in bookcases that framed her 70" flatscreen. The movers had done a great job of hanging the TV for her, and with her deep, comfortable couch and live-edge coffee table, her living room, at least, was ready for some epic Sunday football-watching parties with her friends.

"Assuming we make some friends," she said to Zzumo, who thumped his tail against the floor and then looked pointedly toward the kitchen. That room wasn't nearly as far along as the living room. Her dishes had been unpacked, but as she hadn't figured out exactly how she wanted to organize her cupboards yet, they still stood in neat, paper-lined stacks on her counters.

However, she and Zzumo still needed to eat. Jaylin pushed herself up to her feet with a sigh and walked barefoot across the gorgeous original hardwood floor and stepped into the kitchen right out of the 1970s.

She'd kept Zzumo's bowls out and carried them in the car, so they were already neatly placed beside the pantry door. She refreshed his water, and then scooped out an appropriate amount of kibble. As soon as they were settled, she planned to look into getting him on a raw food diet, but Zzumo was a war dog. He knew how to eat what he was given when the really good stuff wasn't available.

As he'd been trained to do, he sat quietly while she finished her preparations. She stepped back from the bowls and watched him watching her for just a moment before nodding and saying "Go for it." With that, he lunged forward and began noisily crunching on his meal.

Jaylin couldn't keep herself from an amused smile and a headshake. Sure, her dog was a trained warrior, hard as steel... but still and always a puppy when it came time to eat.

"Next question," she murmured to herself, smiling as she recognized a phrase from the book she was reading. "What in hell do *I* eat?"

That was harder. She hadn't even thought about going to the grocery store, and the harvest gold refrigerator was completely empty. However, her eyes fell on the white bakery bag she'd carried in from the car, and relief flashed through her.

"God bless generous southern ladies," she murmured as she opened the bag and looked in to see a pair of blueberry scones nestled within thin scraps of waxy paper. She took one out and inhaled. Even cold, it smelled divine. She couldn't resist popping a corner of the treat into her mouth while she found a small plate. She put the remaining scone and three quarters on the plate and put the whole thing in the house's ancient microwave. It let out a horrendous grindy hum, and the lights may have flickered overhead, but fifteen seconds later, the scones were warm, and Jaylin closed her eyes in delight as she devoured them.

She'd just shoved the last bite in her mouth when someone knocked heavily on her front door.

Zzumo's head snapped up, posture instantly reverting back to alert. Jaylin knew her reaction wasn't much different, but she forced herself to take a deep breath and try to relax as she oh-so-casually drew her Walther PPS from the belly band holster she'd worn all day.

The craftsman's door didn't have a peep hole, but she flipped on the porch light and looked out the front window to see the sheriff's cruiser parked behind her car.

She craned her head a little, and at that moment, Sheriff Ethan himself stepped back from her door, glanced over at her, and waved.

Jaylin took a deep breath, re-holstered her weapon, and called Zzumo to her side. Then she carefully unlocked the brand-new deadbolt Suzie had had installed and eased the door open just enough to see the man on her porch, but not enough to let Zzumo get out at him.

Not that he would. Not without a command.

"Evenin'," Ethan said, smiling a little. It didn't touch his eyes.

"Good evening, Sheriff. Something I can help you with?"

"Ah, maybe. I'm real sorry to bother you tonight, Ms. Brendle–"

"Jaylin," she said with a tiny smile. "You can call me Jaylin. We've had lunch together, after all."

"Right, Jaylin." His smile deepened just a little bit. "Like I said, I'm sorry to bother you. I wouldn't have if it weren't an emergency, but…"

"What's up?" she prompted him.

"Is Zzumo… can he track?"

"It's not his specialty, but he knows the basics. He specialized in explosives detection. Why?"

"Billy Meyer is missing," Ethan said, his eyes going grim. "He's a kid from around here, has kind of a rough life. No one has seen him since yesterday."

"If his life is that rough, maybe he took off?"

Ethan grimaced and turned his head a little to the side. "Eh, I don't think so," he said. "Billy's got a little sister he cares for. I don't think he'd leave Annabelle willingly. His parents aren't the most responsible pair. Billy looks out for her."

"You think something happened to Billy?"

"His neighbors are adamant something's off, and I've been out looking for him. Call it a hunch – I have this feeling that if we're gonna find him, we need to get on it."

Jaylin stared at the cop on her porch for a long moment, and then nodded. She knew that kind of feeling. Ignoring one had nearly cost her Zzumo's life, once. She wouldn't make that mistake again.

"Come on in," she said, swinging the door open. She reached down with her free hand and tapped Zzumo's head lightly, and then stepped back to let Ethan in. "I'll grab Zzumo's vest. Do you have something with Billy's scent on it?"

"Yeah, I stopped by his house on the way over here," he said. "Grabbed a shirt of his and took Annabelle to a friend's for the night."

"How old is she?"

"Annabelle? Six."

Damn. "And Billy?"

"He's eleven."

Just a baby, trying to take care of his baby sister. Okay, kid, we'll do our best.

Before long, they were loaded up in the Sheriff's cruiser and headed to Billy's last known location: a playground on the edge of town where he'd taken Annabelle to play the afternoon before last. Apparently, their mom had shown up and taken Annabelle home with her, but Billy had stayed.

And then never come home.

The streetlights studding the edges of the playground were an oddly toned purple, each with an audible buzz slightly off-tune from the next. The center of the park wasn't as well lit, shadows heavy over the dim shapes of slides and climbing equipment.

Zzumo remained pressed to her side as they walked, his ears on a swivel well before Jaylin picked up the movement and muttering on the other side of the swings.

"I told them to stay on the outskirts of the park," Ethan said, before making a visible effort to erase his frustration and present a blank cop-face. He did not clarify who 'they' were, other than human-shaped figures in the night, but instead pulled out an airtight evidence bag. "Hopefully they won't be a distraction for Zzumo."

Jaylin lifted a shoulder, as it was more likely they'd be a distraction to her, rather than Zzumo. This already wasn't ideal – SAR dogs often ranged ahead to better locate their target, and Zzumo would not willingly leave her behind – but this was the play. A kid was missing, and they were the option.

She took the bag and broke the seal, holding it close to Zzumo. He looked at her, then the bag, then her again. "Find it."

His tail lifted and his eyes locked forward. He scented around the bag, then pushed his muzzle inside. Nose lifted, he strode a few steps forward, then paused, his ears flicking back toward her as he covered the 180 degrees ahead of him. After a long handful of seconds, he took a step toward the space between the spinning circle of death called a merry-go-round and the tallest of the slides.

"You follow him, and I'll follow you - I'll get the others to stretch out and stay behind." The sheriff knew what he was about, anticipating her request, and it relaxed a small measure of the tension across her shoulders. She'd already told him she was armed on the ride over, and he'd laughed and said it was likely everyone would be, and that he trusted her training to keep it handled.

She'd trust him too, to wrangle the civilians and watch her back. This didn't feel like an elaborate hazing ritual or way for her new town to get rid of her. *Did it?*

No. She pushed the thought away – the ridiculous, ridiculous thought - and moved after Zzumo. The moment he heard her weight shift, he was off, at a steady pace she could easily match. Jaylin didn't glance back to see the townspeople get wrangled, and in a moment, they were through the playground and into the tree growth on the other side.

As she broke the tree line, her ears popped and Zzumo paused for a full-body shake before continuing. She opened her mouth and opened her jaw to reset the pressure in her ears and was rewarded with the faint ping of her old friend tinnitus. Only once that ebbed could she catch the susurrus of night bugs filling the air around her.

Crossing beams of others' flashlights cut across the trees at varying heights, but if anyone was speaking it was too low to catch, and there was only the occasional snap of a branch. These were people who knew their woods.

The darkness writhed around the beams of light, and the sound of furious insects rose and fell without a discernible pattern. The more she focused on following Zzumo, the more her mind beat against her discipline, surfacing unhelpful thoughts that threatened to spiral into an overwhelmed worry.

Zzumo slowed ahead, and Jaylin took in a deep breath, held it, and breathed in once more before releasing it. She timed her breathing to her pace, reminded herself they were doing the best they could. Zzumo was on target, and nothing she did in the meantime would help direct the outcome. But she *would* remain calm, and she would *not* distract her working partner, and they *would* accomplish the optimum result available. She couldn't control everything, but she could handle what she did, and trust Zzumo with the rest.

Periodically, one of the walkers would call, "Billy!" and they would all step even more softly, listening for an answer. Would they even hear anything over the buzzing roar?

Zzumo stopped, circled an immense old growth tree, and turned hard left.

"Billy!" Someone shouted from behind, and an immense *crack* rode the heels of the sound. Zzumo didn't hesitate, and Jaylin's free hand dropped closer to her holster as she followed.

"Billy!" someone else cried, this voice a higher register. "Is that you?"

A smaller crack, then a pop, a series of tearing sounds, and –

"SHIT!"

"GET BACK!"

Somewhere ahead, in the direction they had been going, a giant branch or an entire tree fell, sizable enough even the omnipresent hum of the bugs hitched into a pause.

"Jaylin?"

She signaled low and behind her with the flashlight – she should have when Zzumo turned but had assumed they'd continue to follow as they had so far.

Zzumo growled, low but carrying in the absence of sound without the insects. A sharp scent stung the inside of her nose, and she rapidly blinked her eyes clear.

"Hold," she said, for Zzumo and Ethan both, and coolness flooded along her nerves, calm locking down in the face of a possible threat.

Leaves rustled ahead, not the separated sound of steps, more a dragging, sliding, slither sort of sound. Her gut tightened. Predator.

She eased forward, flashlight low, until her hand brushed Zzumo's harness. He vibrated with his growl, the sound below her hearing, intent on some pool of shadow in front of them.

The sound ceased a breath later, but neither she nor Zzumo relaxed.

"Jaylin?" Ethan's voice, barely loud enough to carry, and Zzumo sneezed, three sharp repetitions.

She lifted her flashlight, and his followed, but she couldn't make out the enormous rounded figure in front of them. Adrenaline dumped into her system, but she didn't so much as twitch. More beams of light joined their pitiful two, but the darkness resisted logic until, all at once, it snapped into place.

It was a wall of kudzu, tumbled over whatever trees and shrubbery had lived there before the creeping vine had overgrown it all. In the artificial light, it remained a bleached out gray-green, not the vivid jungle bright it would display under the sun.

Zzumo leaned against her, focused steadily ahead, and she considered unholstering her gun. Whatever she'd heard moving could be under those leaves, waiting, watching – but if it were nocturnal, it wouldn't be jumping out into the brightness of a web of flashlights. This part of Georgia didn't have overgrown pythons or forest gators, and she wouldn't have heard a mountain lion. Possibilities thus weighed, she gave Zzumo what he wanted.

"Find it," she repeated, and he lunged forward, into the mass of kudzu. The leaves didn't visibly part, but he disappeared into them nevertheless, without a flicker of motion to show he'd been swallowed whole.

Her mouth opened to call his name, but the sound that came wasn't her voice. Zzumo barked once – a quick, sharp sound – paused, and then twice more.

"He found something," she said, but she had the discipline not to lunge forward. The Sheriff would need to confirm and secure the scene. He brushed her elbow with his as he passed, his steps as silent as Zzumo's had been, and gestured for her to follow

He didn't duck into the kudzu, but studied it a moment, then pulled a machete loose from his thigh strap. Six efficient cuts made an opening, and Jaylin crouched to signal Zzumo if needed.

Again she kept her light low, not wanting to slash across Zzumo's eyes, and was immediately rewarded by a discernible shape. Small. Human. Dirty. A large dog crouched over him, at the ready.

"Contact," she said, and a muffled sob rode the air behind her. She didn't turn but gestured for Zzumo to stand down. He shifted back but fixed his eyes on Ethan as the Sheriff ducked between the remaining vines.

"He's alive," Ethan said, voice still low. "Tad, standard kit."

Jaylin signaled Zzumo to come, and he nudged the still body of the boy once before doing so. She stayed low and buried her hands in his fur, resting her head against his. "Good boy," she murmured. "That's my best boy."

He leaned hard against her, but the low sound in his chest was more worried than pleased.

Billy didn't appear to have any external injuries, other than a welter of scrapes and scratches. Jaylin stood back, holding Zumo still as the town's paramedic crew carried the boy out on a backboard and put him into an ambulance. Sheriff Ethan helped them shut the ambulance doors with a deep "thud," then turned back to Jaylin as the rest of the search crew dispersed.

"Thank you," he said, lifting his iconic Smokey Bear hat with one hand scrubbing the other over his tired, handsome face. "Really, Jaylin. I…thank you."

"No thanks needed," she said, allowing herself a small smile. "We were glad to help. He's going to be okay?" She asked the question because she felt like it was expected, even though she knew very well that depending on what had happened before Zzumo found Billy tangled up in the undergrowth, the kid had a long way to go before being "okay" ever again.

Still, he's alive. That's a victory.

"I think so, eventually," Ethan said, his smile turning a little sad. "I can keep you posted if you like."

"That would be great," Jaylin said. "Thanks." She hesitated, wanting to say more but not finding the right words. An awkward silence descended, broken eventually by the sound of booted feet approaching.

"Sheriff! Do you need anything else? I wanted to get Amira home for school…" The woman who approached wore a hip-length coat, and what at first looked like a stocking cap. But as she drew closer to the area lit by the ambulance's scene lights, Jaylin could see that it was a hijab.

"Maryam, yes. Let me introduce you to your new neighbor. Jaylin, this is Maryam Little. She and her daughter Amira live a few doors down from you. They're also our local SAR team coordinators. Maryam, this is Jaylin Brendle, and her service dog, Zzumo."

Maryam stuck her hand out in greeting, and Jaylin took it and shook.

"Any relation to Jay Brendle?" Maryam asked.

"My dad," Jaylin said with a smile.

"Nice. My late husband was a big fan."

"Maryam, I was hoping you could take Jaylin and Zzumo home. I need to finish up some things before I'm done, and you guys live almost next door."

"Sure, no problem."

"Is that okay?" Ethan said, turning back to Jaylin. "I hate to abandon you, but—"

"It's fine," Jaylin said. "Zzumo, let's go."

By the time Maryam dropped her off, several things had happened.

First, the adrenaline rush of the search had worn off, leaving her exhausted and unsettled, wondering how, exactly, an eleven-year-old boy had found himself trapped in a ball of kudzu out in the woods. Jaylin hadn't been a detective, but all of her training and instincts screamed at her that there was more to this. She would have liked to spend the ride in quiet contemplation, but the second thing that happened made that impossible.

The second thing was Maryam's daughter, Amira.

Like her mother, Amira had large, long-lashed brown eyes that stood out under her hijab. Unlike her mother, Amira's skin tone didn't wash pale in the moonlight. Instead, it carried a similar warmth to Jaylin's own.

But, if Jaylin had had any concerns for a biracial hijabi teenage girl growing up in this small town in Georgia, Amira quickly laid them to rest. The entire way home, she effervesced about the excitement of the search, how happy she was that they'd found Billy and that he was safe, how wonderful Zzumo was, how excited her many, many friends would be at school, and how cool it would be to tell them all about her new badass neighbor and friend.

"We should make that a 4H project, Mom, training search and rescue dogs, don't you think? Oh! I just thought of something!" Amira gushed as Maryam turned a corner and Jaylin abruptly realized that they were only a block from her house. "I'm supposed to go flying with Uncle Ahmed tomorrow after school, before he leaves on his trip. You and Zzumo should come meet him! He was in the Army, too."

"My brother," Maryam supplied from the driver's seat. "He works out at the little airstrip on the edge of town. He's been teaching Amira how to fly his airplanes."

"That's cool," Jaylin said, impressed. "I always thought it would be cool to learn to fly."

"Not me," Maryam shuddered. "But Amira loves it."

"Please say you'll come," Amira said, turning to hit Jaylin with her big, pleading eyes.

"I'm not sure I can tomorrow," Jaylin said, reaching over to stroke the top of Zzumo's head where he rested it on the seat next to her. "But I will definitely take a raincheck."

"Lots of unpacking to do?" Maryam asked.

"Oh! Yes. Packing and unpacking, actually. There are a bunch of old dolls and things in the attic that I need to haul down and take to Goodwill or something."

"Ewww, Miss Parker's creepy dolls!" Amira wrinkled her nose and shuddered just as her mother had done a minute before.

"Amira, be kind." Maryam murmured.

"Sorry, Momma, but it's true. She used to set them up in her windows like mannequins in a store display. She had little furniture for them and everything, and she'd change it every day, so it was like they moved." Another shudder. "Freaked everyone out. We used to dare each other to walk by the windows."

"Eveline Parker was a bit of an eccentric," Maryam said, meeting Jaylin's eyes in the rearview mirror. "But she was a good woman."

"I'll take that combination any day," Jaylin said with a smile.

"Me too," Maryam spun the wheel to pull into Jaylin's driveway behind her car. "Well, here you go, Jaylin, it was wonderful to meet you and Zzumo. We can't thank you enough for helping with the effort tonight."

"Thank you both for the ride home. Have fun at school tomorrow, Amira."

"Thank you, Ms. Jaylin! Good luck with the creepy dolls!"

"We're right down the street," Maryam said, pointing to a lovely white Victorian two houses down on the opposite side of the road from Jaylin's craftsman. "If you need anything."

"Thank you. Come on, Zzumo, let's go home."

Jaylin let herself and Zzumo out, closed the door behind her, and walked up her front porch. She unlocked the deadbolt, then turned with a wave to let Maryam and Amira know she'd gotten inside. Maryam and her daughter both lifted a hand in farewell, and Maryam backed out into the street again.

"I think we might have just been adopted, Zzumo," Jaylin said as she swung the door wide. Zzumo flicked his tail as he went in, which she took as a sign that he agreed. She locked the door behind her and then turned to her half-unpacked house with a sigh.

"Well," she said as she led her dog up the stairs toward her bedroom. "I suppose there are worse fates than having sweet neighbors."

Zzumo let out a huff which sounded like more agreement, and then waited patiently while Jaylin washed her face and brushed her teeth before falling into bed and the sweet oblivion of sleep.

The next morning, Jaylin and Zzumo climbed up into the low-ceilinged attic to tackle the task of cataloging the contents of the dusty boxes stacked in haphazard rows. Without the insulation protection of the rest of the house, the Georgia sun turned the entire space into an oven, and Jaylin had only gotten through two boxes before Zzumo's whine warned her he needed a break.

"Yeah, bud, me too," she said, swiping a sleeve across her face. It came away soaked with sweat. Jaylin forced an inhale, though it felt like someone was holding a wet washcloth over her nose and mouth, and turned toward the trapdoor that would lead back down into the air-conditioned rest of her home.

She blinked.

A web of broad-leaved vines stretched across the opening, obscuring the view of the ladder heading down. Jaylin reached out to pull them away, but more tendrils snaked across, weaving in and out of the rafters, winding their way towards her ankles, her hands.

Something shuffled behind her.

Jaylin spun, only to see a tiny, porcelain hand reach out of one of the boxes and grip the edge. Something tickled her leg, and she glanced down to see that the vines had wound their way around her ankles and reached up toward her thighs, anchoring her in place.

"Zzumo," she gasped, or tried to. The sound wouldn't issue from her mouth, and so she stood motionless and mute as first one doll, and then another and another climbed out of the boxes that hemmed her in like prison walls.

The first doll turned to look at her, its glass eyes glinting green in the sweltering light from the attic window. Once again, Jaylin fought to open her mouth, to call out to Zzumo, to anyone, but she couldn't make the sound come. The doll oozed toward her, moving as the vine had done: a snake slithering across the attic rafters.

Jaylin blinked.

The doll was closer. Little hands reached out for her. Little vines reaching out from behind glass eyes, writhing through the stifling air, poking her in the side…

Jaylin sat up, drenched in sweat. The morning sun blazed through her open bedroom window, shining directly across her bed.

Zzumo nudged her in the side again, letting out a tiny whine of inquiry.

"I'm okay, bud. Just a nightmare," Jaylin said, reaching out to scratch his ears. "Too much talk of creepy dolls and kudzu last night."

Zzumo pushed his skull up into her hand, and patiently waited for Jaylin to collect herself and get out of the bed.

"I know two things, though," she said, spine popping as she stretched her arms up overhead. "One, we're getting some curtains for that damn window and two, I'm going to call Ms. Suzie's movers back and have them haul that shit out of the attic. I'll go through it in the air conditioning."

Zzumo thumped his tail against the bed and then hopped down to join Jaylin as she stripped off her sweat-soaked sleep tank and got dressed for her morning workout.

Workout, shower, breakfast, more unpacking. We got this, she told herself. *One down at a time.*

Lunch at Arrowroot?

Jaylin regarded the text from Ethan, fully aware she was smiling like an idiot. She refused to be embarrassed – Zzumo wouldn't tell anyone. Her phone buzzed again in a quick series.

A thank you and an update.

And a date date.

Just to be clear.

"A man who says what he means," she said aloud, and Zzumo regarded her non-judgmentally, stretched across the couch with head on his paws.

"And we've gotten enough done to take a break." While that wasn't entirely true, given her goals for the day, she did have to go into town and pick up curtains, so it was an excellent use of time. Nothing to do with putting a bit more distance between them and the attic before Ms. Suzie's guys could come by in the early evening and clear it out.

"You deserve a little treat, and I should probably pick up easy-prep food for the next few days."

Zzumo sighed as though his life were crushingly difficult, and flopped to the side, which Jaylin took to mean 'get on with it already.' So she did. She texted her acceptance and a suggested time to Ethan, rubbed Zzumo's proffered belly, and resolved to get two more boxes worth of assorted sundries clear before it was time to go.

Arrowroot's proprietress, Nina, had a dog bowl with clear water already placed in the corner they'd last sat in, and an assortment of treats in an artful display across the table. Ethan gestured at it with an unfairly charming smile even as Nina came around the counter and spread her hands, beaming somehow more brilliantly than the day before.

"We are so lucky you're here. Got the full report on how invaluable your Zzumo was in finding Billy, Jaylin, and if you'd please thank him for us, I'd appreciate it."

"Mentioned you were coming," Ethan added, not quite under his breath. He stood by the table, in unwrinkled khakis and a red polo shirt, looking about as delicious as anything in the display case.

"Oh." Pressure in her chest, for no reason she cared to pinpoint. The kindness, and the warmth of the welcome... Jaylin dropped to a crouch and unfastened Zzumo's vest. "This is for you, too, bud. Off." He stared up at her, then slowly waved his tail, and she stood. "Ms. Nina, if you'd like to thank him yourself, he can have..." She glanced over the pyramid of baked dog cookies and grinned. "Two of your choice. And you can pet him and tell him how good he is directly, if you want."

Nina made a noise rather like a swallowed squeal, and impressed Jaylin all over again by tamping back her excitement and keeping her motions steady. While enthusiastic, she didn't get overly grabby or linger overlong. Instead she offered

Zzumo a treat, which he took like the well-trained gentleman he was, then scratched behind his ears, and gave him a second one, murmuring what an excellent boy he was throughout. Zzumo found the whole thing as delightful as Nina did, his tail waving and tongue lolling.

After a few moments Nina straightened and winked. "Well that's my day made. Let me know when you're ready to order and I'll leave you be. And I'll bring you a bag so you can bring the rest of those home later."

Zzumo huffed up at her, glanced back at the additional treats still on top of the table, then stretched hugely and laid at Jaylin's feet.

Ethan pointed his chin inquiringly toward Zzumo's vest and Jaylin laughed. "No, I'll leave it off for a bit – why, do you want to pet him too?"

"Do people usually say no to that question?" His chuckle snagged something low in her gut, and she spread her hands in a 'by all means' gesture.

She leaned over to watch and was rewarded with Zzumo flopping over to reveal to Ethan that he did, in fact, have a belly, and that it should, in fact, be scratched.

Well shit. The cuteness was all but overwhelming, and she sat up before she started offering her heart and her underpants to the Sheriff on a platter.

"Billy's ok?" she asked softly, not wanting to interrupt the moment but also needing to haul her wayward thoughts back on track.

"He's still in the hospital." Ethan's voice remained calm, but veered close to Cop Neutral, and Jaylin put her elbows on the table to keep from ducking to look at him again.

"When you said update, please know I'm not expecting the active investigation report. Just want to make sure he's doing as well as can be expected."

"He is." Ethan straightened back to the table, much to Zzumo's audible disappointment. "And I'm not trying to be cagey, it's just…" He ran a hand through his hair. "They can't release him until his body temp stabilizes – it's just outside of hypothermia and they can't raise it."

"And…emotionally?"

"He doesn't remember anything." Ethan sighed. "Which is potentially better for him, but it means there's not much of an active investigation. Nothing at the scene to indicate anyone else was there, but that alone is suspicious because beyond what Zzumo followed to find him, there are no marks of his passage."

"Which makes it unlikely he just wandered off."

"And the bruising around his arms make it likely he was grabbed and carried there."

She dropped her chin in her hands. "Not a common problem around here, I'd guess?"

"No." One side of his mouth quirked up. "But checks out I'd get a frustrating case the moment a beautiful girl moves to town."

"Smooth," she said with a laugh, letting 'update' move right on over to 'date date,' which took them nicely through an excellent lunch.

As they lingered over their empty plates, the door juddered open, bell tinkling discordantly, and every vertebrae along Jaylin's spine locked into place.

Missy stumbled inside, her face subtly off. Allergies, judging from the tissue she kept alternating between her eyes and her nose.

Ew.

Nina crossed her arms. "Missy Archer, how many times have I told you, if you're sick, stay home. You call and I'll get someone to bring you something over."

"Not sick." She brandished the tissue. "Just spring." Her voice was thicker than the day before, and Jaylin resisted the urge to clear her own throat in sympathy. "Doug's… he's feeling worse. Can we get some soup?"

"Soup of the day is pearl barley - go sit outside and rest, I'll package you up a few extra in just a minute."

Missy turned, the motion unwieldy, and her dull eyes passed over their occupied corner. Jaylin tensed, but the other woman's gaze didn't so much as twitch at the sight of either dog or evident date. Poor thing, she had to be miserable - the run-off from her allergies was tinged green, probably some sort of sinus infection.

Ethan's radio crackled, and he answered in terse acronyms. As he clipped it back into place, he met Jaylin's eyes sheepishly. "Unfortunately, even a day off isn't entirely a day off."

"I know how that goes."

"I was going to offer to walk you home," he added, his drawl intensifying in exactly the sort of way to damage her calm.

"Well, I drove, so…" But she returned his drawl with a slow smile that made his eyes widen appreciatively.

"Benny, bring those out and help Missy back to her car, please," Nina called, interrupting their almost-moment.

"I'll get the door, Benny." Ethan stood and let his gaze linger on Jaylin's face. "Maybe we can do this again soon."

"Maybe." She fastened Zzumo's vest and chatted with Nina about Zzumo's training for a bit while the woman packaged some food to get Jaylin through the next few meals before grocery shopping.

The rest of the afternoon passed easily – curtains obtained, snacks procured – and Zzumo actually laid down in the back seat instead of staring out the window. He stood up again a few turns later, as they navigated down a new road a few blocks from their house.

"Ms. Suzie didn't point that one out when she was talking up the neighborhood." Jaylin slowed as she approached the next stop sign and regarded the long-abandoned building on the corner. Draped in sheets of kudzu, it was more a suggestion of a house than an actual dwelling, as though the plants had formed a suggestion of corners and structure under their long vines. A glint in the apparent second story indicated at least part of a window was left, but looking at it too long made all the tiny hairs on her arms bristle uncomfortably.

She made a face, ensured there was no on-coming traffic, and continued on her way. She had work to do before Ms. Suzie's guys came by to bring the creepy contents of her attic down into the main house.

Jaylin ran a hand down her arm to shove off the static electricity feeling and drove.

The following morning, she decided that coffee needed to be the first order of business. Despite yesterday having been a good day, she hadn't slept well again after Ms. Suzie's boys no-showed and Ms. Suzie herself didn't answer her texts. Zzumo hadn't had to wake her from any more nightmares about creepy dolls, thank all that was good, but she woke with an unrelenting sense of dread that was only partially dispelled by the morning sunlight streaming through her newly curtained window.

So. Quick workout, shower, and then Jaylin reached for her phone and texted Ethan.

Coffee?

Three dots immediately popped up, indicating he was responding. Jaylin felt her lips curve in a smile when his text came through.

I thought you'd never ask. Arrowroot?

Sounds good. She considered her current state. *Meet you there in 10.*

I'll be there in 5, text me your order.

"Zzumo, I might be in trouble. I think I really like this guy," Jaylin said. Zzumo pressed his bulk against her thigh and dropped his jaw in a doggy smile.

"You like him too? Fuck, I'm really in trouble, then." Her smile grew into a full grin as she typed out her coffee order.

You asked for it. Triple chocolate mocha frap with caffeinated whip cream and chocolate drizzle.

His response took a minute. Long enough for Jaylin to throw on her walking shoes and get Zzumo's vest and leash ready.

I want to make fun of you for that, but TBH I'm a little impressed. That's a lot of caffeine and sugar! I see you don't F around when it comes to coffee.

Jaylin snorted. *Life's too short to F around. See you in a bit! ;)*

With that, she shoved her phone in the back pocket of her jeans, pulled a Steelers cap on over her ponytail, and headed out into the Georgia morning.

The walk to Arrowroot wasn't far, but Jaylin was glad it was still early. The warm air wrapped around her, holding the promise of punishing heat to come. She toyed with the idea of asking Ethan to give her a ride home after coffee and decided to make that call in real time.

"This sure is a pretty town, Zzumo," she murmured as they walked. The morning light gilded the air, and the surrounding foliage almost seemed to glow with a deep, vibrant emerald green. All along the way, Jaylin spotted tendrils of creeping kudzu wrapped around streetlamps, poised against the foundations of buildings…and in some cases more than that. She thought back to the abandoned house she'd seen the night before at the end of the street. How long had it taken for that invasive, aggressive weed to engulf the structure? How long until the weight of the kudzu made the whole thing collapse?

Despite the rising heat and the growing humidity, an icy chill shivered down Jaylin's spine, causing Zzumo's head to snap up toward her.

"I'm okay, bud," she said, stroking the top of his head. "Just morbid thoughts. I'll feel better once I get some coffee in me."

And when I see those damn dimples of Ethan's… Ugh. Jayjay. You've got it bad, girl! You'd best simmer down and stay focused. The last thing your life needs right now is more complications…

Even if those complications do look awfully good in a sheriff's uniform…

Jaylin shook her head at herself and pushed forward into a faster walk. Overhead, a hot wind whistled through the trees, rustling the kudzu leaves that clung to the tall trunks and wound their way up into the overhead powerlines. The scent of warm, decaying greenery wafted her way, making her empty stomach churn.

"Maybe we'll get one of Ms. Nina's scones, too, hmm?" she said to Zzumo. "I should eat, and you can probably have a treat… but first, coffee."

They rounded the corner and Jaylin saw Ethan leaning against the hood of his cruiser, a drink tray sitting next to him as he smiled down at his phone. She approached, and he looked up, his smile deepening as he hit her with those damn dimples.

"Hey," he said.

"Hey," she replied.

"I got your coffee." He reached over and handed her a tall to-go cup with the Arrowroot logo on the side. "Ms. Nina was a little awed at your order, but she says she pulled it off."

"Even the caffeinated whip?" Jaylin removed the top and took an appreciative sniff.

"Yup. She said they had some anyway for another special they're about to run. Your timing was impeccable."

"Hmm. Sometimes things work out." She lifted the cup to her lips and took a slow sip, savoring the bitter notes of chocolate and espresso as they filled her mouth and rolled over her tongue.

"I'm really glad you texted me," Ethan said. "I was hoping you would. After our date date."

Jaylin opened her eyes and smiled at him, then licked a fleck of whipped cream from the corner of her mouth. She didn't miss the way Ethan's eyes tracked to her tongue, nor the dark and hungry expression that flashed through them for just an instant.

"Well," she said. "Turns out, I like you, Sheriff Ethan."

"That so? Well. I like you too, Ms. Jaylin." He flashed his dimples at her again and lifted his own coffee from the drink tray. "So…the question then becomes, what do we do about that?"

"About you liking me?"

"And you liking me."

Jaylin smirked a little behind her cup. "You don't waste time, do you?"

"Someone told me once that life's too short to F around. So I figure it's best to lay it all out. You're beautiful and competent, two things that are kinda my kryptonite. So…what the hell. Wanna be my girlfriend, Jaylin Brendle?"

Jaylin's smirk morphed into a slow smile. "You haven't even kissed me yet."

"Eh. Call me old-fashioned."

"What does that mean?"

"It means I'll kiss you when you're my girlfriend."

Jaylin laughed and set her drink down on the hood of the cruiser.

"Well, fine then. Sheriff. I'd love to be your girlfriend."

"Yeah?"

"Sure," she said, shrugging as if her heart weren't pounding out a tattoo inside of her chest. "I mean, why not? Zzumo likes you, and he's pretty picky, so—"

She never got to finish the rest of that sentence, because all of a sudden, Ethan's hands wrapped around her waist, pulling her in close. He bent as if to take her mouth with his own, but stopped short, his lips millimeters from hers.

"Now that you're my girlfriend, I don't mind telling you that I've been *dying* to kiss you. Is now good?" he whispered.

"Now is great," she breathed back, flattening her hands against the swell of his pectoral muscles under his uniform shirt. In the back of her mind, Jaylin wondered if maybe he shouldn't be making out with her in uniform in public, but then she figured that he was the Sheriff…who was going to tell him not to?

Then she couldn't hold any coherent thoughts at all, because she was drowning in the taste and feel of him as he claimed her mouth with his own.

He tasted like chocolate and coffee and something else, something indefinably *male* that she couldn't name, but knew that she very, very much liked. She reached up, winding her arms around his neck and threading her fingertips through the short hair at the base of his skull. His arms tightened around her, and he leaned into the kiss just as a scream split the air behind them.

Jaylin jumped back, gasping, reaching for the Walther in her belly band with one hand and Zzumo's lead with the other. The dog stood on high alert, his back to Jaylin and Ethan, a low, warning growl rumbling from him as he stared at the door to Arrowroot.

"Stay here, okay?" Ethan said, pushing past Jaylin and flipping open the retention lock on his holster. He didn't draw, but he kept his hand right there as he stepped toward the door and reached to open it.

The door burst open, and Nina came out, screaming, tears running down her face. She ran right into Ethan, who gripped her with his free hand and backed up a step.

"Shhh, Nina… Nina, what is it?" Ethan asked.

"B-benny…" she sobbed, curling into his chest. Ethan looked over at Jaylin, his eyes troubled.

"Give her to me," Jaylin said, reholstering her Walther and reaching out. "Go check it out."

Ethan nodded, and gently persuaded Nina to allow him to hand her off to Jaylin, who wrapped her arms around the older woman and just let her sob. Behind Nina, the Arrowroot door burst open, and Benny stumbled out.

At first, Jaylin wondered if he'd been injured– an accidental cut or a fall on a not-quite-dry kitchen floor– but then Benny looked up at them, and she couldn't keep from gasping.

The whites of Benny's eyes had gone completely green, and as she watched, tiny tendrils unfurled from the corners of his eye sockets, reaching out and uncurling what looked like tiny kudzu leaves. He let out a weird sort of coughing moan, and another vine snaked out of his mouth, curving downward over his chin and winding around his throat as they watched.

"Benny. Benny, put down the knife." Ethan said, his voice hard and demanding. Jaylin blinked and refocused on Benny's hands. He held a big kitchen knife in his right hand, his fingernails glinting green. Jaylin felt her stomach churning again as another vine popped through the skin under his middle finger and snaked back over his hand to wrap around the hilt of the knife as he turned to point it menacingly at Ethan.

"Benny. Put the knife down." Ethan said again, drawing his pistol. "Come on, Ben. You know me. It's Ethan. Put the knife down. Benny. *Benny!*"

Benny lunged towards Ethan. The morning sun glinted off the knife as he brought it up. Zzumo barked, pulling against the lead as he fought to defend Ethan.

Ethan fired once. Twice. Three times.

The world went quiet, silence broken only by the high, buzzing ring of tinnitus.

Benny stumbled, then fell to his knees. Green liquid oozed from the exit wounds on his back. He slumped forward onto his face.

Nina screamed, the sound barely registering over the tinnitus. Jaylin hugged her close and turned her away as she just kept screaming.

Slowly, the buzz retreated, and more sound registered. Nina's screams had devolved to sobs. Jaylin patted her back, trying to comfort her as Ethan got on his radio to report the shooting.

Or tried to, anyway.

Jaylin met his eyes as he looked up at her from where he knelt next to Benny's body.

"Dispatch isn't answering," he said, worry thick in his voice. "Something's not right."

"More than one thing, I'd say." Jaylin kept her voice calm and empty, but inside her head, she felt like screaming along with Nina.

"Let's get Nina settled in my car," Ethan said, straightening up. He stepped over and opened the rear door to the cruiser "And I'll try the car rad—"

Glass shattered as a human-shaped figure lurched through the display window next door. Zzumo lunged forward, in a cacophony of barks and growls as the figure turned and rushed them, green vines protruding from obliterated eye sockets and snaking forth out of the mouth. Because she held Nina, Jaylin couldn't keep hold of Zzumo's lead, and he launched himself at this new threat.

"Zzumo!" Jaylin screamed, as Ethan grabbed the still-sobbing Nina and pushed her into the back seat. Without meaning to do so, Jaylin fell back on her military training, drawing her Walther in a smooth motion and sighting along the barrel at the figure's head. It had collapsed under Zzumo's weight, but its green-tipped hands clawed at her dog, spreading what looked like sap all over his harness.

Jaylin approached close enough to be sure of not hitting her partner, and then fired twice into the forehead of what may have once been a human. As with Benny, the thing on the ground didn't bleed red. Rather, more green stickiness oozed out of the back of its skull, and the strong scent of newly mown foliage filled the air.

"Jay, you okay?" Ethan asked, breathless. She nodded, her breathing accelerating as the adrenaline dump hit. She reholstered her weapon and grabbed Zzumo's lead.

"Leave it, Zzumo. Good. That's my good boy."

"Hard to tell… but I think that may have been Nathan Saville. He owns — owned– this furniture shop." Ethan gestured to the window through which maybe-Nathan had crashed. His voice sounded like Jaylin's own: calm, but with that careful undercurrent that said he was busy compartmentalizing like a boss.

"I had to shoot," she said quietly. "He was a threat."

"I know," Ethan said. "I'm not–let's just get to the station, and we can figure this shit out, okay?"

Jaylin nodded and let him help her into the passenger seat of the cruiser, with Zzumo crammed between them and Nina still sobbing in the back.

Ethan couldn't raise dispatch on the car's radio either. He looked over at her with a grim smile as he started the engine, and then wheeled the cruiser around to head out toward the edge of town where the sheriff's office sat next to the Grantsbury High School football field.

Between Nina's muffled sobs in the back and Ethan's cursing at the radio, it took Jaylin a moment to realize what she was seeing. But sure enough, as she sat there and watched, first one vine, and then another snaked toward the nondescript building with the "Grant County Sheriff" sign out front.

Jaylin tightened her trembling hands in Zzumo's fur.

"Ethan," she said, her voice low but steady. "I don't think we should go to the station."

"What?" he asked, looking up from the radio. He'd been driving with one hand on the wheel, glancing out the windshield at the road. She saw him focus on their destination and jam on the breaks, sending her and Zzumo jolting forward against their restraints.

"What the everloving fuck?" Ethan muttered, and despite herself, Jaylin grinned to hear the profanity he'd been censoring the entire time she knew him. As they watched, a vine burst through the front window of the station and eeled its way up toward the roof, winding around the radio antenna mounted there.

Jaylin looked over her shoulder.

"The high school looks clear, and there are cars in the parking lot, maybe there's people there with some idea of what's happening."

"Got it," Ethan said, and threw the cruiser into reverse, spinning the wheel to turn them around before rocketing in that direction.

They pulled into the parking lot and right up to the curb. Ethan killed the engine, and then hopped out to head to the trunk. Jaylin got Zzumo out, and then opened the back to find Nina's sobs had quieted to despairing sniffles.

"Ms. Nina," she said softly. "Come on out now, we're going to go see if we can't find some others, all right?"

"O-okay," Nina said, her voice quavering. "Wh-what's happening?"

"That's what we're trying to figure out. Just come on out now and we're going to see who's here at the high school."

Nina put her hand in Jaylin's and allowed herself to be pulled from the car. When Nina straightened up, Ethan was there, holding a Kevlar vest with the word Sheriff blazoned across the front and back.

"Here," he said, handing it to Jaylin. "I'm deputizing you and Zzumo. I don't know what this is but fuck if I can handle it alone."

Jaylin pulled the vest on, grateful to see it was a smaller size and a design not too dissimilar to her old USAF battle rattle. When she had it in place, Ethan handed her a Mossberg shotgun and a pouch of shells. She mounted the pouch on her vest and slung the shotgun. It wasn't the M-4 she was used to, but she would make do.

Zzumo recognized the preparations, because his body language shifted away from "service dog monitoring his person" to "working dog protecting his handler and team". After a moment's thought, Jaylin pulled his "doggles" out of the pocket of his vest and fitted them over his eyes. Better safe than sorry.

"Can you do that? Just deputize us?" She asked as she tightened the strap on the doggles. *Especially since I'm your girlfriend?*

"There's paperwork, but we'll figure it out later. If he's good to go, let's move. Stay close."

Ethan turned and led the way to the front doors. Jaylin gestured for Ms. Nina to follow, while she and Zzumo brought up the rear. Zzumo really should have been in the lead, since he would sense threats the fastest, but something in Jaylin's gut told her that the threat was greater outdoors than in.

"Sheriff!"

Jaylin blinked in the interior dimness. As soon as her eyes adjusted, she made out the figure of Maryam hurrying forward, arms outstretched in welcome, worry on her face.

"Maryam, thank God you're here."

"Yes, thank God indeed," she said. "It was a near thing. There is something very wrong with the—"

"The kudzu. Yeah, we saw it. It killed Benny, and Nathan Saville, and is in the process of engulfing the Sheriff's station."

"It took Principal Louvers, too. The back quad is fully infested. I've gathered up the students from both junior and senior high sides and brought everyone to the gym."

"Have you heard anything from the elementary school?"

"Yes, they're all right. They're further out of town with that new building of theirs. No problems so far."

Ethan let out a sigh of relief. He opened his mouth as if to say something else, but Zzumo alerted, letting out a low, menacing growl. Jaylin turned to see a woman through the windows of the school. She was walking, stumbling toward the front doors.

Missy Archer.

To her credit, she didn't have vines growing out of her eyes, though her skin did have a distinct greenish tint. Jaylin unslung the shotgun and she and Zzumo moved to intercept just as Missy reached for the front door.

"Stop where you are!" Jaylin ordered as she pushed the door open and charged out. Missy stumbled backward a few steps, and then looked up. A look of naked hatred crossed her face. The whites of her eyes glowed green.

"You! This is all your fault!" The woman leaned forward, her face twisting into an ugly sneer. Zzumo snarled and barked a warning.

"Don't move, Missy. Have you been in contact with the vin–? "

Missy cut her off with a wild, despairing laugh.

"Have I been in contact with the vines? Oh, yes! The vines! The vines are just as angry at you as I am! Why did you have to come here, you stupid bitch? You and your dog ruined everything!" She lurched forward another step and then stopped, swaying.

"Missy, I don't know what you're talking about, but if you don't stop–"

"*You found the sacrifice!* No one was going to miss that nasty kid, and the vines would have been happy. But you found him and stole him and now we're all going to die writhing! Why couldn't you just stay home? Why did Ethan come to you?"

Jaylin blinked, processing all of this as the door opened behind her and Ethan stepped out.

"Missy," he said, his voice pitched to calm. "Slow down. We don't need to fight. What happened here? Where's Doug?"

"Doug's gone," she said, her voice breaking on a sob. "The vines took him when you and that whore stole the sacrifice."

"What sacrifice?" Ethan asked, stepping up next to Jaylin. "And don't call my girlfriend a whore."

"Girlfriend?" Missy's eyes widened, enough that Jaylin could see tiny green tendrils twisting behind her eyelids. She let out a feral shriek and launched herself at Jaylin, hands swinging, fingers clawed.

Zzumo leapt without a sound and took her by the throat. Green liquid splashed over his muzzle as his powerful jaws ripped through her flesh. As with Nathan before, the weight of Zzumo's body forced Missy to the ground, her legs crumpling in odd angles beneath her.

She let out a gurgling scream and tried to claw at Zzumo's face, but Jaylin was already there, shotgun in hand. She put the barrel against Missy's forehead and pulled the trigger, obliterating her skull into a fine, acid green mist.

Zzumo let go and shook his body, as if he didn't like the taste of the dead woman's… not flesh exactly, Jaylin realized as she looked at what was left of Missy Archer's skull. There was no bone, no blood, no muscle. Only fibrous plant material, crisped and burning as the scent of fresh-cut grass filled the air.

"You okay?" Ethan asked, walking up close and putting a gentle hand on her shoulder.

"Yeah…" she said. "At some point, I'm going to feel real bad about killing two of my new neighbors within a week of moving in… but not just yet."

Ethan let out a snort of mirthless laughter and met her eyes in a smile. "Dark humor as a coping mechanism. I knew you were the woman for me. Let's get inside. I think Maryam might have the beginnings of a plan."

The multitalented vice principal, chemistry teacher, and community SAR coordinator did, in fact, have the beginnings of a plan. And a middle. And an end.

Jaylin had swiped a pack of baby wipes from the nurse's office and used them to clean the sticky green sap off of Zzumo's face and fur while she listened and tried not to feel inadequate next to her neighbor. While they'd been fighting to stay alive, Maryam and the remaining staff and some of the students of Grantsbury High had compared notes and come up with a few possible solutions.

Namely, goats and airplanes.

"These vines are a form of kudzu," Amira explained in her rapid-fire, enthusiastic teenager manner as they gathered in a corner of the gym. They spoke quickly as other high school students led the gathered middle-schoolers in hastily assembled activities. "Granted, a particularly aggressive form that can turn humans into plant-zombies, but kudzu nonetheless. We've got a whole herd of goats out in the Ag barn, and goats *love* kudzu. We set a few loose in the back quad, and they cleared it out right quick – it didn't even try to wrap around them. Too late for Principal Louvers, though. He was just a green shell; it was super gross." She wrinkled her nose and shuddered, and then moved on with a quickness that Jaylin found surprising, even as she was grateful for the kid's resilient nature.

"So that's step one, release the goats. Step two is a bit more difficult. Mom and the other adults will head out in pairs with machetes and try to rescue any other townsfolk. We've also got the school radio station broadcasting on the emergency frequency to tell people to rally up here. Meanwhile…" she pulled in a deep breath, and just for a moment, she looked like the scared high school kid she really was.

"Meanwhile what, Amira?" the Sheriff asked, his tone gentle.

"Meanwhile, we need you and Ms. Jaylin and Zzumo to take me to the airport. Uncle Ahmed's been playing with some different herbicides, and his Piper is all loaded up with the latest batch. He left for Jordan last night, but I know how to fly. I'll dust the town, and that should help a lot."

"Maybe buy us some time to rig some good flamethrowers," one of the other students interjected, all but rubbing his hands together.

"Amira, are you sure?" Ethan asked. The teenager cut her eyes to him and nodded, squaring her shoulders.

"This is my town, Sheriff. My friends are trapped out there. I'll do whatever it takes."

Good for you, girl. Jaylin found herself thinking. She shot Amira a tight smile and straightened up to toss the ball of used baby wipes into a nearby trash can.

"I'm in. Let's go."

"We'll take the cruiser," Ethan said, and they headed outside to the front. Someone had moved Missy's body, but a greenish stain still slicked the sidewalk in front of the school. They all stepped carefully around it and climbed on in. Ethan started the engine and pulled out of the parking lot.

"Look! There's one of the goats!" Amira cried out about five minutes into the ten minute drive across Grantsbury. Jaylin had been staring in horror at the buildings lining main street. All of them sported thick, creeping vines visibly winding their way over them, in through the windows, and out through the doors. At Amira's call, she turned to look where the teenager pointed, and sure enough, there was a small, valiant figure chomping away at the vines that tangled around one of the streetlights. A mostly clear path stretched behind the animal, paralleling their route from the high school.

"Why don't the vines fill in behind the goat?" Jaylin asked.

"I don't know," Ethan said. "Maybe they don't like the feeling of being eaten?"

Sure enough, as she watched, four tendrils that had been reaching for the streetlight actually retracted, slithering back across the sidewalk and into a narrow alley between a bicycle shop and the ice-cream parlor.

"This is wild," Jaylin murmured, and then inwardly laughed at herself. *Understatement of the year, that.*

"Airfield is just ahead," Ethan said, turning the wheel to head down a street Jaylin hadn't explored yet. "We can try something else, Amira. The hangar looks completely overgrown."

"I just need to get to the Piper. It's outside, on the ramp, all fueled and everything."

"All right," Ethan said, glancing over at Jaylin as he pulled into the parking lot of the tiny terminal of the Grant County Regional Airport. The building was wreathed in green, tangled vines obscuring the revolving door and reaching out of the windows.

"I don't think we should try to go through that," Jaylin said.

"Yeah," Amira answered, worry threading through her voice. She scooted over into the middle of the backseat and leaned forward to point through the mesh that separated the front and back of the cruiser. "The Piper is parked over there. The fence isn't fully covered, if we can cut through it, I can make a run for the airplane."

"If the airplane isn't engulfed," Ethan said.

"True. But it's filled with herbicide and avgas. I'd be surprised if the kudzu was anywhere near it."

"Fair point." Ethan gunned the engine and piloted the cruiser up over the curb and onto the sidewalk. From there, he drove along the chain-link fence until they had passed the corner of the terminal building. He stopped the car and slewed around in his seat to look at Amira.

"Can you see the plane from here?"

"Yes," Amira said. "She's right there."

"Okay. Stay here until I call for you. I've got bolt cutters in the trunk. Jaylin and I will clear a hole for you. Jay, you and Zzumo cover my ass."

And such a nice ass it is… Out of respect for Amira, Jaylin didn't give voice to her irreverent thoughts. But she continued to let herself think them as she followed Ethan to the trunk of the car to get the bolt cutters and two machetes, and then to the fence where he started hacking at the vines. She let herself take a good, long, appreciative look before she joined in the work.

"Checking me out, Brendle?" Ethan murmured as he methodically cut and pulled at the vines.

"I figured it was better to look at your ass than it was to visualize killing Missy over and over again," she said, forcing a little levity into her tone. "Or the other guy. Nathan. I never even got to meet him."

"We're going to make it through this," Ethan said. "And then I promise you can check out my ass as much as you like."

"Ditto, Sheriff. For sure."

"Oh, I already have been."

He smirked at her and dropped his knife to the ground, then picked up the bolt cutters and made four neat cuts in the chain link. He reared back and kicked the fence twice, and a gap opened up.

"I'll hold this here," he said. "Get Amira."

Jaylin nodded, stuck her own knife through her belt as if it were some kind of damn pirate sword and sprinted back to the cruiser, Zzumo right beside her.

The vines had started to creep towards the car's tires, and she took a moment to savagely slash at them before opening the door and beckoning the teenager out.

"Better run," she said. "They're moving faster every minute."

Amira nodded, and then shot out the rear door as if it were the starting gate at a high school track meet. Jaylin followed, and as the vines slithered after the girl, she drew her knife to slash at them again and again and keep moving.

Zzumo's growling bark was her only warning. Jaylin spun to see that a vine had snaked around his middle and was pulling him away from her. He snarled and snapped, but the angle was wrong, and he couldn't get a bite on the vine. Jaylin lunged after him, pulling her knife only to find vines wrapped tightly around her booted ankles, rooting her to the spot.

"Zzumo, get it!" she yelled, releasing Zzumo to fight as best he could. She heard a flurry of snaps and snarls as she bent to saw through the wrist-thick vines that bound her in place.

It took forever, and more of the sticky sap covered her hands before she was done, but she got free and lunged toward her dog. More vines snagged at her boots, and she fell forward, but her reach was enough to bring the knife blade down hard on the vine that held Zzumo. She severed it, and an acid green spray burst into the air, searing her face and eyes as it coated her.

Don't let this be how it colonizes people.

"Zzumo, Here!" Jaylin called, and a breath later she felt the impact of her dog leaping into her arms. She dropped her knife before she accidentally cut her partner, and then tucked her body and rolled around him, away from the car. As she rolled, she buried her face in Zzumo's warm fur, trying to clear her eyes of the sap so that she could *see.*

She felt Zzumo's body quivering as more deep growls rumbled forth. She came to rest on her elbows and knees, her back arching above him. She opened her eyes into sudden, green-tinged darkness and craned her neck to look up…only to find the sky blotted out by wide, flat, three-lobed leaves.

"Fuck," she breathed, loosening her arms from around Zzumo. The vines surrounded them in a ball like the one that had held Billy a few nights ago. Billy, whom nutball Missy had referred to as "the sacrifice."

Zzumo growled again and snapped at a tendril that reached out from the ball toward his face. He snapped the tendril in half, but another one writhed out from the curving wall of vines that held them captive.

"Fuck this," she said then. "I'm not a damn sacrifice to some asshole weed!" She'd left the shotgun in the cruiser, but she still had her Walther. She drew it, turned her body away from Zzumo, and began firing as fast as the little semi-auto would cycle.

Eight rounds later, the magazine was empty, and her slide locked back. She'd managed to create only a fist-sized hole in the wall of vines, and despair threatened as she watched it close. Behind her, Zzumo pressed against her legs.

"Damnit," she cursed again, and then turned to lift her dog in her arms. If she was going to die, it was going to be holding the one being who had never let her down…who had always been the perfect partner, the very embodiment of love.

The vines overhead contracted, driving Jaylin to her knees. Zzumo let out a whine, and she buried her face against his shoulder again.

"I'm sorry, bud," she murmured. "I love you so much. You're the best boy. The best boy ever–"

Ma-a-a-a-a-a. Maa-a—a-a-a-a-a!

Jaylin froze. Was that–?

The ball of vines around her shuddered and contracted even tighter. The distant bleating sound drew closer, and over it, Jaylin heard something else. A distant, rumbling buzz… like that of an airplane engine.

"Brilliant, Amira." The bleating intensified, and suddenly, a hole opened in the top of the ball that held her as the vines contracted still more. Jaylin craned her head to look up and saw the startlingly low belly of a small airplane as it soared overhead, spraying a fine mist in its wake.

She had the presence of mind to duck her head and cover Zzumo's mouth and nose, so they didn't breathe in the herbicide, but just as the sticky sap had sprayed them earlier, so too did the cropduster's aerosolized mist drift down all over them. The vines surrounding her convulsed. Then, slowly at first, but with accelerating rapidity, they withered and wilted until they lay in tangled ruins all around her.

Ma-a-a-a-a.

Jaylin looked up into the vertical slit pupils of one of the school's goats. He stared at her, as if angry that she'd made all the delicious vines die before he was done eating them, and then turned and stalked away on his spindly legs. In her arms, Zzumo let out a rumbling growl, but Jaylin blinked… and then laughed. And laughed.

She was still laughing, tears streaming down her cheeks, holding on to Zzumo for dear life when Ethan found her a few minutes later.

"Jay? Sweetheart?" Ethan asked, his voice tentative and sick with worry. "Look at me. I need to see your eyes."

"I'm all right," she gasped, turning to look at him, opening her eyes wide so he could see the lack of green therein. No leaf-whispers in her head. No urge to pollinate or photosynthesize or kidnap small children. "Amira did it. She and the goats. They got to us in time. Zumo and I are all right."

Epilogue

The elementary school, on the outskirts of town, had remained untouched by the kudzu and served as a temporary dwelling for the survivors over the last weeks.

The well-fattened goats were making inroads – and literally re-finding roads – but it would be a while before the vast majority of Grantsbury was safe for habitation. While the kudzu no longer pressed forward or seemed animated, no one wanted to tromp through it – or sleep amidst it – either.

Ethan lived in a two-story loft above Nina's sister's restaurant cattycorner from the elementary school, which meant his building had survived where Jaylin's old craftsman had not. After five seconds of consideration, Jaylin and Zzumo lived there too, with the addition of Maryam and Amira for more than a few days.

They'd reclaimed enough houses that Maryam and Amira had their own space again, and Ethan agreed it was safe enough to bring Jaylin's worried dad and his nurse for a visit. His memory came and went, but for some reason the loss of her new house to a kudzu demon had rooted into the forefront of his thoughts.

"He'll be better able to settle once he puts eyes on me and knows that we're ok."

"Besides, it'll be a morale boost, bringing a legendary Dawg round to shake hands and pat heads. If he's up for it."

"Tahani said he's been having great mornings." Jaylin said, setting aside the leather harness she'd finished repairing and standing with a stretch. "And I think talking with some Georgia Bulldog fans will do him some good."

"Want to wait for them outside?"

She didn't. Outside still felt vaguely threatening, every unidentified sharp foliage scent in the air and any unexpected brush of air through leaves heralding potential violence. Zumo pivoted to stare at her, catching some shift of her internal chemistry.

She didn't want to go outside.

All the more reason to go.

The three of them sat on the sidewalk outside, exchanging warm pleasantries with their neighbors, until a silver SUV pulled to the curb.

Tahani waved from the driver's seat, and Zzumo sat up with interest.

Jay Brendle swung out of the backseat, his eyes intent on his daughter. "You ok, Jayjay?"

"Take more than plants to keep me down," she answered, her voice almost entirely steady. "Hey daddy."

He crushed her against him, stronger than he'd been in years, and she stayed in his arms until her eyes cleared. "Dad, this is my boyfriend, Ethan. He's the Sheriff who helped keep the town together."

"Lot of that credit goes to a teenage pilot, but it's an honor to meet you, sir." Ethan held out his hand and Jay grabbed it without delay. There was no sizing-up in his regard to the younger man, only admiration.

"Takes a team." His voice rough, her father pulled her boyfriend into a backslapping hug. "Good on you, son."

Tahani had hung back but stepped forward to embrace Jaylin and be introduced in turn. "Maybe a walk?" she suggested. "A little exercise would be welcome."

"Of course."

The surrounding streets had been meticulously cleared, but a block away there was still kudzu trailing from high branches and roof peaks. Jaylin had joked about bringing in mountain goats, and one of the farmers from a town over was on the verge of making it happen. In the meantime, their own 4H herds, saved from the year's upcoming auction, patrolled throughout the populated parts of town. Since that awful night, the vines had remained inert, but no one was ready to take that for granted.

Zzumo watched a trio of goats cross the street ahead, his tail wagging low and soft.

"Hey bud," Jaylin said softly, crouching down and unclipping his vest. "Off. Why don't you say hi to dad and go play?"

Zzumo touched her cheek with his nose, shoved his head under Jay's hand for a solid scratch, and then bounded ahead with a little yip of warning to the goats.

The largest of them wheeled around and play-charged, and Zzumo leapt over it with another happy sound.

Jay laughed, a deep belly laugh, joy in his eyes and shoulders relaxed. "This is life in your new town, huh? Goats and sheriffs and running the streets?"

"Just the one Sheriff. But otherwise…yeah."

"You trusting it all to the goats?"

"We've got some rigged up fire-throwers now too. Just in case."

"Enough to be safe and happy?"

"That's the play, dad."

"Yeah." He patted her arm and beamed down at her. "That's the play."

"If you have a green thumb, this is the floor for you. Our residents on this story are not all vegans, but they are very thoughtful of their food, and grow much of their own. The roots here run deep – I hear they share cuttings quite often."

* * * *

The Call of the Temple
by Dan Bridgwater

Alacon System
Unnamed 2nd Continent of Alacon III
Exo-Archeology Expedition

Day 1

The shuttle landed right on target. As dust blew around the lowered cargo ramp, archaeologists Dr. Mark Davos and Dr. Peter Jefferson, followed by the rest of the dig team and a 12-man naval support detachment, descended to stand under an alien sun. They looked across the stone ruins, unlike anything they'd seen on Earth. Sharp, curved towers dominated the skyline, with occasional gaps where a structure had surrendered to the depredations of time. Rounded openings, like empty eye sockets, decorated the sides of each structure. Five large structures formed a central core, and a dozen or more smaller buildings were scattered among them. Gigantic tree-like vegetation, its foliage a strange, deep purple-green, ringed the clearing that formed the site. All of it spoke of age, something ancient beyond that of the pyramids of Giza on Earth.

"I can't believe you convinced the captain to let us do this, Mark," Peter said, his dirty-blond hair unkempt and blown around his face by a hot, dusty wind. He clapped a hand on his taller friend's shoulder. "This is going to change everything we think we understand about the universe."

Mark looked down at Peter and grinned. "She owed me, and I called it in. We were going to do this anyway but dropping us off before she does the outer system survey just means we get an extra six or eight weeks on site. Can you imagine how much more we could discover?"

According to the perfunctory survey conducted by the Explorer Corps a decade before, the stone ruins before them had been abandoned since before man had domesticated the horse. No other trace of the builders had been found—no other cities, and no evidence this planet was anything other than a marginally habitable world with liquid water and life forms with only simple animal intelligence.

"Hey, you slackers! Quit staring and help unload!" The female voice jerked them out of their reverie and back to the task at hand. Behind them, Dr. Lisa Daniels waved them toward the cargo containers being trundled down the ramp. "We've got plenty of time for that"—she gestured toward the ruins— "later. But first, we need to get the shelters set up, and a tent for the analysis work, and a place to store whatever we find."

Mark covered his mouth and leaned toward Peter, "I thought I was in charge," he said quietly to his grinning friend.

"She lets you think that because she likes you, and she'll let you pretend to be in charge, but…" Peter shrugged, a concession to the inevitable ways of the universe.

"I still can't believe you two are dating," Mark whispered.

"Opposites attract. And she loves my cooking. And it doesn't hurt my productivity that she is so very organized," Peter said.

Mark watched Lisa approach and smiled. He took a deep breath and let it out slowly. "We're here," he said to Peter. "We've been planning this for months but now, we're here." He bent down and ran his hand across the patchy grey-green lichen and then grabbed a handful of rocky sand. He let it run through his fingers and watched the wind carry the granules away. "I talked to Captain Mazen while we were waiting to open the ramp. She wished us luck, and she'll be breaking orbit in about two hours."

"I know she wouldn't have done it," Peter said, "but there was a little voice in my head just waiting for the captain to cancel this and bring us all back up."

Lisa smiled as she joined them and shook her head. "You worry too much, Peter." The tall brunette looked at Mark and Peter and went on. "Time to change the subject. I've organized three teams for the initial site survey. Seven people per team. Pretty good balance of skills and backgrounds."

Day 5

"I can't believe the amount of paperwork I have to do," Mark mumbled to himself as he reviewed the notes from the previous day's work. He and his team had been working the site for two days, and so far, the finds had staggered him. He looked over at the table covered with small stone artifacts and tools recovered from Site 1, the structure originally found by the Explorer Corps survey. A few pieces were obviously cutting instruments of some sort, but the handles were odd and awkwardly shaped. He didn't know who had built the structure, but he was pretty sure whatever they used to hold the tools didn't look anything like a human hand. By far, the most interesting piece they'd found was a palm-sized stylized stone disk with three rays protruding from it. They'd seen a similar design drawn in several places around the ruins, but this was currently the only artifact of its kind they'd discovered.

A cough from the door of the tent drew Mark's attention, and Peter stuck his head in. "Hey boss! How's it going?"

"Horrible. I'm spending more time in this tent writing up and then uploading the files to the ship database than I am actually out on the site. This is not what I signed up for."

"Well, at least we can still talk to the ship. What's the delay at now?"

"Currently about 95 minutes. But they are about to pass behind the system sun, and we're going to have to start bouncing the signal off one of the probes. That's going to add a bunch. And according to their last update, there might be a period of several hours, up to eight, I think, that we won't be able to talk to them at all."

His comm unit chimed and he pressed the answer key. "Yes?" he asked.

"Doctor Davos, we've had an incident… when we opened access to the corridor off the back of anteroom C-17, the one they're calling the West Temple." The voice belonged to Commander Jason Bayland, a medical doctor and the senior member of the 12-man naval detachment that supported the archeology team.

Mark picked up the device and spoke into the microphone. "An incident? What kind of incident?"

"It's Doctor Daniels, sir. She's been injured." Commander Bayland responded.

"Lisa?" Peter blurted and ran out the tent flap.

"Crap," Mark growled. "Do I need to bring you a kit?"

"No, sir. She's cut her hand. I've bandaged it, and she's going to need maybe four or five stitches, but there has been some contamination on the site."

"Right," Mark replied. "I'll be right down."

"So, what happened?" Mark asked when he arrived in the corridor. Peter crouched next to a seated Lisa, who looked angry and a little bit embarrassed. Standing over them both was Commander Bayland, a slightly bored look on his face.

"My foot caught the edge of the door as I came in," Lisa said. "I caught myself on the wall and cut my hand on that," she said and pointed with her right hand. Her bandaged left hand she cradled at her waist.

Out of the wall bulged a large, oval nodule, probably three feet across.

"What the hell is that?" Mark asked and leaned closer to the object. He pulled out his flashlight and switched it on. Up close, he could see shining reflections on the sharply ridged surface, like tiny, jagged crystals. As he played his light across it, he could see the dark spot, damp with blood, where Lisa had cut her hand.

"Never seen anything like it in any other part of the complex. It almost looks like some sort of large geode," Lisa said.

"If it is," Peter said from beside her, "then it's pretty damn big. One of the biggest I've ever seen." In addition to his doctorate in Archeology, Peter had a degree in Geology.

"I'll take your word for it," Mark said. He straightened and played the light down the passage. The walls were beige shot through with dark-brown veins and glass-smooth. About five meters from the first nodule, he saw another lump where a second nodule protruded. "Some kind of natural occurrence?" he asked.

Peter stood and walked to the next node. "Not likely," he said and pointed at the second one. "It's too uniform. As near as I can tell, same size as the first, same height off the floor."

"Decoration, then?" Mark asked.

"Maybe. Let's see how many there are." Peter pulled out his own flashlight and started down the corridor. He walked about five more meters and found another. "Same height, same size," he said. He continued for a short distance and stopped. "End of the line."

Mark moved toward Peter, focusing his light past the shorter man, and saw what he meant. The corridor ended in a rough, stone wall. He stepped toward the wall and examined the stone. "Looks wrong. Slid into place after the fact, maybe? I wonder…" He shook his head. "We're getting sidetracked. Let's get Lisa out of here and into medical. We'll mark this for later."

They walked back to the still-seated young woman. Peter offered his hand. "Come on, hun. Let's go." She continued to sit and stare off into space. He raised an eyebrow and leaned into her line of sight. "Lisa?"

She started, as if she were seeing Peter and Mark for the first time. "Sorry, I zoned out for a second. Do you guys hear humming? Like, a really faint hum?"

The men looked at each other and back to Lisa. "I hear some wind noise," Peter said, "and I think I can hear one of the cargo sleds. Is that what you hear?"

"No. I hear the sled, too. This is fainter." She shook her head and rubbed her ear. "I probably just banged my head. Either that or it's the pain killer Commander Bayland gave me." She reached up with her uninjured hand and grabbed Peter's. "Let's get out of here."

Back in sick bay, Bayland had Lisa sit on his diagnostics table while Mark and an anxious Peter watched from the door. He unwrapped the bandage from her left hand and examined the injury. "Well…" he said. "The cut is about an inch under your index finger toward the thumb. It's pretty ragged, but the bleeding has slowed considerably. Fortunately, it's nowhere near the tendons, there's no damage to your nerves, and three stitches ought to do it. It may scar, but we can always take care of that later. You should have full use back in three weeks or so."

"Oh, that's great, Doc," Lisa said.

Peter started across the room toward Lisa but was stopped by the doctor's upraised hand.

"Get out," Bayless said.

"What?" Peter asked, shocked into stillness.

"Get out. I still need to clean this properly, get a deeper scan to verify my diagnosis, and then stitch it up. I don't need you looking over my shoulder in this tiny room. We'll be finished in probably 30 minutes. Go somewhere else."

Mark grabbed Peter by the shoulder. "Come on, buddy. She'll be fine. In fact," he said, eyeing Lisa and then Peter, "I think she's doing better than you are. Come on, we'll go to my office. I have some medicinal scotch that'll help settle you out."

About an hour later, Lisa joined them in the Director's office. Peter rose, crossed the room, and reached for her uninjured hand. "So?" he asked. "What'd the doctor say?"

She held up her hand and showed them the clearskin bandage. "He said I was fairly lucky. No nerve or tendon damage, but he did remove some crystal shards." She shuddered as she said it. "He said, and I quote, 'Probably got them all. Best I can do with the primitive tools we have here. When we get back to the ship, we'll run you through a real scanner.'" She flexed her fingers. "Everything works, and it doesn't hurt. Itches like crazy though. And I still feel like my ears are buzzing. It's really weird. But the commander says the itching is normal, and it should fade in a few days."

Mark poured a glass and handed it to her. "Well, congratulations. You're our first, and hopefully only injury. So far, I guess." The three of them clinked glasses and sipped the golden liquid. "I will say, however, I'd appreciate it if you'd refrain from bleeding anywhere else on my dig."

"Hear, hear," Peter agreed.

Lisa laughed and raised her glass. "I'll do what I can," she said and rubbed her left hand on her pant leg.

Day 8

"How did I get myself into this?" Mark asked himself as he signed off and filed another field report. "I'm supposed to be an archeologist, and I am sitting on my ass while my friends are working the most exciting dig I've ever heard of. We should have hired an admin." Tapping from the door frame startled him. Mark jumped and turned, biting back a curse.

"Sorry, sir," the young petty officer said from the entrance as she held back a grin. "Didn't mean to startle you. It's the boots. They just make no noise."

"Can I help you, Janice?" Mark said through gritted teeth and a pasted-on smile. Petty Officer Janice Rogers had been assigned as logistics support for the dig. Mark knew he had signed for a substantial amount of navy property when they left the ship, and the credit value was eye watering. Most of the time he appreciated PO Rogers's work and her attention to detail, but she was one of the quietest people he'd ever met. She held up a folder and Mark fought back a grimace. "More paperwork? How does the navy get anything done?"

She shrugged. "You get used to it. I do have a small issue, though."

Mark sighed and indicated she should continue.

"I was doing inventory. We're missing some gear. Nothing important," she said when she saw his look of alarm. "Just some portable power cells, some protein packs, and a trauma bag."

"A trauma bag sounds important."

"Not really. We have several, and now that Doc Bayless has his med bay set up, I doubt we'll need any of them. But it's missing, and that bothers me."

Mark sat back in his chair and chewed his stylus. "And you're sure we had 'em when we came down?"

"Definitely. We're talking about three separate sealed crates."

"I could almost understand the power cells," Mark said after a moment of silence. "And I'm sure a trauma bag has useful tools and whatnot in it, but why on Earth would anyone take the protein packs?" Before the mission, the navy had put the archeology team through a survival exercise affectionately known as "Starve-Ex." After three days of failed attempts to fish or trap, the group had been given the emergency protein rations packs. Despite their hunger, very few of the academics managed to finish a single ration.

Rogers nodded her head in agreement and then went on. "The power cells and the protein are considered expendables. We normally don't track the protein, and we only track the power cells, so we know when we need to break out another crate."

"Recommendations?" he asked.

"If it were a navy crew, I'd recommend a shake-down. Probably wouldn't find anything, but it lets the kleptos know you're watching. That's usually enough to keep it down to a minimum."

"A lot of issues like this in the navy?" Mark asked with a smile.

"Oh, you have no idea, sir. Petty stuff as a rule, no one actually wants to endanger the ship. But there's always someone who's trying to get one over."

"Well, I can't do a shakedown on this lot. They'd lose their minds," Mark said. "It'd be all, 'You're invading my privacy, you don't trust me, I can't work under these conditions.' Like we aren't all a bunch of pack rats." He made a disgusted noise.

"Wow, really?" Rogers asked.

"Oh, you have no idea," he said, giving her phrase back to her. "Academics are like a bad soap opera." He shook his head. "Here's what I can do. I'll let everyone know there's stuff missing and let them know that while they will get whatever they need, it still needs to be issued out properly. Not saying that'll fix it, but it should remind people there is a process for getting equipment. Heck, whoever took the trauma bag might even bring it back. If they do, tell me… and inventory the heck out of the bag."

The PO gave him a mock salute. "You got it, chief," she said and turned to leave.

Mark raised his hand for her attention. "Oh, one more thing. Thank you. We're a bunch of grumpy academics, and we aren't going to say it, but we appreciate what you're doing for us."

Rogers smiled, nodded, and headed back toward her work area.

"And now I have petty thieves," Mark said to himself once he was sure she was out of earshot.

He had made it through two more pages of Team 2's work log before there was another tapping at the door.

"You sound sad," Peter's voice came from the tent entrance. "Your annoyed grunting is audible a full ten feet from the door. You should hear yourself."

"I do hear myself," Mark replied testily. "You wouldn't believe the requirements the navy's put on us. If this is normal, I don't know how they get anything done. And on top of all the required work logs, I now apparently have petty thievery to deal with."

"What? Petty—" Peter shook his head and made a negating gesture. "No. I'm not going to let you sidetrack me. I've come to share glad tidings and something amazing." Peter smiled wide. From behind his back, he pulled a slate and a holo projector. "I've not said a word on the radio, and I swore Giorgio and Michael to secrecy until we got to you."

Mark's eyes lit up. "You… you found something unexpected?" It came out as more of a statement than a question.

Peter nodded. "Unprecedented." He laid the slate down on Mark's desk and began to set up the projector. "The… well, let's call them geodes for right now, since that's what I thought they were… the geodes bothered me. What we found just couldn't be a natural formation. Geodes can form in clusters, but not like those three." Satisfied with his adjustments, he hooked a wire from the projector into the slate. The air above the projector sparkled, and an image of one of the geodes formed, slowly spinning in space. "Wanted a better look, so I borrowed one of the hi-rez scanners and took it down to the corridor. This is what we found." He pressed a button on the slate.

The geode stopped, and the outer shell shimmered and became transparent. Inside, a curled shape was revealed.

"What is it?" Mark asked as he rose from his seat to get a better look.

"It's an egg. A three-foot egg. Fossilized, maybe? But weird. The crystals almost look organic. This temple may be way, way older than we think. I know what you're going to say, but we don't know what erosion might look like here, so whatever the Explorers might have said, we really don't know how long the ruins have been sitting here. But what we do know is that we've found similar things on Earth. Giorgio is the closest thing we have to a paleontologist, and that was his conclusion, as well as mine."

Mark looked closely at the image and then reached for the slate. He made some adjustments and the "geode" flipped over. He pointed at the image. "That's a head," he said excitedly. "Some sort of massive insect equivalent? Look there. Mandibles, compound eyes… those could be antennae."

Peter nodded. "That's what I thought. I got these images with the hand-held. Imagine what we're going to get once the ship comes back and we get one of these up to the Labs."

Mark sat back down, all his earlier frustrations forgotten. "This is amazing." He felt the grin growing. "My God, the paper on this is going to absolutely make your name, Peter. What's next?"

"Part of why I'm here. I want your permission to dig them out of the wall, and I want to break one open. You're the director of this dig, and there's no way I can proceed without your permission. Besides, you've got to be there when—"

Mark's comm set sounded, interrupting Peter. The normal chime had been replaced by the two-tone buzz that indicated a call from the security team. Mark looked down in surprise. "It's Hill. Crap. Why would security be calling?"

Jacob Hill was the security lead for the expedition, a solidly built retired Fleet Marine making a second career as a Navy Warrant Officer. He'd been added to the expedition at Captain Mazen's insistence. His job, along with his 5-man team, was to ride herd on the dig team and keep them out of trouble.

Mark activated the comm. "Hey, Jake. You're on speaker. What's up?"

"Who's with you, sir?" the gruff voice asked.

"It's just me and Peter Jefferson. Why?"

Mark heard the sigh at the other end of the link. "I need you to come down to the drainage channel. The tower closest to the landing pad. You know the one?"

"Yes. Why?"

"I'll meet you there, and I ask that you not tell anyone besides Dr. Jefferson. There's been an incident with Dr. Rahman."

"What's happened? Is it bad?"

"Yes, sir. He's dead."

Hill led Mark and Peter toward a cluster of purple-red bushes near the stream at the base of the drainage channel. They stepped through the bushes into a small clearing where the rest of Hill's force stood by the still form of Dr. Rahman. The sprawled body lay face down, clothes damp and legs partially in the slow-moving water. The left arm, splayed above his head, ended in ragged streamers of red flesh and pinkish white bone just below the elbow, as if something had dragged him from the stream and then ripped the forearm and hand away. Icy sweat exploded down his back and legs and Mark fought for control of his stomach. Behind him, he heard Peter being noisily sick in the bushes off the path.

"Oh my God, what happened?" Mark asked, one hand involuntarily rose to cover his mouth. He could feel his stomach twist and he tried to focus on Dr. Rahman's pale face.

"We've seen a few things that seem to live along the water. Sort of a cross between a dog and an alligator," Hill said. "Slow, probably an ambush predator. For the most part, the locals have gone out of their way to avoid people, but we've warned your team about coming down here. Still, people have relaxed. We think he just came down here on a break and maybe surprised one."

Mark looked at the body again. The arm could have been bitten off, and a deep slash between the right shoulder and neck gaped open. "Why… why didn't it… eat him?" He asked. He heard Peter retch again.

"We probably don't taste good," Hill replied. "From talking to Dr. Bayless, we aren't digestible to the local wildlife. Doesn't mean they aren't willing to give it a try though."

"I can't believe this is happening," Mark whispered. "It was supposed to just be another dig, no real danger."

"It isn't your fault, boss," Hill said quietly. "Everybody got the brief before we got on the shuttle; everybody got another brief once we got down here and saw the local wildlife. He was told not to wander off, especially not alone."

"What now?" Mark asked.

"Your call, sir. I'd recommend we bag the body, get it up to sick bay. Let Cmdr. Bayless have a look at it. We'll get a thorough scan of everything before we move him. After we get him up to the Commander, me and my boys'll break out some rifles and clear the area. From what we've seen there can't be more than three, maybe four of the gators near camp."

"That sounds good," Mark whispered. "Crap, how are we going to tell the team? I have never had a fatality, ever, in all the sites I've ever dug. Broken bones, sure, a heart attack once, but never anything like this."

"If I may, sir?" Hill asked. Mark nodded. "Don't sit on this. People are going to notice he's missing pretty quick, if they haven't already. If you do anything other than be as open as you can, you're going to start rumors, and that will eat away at morale. New planets and exploration are a dangerous business. We're dealing with the unknown, and everyone knows it. Tell 'em what happened and honor your dead. Then tell 'em what you're going to do to mitigate the risk, what they can do to protect themselves. And unless you're going to pack 'em all back into the shuttle and wait 'til the captain gets back, get 'em back to work. It'll be tough for a day or two, but work's the best thing for 'em."

Peter nodded and said, "He's right, Mark. The team deserves to know." He grabbed Mark's shoulder and shook it gently.

Mark nodded. Peter's face was as pale as he'd ever seen it. "Come on. Let's get back up to the communications shack. We need to get everybody back into the camp for an all-hands meeting. The cafeteria, I think. It's the only place big enough, really. After the meeting, I'll need to let Captain Mazen know. They're in the outer gas giants, and any message will take about six hours or so. Not that there's anything she can do about it."

Day 10

"Director Davos, could I see you in medbay?"

The tone of his comm unit jolted Mark back to the present. He'd been working on a report for a while, but as was often the case over the last two days, he was distracted by Dr. Rahman's death; he'd been remembering his last interactions with Dr. Rahman and, of course, the discovery of the body. He hit the answer key. "This is Davos. I'm sorry, what was that?"

"It's Commander Bayless, Director. I'd appreciate it if you could come down to med bay. I have some questions for you, and it would be easier to do here rather than at your office."

Easier for you, Mark thought. On the trip out, he hadn't interacted much with Bayless. Now that they were on planet, he spoke to him practically every day. He was coming to suspect that Captain Mazen had not been terribly disappointed when the good commander had been tapped to join the expedition. "Give me five minutes."

"Thank you, Director."

On the walk over, he saw clouds building in the distance. Hill had warned him they were likely to have weather this evening, and he couldn't argue. Mark had grown up on the plains of North America and recognized a supercell when he saw one.

When he arrived at the med center, he was surprised to see Jake Hill already there, along with Bayless, seated behind his desk.

"Thank you for coming so quickly, Director," Bayless said. "It's about Rahman. I've completed the autopsy and there are some"—he hesitated for a moment—"issues."

Mark looked at Hill, who shook his head and shrugged. He returned his attention to Bayless. "What do you mean?" he asked.

"I'll get right to the point. Rahman died of trauma and blood loss. No surprise there. The question is, where is the blood? I've already spoken to Hill about it and looked at the video of the recovery. There should have been a pool of blood around the body."

"He was partially in the stream," Mark said. "Maybe it just washed away?"

"That would make sense if the body was completely in the water, or if the site of the major trauma was in the water," the commander answered. "Both the arm and the laceration across the neck and shoulder were well out of the water."

"His clothes were wet," Mark said. "Maybe he'd pulled himself out of the stream?"

"That could account for some of it, but there should still be more blood," Bayless replied.

"It's possible that whatever killed him, killed him in the water, and then pulled him out to eat him," Hill volunteered, "but that wouldn't make much sense either. The scene would have been much more disturbed."

Mark looked sharply at the stocky security chief. "Wait a sec. You just said, 'whatever.' You're not thinking croc anymore?"

Hill shrugged again. "Me and my boys swept through the area, we didn't find any crocs. They might be migratory, or maybe they just decided to leave when we showed up. All I know is we saw a few the first couple days and haven't seen any since we found Dr. Rahman. Might be there's something else out there, something that made the crocs want to be somewhere else."

Mark looked from the commander to the security chief and back. "Well, where does that leave us?" he asked.

"It means what we thought we knew about Rahman's death might not be what happened. All I can tell you at this point is that what we're doing is inherently dangerous. You need to emphasize it to your people and make damn sure no one goes out anywhere by themselves."

"I think we have that part covered," Mark said. "I can hardly get the teams to leave the camp right now. They're all finding reasons to stay put, either working in the main tent sorting and cataloging finds or writing reports that had been put off."

"Probably best," Hill said. "At least until we get a better line on what happened to Rahman. They'd need to stay close tonight anyway. The weather satellites the ship left in orbit say the storm's going to hit us just before sunset, and if the weather here acts anything like weather on Earth, it looks like it's going to be a good one. You'll want your people in close."

"Are the tents sturdy enough?" Mark asked.

"We should be fine," Hill assured him. "The tents are Fleet Marines issue. But if it looks like it's going to go really bad, we can retreat into the shuttle. In fact, you might want to consider moving some of your more delicate equipment into the bay anyway. Along with any artifacts you think need to stay dry. The tents are good," he shrugged, "but military grade doesn't mean one hundred percent waterproof."

The storm billowed and grew, an enormous black anvil that dropped the ruins and dig site into its massive shadow. From a small rise on the western edge of the camp, Ken Baker watched it with some contentment. He'd grown up only an hour's drive south of the city of Omaha, and he'd always loved the thunderstorms of the Great Plains. There had even been a point in his life when he'd considered meteorology as a career. As he watched, he heard movement behind him, the sound of stones falling against each other. He whirled to see Lisa coming up the trail. "Ah, Dr. Daniels. You gave me a bit of a start."

"Sorry about that," Lisa said with an impish grin. "I honestly didn't mean to. I am glad I found you, though."

"Really? What can I do for you?" he asked, and his craggy face creased into a smile. He hadn't interacted with Lisa often on the dig, they'd been assigned to different teams. But during the conversations he'd had with her, he'd found her to be quick-witted and very well-read on his own specialty, Pre-Columbian Mesoamerican culture.

"I need some help. I need to retrieve some equipment before that"—she pointed at the thunderhead—"ruins it. Since we can't go out alone, I need a buddy. You busy?" Absently, she rubbed her hand down her pant leg.

Ken noticed the movement. "Hand still bothering you?" he asked.

She looked startled and glanced down. "Well, yeah. It still itches like crazy. Bayless said it's probably psychosomatic. He might be right, but I'm starting to think while *Commander* Bayless may be a fine naval officer, *Doctor* Bayless would not be my first choice as a primary care physician." She rubbed her hand again. "Anyway, can you help me out?"

"Well, you caught me standing here watching a storm blow up, so you know I'm not busy. I'd be happy to help."

"Great. It's over by the entrance to B-3," she said and pointed to a structure about a kilometer away.

"Ah, the Library," Ken exclaimed. "That's what some of the others decided it was."

Lisa looked thoughtful. "I could see that. Several rows of what look like shelves, unfortunately empty." She started walking. "Come on. I think we have about an hour before the storm breaks, but I could be wrong. I grew up in California. What do I know about big thunderstorms?"

They continued on in companionable silence for the 10 minutes or so it took to get to the building. Ken looked around and tried to spot the equipment. He turned toward Lisa, who had stopped and was staring at the tree line about 10 meters away. Once again, her left hand was rubbing up and down on her pant leg. "What is it, Lisa?"

Her head swiveled to look over her shoulder at him, a strange expression on her face. "I really appreciate you coming with me, Ken. You have no idea how helpful you're going to be."

The way she had phrased it seemed odd, and he felt a growing unease in his spine, like he was being watched. "It's no problem, Lis— What was that?" he exclaimed and pointed toward the trees. Between two of the strange, purple-barked trees, something had jumped? Flown?

Lisa slowly walked over to Ken, looked into his eyes, and gently rubbed her bandaged hand on his arm. "I think if you could hear the humming, you'd understand," she said earnestly. "Thank you."

The dull rumble of an almost ceaseless thunder accompanied the storm's approach. The calmness of the previous hours was broken by the sudden arrival of a powerful gust front.

"I've changed my mind, boss," Hill said from behind Mark's right shoulder. "I'm going to recommend everybody get in the shuttle until this blows past."

Mark looked back and saw the old Marine's eyes tracking whisps of cloud as it was torn apart by the storm's violence. "How much time have we got?" he asked.

"Shuttle's radar says twelve minutes, fifteen on the outside."

Mark nodded sharply and brought his comm unit to his lips. "All hands. Shelter in the shuttle. Now."

Peter walked up to him, a troubled look on his face. "Have you seen Ken Baker?"

Mark shook his head. "I've been with Hill and Bayless the last hour or so. Where did you see him last?"

"He helped me box up some of the artifacts," Peter replied. "That was about an hour or so ago. We finished, and he said he wanted to get some of his gear into the shuttle before the storm hit. I talked to his tent partner, and he said he hasn't been there. Tried his comm and he's not answering."

"Crap," Mark hissed. He looked over at Chief Hill. "Can you find him for me?" he asked.

"No problem," The chief replied, and pulled out his own comm unit and made a call.

"Security Offices. Scott speaking," the answering voice said.

"Scott? It's Chief Hill. I need you to locate Dr. Ken Baker."

"Hold on, Chief," Scott said, and Mark heard the sound of a separate computer being activated. There was a bell tone and Scott's voice came back. "His comm location is out in the southwest portion of the dig. Near B-3."

"Anyone else with him?" Hill asked.

"No, Chief."

"Hill, I need you to go retrieve him," Mark said.

"Not a problem, boss," Hill answered. He raised his comm again. "Scott, put someone else on the comms and meet me at the Quads."

"Aye aye, Chief. Be there in two minutes."

Hill jogged off, and after a short pause, Mark heard two quad bikes firing up and bolting into the distance. The sharp hum of the electric engines quickly faded into the background noise of the approaching storm.

Peter nervously paced back and forth, his hands rubbing together. "There's an explanation," Mark heard him mutter to himself. "No reason Ken would run off by himself."

Mark's body buzzed with the adrenaline surge caused by the latest emergency, and he fought his own desire to run out to the site, to see for himself what had happened. In his mind he could hear the echo of Chief Hill's earlier warning. *Might be there's something else out there.*

It didn't take long for the quads to cover the kilometer distance, and Mark's comm buzzed.

"Yes?" he asked.

"We found him, sir."

Mark felt visceral relief wash through his chest. He felt the beginnings of a smile start and he said, "Great. Everybody back—"

Hill's voice interrupted him. "Dr. Davos, he's dead."

Hill brought the body to the shuttle med bay, where Mark, Peter and Bayless waited. He put the long bundle on the diagnostic table and unzipped it. "It's bad," he said. "There are at least three serious puncture wounds, two in the chest and one in the lower back, right in the kidney, it looks like. His arms have several shallow cuts, defensive wounds most likely. It looks like it happened fast, all three wounds would have been critical."

Bayless leaned over the table, examining the wounds. "Deep," he said, "and clean. Really clean." He looked over to Hill. "What about the site? Where you found the body?" he asked.

Hill's lips twitched, like he was trying to suppress anger. "His were the only clean tracks. Of course, there are a lot of other boot prints, it's a pretty trafficked area of the site. No tracks I didn't recognize, no animals. And no blood."

Bayless nodded, as if he had expected that answer. He addressed Mark. "Despite these severe punctures, no blood at the site. And I can tell just on initial observation that there is damn little blood in this body."

"What the hell could be doing this?" Mark burst out.

Bayless straightened and rubbed his eyes. "There are any number of animals on Earth that subsist on blood. Mostly parasites, but a few higher animals as well. But this," he pointed to the punctures. "This is almost unbelievable."

Mark raised his hand and dropped it, at a loss for words. He paused and tried again. "Do the autopsy, Commander. See if you can… find anything," he finished in a rush.

Bayless nodded. "I'll get started," he replied. "I'd recommend you two get back to your people, let them know what has happened."

As Mark and Peter left medbay, metallic pings could be heard in the corridor, announcing the arrival of the storm, accompanied by driving hail. They walked to the ramp and looked out into the storm. Hailstones, many as large as apples, bounced off the tents or shattered on the hard ground of the camp area. A brilliant stroke of lightning almost instantly followed a tremendous crash of thunder that stunned them and sent them back deeper into the shuttle's protection.

"Shit," exclaimed Mark as the blue streak across his vision started to fade. "That was really close."

Peter shook his head, not in disagreement, but in morose acceptance of the situation. "Come on. Everyone should be in the cargo bay. Let's go check on them."

Once in the bay, Mark used his comm to access the loudspeakers. "Hey everybody. I need your attention." He waited for the conversations to die down and then looked out across the assembled people. The ones closest saw the expression on his face and grew pale in concern. "I am very sorry to say we've had another fatality." There was a collective gasp across the room. "Ken Baker was found dead near Site B-3. We don't know exactly how he died, but it looks like it may have been another animal attack. I need—" He paused, then raised his voice over the increasing volume of the shocked conversations that had started on the heels of his announcement. "I need a head count soonest! Team leads, get your people together. I need to know that everyone's here, and nobody got stuck out in that," he said and jerked his thumb back to indicate the storm raging outside. As if to punctuate his words, another wave of hail impacts crashed across the ship, followed by another roll of thunder.

As the existing groups began to break up and reorganize into their team divisions, Peter darted up to his side. "She's not here," he blurted.

"What?" Mark asked, confused.

"She's not here," Peter said again. "Lisa. I can't find her anywhere, and she's not answering her comms."

"Shit," Mark hissed. He activated his own comm. "Chief Hill. I need Dr. Daniel's location right now."

"Yes, sir." There was no hesitation in the chief's response. "Got her. Site C. West Temple. Past the anteroom and the corridor behind it. She must have gone in to shelter from the storm."

"Anyone else in there with her?" Mark asked.

There was a pause as Chief Hill adjusted his search. "Ah, no sir. She's in there by herself."

"What the hell is she doing out there alone?" Mark whispered to Peter.

Peter shrugged; relief warred with new worry on his face. "She could have lost track of time, gotten too focused on whatever she's working on, and there are some areas where the comm is spotty, but she still shouldn't be out there by herself. We need to go get her."

Mark nodded. He brought his comm up again. "Chief, put one of your boys on weather watch. I need you here. As soon as there's a break, we're going to get her and bring her in."

"Got it, sir. I'll be there in five."

Unsurprisingly, Chief Hill joined Mark and Peter in three minutes. He'd also managed to don a light combat vest, and the short carbine in his hands was a match for the pistol at his waist.

"Ready when you are, boss. I know you're both checked out on the quads, but you're going to need to follow my lead on this. If you can't, I'm going to leave you here and take a couple of my boys to go get her. Understood?"

Peter nodded jerkily and Mark hesitated, but then nodded as well. Administratively, he might be the leader of the expedition, but Chief Hill was wildly more qualified to oversee what they were about to do.

Once he'd seen both acknowledge his authority, Hill went on. "Scott's on the radar, and he said this line is about ready to pass us. We'll have about ten minutes before the next band, so we might not have time to grab her and get back. If that's the case, we just hunker down and wait for the next break. Understood?" Both men nodded, and Hill nodded in response. "Good. Follow me. We'll wait by the ramp for the break. Run for the quads and then go get Dr. Daniels."

They proceeded to the ramp and prepared to wait. After a few minutes, Hill put a hand over one ear and whispered into a throat mike. He nodded and looked out across the camp. For the most part, the hail had stopped and what was left was much smaller than the deadly stones that had been falling less than ten minutes earlier. The rain slackened and Hill said, "Time to go."

They dashed to the shed where the quad bikes were stored, mounted, and sped single file into the rain. Once at the West Temple site, Hill slowed, turned, and drove into the arched doorway. Mark and Peter followed, and once inside, parked in the entry area.

"I know this is a dig," Hill said and wiped the water from his face. "But I'm not leaving the bikes out in that."

The storm had lessened, but all three men dripped water onto the floor, soaked to the skin by the still heavy rain. As if to punctuate Hill's statement, there was another white flash of lightning, followed immediately by the deafening crack of thunder. "Let's move," Hill said, bringing his carbine to a ready position. He moved smoothly into the first chamber, his weapon tracking across and up, checking the large oval room. The storm sounds faded as they moved deeper into the building. Shadows flowed back as all three men activated lamps, and light bounced off the glass-smooth walls.

"Lisa!" called Peter. "Lisa, are you in here?"

"Quiet!" Hill hissed. "She's in here. Let's just keep moving forward."

They came to the corridor where they'd found the geode-like eggs. As Hill stepped into it, he flashed his light along the floor. "Oh, hell," he said quietly.

"What?" Mark asked.

"Her comm unit. Right there on the floor by the first nodule." Hill replied.

Peter pushed forward and fell to his knees, snatching up the comm unit. "Now what?" He asked. "Where is she?"

"Don't borrow trouble, Dr. Jefferson," Hill said soothingly. "We'll find her."

Mark looked down the corridor and saw a black shadow where a rough stone wall had been previously. Goosebumps flowed across his skin, and he asked, "Wasn't that blocked before?"

Peter's head spun to see what he was looking at. "Yes," he said, climbing back to his feet. "It was blocked. She must be down there, come on!" He dashed away before the Chief could grab him.

"Dammit, Dr. Jefferson, wait! Get behind me," Hill snapped.

It was too late. Peter had disappeared into the gap.

Mark looked at Hill. "We can't let him go alone."

Hill looked like he was about to protest but bit it back. Instead, he nodded and said, "Fine. But you, at least, will stay behind me. Got it?" he asked, a finger pointed in Mark's face.

"Right behind you," Mark answered.

They moved forward, and Hill stopped abruptly. "You see this, Doc?" he asked and pointed up at the wall near the new opening.

Mark's eyes followed the line Hill indicated and his eyebrows rose in surprise. High on the wall, protruding from the stone, was the three-rayed disk that had been among the collected artifacts. On its surface, he could see the ID tag that marked the date and location where it was found. One ray of the disk was fit securely into a narrow slot near the opening. "My God, I think it's some kind of key or release mechanism. It must have let her open the passage."

Hill looked worried and asked, "How did she know?"

Mark stopped and considered. Then he shook his head and answered. "I… don't know. We'll ask her when we find her, but first, we have to find her."

Hill nodded and continued forward. Mark fell in behind the Chief. They moved through the opening into surprisingly stagnant and damp air that was a harsh contrast to the dry and dusty corridor. The Chief's carbine once again tracked left and right as he sought out threats. Once through, they immediately saw Peter, who had stopped and was staring in wonder at a thick, knobby, reddish-brown column in front of him.

"It's more eggs," he said, as Mark moved up to join him. Hill stepped to one side and tried to keep a clear line of fire into the vast darkness of what appeared to be an enormous chamber. "Look at it, Mark. It… I don't have the words." Peter moved his lamp around, and Mark could see there were several, possibly dozens of identical columns around them.

Mark returned his attention to the column in front of Peter. Something about it greatly disturbed him, and he wasn't sure what it was. As he moved closer, shadows flickered around it, revealing and concealing more columns that disappeared as the light from his lamp shifted. It suddenly struck him that these nodules did not look like stone and crystal. In the shadows, the eggs almost appeared leathery. His hand shook as he reached out and touched it. He gasped. "Should it be… moist?" he asked.

Peter opened his mouth to answer when a strange humming filled the room. They peered into the darkness around them and saw a faint glow further into the chamber. "Lisa!" Peter exclaimed and ran toward the light.

"Dammit, Peter!" Mark shouted and chased after Peter's bobbing lamp.

Mark saw that Peter had stopped at the edge of the lit area. He shuddered to a stop beside him and stared. The light came from one of the archeology team's camp lanterns, and it illuminated an enormous statue, which towered nearly 10 meters to the ceiling of the chamber. The stone figure looked almost human, like a gigantic man crouched on his heels with his arms draped around his knees. But that was where the explainable stopped. Out of the statue's back rose two tattered bat-like wings, and in place of a head, a tentacle monstrosity sat on the creature's shoulders. Peter's mouth gaped in apparent shock. "That… that can't be right."

"It looks almost human," Mark said. "How would that even happen? Some other species gone extinct, maybe?"

Peter looked over at Mark, horror in his eyes. "Oh, Mark, it's so much worse," he said in a hoarse whisper. "I've… seen this… back on Earth. In a museum in Louisiana." His wide-eyed gaze floated back to the monstrosity. "Not on display, in the back. But it was only this tall." He held his hands about 20 centimeters apart. "I know what this is, or what it would be back home. It's something ancient from the oldest prehistory of Earth. Before humanity even got to the point of worshiping anthropomorphic gods, we worshiped older things, mad things, ancient, horrible things that are best forgotten, Old Ones. C—"

"Don't say it, Peter," Lisa's voice cut him off. "Do not speak it! Don't get his attention."

The men jumped and saw Lisa emerge from the shadows to the right of the statue. She smiled at them and moved toward another of the nodule-covered columns that rose throughout the chamber. In her hands she bore a stone bowl.

"Lisa! What're you doing?" Peter asked. He seemed to be shifting his weight, as if he wanted to go to her but couldn't move. "We need to get back to the shuttle."

"Don't worry, Peter," she said as she shifted the bowl to her right hand. With her left she reached out and caressed the column of eggs. "I'm perfectly safe. In this chamber, the humming is almost soothing, less disruptive." She shifted the bowl again and gently poured a thick, dark liquid over the column. Some spilled across her hands and the coppery smell of blood assailed their noses. The low humming grew stronger and filled the chamber.

As she moved past the column, Mark noticed a rectangular shape near the base. He moved his flashlight's beam and illuminated the black box at the base of the pillar. Wires ran from the box, twisted around the pillar, and disappeared into an egg. "That's a power pack."

Lisa stopped and looked at him. "Very observant, Mark. With everything going on you still see the basics. That's useful." She paused, a thoughtful look on her face. Finally, she nodded to herself and continued. "Yes. The power banks and the protein supplements were very nearly enough. Enough to bring them to the surface of sleep, almost awake, but still dreaming." She shrugged. "But in the end," she went on, "it was blood. Always blood to finish the task."

"Oh God, Lisa, what have you done?" Peter whispered. His voice cracked and a tear ran down his cheek.

Lisa ignored him and moved to another column. "You know, I can almost understand the humming," she said. "I know what they want, and I know what needs to be done, but it's more images and impressions. In here, with the statue, it's so much clearer."

"I don't care what you think is going on, but you are going to stop right now." Chief Hill's voice was as firm as battle steel as he emerged from the shadows, his carbine trained on Lisa.

"Chief, no!" Peter burst out.

"Sorry, doc," the chief said. "This must stop. She's lost it and as far as I can tell, she's already killed two people."

"No," Lisa protested. "I didn't kill Ken. I didn't need to. But Dr. Rahman…" she trailed off. "I needed the blood."

"That's it," Hill spat. "Put the bowl down and hold your hands where I can see them."

"I'm sorry, Jacob. I wish you understood," she said sadly.

The humming shifted to a jarring, discordant note, and a harsh chittering shrilled out of the darkness. Chief Hill jerked the carbine toward movement in the shadows. Half a dozen flying shapes bolted into the light and struck him, knocking him back and onto the ground. The chief rolled onto his stomach and struggled to get back to his feet when something like an immense praying mantis slammed into the chief's shoulders. A sharp, narrow rod extended from the monster's head and jabbed into the chief's neck, just above the armor. Hill's hoarse scream was cut off with an abrupt finality.

Mark and Peter stared in stunned shock. Several more insect-like monsters emerged into the light. With a strange grace, one walked to Lisa, rose onto four legs, and folded its blood-splattered claws in front of its chest. Lisa reached out, shoulder level, and gently caressed its head.

It buzzed at her, and she nodded. "Yes," she said, as if she was answering the creature. "We will be able to put many eggs on the shuttle, and the Navy will want that shuttle back, no matter what happens to the expedition." She smiled and caressed its head again, then faced Mark and Peter. "I should thank you. None of this would have been possible without your help." She stepped forward and with one bloody hand touched Peter's face. She smiled sadly at the tears that streamed down his cheeks.

"Lisa, no. You've got to stop this," Peter pleaded. He reached out and took her hands into his.

Lisa leaned forward and kissed Peter gently. "Don't worry, darling," she whispered. "It'll be quick."

Peter suddenly jerked forward. He choked and fell limp to the floor, like a puppet with its strings cut, his eyes already glazed in death. The large mantis creature behind him moved forward, its head cocked as if it was examining its work.

Mark wanted to run, but the humming increased in volume and obliterated his thoughts. He could feel the panic rising in his mind, and he could almost make out words in the hum. "Lisa, wait," he gritted out. His knees buckled and he collapsed to the floor. A pair of clawed pincers grabbed his shoulders and pulled him to kneel in front of the woman. "Wait," he cried out, desperately telling his arms and legs to move, but none of his limbs would respond.

The humming crescendoed, rising into a hammering noise he could feel as it crashed into his chest, and his mind was assailed by alien images and incomprehensible thoughts. Lisa leaned down. "It's okay, Mark," she said in a comforting tone. "Like I said, you're useful. You are disciplined and observant in ways a lot of the others aren't. And as the director of the expedition, your authorizations will be a benefit when the ship returns. We need you if we're going to get off this planet." More of the insect creatures, half concealed in the shadows, moved behind her as she spoke. "You are going to help us, and just like me, you're going to be overjoyed to do it. You might resist now, but every religion needs a prophet, and I have chosen you."

She reached out her left hand and her fingers caressed his cheek. At her touch, agony and fire blossomed in his brain, and the whispers became screams.

"Archaeology is such an interesting field of work, don't you agree? You never know what old bones will tell you, when a civilization has been long forgotten. Not that they bring their work home with them, of course. Only the tales…"

* * * *

Dream of Distant Shores
by Mark Wandrey

A Turning Point story
Present

"No, no, no," she cried repeatedly as she ran. It took all her will not to look back over her shoulder. Her legs were rubbery and hurt with every step. Coopersmith, less fatigued despite his age, was just ahead of her, shotgun against his shoulder as he ran. Sticky green blood flew off his suit with every step.

As they reached the next corner Horner and Benton were waiting. Benton was still armed; Horner was hobbling badly. His ankle might be broken. They were alone.

"Where's Rico and Peron?" Coopersmith asked as he came to a stop next to her.

Benton shook his head inside his open helmet. "Urvi, Sotos, and Komatsu?"

She shook her own head in reply.

"We need to go back," he said timidly.

"No time," she said.

"We gotta get the fuck outta here," Horner said, gasping for breath. "We're fucked, Skipper. *Please.*"

"What do you think we're trying to do?" Coopersmith snarled. "Keep it together, Mr. Horner."

A blood-curdling scream made them all spin around. The sound was something a human's throat could never produce in a million years. Claws scraped on the deck as the horrors raced towards them.

Benton cried out and raised his shotgun. *Click.* "Fuck!" he snarled and struggled to get a hand into his ammo pouch.

"God damn it," Coopersmith cursed, raised his own shotgun, and fired. He aimed low, the buckshot throwing sparks off the deck as it destroyed claws and underbelly. One of the creatures fell with an equally horrible screech. A moment later its cohorts fell upon it, ripping the creature apart. The monster had a harness, and on the harness was what could have been a weapon. It made no attempt to reach for it.

"That'll buy us a minute at most," Coopersmith said as he shakily fumbled another shell into his shotgun. "Low!"

"Move, move, move!" Tina yelled, pushing Horner into stumbling forward motion, away from the flying blood and dismembering attack. Already one was moving past the meal, this one furred with too many eyes and long clawed arms. Blood of various colors dripped from massive fangs.

Behind the creature, Tina's eyes went wide when she saw a green engineers' spacesuit, an arm torn away, and the helmet missing. Rico's familiar facial features were distorted in incomprehensible rage and hunger. He locked eyes with her and howled. A prayer escaped her lips and tears fell from her eyes as she ran.

Two Days Earlier

"Official Log, April 19th, 2049, Lieutenant Commander Tina Pendleton in command. *Acheron* continues to function well. Better than many would expect as the first of the *Azanti*-class frontier ships. As of this morning our distance from Sol is estimated at 12 light years. This is our…pause log." Tina checked the tablet computer strapped to her thigh board. "Resume log. This is our 11th jump using the Supraluminal Gravity Distortion drive and the astrophysics team believes they have the calibration down to plus/minus 1 million klicks per second.

"The unfortunate nature of the SGD means every ship equipped with one will cruise at a different speed. We've resorted to doing practice jumps and calculating distance and time coefficients based on observations after a jump." She shrugged. "If the Vulpes had helped our understanding, maybe things would have been different. Instead, we're children learning how to operate a shotgun, in the dark."

"And wearing gloves."

"Ignore my pilot's input, it's not an official log," Tina said, giving Lieutenant Peltz a commander's steely- eyed stare.

"It is now," Peltz said with a chuckle.

"Astrogation says we'll drop out of jump in just under an hour, at which point we'll begin adjusting calibrations. If they match the last jump, *Acheron's* speed in jump will be confirmed at 62.2 million kilometers per second, or about 32 hours per light year."

"Forty-two," Peltz corrected.

"Mind your own business flyboy," she growled.

"Fine, enter the wrong number in the log," Peltz said and shrugged.

Tina scowled and ran the division of 9.454252 trillion by 62.2 million, then divided the sum by 60 twice. *Shit.* "Correction log, 42 hours per light year." Even though she couldn't see him, she could feel Peltz grinning. *Prick.* "Anyway, if the numbers hold out after we spend a day in normal space to calculate, that means we'll only need a couple more hours to reach Wolf 1061. Before I was born my parents dreamed about one day traveling to Mars. Now we can go from Earth to Mars at over 200 times the speed of light, or a couple of seconds."

"I don't know about you, Skipper, but my old man would rather have kept the planet and never gone FTL."

"Mine too," she agreed, then turned back to the log. "No other items to note. Acknowledge the pursers report on stores, and E3 Hartwell's case of appendicitis was confirmed. Ships' surgeon Dr. Ortiz is waiting until we are out of supraluminal before surgery. Mr. Hartwell is stable on antibiotics and in no serious danger. Conclude log."

"Log concluded, Captain," the computer responded with its normal contralto. Since all SGD equipped ships to date had male captains, the female computer voice was considered calming, for some matronly bullshit reasons. Tina's mental image was of a nosy neighbor woman on the block where she'd grown up. In other words, an interfering bitch. "Shall I file the log?"

"Confirmed, file the log."

"Log filed, Captain."

Acheron's small bridge would be fully staffed in a few hours, for now it was almost deserted. "Mr. Peltz, you have the conn."

"Aye-aye, I have the conn."

She unbuckled the seatbelt and climbed to her feet. The SGD provided constant gravity while it operated, even out of supraluminal. The sci-fi movies of her parents always showed artificial gravity. They'd done that to save money making movies. Turned out it was just the way you flew between the stars.

"I'll be back after a shower."

"Take your time," Peltz said. "I like the big chair."

"Same as yours," she said as she left the bridge.

Moving back from the bridge led her to the central hallway, running forward to the avionic and all the way aft to the engine room. *Acheron* was a flattened cylinder 112 meters long, 12 meters and three decks tall, and 22 meters wide. Thanks to the SGD the ship only needed nominal aerodynamics to land on a planet. She couldn't wait.

Because of its artificial gravity *Acheron* was a lot like an old terrestrial navy ship crossed with an aircraft. Because the SGD also generated an impenetrable field around the ship entering an atmosphere was simply a matter of flying down to just above the surface, turning off the SGD, and landing with thrusters.

The captains' quarters were intentionally close to the bridge. In an SGD powered ship, it didn't matter much to be further from the engine room. There were no rockets to keep you awake, or massive power plants thrumming the entire vessel.

Acheron was a quiet ship with the predominant sounds being crew moving about and air recycling fans working.

In Tina's quarters she grabbed a quick shower then spent a few minutes relaxing with a book. On her little desk were various pictures of previous missions before she was assigned to *Acheron*. There were other, earlier memories as well. One showed Tina on the terraforming station above Venus, another was with her mom and dad at the newly completed Mars Space Elevator, then with friends in college skiing at Titan.

The last picture was her mother and father with her at the commissioning ceremony of *Acheron*. Did they have some sway in getting their newly-promoted to lieutenant commander daughter assigned to the first in class explorer ship? Sure, maybe. Did she care? Fuck no. She was 12 light years from Sol, further and faster than any human had ever traveled.

Without time for a meal, Tina grabbed a protein bar and munched while she reviewed the shakedown cruise master report. There was a laundry list of things she wanted to report to the shipyard in Martian orbit. Most were minor except for a problem with the main docking collar. It was quite finicky, which was likely because it was a legacy design given to them by their custodians, the Vulpes. By the book it could allow *Acheron* to dock with just about any ship. In practice it was a kludge.

"Ten minutes, Captain," Peltz' voice came out of her quarters PA.

"Roger that," she said, popped the last of her snack in her mouth, cleaned the crumbs from her uniform tunic, and headed back to the bridge.

"Captain on the Bridge!"

"I have the con, Mr. Komatsu."

"Roger that, Captain has the con."

Tina took her center seat on the semi-circular bridge, the best position to do any of the jobs, if necessary, and in the middle of anything that might go wrong. All stations were now manned. Peltz was still at the helm, Lieutenant Akio Komatsu, her XO, at sensors and science. Ensign Beth Albertson was at nav, with Chief Bary Coopersmith as chief engineer. The remainder of her 23-person crew would all be at their duty stations. Nothing had ever happened to a ship coming out of supraluminal, yet it remained the most dangerous moment of flight owing to not being able to see the space you were decelerating into.

"Cameras front," Tina ordered. Two LCD screens mounted to either side of the currently shuttered front windows came alight with a view like no other. Stars and distant galaxies moved at various speeds, all visible in some shade of blue. Closer stars would move subtly quicker as they approached the edge of the view, while distant objects did not appear to move at all. Out the rear everything would appear red.

A single star, dead center of the view, showed no sign of movement as it grew larger. Wolf 1061, the last leg of their shakedown cruise, was just ahead. Ensign Albertson spoke up.

"Prepare to disengage SGD," she said and consulted her computer. "In five…four…three…two…one…disengage!" The camera view dissolved into static and a moment later resolved into a view of space most unlike their home star system. The navigator was silent for a moment as she used instruments. "Welcome to Wolf 1061."

Everyone on the bridge, Tina included, applauded. "Well done, Ensign," she said. "Distance from primary?"

"Distance approximately 11 million kilometers. "I'll have it refined in a few hours."

Tina became aware they weren't alone, a dozen or more of the crew were crowding in the rear of the bridge. She considered saying something, then shook her head. "Mr. Peltz, release the bridge shutters."

"Release the bridge shutters, aye." With a mechanical whir of motors, the heavy steel shutters retracted from the forward viewports and dark, blood red starlight flooded in.

Amazingly, despite being bright, it didn't make her squint. At 11 million kilometers from their sun, *Acheron* would have been cooked by radiation. Earth orbited 151 million kilometers from the sun. Even Mercury was 69 million kilometers. But Wolf 1061's radius was a mere 212 thousand kilometers, compared to Sol's 700,000 kilometers. Wolf 1061 was a red dwarf, so it lacked the luminosity of Sol and was quite small. Despite being just 13 light years away, it was invisible from home without a telescope.

"The light is so cool," one of the visiting crew said.

"Would we die without the SGD screen?" someone else asked.

"Negative," Lieutenant Komatsu said. "The radiation would be considerable; however, *Acheron's* hull plating would be enough to reduce gamma ray flux enough for us to remain for many hours."

"Just the same," Tina said and turned to Coopersmith, "let's be sure the drive stays powered during our brief visit?"

"Absolutely Captain," he said. "Schedule is for 18 hours of scientific observation?" She nodded in agreement. "I'd like the time to power the fuel cells and recharge the capacitor banks."

Tina glanced at Komatsu. "Would it interfere with scientific study?"

"No, Captain, the fuel cells do not generate enough RF to interfere with my instruments."

"Very well. Once we've fixed our position and are sure nothing is going to conflict with our orbit, let's recharge." The general hubbub behind her made her add to the orders. "You can also unshutter the observation viewport and allow extra time off so all the crew can see the wonders of Wolf 1061." A light applause behind her made the captain smile. "That's enough, get off my bridge," she said with mock sternness.

In a moment the bridge crew was alone again as everyone began working on their various tasks. Tina stared at the almost hypnotic blood-red glow of Wolf 1061 and sighed. For a short time, at least, she would be the captain who'd flown the furthest from Sol of any human. She decided to enjoy it while she could. Still, the sun's light made her feel off, as if something were watching. Something which didn't like being disturbed.

"Afternoon, Skipper," Peltz said as Tina walked onto the bridge, steaming coffee in one hand and toast in the other. "No breakfast?"

"Inedible," she mumbled around a mouthful of bread.

"I hope Hartwell comes out of sickbay soon," Peltz agreed.

Tina grunted as she took her seat, making sure the hot coffee was secured in a holder. You never felt so much as a bump in an SGD equipped vessel, however like all space crews she'd trained in a traditional rocket fitted ship. They said it built character; she wasn't sure if she agreed. Tina only thought Hartwell was an average cook, as naval cooks, or culinary specialists, went. Now he'd been on sick call for four days, her opinion of him had softened somewhat. E2 Bates, Hartwell's part-time assistant, wasn't equipped to take over the job.

"How do you fuck up scrambled eggs?" Peltz wondered, shaking his head.

"It's one of life's mysteries. Status update?"

"Coopersmith says recharging is proceeding on schedule. Capacitor bank two is 90-percent charged and he says we can take the fuel cells offline by midwatch."

"Very good," she said, checking the bridge's master chronometer. Any word from Mr. Komatsu?"

"Spock says his analysis is proceeding." Komatsu's nickname among the senior staff wasn't shared widely. She was sure the Japanese man wouldn't appreciate it. However, in many ways, it fit the taciturn scientist to a "T".

"You see the report on Wolf 1061c?"

Peltz nodded. "Icy but potentially habitable. The brass back on Mars will be excited to see that. If someone doesn't tell them to take it slow, most of humanity will be living in other solar systems."

"Consider yourself lucky, you won't be compelled to stay pregnant 2 years out of three until you're 40."

"Gotta rebuild the human race," Peltz said, casting a sly grin at her over his shoulder. "When are you doing your part for the species?"

"Mind your own business, Lieutenant." Under different circumstances….

The bridge door opened admitting her XO. "Oh, good, Captain. You need to see this."

"Whatcha got, Sp-, XO?" She snarled at herself for almost screwing the pooch.

Komatsu either didn't notice or care. He used a tablet to take control of a front display, wirelessly sending an image. Space was, by its nature, dark. When backlit by stars you could usually see nearby features. In this image a circle darker than the background stood out. As she stared at it, she began to discern features like lines, or bands she realized. "One of the exoplanets found by scientists?"

"Yes," he said, and a label appeared. Wolf 1061c. "This was the planet they figured most likely to be habitable. Mass 4.3 times Earth, diameter about 1.5 times. I've spent a fair amount of time studying it."

"Is it habitable?"

"No," he said, shaking his head. "At least, not to us. Spectral analysis says its average surface temperature hovers around -10c at the equator, and closer to -150 at the poles. And this is planetary summer. We could get around the temperature, but there's a significant amount of ammonia in the atmosphere as well."

"Okay," she said as the data scrolled. "What's so fascinating, then?"

"It's not the planet, it's what's orbiting it."

"Moon?"

"Better by far." The image zoomed in until the planet dominated the entire field, then even further. What she thought was a lens flare or artifact of the image resolved into a geodesic shape reminding her of a snowflake. It slowly spun against the ebony sphere of Wolf 1061c.

"Is that a space station?" she whispered.

"Or a starship. Whatever it is, it isn't natural. Well, unless everything we know about natural laws is completely wrong."

"How long have you been studying that thing?"

"We found it four hours after our arrival here." The gob-smacked look she gave him made the normally somber scientist grin.

"You know, my first officer is supposed to keep me in his confidence."

"We weren't going anywhere until my survey was complete."

"I'm frankly amazed you could spot that thing against the huge infrared signature that planet puts out. Looks like you haven't done much with the survey."

"I have Chief Patel working on it. Wolf 1061b and 1061d are what you Americans call nothingburgers. One's a rock, the other a failed gas giant."

"I'm not American," Tina said darkly. "None of that exists anymore."

"Sure. Sorry, Captain."

"Don't worry about it." She gestured at the display. "Considering you're the first human to find a fucking *alien ship!*"

"That would be Jeremiah Osborne."

Tina turned to Peltz. "What?"

"Jeremiah Osborne found the first alien ship, in the desert. Didn't you go to school?"

"He's right, of course," Komatsu said.

"You never know what to believe from school," Tina mumbled. She hadn't learned it from school, though, she'd learned it from her mother and father. Instead of arguing she pointed at the ship, or whatever it was. "Regardless, that is an alien construct. We need to get home and report this ASAP."

"Captain," Komatsu said. "A moment?" He nodded his head towards the small meeting room just off the bridge.

"Certainly," she said and followed him. Peltz watched them go for a moment then turned to stare at the strange ship.

"Yes, Lieutenant?"

Komatsu closed the hatch before speaking. "Captain, we cannot leave without investigating."

"We most certainly can."

"What if it's gone by the time another ship comes back."

"Akio, we need to be logical about this. *Acheron* is on her shakedown cruise. We're not even at half strength, crew wise, which is why they sent us here instead of a high-prospect world, because we don't have a survey crew."

"With all due respect, ma'am, we don't need a planetary survey crew. That's an alien ship, and we have no idea if it'll be here in two months, which is how long it will take, minimum, to get back here."

She examined the expression on her XO's face. Part of the reason the crew called him Spock was his normally emotionless attitude towards things. This response was extremely out of character for him.

"Is this risking the crew?"

"A simple survey? Slow approach, and if there is any sign of hostile activity, we simply use the SGD to escape."

She nodded. It was minimal risk. While she'd never spoken to one of the Vulpes, she did know from her parents that the aliens had never mentioned hostile races elsewhere in the galaxy. They hadn't actually spoken about *any* other races, only themselves. Behind it all was the elephant in the room; first contact with another alien race. One of her teachers insisted if there were one alien race, there must be another, and more than likely thousands. *What about the Fermi Paradox?* Maybe the answer was right there, just a few hours away.

"Let me check with Mr. Peltz on how long it will take to reach the bogey."

"A little less than three hours," he said, then noticed her expression. "I ran the numbers before coming to you. We can't use supraluminal speeds, it's too close, even with our completed calibrations."

Tina had noted the log entry from Ensign Albertson certifying the speed calculations. At least they could be certain about not flying into the sun or missing their home system entirely when they got there.

"So, we'd have to go point-five of C?"

"That would be wise."

"Alright. If I get chewed out by Admiral Winters when we get back, I'm taking you with me."

A fleeting grin ran across his face. "Understood, Skipper."

"Okay, let's go see this thing up close."

Tina always found the visual effect of traveling at high velocities below C more dramatic than being supraluminal. Above the speed of light, the blueshift coupled with the gravitic 'lens distortion' always made it look unreal. Regulations stated at near or above light speed you shuttered all view ports, which she found amusing. If the SGD ever failed at supraluminal speed, risking a dust impact was the least of their worries. Anyway, the computerized image on the monitors was even stranger. She thought it was due to the computer not being able to process what it was seeing.

"Bring us in slow, Mr. Peltz. E3 Hartwell is in surgery."

"Understood, Skipper."

Acheron stopped relative to the alien construct just 250 kilometers distant. All the ship's sensors scrutinized what lay before them. It was a lot less like a snowflake at 250 kilometers and more like a child's ruined drawing of a snowflake. It spun slowly in space as it orbited Wolf 1061c. What amazed Tina the most was the size of it. At the current range, *Acheron* would be invisible to anything except the most powerful telescope or radar. The alien construct was the size of a baseball through the window.

"It is amazing," Peltz said while managing his controls. "I have rotation."

"Confirmed," Komatsu said. "I was fairly sure when it orbited behind Wolf 1061c. When it came back around, and we were less than a million kilometers distant, it was certain. Looks to be a rotational rate of twice per minute. At 10 kilometers across, the object will have nearly a full G on the outer rim."

"Power?" Tina asked.

"Several energy sources registering on the EM spectrum. Nothing like the drive modules we have here, or the fuel cells."

"So, what is it?"

Komatsu shrugged. "The planet is putting out a fair amount of radiation, and with Wolf 1061 spewing out so much gamma radiation, everything is muddled. I'd like to be under 50 kilometers and in the same orbit. When it goes around the side opposite to the sun…"

"There's more risk," she countered.

"There's been no response," Ensign Albertson said at navigation. "I haven't seen so much as a radar wave. Radio either. I think it's a ghost ship."

"You're not the scientist," she reminded her.

"I agree with navigator Albertson," Komatsu said.

Tina chuckled. "Of course, you do. Chief Coopersmith, can you detect any serious threat?"

The older man rubbed his stubbly cheeks and made a grunting sound. "Nothing I can see."

"What about what you *can't* see?" she asked him.

He shrugged. "We're in unknown territory, skipper. You're asking me to be a psychic, not an engineer." He pointed at the alien construct blown up on a monitor, taking up the entire display. "That doesn't look like any spaceship I could imagine. If you're asking my opinion, it's a space station."

She turned to squint at the station. It lacked the uniformity of a snowflake. The various connections between the five major lobes extending from the hub were all distinct, like a sculpture.

She sighed. *First command and I get shit like this.* First command, last command, you had to take your chances. "Bring us in like XO says."

"Roger that, skipper," Peltz said and started the ship moving. There was no sensation with the SGD. A hundred miles an hour or a billion felt the same; nothing. "We'll get in a lower orbit and come up from astern."

"Sounds fine," Tina said.

"Captain Pendleton?"

Tina clicked on the nearest intercom. "Dr. Ortiz?"

"Yes, sir."

"How is E3 Hartwell."

"He's dead, sir."

Tina blinked. Confused. "Sorry, did you say he's dead?"

"Yes, I'm sorry."

"You said it was a routine appendectomy." Everyone else on the bridge stared in shock.

"It was, and everything was going fine. Then he coded, and we couldn't resuscitate him. Anesthesia has a degree of risk. We forget about that with starships and such, living on Mars and Venus." The doctor gave an audible sigh. "Maybe if we were back on Mars? By the time I diagnosed his condition we were almost here, and too far out to get back. Sorry, Captain."

"Not your fault, doc. You're an excellent doctor."

"I was back before the world destroyed itself. Now I feel like a primitive."

"Get me the death certificate ASAP so I can enter it in the log."

"Will do."

As *Acheron* began maneuvering for its rendezvous with the alien construct, sunrise dawned over the planet below. Dazzling, blood red light from the star filled the bridge, and everyone's thoughts.

As *Acheron* slowly gained on the alien construct Tina added E3 Hartwell's death certificate to the official log, and her list of firsts as a commander. Cause of death was noted as preliminary, and likely from a stroke. Dr. Ortiz had elected to freeze the corpse for an autopsy back on Mars, stating he lacked the necessary equipment.

Observations of the approaching construct, while still exciting amongst the crew, were now more somber because of Hartwell's untimely death. It wasn't just because he'd been the ship's cook. Hartwell had been popular, a friendly man of contagious exuberance who never failed to give a wave or kind word each day when you met.

Her report completed, she returned to the bridge. The alien artifact, once small and indistinct by the naked eye, had grown to consume much of the forward window and smaller details were becoming visible. "What are those spots?" she asked pointing and squinting.

Komatsu glanced up from his computers, grinning. "See for yourself." One of the main monitors flicked to a zoomed view of the artifact. The material of it was similar in color to lightly cooked marshmallows. In places the color varied from darker brown to lighter white. There was no way to tell which was normal. The interesting part was centered, a mottled green sphere.

"What is it?" she asked.

"Not positive," Komatsu said, "but it gives off the right readings to have a breathable atmosphere as well as a high likelihood of photosynthesis ongoing."

"Plant life?" she asked. He nodded. "Maybe animal life?" This time he shrugged. "You already suspected this."

"It was too inconclusive at that range. I rolled the dice."

"How do we get aboard?" she asked without giving it a second's thought.

"You sure?"

"Be nice to go home with something more than photos of a giant alien ice crystal."

He grinned even bigger. "We've found dozens of docking ports."

"Pick one next to a dome."

Docking proved easier than the approach. Bringing a ship the size of *Acheron* up alongside a station nearly as big as Phobos could be challenging. Phobos had the advantage, it didn't spin twice a minute. The docking points were all near the center, so they all rotated rapidly.

Peltz had *Acheron* down to 5 meters per second as he began spinning the ship to match the station. After a few minutes he was satisfied. "Spin is matched, we're 45 meters out. Ready for docking."

Tina nodded and turned to Coopersmith. "Chief, disengage the SGD."

"Roger that, Captain." He used his controls and an alarm sounded. "All hands, prepare for freefall." A second later the miracle drive disengaged, and they were in space's normal way of being.

Tina swallowed and resisted grabbing her chair as she drifted up until the belts caught her. She swallowed again and suppressed a moan. It had been quite a while since she'd zero-G qualified.

"All good, Skipper?" Peltz asked.

"Just get us docked, helmsman."

"Get docked, aye, aye." He had a little smirk on his face as he maneuvered the ship.

The closer they got the more it looked like Phobos. A strange, pale white tinged in blood red light stretched out of view in either direction. Tina concentrated on not puking as the ship crept closer, slowed, closer, slowed more, then stopped.

"Docking collar shows green," he said. "We have a hard dock."

Tina nodded. The system provided by the Vulpes was supposed to be universal. It appeared to be. But that also meant whoever built this station shared a technology base. A lingering concern floated to the surface in the back of her mind. "Try the drive," she said, and settled back into her seat. "That was fast."

"It wasn't me, Skipper," Coopersmith said, touching controls. "The station extended its field through the docking collar. Jesus Christ, *undocking!*"

The concern began to grow out of control. *What's he afraid of?*

He touched his controls, much faster than before. The same free-fall alarm sounded, except gravity didn't go away. He glanced at her and activated the sequence again with the same results. "Shit, shit, *shit*," he snarled and was out of his seat, heading aft.

Tina sat for a minute, her breath racing and cold sweat on her back. The sun rose again over the planet and flooded the bridge with blood red light. She hissed under her breath. A minute later she went aft to follow her engineer. She found him with the three other engineers under him, all the access panels around the airlock were stacked on the floor and test equipment was set up to the various cables and other parts.

"Anything yet?"

"Nothing good," Coopersmith said, shaking his head at some sort of oscilloscope. "It's going to take a few minutes to be sure, but…"

"But what, chief. Tell me."

"The station has taken control from our SGD. We're stuck here."

She made eye contact with each of her senior staff in turn, landing on Chief Coopersmith. "I need a timeline," she said. He didn't make eye contact. "Bary!" she snapped, and his eyes jerked to hers. "Timeline?"

"I can't say."

"You know more about the SGD than anyone aboard."

"Which is damned little."

Tina's eyes narrowed.

"You think I'm kidding? Skipper, where were you born?"

"Shangri la, Mars, 2020."

"I figured somewhere there abouts. You and most of this crew. I was born in Albuquerque, New Mexico. I was 10 when it hit. I went from grade schooler to survivor in the aftermath, all in a day, watching the world tear itself apart."

"Jesus, Chief, I didn't know. Everyone on the crew over 30 had to have been a refugee."

Komatsu raised his hand. "I was only four, but don't remember. Shrinks said PTSD."

"I was 25," Ortiz said. He was the oldest on the crew. "I was a corpsman on the *John Paul Jones*, a guided missile destroyer. Only been in the Navy 2 years. Was going to use my GI bill for medical school." He shrugged. "*Jonesy* was in the west coast flotilla and assisted in the Coronado operation. We had an outbreak of Strain Delta. A total of 29 crewmen died. One was my best friend. I used a scalpel to sever his spinal column. You never forget the howls the infected used to communicate. Never."

"There were 7.8 billion humans on Earth in 2020," Chief Coopersmith continued, his eyes wide. "A month later there were maybe a hundred thousand. If the Vulpes hadn't shown up in the middle of it all, we'd never have left the planet. You've seen satellite images?"

"I ran a salvage ship before being assigned to exploration," Tina said. "Part of the captain's track." The flights over decaying cities, crumbling bridges, busted damns. Radioactive plumes a hundred times worse than Chernobyl from Chinese reactors missing the safeties of their western counterparts. There were no survivors from that region of the planet. None.

Of everything, it was the hunters she remembered most vividly. Flying cover over salvage teams as packs of zombies they called "hunters" made attack after attack trying to reach them. Still driven by the same insanity that Strain Delta infused in them. The planet was lost, forever, returned to a primordial wilderness.

"Right," Coopersmith said. "I got my start working on those ships. We got 120 SGDs from the Vulpes. I worked with one of them, I think it was Glambring?" He shrugged. "Doesn't matter. They gave us just enough help so we didn't blow the fuck out of ourselves or fly a damned ship into a planet at supraluminal. I asked it once, what would happen if we flew into a star at that speed? You know what it did? Laughed. *No more star,* it said in its squeaky little fox voice. I think it was amused."

He looked into the distance for a moment, then shrugged. "They never gave us any of the physics behind the technology. How to stretch their abilities, or even calibrate them. But you know that, it's why we're out here 14 light years from home. We're like a couple monkeys that some dude gave the keys to his Corvette." Ortiz grunted and gave a half smile.

"What's a corvette?" Peltz asked, voicing the same question Tina had.

"It was an automobile."

"Oh," Tina said. "So, what are you trying to say about the reason we're stuck here?"

Coopersmith ground his teeth and spoke. "If you dock with another ship and link your SGD systems, the first ship to engage theirs controls both. It's something inside the alien cube that runs it all. They warned us about it, and we tested it to be sure. It's the absolute truth."

"Why didn't you warn me?"

"That thing didn't have a working SGD until *after* we docked. I think we accidentally activated it. Turning off our SGD is procedure because fields can act weird in contact with each other."

"So can you get us out or not?" Tina asked.

"I can sever the connections."

"Then do it," she ordered.

"If I do sever the connections, I can't fix them. The field gradient lines are made by a machine the Vulpes gave us. We haven't figured that out yet either. If I sever the connections, we'll get loose, sure..."

"And only have the rocket engines," Peltz said with a sigh. "I can get us up to 150 kilometers per second before the fuel runs out." He looked at her. "At that speed we'll be home in about a million years."

Tina cursed for a long time then looked down. Her tablet showed an image of the snowflake-like alien construct. "Any sign of life?"

"Just the SGD," Komatsu confirmed. "This isn't Star Trek; I don't have a magic life scanner. My people have been looking all over it for any movement. There aren't any windows except the domes, and they are opaque."

"Why?"

"Maybe to filter the light? Not sure."

She turned back to Coopersmith. "You confident you can deactivate any SGD?"

"Super easy, barely an inconvenience."

"Okay. Akio, let's get a boarding party together."

"What?"

"You heard me, XO. We go aboard, find the SGD, and turn it off." Komatsu looked floored. "Will that do it?" she asked her engineer.

"Yeah, it should. As long as ours is shut off."

"Okay. XO, let's get going."

"We are a skeleton crew," he complained.

"Many have cross training. Dismissed."

Tina was back to the airlock an hour later in her space suit, helmet clipped to her equipment belt. She found Coopersmith with seven other crewmen. With a ship as small as *Acheron,* she knew everyone aboard. Horner and Benton were both under Coopersmith in engineering. Specialist Alice Rico from supply, and Peron was a general mechanic. The last were friends, Bates, perpetrator of burned eggs, Kristina Urvi who was a maintenance rating, and Terry Sotos was an electrician.

The entire team was suited, like she was. Four of them carried pump shotguns from the ship's meager arms locker. She had an old Baretta semi-auto pistol with one extra magazine holstered on her equipment belt. The gun probably went back to the evacuation from earth. The surprise was seeing Komatsu come from the other direction. She immediately shook her head.

"We can't have both senior officers on this boarding party."

"With all due respect, Captain, I'm more qualified for this sort of mission than you are. I doubt you have more than a cursory class in xenobiology while it's one of my areas of study. So, unless you'd like me to insist you stay behind while I lead the boarding party…"

"Well played," she said. "You armed?" He patted a holster identical to hers. "Okay, let's get this over with. Coopersmith, you're in the lead."

"Yes ma'am," he said, lifting a portable instrument he'd taken from engineering. She knew it had something to do with the SGD, though God knew what that might be. "We need to get past the field interface so I can start figuring out where to go."

She turned to Komatsu. "The extra guns necessary?"

"We're in unknown territory. Nothing in the manual. Nothing from the Vulpes on who else might be out here." He shrugged.

"Point." She gestured at the airlock. "Let's get this done."

It opened faster than they did on the Mars stations. Maybe the lock was the Vulpes design, she wasn't sure. As it cycled there was room for five people at a time, so they entered in two groups. Coopersmith and his two engineers, Peron and Rico went through first. It took five minutes for it to pump out *Acheron's* atmo and refill it with the alien air. Coopersmith reported right away.

"All good," he said from only a few meters away. "Place is empty."

As soon as the lock cycled the rest went through. As the lock opened, she did her best to remain calm. They were entering an alien construct 14 light years from home. The door opened and she walked in. Her suit sensors said the atmosphere was breathable, high in oxygen while low in nitrogen. There was an unusual amount of argon.

The interior was…unremarkable. Nearly completely round and lit only by 10 wildly swinging suit lights. To Tina, the color shifted, no matter how she looked at it the tones seemed to change. Iridescent hues of green, or blue, or violet.

"It's pretty," Rico said, catching Tina's eye. The young E2 supply specialist grinned nervously.

Tina grunted and nodded. It was kind of pretty, she supposed. What amazed her more was how it could have been something humans made. She'd seen pictures of ancient space stations around Earth. They looked like a surplus storage bay on Mars, every square inch covered with bags of gear and everything else pillaged from a dead world to aid in their survival. This? This was more artistic than utilitarian. As Rico said, "pretty." Some of the nervousness fell away.

"Point the way, Coopersmith."

"Aye, aye, skipper."

The alien corridors managed to somehow convey comfort while simultaneously feeling wrong. You couldn't breathe the atmosphere of Mars, yet, so you went outdoors in an environment suit. Less bulky and capable than the spacesuits they currently wore, though you could never forget you were wearing one. The suit sensors kept reminding her she was wasting life support because the atmosphere outside was breathable. She silenced the alarm.

Most of her generation suffered from agoraphobia to one degree or another. Space didn't bother them as they commonly took their first trip off planet before they could walk. The alien corridors were so large it was triggering her own fear of open spaces. It just wasn't *natural* to have such an open space.

"I don't understand this place," Rico said, shaking her head. Others in the team nodded.

"Feels like someone is watching me," Peron agreed.

They'd only walked a few meters before Komatsu stopped.

"What's wrong?" Tina asked.

"We've lost comms with *Acheron*," he said, turning around and holding up an instrument.

Tina took a few steps back towards the airlock and tried her comms. "*Acheron*, boarding party, do you read me?" When nobody responded she took a few steps closer to the airlock and tried again. "*Acheron*, boarding party, please respond."

"*Acheron*, go skipper," Peltz voice responded. Just a meter closer and reception was perfect. She glanced at Komatsu who looked completely baffled.

"Aliens" he mouthed, and she let a little laugh escape.

"Radio check," she called. As the helmsman started calling out, Tina backed up. Halfway through the count the voice suddenly stopped. It looked like Komatsu was right. She moved back past the barrier, or whatever it was. "*Acheron*, there is some kind of interference, or barrier that's blocking transmission a few meters from the airlock. We're going to be out of comms for an hour or more while we find the SGD and deactivate it."

"Noted Skipper, do you want me to send a team over if you don't check in?"

"Negative, Peltz. There's nothing here, no signs of life yet. I'll send a runner if there's an issue."

"Roger that."

She walked back to the others. "Okay, let's go find the SGD."

Komatsu turned his device and pointed. "This way."

They quickly realized the alien construct was a maze with no sense to its construction. There didn't seem to be any doors at all, just endless curving corridors. Only minutes into the trek the party ran into a dead end. Everyone spent a while feeling along the walls for any hint of a door mechanism without success. They were forced to backtrack all the way to the airlock, then head the opposite direction.

"We're going the wrong way," Komatsu mumbled, shaking his head.

"Well aware of that," Tina said after she used the opportunity for a quick check-in with Peltz.

"Hey," Horner said, shortly after they were out of radio contact again.

"Yes, specialist?" Tina asked.

"Isn't it weird the station is almost exactly our normal gravity?"

"Feels just like *Acheron*," Benton agreed, nodding.

"Every SGD automatically makes this gravity," Komatsu said.

"Why?" Horner asked.

Komatsu cast an abused look at him.

"I mean, there has to be a reason, right?"

"Earth's gravity is 9.8 meters per second," Tina said as if she were reading from a text recording. "SGD's produce a steady 9.4 meters per second. Not quite our gravity. The theory is this was what the Vulpes home world's gravity was."

"Sure," Horner said. "But here we are on an alien ship with the same gravity." He made a gesture at the corridors wide enough for four men to walk abreast with ceilings equally tall. "There's no way this is a Vulpes station."

She was about to tell the engineer to stick to turning wrenches when Komatsu gave a grunt.

"He's got a point. A Vulpes is not much bigger than a terrestrial fox, hence our name for them. Their escape pods that crashed on earth weren't much bigger than a child's toy car. They would never make something this big."

Tina frowned. She'd met a couple of the Vulpes and considered those meetings the principal reason for her becoming an explorer, something her parents grudgingly approved of. The Vulpes were tiny. They could have moved 20 abreast down this corridor. Horner might be a loud-mouth agitator who was on report more often than not, but he had a point.

"Maybe there's a galactic standard gravity?" she suggested.

Komatsu shrugged. "The Vulpes neither confirmed nor denied there were other races out in the galaxy. We've only just begun serious exploration and found this the first time we went more than 10 light years from Sol. We can conclude many planets are colonized."

"But the planet here can't be colonized, you'd die instantly down there," Sotos noted. He'd been born on the Venus colony, using an SGD to float in the dense atmosphere at an altitude where a breathable, if cold, atmosphere existed. The world below was eerily like his world.

"Fascinating discussion," Coopersmith said in a voice dripping in sarcasm, "but maybe all you big brains should look at the door?"

A short distance ahead was the first door they'd encountered. And it was open!

Coopersmith gestured to Rico and Peron, both armed with shotguns, and the pair cautiously crept forward, looking past the doorway into the next compartment. Rico turned back and gestured with her unencumbered arm. "It's clear," she said. "Just as abandoned as the rest."

As everyone walked through the gigantic door, Horner took a second to examine the doorway itself. "Found the controls," he said. A small section of wall, roughly waist high, had slid seamlessly away to reveal touch plates. Komatsu and Tina exchanged looks; the controls were identical to the ones on the Vulpes ships. Tiny glowing glyphs set against an obsidian-like backing.

"So, this is Vulpes tech," Tina said.

"Or like I said, shared technology," he replied. "Coopersmith, you've got the most time with this tech?"

"Horner has more than I do. I'm more of an old-school rocket-jock. Horner, figure that out."

"Oh, don't ask much, do ya, chief?"

Horner griped a lot, but he was indeed able. After only a few moments and a couple experimental taps he figured out the process. When the door slid closed, so did the access.

"Uhm…" Tina said.

"No biggie," Horner replied with a chuckle. He placed his palm flat on the spot where the access used to be, and it reappeared. "The Vulpes tech is extremely user friendly, once you get the basics down." He looked the wall up and down, memorizing. "As long as we can guess where a door is, I can open it now."

When they continued, Horner started finding other doors intermittently, and the rooms they revealed were neither uniform, nor useful. It took another 15 minutes to find a cross corridor which finally led them in the correct direction, as indicated by Komatsu's device.

"I didn't know those things existed," Tina mentioned to her science officer while they waited for Horner to open another doorway.

"It's just a field effect sensor," Komatsu said with a shrug. "I grabbed it and adapted the system for our needs."

It was a simple explanation matching the situation. But over the next few minutes she got closer looks at the device. It didn't look adapted, it looked refined, and the question remained in her mind.

"We're getting close," Komatsu said when he noticed her looking at the device. At that moment, Horner found another door which opened to reveal neither another small unknown room nor a corridor. Reddish light flooded out as the door slid aside, casting the boarding team in a sickly, ethereal glow. They'd found one of the domes.

The interior was not so much a forest as a dense jungle of fronds, strange trees with leaves bigger than a man, and nearly impenetrable undergrowth, all of which appeared in shades of gray.

"In there?" Tina asked in a bemused tone.

"Yes," Komatsu replied.

"It's an alien jungle!" Rico said. She sounded almost giddy, and without asking, immediately ran inside.

"Hey!" Coopersmith barked. Too late, everyone except him, Tina, and stoic Komatsu had already followed her.

"Damn it," Tina said, then yelled. "Stay within view of each other."

"Looks like a park," Komatsu noted as he walked inside, following his enigmatic sensor device.

Tina and Coopersmith flanked to either side of the scientist, trying somewhat in vain to keep the rest of the team in sight. They'd only been in the dome for a moment when Komatsu's device let out a keening sound. It was instantly familiar to Tina, though not familiar enough to place. Her science officer turned, using the device like a compass, and set off.

"Slow up," she said and trotted after him. All the while she was taking in the alien plant life. *Alien* plant life. Her first mission and she'd located alien life. But who'd put it here, and why?

Tina lost view of Komatsu for a moment and abandoned her observation of the botanical menagerie to catch up to him. She'd been expecting some equipment, the control for the station's SGD. Instead, it was just Komatsu kneeling in a glade, the blood red light of Wolf 1061 flooded through the massive dome mixing with the various plant colors to create a truly alien tableau. Her science officer was kneeling over…something?

She approached quietly, the grass muffling her steps. Komatsu had set aside his instrument and instead had a material samples case. She blinked in confusion until she saw what he was leaning over. While confusing in its outlines, there was no mistaking decay and rot. Something was dead, something that had never seen the yellow sun of Sol.

"We hoped," he was mumbling under his breath, apparently not aware he was broadcasting on their private channel. "But I never thought we'd actually find a specimen."

"What are you doing?" she asked.

Komatsu gave a little jump at her voice, then continued with his task without interruption.

"I asked you a question, mister," Tina repeated with ice in her voice.

Komatsu gave a grunting sound as he used a pair of tongs to tear at the creature's skin. Only she realized it wasn't skin, it was clothing or a space suit. Whatever it was, it tore to expose grayish flesh. "Remember you noted how surprising it was I found this station?"

"Yes," she said impatiently.

"It was no coincidence," Komatsu said, using a scalpel to slice into the being and expertly excise a chunk of the strange colored flesh. "We're not the first ship out this far. Our scouts have been doing quick surveys of all the systems around us looking for any signs of ships or intelligent life. They found this station last year, but there were only two people on each scout. Not nearly enough to go aboard."

"Our scouts?" Tina asked, varying between confusion and disbelief.

"Well, yes. I work for Project Genesis." He'd split the sample into three pieces and secured it in three identical tubes, carefully sealing them before placing each in a belt pouch. "I know, you've never heard of it." He shrugged. "We've been around since the 1940s."

"You said yourself, you were a kid when the plague hit."

"I was using the empirical. I was recruited on Mars while in school, about the time you were born. Like I said, they were around since the 40s when the first aliens showed up."

Tina gawked; Komatsu shrugged. "Yeah, they called the Vulpes to Earth."

"And the Vulpes brought the plague that turned seven billion people into flesh eating zombies!"

Komatsu stood up and stared at her. "They said it was an accident. Maybe, but now we have a copy of Strain Delta not from Earth."

"How do you know that…alien had the zombie virus?"

"I said there weren't enough crew to board on the scout, I didn't say they failed to verify." He drew his pistol and in one smooth motion fired it into the ground twice.

Tina jumped in surprise as the rounds thudded into the dirt and loam, the sound of the blasts reverberated inside the dome. "What the hell are you doing?" she screamed.

His smile chilled her to the bone. "Clearing the way."

An alien screech reverberated through the dome, and then repeated by a different sounding scream, and another, and another.

Tina spun, searching for the source. She clumsily drew her own firearm.

"We saw them from through the windows," Komatsu explained. "It's a ghost station or ship, full of zombies."

"Why? Why kill yourself and all of us too?"

"Nobody is supposed to know," he said, then shrugged. "Orders, Skipper. But it didn't include killing myself." He took out a small apparatus and touched a control.

Her anger turned to shock as her suit hissed and the faceplate popped open. Alien air and the stench of decay flooded in as she held her breath and tried desperately to pull the visor back down.

"Captain, our suits are open!" Rico yelled.

"What the fuck?" Coopersmith said. "Me too!"

The air! The air would be full of the virus, they were all in danger of turning! All other thoughts blew out of her mind as she struggled to get the visor closed, but nothing worked. It wasn't until she heard one of her people scream, followed by the blast of a shotgun, that she remembered the more immediate threat. It was then she noticed Komatsu was gone.

"Get it!" she heard Coopersmith yell, followed by the boom of his shotgun.

"Coopersmith, on me!" she called back, and drew her ancient Beretta. It took a fumbling moment to remember her orientation class, and another to check the chamber. By the time she looked up from the now-loaded weapon Coopersmith was loping towards her with Sotos, Urvi, and Bates in tow.

"Where are the rest?" Tina asked.

"On the other side of the dome," he said, out of breath. He pointed. "There's another door, but these monkey things came down between us. They're just like the fucking zombies on Earth," he said. The older man, normally calm and collect, was white faced and his eyes were as big as saucers. An ancient terror was stalking him again.

"Can you hold it together?" she asked as he stopped next to them.

"You…you weren't there," he said. "You didn't near the armies of them, hunting, stalking, screeching."

Tina gripped the front of his open helmet and jerked, *hard*. "God damnit, mister, if we don't work together that will be the last thing you hear!"

It seemed to jar something loose. The man nodded and visibly struggled with himself. His eyes cast about. "Where's Komatsu?"

"Later," she snarled just as a hooting scream echoed from the nearest tree and a trio of the monkey things Coopersmith had mentioned came swinging at them. "Jesus!" She raised the pistol and jerked the trigger. Nothing. The hammer hadn't moved. *Safety,* she admonished herself and flicked it off with her thumb. The advanced spacesuits they wore weren't like the ancient ones before the Vulpes, when someone could barely hold a screwdriver. These were medium thick gloves. Even so, holding the weapon while moving her thumb up to snap the safety down took concentration.

As the safety finally clicked off, Coopersmith fired from hip level, his big 12-gauge shotgun sounding like a cannon right next to her. Tina jumped despite herself. One of the monkeys disintegrated in a storm of meat and green blood.

She raised her pistol at the second one, sights lining up on its head. It had a single huge eye with a wide slit pupil, like a reptile. She squeezed the trigger, a double-action shot they called it, and the Baretta bucked. It wasn't nearly as loud as the shotgun, yet it still put the alien creature down. The last of the three crashed right into Sotos' face.

Strangely jointed limbs moved in a blur and this time red blood flew. The electrician screamed and grabbed at the alien, trying to jerk it clear. Tina had just begun to move when Coopersmith's shotgun fired. *Boom!* The monkey thing was torn apart, along with half of Sotos' head, ending his screams.

"Coopersmith, what the fuck?" she screamed.

"They're infected, damn it!"

"Oh god," Urvi said over and over. "This can't be real."

Coopersmith mechanically fed shells into his gun, his mouth a thin white line.

"The door," she said. "Move it!" She started to take the lead.

"Let me, Skipper," Coopersmith said, raising the shotgun and trotting ahead of her.

Tina moved behind Urvi, taking the rear as they ran through the undergrowth and past alien trees. Her breath came in gasps, each intake bringing more of the unearthly smells to her nose along with more of the virus.

"Door," Coopersmith said, and they came to a stop behind him.

"Can you open it?"

"I'm pretty sure," he said. "I've watched Horner do it a dozen times now."

He got it, but only after a half dozen attempts. There was something, some component to working the mechanism Coopersmith struggled with. The door finally slid aside with the same silent motion as all the others, and they were back in the corridor. When Coopersmith went to close the door, he found the control smashed.

"Komatsu, you son of a bitch," Tina snarled and punched the wall just as a creature that was all legs and long arms with curved blades for fingers shot from the still open doorway and crashed into Kristina Urvi, sinking a dozen razor sharp claws into her chest.

Coopersmith grabbed Urvi's arm and tried to snatch her away from the attack. The claws had turned inwards so when Coopersmith yanked her back, they hooked and pulled out, eviscerating the maintenance technician who died in a spray of blood, organs, and a scream cut frighteningly short.

The creature tore into the spasming body, blood and gore flying in all directions. Coopersmith landed on his butt and raised his shotgun.

"Save it," Tina said, and hauled him to his feet. "Back to the ship, and I think it's this way. Move it!" As she got him up and moving, the sound of screeches grew louder from the dome they'd just left. She pushed Coopersmith into a run.

Just like the tales and rare videos from Earth, the zombies were relentless. The infected aliens hunted them, driven insane by the virus, motivated by some deep instinct to hunt, kill, and infect others.

"They're gaining on us," Coopersmith panted as he ran.

Tina could only nod, out of breath herself. She couldn't imagine what space missions were like before the SGD's gave basically free artificial gravity to any ship equipped with one. Just a couple weeks in zero-G made it stressful to even walk. She made a mental note to suggest deep space operations require a workout, then almost laughed out loud. Immediate survival was questionable, she'd worry about notes to command if she made it.

"I think this is it," Coopersmith said, huffing as he came to a stop. "The corridor leading to *Acheron* should be through here." The strategy to keep moving outwards had hopefully paid off. If they were right, of course.

Both quickly felt along the walls for an access panel. Tina cursed whatever alien had designed the damned station with hidden doors and controls. Maybe they weren't invisible to the aliens, or they just instinctively knew where to look? The wall suddenly moved under her fingers.

"Got it!" she called out.

Coopersmith ran over and entered a cryptic series of codes he'd seen Horner use. The door opened and they burst through. Coopersmith paused just long enough to unleash a blast down the corridor towards their pursuers. An alien scream told her he'd at least wounded one.

"This way," she said and forced her burning leg muscles into a run.

Present

The shotgun roared. In the close quarters of the corridor Tina felt it like a punch in the ears every time.

"Four rounds left!" Coopersmith yelled.

Benton tossed him a shell. "Now we're even," he said.

"I wouldn't go that far."

Tina touched the place on the door which had opened every other one so far, and nothing happened. They were blocked, again. Worst, she was certain this was the last door. At least she prayed it was. "Help!" she called.

Coopersmith glanced back at her, then at Benton, making a face. "Shit. Horner?"

"What?" Horner asked, his voice reedy and strained. His face was a white rictus of pain from his fractured ankle.

"Get the god-damned door."

"I...I can't."

"You can't hold a gun and shoot, so get the fucking door!" He stared at the Chief, eyes not focusing. "DO IT!" Coopersmith roared, and Horner stumbled past Tina, shoving her out of the way. Any thought of who he was shoving was gone from his mind, washed away by the agony in his leg. His face was ashen and sweating even in the cool alien atmosphere.

"I got it," Horner said, relief in his voice as the door slid open. He gave a little start and took a half-step back. "Rico?"

"Get back!" Tina screamed, raising her pistol and trying to slide sideways around Horner.

"Alice?" Horner said. "We thought you were dead!"

The person formally known as Alice Rico, supply specialist, looked at Horner, eyes wide and staring, their former blue now red with the bloody tears running from them. She cocked her head at his voice, never looking away.

"Rico, I-" Horner never finished what he was going to say because Rico lunged forward, expertly seized his head, and sank her teeth into his neck. The crunch of cartilage and ripping flesh was drowned out by gurgling screams.

"NO!" Tina cried and fired. The ancient pistol's recoil was surprisingly light. A tiny red hole appeared in Rico's forehead and a mist of blood sprayed from the back as her former supply clerk's life ended forever. Horner fell, spasming, his neck spraying blood like a shower head.

"Horner, buddy!" Benton yelled and sat the shotgun down to help his friend. A tentacle wrapped around his neck from behind and jerked him back and off his feet. It suckers must have been serrated, because blood poured from around the grasping appendage. Benton gurgled more blood and reached up, trying in vain to staunch the flow.

Coopersmith raised his gun at the squid-like monster reeling Benton in and squeezed the trigger. *Click.* "Fuck!" he snarled, dropping his empty gun and diving for the discarded shotgun.

Tina fired at the monster three times with no apparent effect as Benton reached its body and more tentacles began to rip him apart like someone tearing into a turkey dinner.

"Go!" Coopersmith yelled, pushing her towards the door where Rico and Horner's bodies lay. He blasted a round of buckshot into the horror shredding Benton and worked the pump. The creature screamed, threw the rest of the former engineer's body aside and swarmed towards him. "Get to the ship!" he yelled and fired again.

"I can't just leave you…"

"I'll catch up," he said, backing away from the creature and firing. "God damn it, get to the ship!"

Tina didn't remember jumping over the bodies of her former crew, or even which direction she turned. But somehow, she was at the alien ship's airlock alone. Only the distant sounds of the virus afflicted creatures reached her, and she couldn't tell if they were getting closer or not.

As she reached for her radio to have the crew open the outside lock, she saw it was already open. Approaching cautiously, Tina could see the inside door was open too. She lifted the pistol and stepped carefully into the ship just as the lock closed behind her. *Acheron* gave a bump as she undocked easily and began to maneuver. They'd never found the alien ship's SGD. There'd never been a problem after all. Another of Komatsu's lies. She punched the closed door once, rage filling her. Coopersmith could still be alive.

Tina turned towards the bridge, her pace quickening along with her anger. She didn't notice the corridors were empty as she moved. When she reached the bridge, she found it empty except for her XO. He turned at the sound of her entering the bridge. Her recognition of her XO also brought the realization that the ship's extra spacesuits had not been in the lock as they were when their boarding party left.

"You made it," he said, genuinely surprised, then focused on the gun she was still holding.

"Figured I'd be dead?"

"Honestly, yes."

"Where's the rest of my crew?"

"No clue, lock was open when I got here." He shrugged. "I think they went in after us."

Tina looked out at the front view that was still open. The blueshift of supraluminal speed was visible. "Turn us around, right now."

"Not happening, Captain. I have orders from higher-up."

She raised the gun and pointed at his chest. "That's an order, mister."

His eyes narrowed and she saw a side of him she'd never seen. Not quite anger, more like self-assured control. "Put the gun down," he said. "You made it, we're going home."

"We're infected," she said. "The whole ship was exposed. We don't dare go home."

"They'll have a Februus Device," he said, trying to sound comforting and taking a step closer. "They can neutralize the virus. Yeah, there's some risk…"

"More than some risk," she said as he took another step.

"So, we'll play it safe," he said. Another step. "Stop in the outer system and go through quarantine. What matters is we made it, and I have the undifferentiated virus." Another step and his eyes gleamed. "With this, Project Genesis can figure out how to control the infected."

"Control?"

"Think of it, an army of zombies fighting for us. Unfeeling, unstoppable warriors."

"And a ship full of dozens of aliens, all just as crazy as the infected we're used to, doesn't even give you pause?"

"I'll worry about that later." A final step. "Give me the gun, Captain," he said and lunged.

She was used to the sound of a gunshot in close quarters now. Komatsu staggered back, his eyes wide as his own gun fell from his left hand where he'd held behind his back. His right reached up to his chest to cover the red spreading quickly on his uniform.

"Y-you don't understand," he said, coughing and slowly falling to his knees.

"No," she said, "I don't care."

His eyes looked past her and his head shook. "I guess this is better," he said, almost a whisper, just before flopping face first onto the deck.

Tina took a step towards the helm controls then stopped. What had he seen? She spun around. Peltz was standing at the bridge entrance, staring.

"There you are," she said, holstering the gun. "Komatsu was…" her voice tapered off as Peltz cocked his head as if her voice was a strange sound. "What?" she asked as Peltz gave a primal scream and lunged for her. Tina cried out as she desperately tried to claw the pistol back out of its holster, all the while backpedaling as fast as she could, only to trip over Komatsu's body. Peltz closed. His eyes wide, and teeth gnashing.

"I say again, this is Mars traffic control calling *Acheron*, please respond."

The deck officer entered and crossed to the traffic controller. "What's going on?"

"*Acheron* appeared out of supraluminal five minutes ago. She came to a stop 5,000 kilometers out, just by the book. But they won't respond to hails."

The officer rubbed his stubbled chin, as he hadn't had time to shave before rushing in. "Have *Tempest* divert from its comet."

"They're due to drop tomorrow," the traffic controller reminded him.

"I'm aware, but this should only take a few minutes. Send the order. *Acheron* is the first of its class. Probably a comms malfunction."

"Divert *Tempest*, aye-aye, sir."

The young petty officer walked through the lock to *Acheron*'s outer airlock. The other ship's automated systems didn't respond to their computer's attempt to dock automatically. He plugged his manual comms jack into the receptacle and called twice. "Still no response," he called back to *Tempest's* captain.

"Use the external controls, Petty Officer."

"Activating external controls, aye," he responded. Opening the access door revealed all the correct lighted controls. Two buttons pressed and his ship's airlock latched on finally. With a hard seal, pressure began to return. "Good dock," he told his captain. Another button push, and *Acheron's* outer door slid aside. "We're in."

"Be right there," the captain said. His ship's inner door slid aside, and the captain arrived. "Now we can get some answers." The petty officer cracked his helmet seal with a hiss and racked the helmet in the airlock while the captain went to *Acheron's* inner door and commanded it to open. The door slid aside to reveal an empty corridor. Nobody was waiting for them. "This is odd," he said. "Damned odd."

The petty officer joined him, still in spacesuit but sans helmet. "Weird," he said. The captain nodded. Then the man coughed and backed up. "God, what's that stench?"

"If comms are out, maybe life support failed as well?" He sniffed the air and gagged as well. "Jesus Christ," he hissed and wished he'd suited up. Was everyone dead? Had they just boarded a ghost ship?

"Ahoy, *Acheron*," he yelled.

Only an echoing silence responded. He was about to yell again when a scream echoed.

"What the fuck?" he asked. Another scream. Something clicked. "God, get back aboard *Tempest!* Seal the lock!"

"I don't understand, Skipper? Hey, sounds like someone's coming."

"Move, damnit," the captain yelled and shoved his confused petty officer who promptly fell over the lock combing. The captain jumped over him and slapped the lock close controls, but they didn't respond. Handy sensors had detected the petty officer lying across the door. The captain grabbed his man and bodily dragged him clear.

As soon as the lock was unobstructed, he reached for the controls. A young woman wearing an officer's uniform appeared in *Acheron's* lock. Her eyes were wild and dried blood stained her uniform, including the lieutenant commander's emblem.

"Mother of God," he said.

She cocked her head at his voice, and before he could hit the close control again, she sprang. As the captain was borne to the deck, her nails and teeth ripping at him, two more people appeared in the *Acheron* and set upon the petty officer. The captain didn't have time to warn his crew—or anyone else.

"We're getting high enough in the building that the stars are quite visible from your balcony at night. Who knows what you will see, moving above us. Though she's been on assignment for some time, one of the residents on this floor is a ship's captain. I cannot wait to see what she brings us back from her latest adventure…"

* * * * *

They Burn Witches

by Declan Finn

For readers of the Saint Tommy, NYPD series, the following takes place after **Infernal Affairs,** *but before* **City of Shadows** *(Silver Empire / 2018, Tuscany Bay, 2023)*

I walked out of my partner's house, drinking from his "World's Best Dad" travel mug, when I found the dismembered corpse artistically displayed in the front yard. I didn't blink, flinch, or do a spit take with the insanely hot coffee. I merely sighed and sat down on the front steps. All of my partner's demonic troubles may have made me even more jaded than I had realized. I'd like to think that I was fairly hardened when I started this job, but a demon, a death cult, and a warlock later, very little fazed me anymore.

I grabbed my cell phone and dialed my precinct, only a few blocks away.

"Hey, boss. Packard here. This is me checking in. Could you send people down? Because we've got another body. This time it's out in the front yard. Heh. You think the medical examiner can find Tommy's house without directions by now? Thanks."

My partner was Detective Thomas Nolan, and that man was a saint. He was a Swiss Army knife of saintly superpowers. In the last few months, he had bi-located to put down a prison riot, levitated to escape an exploding building, and smelled evil on a possessed serial killer. When not being shot at, Tommy was known to open his house to any random homeless person he met, volunteer for every church function that didn't involve liturgical terrorists, acted as Eucharistic minister, and stood over the little old ladies who prayed outside of abortion clinics to make certain no one harassed them. Since getting married, he never even noticed other women, unless it was to act like a big brother to them, especially if they were part of a case.

And yet Tommy still wondered why those who knew him were nowhere near surprised that he had literal God-given superpowers. He once tried to explain to me that he had many sinful defects to his character, but I stopped listening before I laughed in his face.

My name? Detective Alex Packard. I am nowhere near a saint, unless I'm riding in a car with Tommy. I accidentally shot someone early on in my career, and never confessed to it until a demon threw it in my face. I had picked up a drinking habit shortly after the shooting. Fortunately, I stopped drinking decades ago, though I'm not against smoking, or partying on a Friday night. While I didn't have much outside of the job anymore (I hadn't seen my ex-wife or children in decades), I had picked up new hobbies—like chemistry and magic tricks. You might think those are odd things for a man my age to pick up. However, I didn't have any of Tommy's superpowers (okay, they're called charisms; I looked it up) and I was usually right next to him when he went up against bulletproof bokors, demonic serial killers, and warlocks. When the odds stack up like that, I prefer to have a homemade hand grenade in my back pocket.

Of course, being so good, pure and virtuous, Tommy made so many powerful enemies that he had to leave New York City. Hey, find me a politician that *couldn't* be easily mistaken for Satan and get back to me. Though Tommy and I had found so many Satanic left-wingers I had taken to calling them Demoncrats (in New York City, you try finding a Republican, Satanic or not). The only politician I ever voted for anymore was a Queens councilwoman who had sung "God Bless America" in public. I presumed she wasn't possessed, but that was as far as I got.

As Tommy went around the world on "intelligence work," I stayed in his home. His stint abroad was only supposed to be until every dark-web bounty on his head had been pulled down, or everyone knew that the man who had posted the bounty was deader than disco. I should know—I had seen him dragged to Hell.

The first patrol cars showed up in a matter of minutes. It wasn't surprising. Since I had started house sitting, it had become a common call out. Every week or two, someone came knocking, usually armed.

This was the first time someone else had been left on the doorstep.

I lit a cigarette and watched as the patrolmen secured the scene. If this had been yet another attempted assassination on Tommy, very little about the scene made sense.

Why kill someone here? I thought. *I didn't know there was a range on magic. If this was a hit on who was in the house, why don't I even feel ill?*

Once the crime-scene tape went up, I downed the last of my coffee, placed the mug on the stairs, and rose. *Time to make the doughnuts.*

I strode to within a few feet of the corpse. When I said it was decorative, I wasn't joking. The mutilated corpse had been stripped and disarticulated. The body parts had been arranged similarly to da Vinci's *Vitruvian Man*. There were markings carved into the skin, from the soles of the feet to the palms. At a guess, they were made with X-Acto knife. If I were forced to describe the markings, I would say that the last time I had seen something like it, it had been the markings on Sauron's One Ring… or on Northern Parkway in the Hasidic neighborhoods.

Given the streaks of blood, the victim had been alive when she, he, or it had started cutting. I immediately made a note that I wanted the ME to run a toxicology screen. There was no way someone could be this exact with a live, struggling victim. Though a good dose of ketamine or curare would have done a good job of keeping everything still.

You'll note at this point that I have not yet referred to the victim as a he or a she. There's a good reason for that—all the relevant parts were missing. On the chest, two bloody gashes of skin were missing. There was no groin. Someone had cut from hip to hip and removed that part of the lower trunk. Also, did I mention that the head was missing?

The corpse … okay, the pieces of corpse … lay in the center of a circle on top of a pentagram. The mark was probably made with human blood, given how it turned from red to black. I didn't start joking about witches just yet … I needed to save the remarks for someone who could appreciate them. Tommy may not have enjoyed my snark, but he at least understood what I was talking about.

Luckily, within 30 minutes, Doctor Sinead Holland, Medical Examiner, pulled up. I must admit to a deep and abiding crush on the good doctor. She had a heart-shaped face, brunette hair down to her shoulder blades, and distinct smile lines whenever she was happy. Her dark chocolate eyes contrasted with the ME's office pale. And for being somewhere in her forties, "shapely" is the best, cleanest word to describe her figure.

Sinead gave me a smile and a wave as she slung the pack over her shoulder. As she closed, she could see the corpse, and her smiled faded. Her face was neutral as she approached. She came to a stop just outside the tape, and looked from the corpse to me, and back again.

Sinead sighed. "Why is it that you never get *normal* cases anymore?"

I shrugged. "I blame Tommy."

Sinead rolled her eyes and crossed the tape. "He didn't cause anyone to dabble in the demonic."

"I know that. I just said I blamed him."

Sinead stepped around the crime scene and the Crimes Scene Unit. She studied the corpse closely.

"Does Ziplock make body bags in 'arm' and 'femur' sizes?" I asked.

Sinead ignored me. That was for the best. She didn't want to wet herself from laughing too hard.

I looked around, considering the street. It was a knight's jump away from a major intersection, which meant that the street was two houses off of one main road and paralleled another. At five in the morning, when I fell out of bed, I hadn't heard anyone outside—and after the first bounty hunter knocked at the front door, trust me, one noticed such things.

I hovered while Sinead examined the body up close.

Figuring that the best time to do this would be at … two in the morning? The best way would be to kill the victim elsewhere, drain the blood, bring the parts, do some arts and crafts on the sidewalk, layout the parts, then drive away. If the location was so important to them that the body had to be placed right here, *I wonder if all this ritual had to be done nearby. If not, then the crime scene could be anywhere. If it needed to be nearby, then I'm looking for a mobile crime scene.*

I grabbed one of the uniforms and read his name tag quickly. "Tinney, I want you, your partner, and any other unis you can get your hands on to go out, canvass the neighborhood, and find any of those little doorbell cameras, home security cameras, something. We'll need their footage. I think we're looking for a panel van, or some kind of covered truck."

Tinney frowned. "Why?"

I gave him a look. "Are you new here?"

"Um … yes?"

I glared at him. "Are you asking me or telling me?"

Amy Gibbons, who I knew on sight, strolled up. "Leave my boot alone, Packard. You're not allowed to ruin his life. That's my job."

I sighed. He was a rookie. *Geez.* "Sorry, at my age, all you kids look alike."

Amy rolled her eyes. "Come on, boot."

Tinney raised a hand. "Why are we looking for a van?"

I pointed at the pieces. "If he was cut up nearby, you don't want to try it in the back seat of your sedan. Any other questions?"

Tinney looked to his training officer. "We're going to cover the *entire* neighborhood?"

Good God, I hope I was never this stupid. I pointed. "The nearest highway is three blocks that way. How about you canvass every possible route from here to there?"

Gibbons took Tinney away before the conversation went dumber. Hopefully, the kid learned something eventually.

I sat on the front steps, then I went into my smartphone and scanned recent police reports. Some news made it back to me. Some didn't. My precinct was small, and on the outer edge of New York City—Eastern Queens, to be precise. We referred to Manhattan as "the city." My last source for really juicy gossip across the city had been gunned down in the lobby of our precinct by Internal Affairs when she'd tried to claim the bounty on my partner.

It took me about fifteen minutes of searching to find something that piqued my interest. I looked up and called over, "Hey, Sinead. Come here a second."

She waved her assistants to continue bagging and tagging the body parts. "What is it?"

I turned my phone around to show her. "Any idea what this is?"

Sinead took the phone and studied the police reports. "Stupid kids playing stupid games is what it looks like."

I shook my head. "Stupid kids only vandalize graves during October, not January. The ground's too cold and too hard to go digging. What if I told you that the last time something like that happened, in that graveyard, was the same day that you came over for dinner and we had uninvited guests?"

Sinead became very still and very silent. She didn't need to think about it very hard. Sinead had come over to dinner that night because The Incident in question was when a bokor—a Voodoo necromancer—had broken in, bringing a small squad of zombies with him. It would have ended very differently if a local truck driver hadn't been speeding through the intersection and turned the zombies into paste.

The zombies in question had all come from Mount Olivet Cemetery. According to my internet search, Mount Olivet Cemetery had just been vandalized the other night.

Sinead nodded to the corpse on the sidewalk. "This one can't be from a cemetery. It's too fresh."

"I know. Which makes me worried."

I glanced over at the body. Who else was connected to the zombie attack? Tommy and his family were out of town. I was still alive. So was Sinead. It was too small to be the corpse of the truck driver who'd come in at the last minute and saved us from being murdered. But that didn't mean anything. He could have been next.

"One second," I told her. I texted Internal Affairs Detective McNally. He and his partner Horowitz were on almost-permanent assignment to my partner's life. If anyone had the contact information we wanted for the truck driver, it would be them. I looked back to Sinead. "That'll take a minute. If you had to guess on who or what that was, what would it be?"

"Male. I think," she told me. "Other than that, I don't have a guess. I may be able to reconstruct the fingerprints. They were also carved into."

I frowned, not liking any of this. "When would you be available to carve into the body yourself?"

Sinead paused. The usual speed on autopsies in New York was variable. On the one hand, they were time consuming. On the other, New York City's murder rate was under 300 a year. The paperwork alone would crush some people.

Finally, Sinead answered, "Four hours? Maybe five? I'll have to move things around. I know when this stuff happens, it's more of a rush job than usual."

I concurred. When this happened, someone was going to be shooting at me soon. "I'll have Father Freeman meet us there. He might be able to translate some of those symbols for us."

My phone vibrated. McNally had gotten back to me with the number for the truck driver mentioned above.

I dialed. It took a moment.

Then a police officer answered the phone.

Truck driver Ben Nettles had had a run-in with someone the night before. And it happened in my precinct's jurisdiction. Homicide Detective Perry Kinney had the case.

I left the crime scene to the CSU and the ME and took a brisk walk to the station. I made it to the front lobby in ten minutes.

Detective Kinney had Ben Nettles in handcuffs, arrested for murder one.

Given the circumstances, my greeting was simple, elegant, and direct.

"What *the fuck* is your problem, Kinney?" I bellowed loud enough so the entire station heard me. "You're not busy fighting off six other lawsuits? You have to go looking for more trouble, you moron?"

Kinney, the weasel-faced fat bastard, scoffed and clapped Ben on the arm. Had he clapped any harder, I would have written him up for physical abuse. "We have this guy! He confessed! He shanked a woman and claimed it was self-defense."

Ben winced and opened his mouth. "But—"

Kinney raised his hands like they were clean, instead of covered in powdered sugar. "Out of my hands. It's the DA's call now." He grinned like he had just pulled one over on somebody. "But his knife is a deadly weapon. Might as well be carrying a gun."

"I'm a trucker," Ben exclaimed. "It's legal in Tennessee. I use it to open boxes! I didn't know you guys were idiots."

Kinney maneuvered his bulk around to his seat. "Ignorance of the law is no excuse," he taunted.

I facepalmed, took a deep, slow breath, and fought the headache building behind my eyes. I wanted to explain that the "ignorance of the law is no excuse" ruling came from a time before there were more laws on the books than there were people in the country. Reason and rationality was not the way to break through to Kinney.

Trucker Ben, however, still thought he could break through to the idiot. "Is it illegal to stop someone from trying to kill me?"

"With *that* knife?" Kinney answered. "Yes."

I slowly let out my breath. *Okay. Fine. Time to play.*

Trucker Ben Nettles was a nice person. A pleasant person. He believed you could break through to people with reason and patience.

I didn't have any patience. It was time to throw rocks. It was the only way to break into the man's head.

"Kinney. Did you … by *any* chance … check up on your 'victim' anytime since last night?"

Kinney looked at me like I was an idiot. "Of course not. Why bother? I got her statement. This man accosted her for sex, she declined, and he attacked her."

I nodded slowly. "And you've talked to the CSU team since then?"

Kinney waved it off. "Why bother? It's open and shut."

I smiled. My headache started to dissipate. I worked better when I gave migraines to other people. "If you had bothered to reach out to any of them—as I did in the ten minutes it took to walk to the station—you would realize that your 'victim' is missing from the hospital, the contact information she gave you belongs to an empty lot, and the CSU team found a Bowie knife under Ben's truck. So you have no 'victim' for Ben's crime. It's likely he's the *actual* victim. And you've arrested the wrong guy and let the criminal go free. Any questions?"

Kinney's mouth hung open. He leaned forward and pointed at me as though ready to deliver the world's most profound retort.

Kinney was spared by his phone ringing.

I clasped my hands behind my back and nodded at the phone. "You're gonna want to pick that up. You see, I also spent ten seconds on the phone with ADA Carlton with all the information I just told you."

Kinney's eyes bugged out of his head as he scrambled for the phone.

While he was busy, I pulled out my handcuff key and unlocked Ben. Kinney was going to be busy for a while. I knew Carlton. He spoke in paragraphs and amicus briefs. I loved the guy, but *man*, could he talk.

I walked Ben over to our station rec room. It was lit with a naked fluorescent bulb, making the bare concrete walls look even less hospitable for human habitation. But that didn't matter—I wasn't human, I was a cop.

"So, Ben," I started, "Tell *me* what happened."

Ben frowned, confused. "Aren't you going to offer me coffee? I thought that's why we were talking here."

I dismissed that with a wave. "Hell no. You want police coffee? Are you a masochist? I think I have a Dunkin' coupon if you want coffee." I reached into the small refrigerator that Tommy had bought the station and offered a Pepsi to Ben. "Now, what happened?"

Ben shrugged. "I'm not sure. I was on my usual route up 222nd last night when a car was pulled over to the side of the road with lights flashing. The plates were … I don't know where they were from, but they weren't local. I figured whoever it was didn't know they were a few blocks from a police station. I got out to tell her, and that's when they both jumped me."

"Two of them?" I asked.

Ben nodded. "They both had really big knives. One was a Bowie, I know that, and the other was … odd. Black handle. Double-edged like a dagger. Though it looked like a six-inch sword. And it had a silver inlay. That was a star with a goat's head inside? I think?"

I made a mental note of that. Then decided to move on. I wanted to know how he got away from the two knife-wielding women. I looked him up and down. He didn't seem too badly beaten, but he moved stiffly from the moment I had taken him out of the chair.

"I know our chairs are uncomfortable, but I didn't think they were that bad. Did they get you any?"

Ben nodded. "I cut one of them with my knife. The one who claims I came after her? She dropped the knife, and the other one slammed me up against the cab of my truck. She was strong for someone her size. I mean, *really* strong. She tossed me one-handed, bro. That was insane. And then …" Ben drifted off, and his eyes became fixed and glassy. I snapped my fingers in front of him to bring him back.

"Yo. Wake up. What is it?"

Ben smiled awkwardly. "You see, I kinda … stopped. The other woman just sorta stared at me, you know? I couldn't do anything."

I kept myself calm as my heart rate spiked. The knife had been a big red warning sign. Now the klaxons went off and the red shirts dove for cover. I wasn't the expert, but *pentagram with goat* and *instant paralysis* changed my hoped-for analysis—that these were idiots playing at being supernatural—and shifted it to the worst case scenario.

Worst case scenario being *Here we go again.*

Which left one question. "So you didn't actually escape?" I asked.

Ben shrugged. "Does a speeding car count?"

I paused and thought about it. One was in the hospital, not two… but there wasn't a second "victim" in Kinney's report. "Who did it hit?"

"Both of them. It was another truck. Damn near hit me, too. One girl went flying, the other didn't."

And they both walked away, I concluded. *Not zombies, they'd be a little more dead. Even Kinney would have noticed if the victim was a mobile rotting corpse. I hope. And zombies don't come with their own power… that I know of. Wendigo? Nah. They're cannibalistic. No bite marks on the victim this morning.*

"Does this have anything to do with that thing from January?" Ben asked.

I opened my mouth to answer him, then paused. *Good question. Maybe I'm looking at this backwards. Perhaps this has less to do with Tommy, and more with the powers brought to bear against him. Power was used to raise the dead in Mount Olivet, there're shenanigans there. Those zombies were destroyed at Tommy's doorstep, so there's a body there …*

I locked onto Ben's stricken expression. *And Ben had run over those zombies with his truck. Perhaps he was supposed to be killed last night… for revenge, or to add pep to whatever they were doing?*

"I have no idea," I told Ben. "But I promise you, I'm going to find out."

I walked Ben back to Kinney's desk. Kinney was full of bluster and halfhearted apologies. I left the two of them to work out what would happen next. With luck, all they would want is Kinney's badge … or his head on a plate. Either worked for me.

I went to work using the greatest investigative tool known to man … DuckDuckGo.

Don't laugh. We didn't need a warrant for things posted on the internet. I await the day when it's common for murderers to live stream their kills on Facebook because they think their privacy settings will protect them.

But twenty minutes later, I had a pattern—and it was disturbing. Most of these were murders that local governments tried to keep quiet. The stories were successfully put down because there were no *local* repeat murders.

There was a body recently discovered at a home in Perth Amboy, New Jersey. It was an overpriced neighborhood, and well hidden, the way some wealthy neighborhoods were. If you didn't know where it was, they didn't want you. The body was desecrated and killed in a ritual similar to the corpse I tripped over.

The home had belonged to a bokor who tried to kill me and Tommy.

A few days later, there was a shanking at Rikers Island, home to ten thousand or so felons. It didn't make the newspapers because … it's a shanking at a jail. Who cared? As for the arts and crafts with blood for the medium? It was written off as a Latin American gang, probably MS-13. Santeria wasn't uncommon among some of the gangs. So pictures were taken, notes were made, and it was promptly kicked over to homicide. Given that there wasn't a lot of pressure to solve the murder of a random skell in the pen, it was investigated for two days, then lost in a file drawer. It wasn't a cover-up, *per se*, just laziness permitted by apathy.

However, Rikers had been the scene of a mass possession and riot. The victim had been a perp Tommy disabled during the riot, one who had been possessed at the time.

Then the desecration of Mount Olivet cemetery.

Then this morning's corpse.

If you're wondering, the bokor I keep mentioning had been dealt with by my latest hobby: chemistry. Chlorine trifluoride burns concrete and sets sand on fire and would ignite at room temperature. It did a neat job on bokors, too.

This was all disturbing. Though, the really disturbing part was that I think I knew where they were going next.

That was the *where*. All that was needed was the who, how, what, and why?

Hopefully, those answers could be found at my appointment with Sinead and Father Richard Freeman.

The next several hours were spent catching up on paperwork. It was a way to keep busy while I waited on the identification of the victim. Or an identification of what was going on with the bizarre rituals.

The last fifteen minutes before I left were spent with my lunch. At least part of my lunch. I had brought in an orange with the rest of my brown bag. It made for great target practice with my playing cards. If you've never seen a trick, the magician takes a pack of playing cards—undoctored, untampered, not unusual at all—and flings them into an orange with a snap of the wrist. The playing card slices into the orange like a knife. If you ever wondered how it's done, the trick is literally all in the wrist motion.

Normally, I would prefer to chew my own arm off than fill out a DD5, or "daily" report. But whenever I worked a supernatural case with Tommy, they were a source of fun. I got to practice my fiction as I converted crazy to fit into the box of red tape we dealt with. I wrote up the case notes and kept the details as sane as I could. No matter how "open minded" New York claimed to be, "cemetery ritually disturbed for zombie attack" didn't fit on a DD5. But "pattern of behavior aligns with scene of the crime for various cases, as cited in the below case files" worked just fine. Ben's assault was written up as "perpetrator held victim at knife point" (true) "until scared off by passerby" (which sounded better than "run over by truck").

Yes. My partner was a saint, but there was a reason I did the paperwork. I could write up the events with a straight face, and bend the truth until it was a pretzel, and not be accused of lying. Tommy was a bit too honest for that.

After the paperwork, I signed out a car to get to the ME's office. Father Richard Freeman met me at the front door of the plain bunker of a building. At the end of the day, every morgue is basically a glorified refrigerator wrapped in concrete.

Father Freeman, however, was dressed in his basic black and dog collar. He was a nebbishy sort of priest. His wire frames were so thin, they were almost invisible. His hair was graying, and his nose looked like it had been stolen off of Woody Allen. He was slender, of medium build, and not all that tall. Or as the ABP would put it, "middle aged Caucasian male, medium height, medium build, starting to gray, wearing a priest's costume, carrying a manila envelope."

We shook hands, and Freeman smiled at me. "At least we know Tommy didn't attract this one."

I scoffed. "Nah. These are rats attracted to the last faint vestiges of Tommy still in the area. So, still his fault."

Freeman rolled his eyes, but with a smile. So he knew where I was coming from. "Shall we?"

I nodded and let him lead the way. This wasn't his first trip here.

We were led to Sinead by one of her staff. She was over our corpse *du jour*, more or less reassembled on her table. "Welcome, all. Have a good trip here?"

I shrugged. "Productive. Whaddaya got?"

"White male. No ID on the body and ketamine in the blood, for starters. Explains why he didn't move while he was being cut."

I winced. It was a glorified paralytic. Someone explained to me how people used it as a street drug, but my eyes glazed over, and I mercifully blacked out. Or I just spent the time remembering the baseball game. Either way…

Freeman winced. "Not crucifixion, but hardly a tickle."

Sinead nodded. "I think they used something like an X-Acto knife. These are some precision cuts, and they took a lot of patience."

I leaned close to some of the incisions and nodded. "And time."

Sinead made a negative hum. "Not quite," she explained. "Look at the thumb on each hand."

I grimaced. "Do I have to?" I asked before I bent over to look at the cut flesh. It was a strange little symbol that looked like a lowercase "m" where the tail end of the letter dropped and formed an inverted capital "T."

One on thumb, the "T" leaned to the left. On the other thumb, it leaned to the right.

"Oh no," I muttered.

Sinead nodded. "Exactly. Two different people, at least. I'd have to get a handwriting expert down here, but if I had to guess, this guy had at least four people working on him at once."

I winced again. I didn't want to imagine what happened to some of the missing body parts. I would have asked, but Sinead had endlessly told me to not ask her about what *wasn't* there. "And you're sure it's a *he?*"

Sinead nodded. "Hips don't lie. Or the ribs. It's easier to see when it's not all covered in blood."

I looked to Freeman. "I think that's your cue. In the immortal words of the bard—dafuq?"

The priest rolled his eyes at my colorful expression. He placed the manila envelope aside. "Those were printouts of the photos you sent me. Though I guess we don't need them. The script is called *passing the river.* It's a Hebraic, Kabbalistic writing system derived from ancient Hebrew—the river being the Euphrates."

I arched a brow. "I'm certain the Hebrew Hammer didn't do this."

Freeman looked at me over his glasses. "Nowadays, if you're not Jewish, it's most likely witches."

Sinead and I exchanged a look. "You mean *Wicca?*" Sinead asked.

Freeman shrugged. "They use it as well, but I don't think your standard hippy-dippy neo-pagan did this. No. They generally don't know what they're doing until it's too late. I mean *witches.* The not-safe-for-network-television kind." He paused. "Okay, Freemasons use it as well, but I don't recall the last time they had a human sacrifice."

I was taken aback, furrowing my brows. "And you get a lot of *witches* killing people?"

Freeman arched a brow. "In Europe? Often enough that they have occult bureaus in police departments throughout the continent. Here? Depends on who you ask."

I think I was better off before I asked that question. "Okay then. Any idea what the end goal of all of this is?"

Freeman shrugged. "I'd need more data. Or more time to translate all of this."

I looked to Sinead. "Doctor?"

She also shrugged. "All I can tell you is that the disarticulation was very neat. Someone either has a medical degree, or a lot of practice."

I sighed. "I can vouch for the practice."

I explained the crime scenes at Perth Amboy, Rikers and Mount Olivet and how they tied in with our body.

When I was done, Sinead frowned. "And no one knows about the connection between the four crimes scenes except for us."

I shrugged. "I wrote it up as being connected by the type of rituals at the crime scene. Obviously, the body in Rikers wasn't nearly as cut up as ours is. That one could have been handled by one person. I…"

I was going to go into a little more detail about the Rikers Island body, but Father Freeman looked pensive. He also hadn't said anything since I explained about the other crime scenes. "Something, Father?"

Freeman's brow was furrowed, and his face locked into a scowl. "The use of an athame dagger, the locations of the murders, the rituals around them ... these witches could take the power of the dead."

I blinked. My brain had gone full blue screen of death. "Um ... define?"

"This is a way of not only taking the power of the victim, but also sucking up any supernatural residue that had been left behind by previous acts. Once they take this power, they absorb it into themselves, and become as strong as the undead, without ever becoming undead."

I blanched. It fit with the attack on Ben, but it was the last thing I wanted to hear. It was bad enough when they had a paralytic touch. I had dealt with one bokor, and barely walked away. This sounded like the threat of ...

"How many?" I asked.

Freeman shrugged. "There's no way to tell. From your description of the attack on Ben, we know at least two of them have already absorbed the power; otherwise one would have bled when Ben cut her. And they both would have died when the truck hit them. Perhaps at least two per body? The energy is absorbed into an elixir. They drink it, they gain the power. The only question becomes if they've spread it around the coven, or if they used it to power individuals."

"That's four crime scenes," I told him. "You telling me that we've got four super-powered witches?"

Pearson nodded. "At least that many. We have no idea how many others are in the coven, or how many other incidents there have been like this nationwide. There's no way for us to tell."

I didn't say anything, because there may have been a way to tell. Ever since my life had become an Urban Fantasy novel without the sex scenes, I had become a connoisseur of insane factoids in news stories. A cult that had built an underground pyramid beneath a health clinic. Rumors about a dragon the size of a cow at a football game in Athens, Georgia. A prison breakout that had looked like a war, but no trace of explosives or artillery. That didn't even count two incidents at Mount Olivet that had happened *before* Tommy had these bizarre powers.

I made a mental note to start scouring the country. If these people had been at it a while, this could be several magnitudes of suck. At least Nazgul-level bad.

"I'm going to need a bigger boat," I muttered. I focused on Sinead and the good Father and said, "At least we know where they're going to go next. They've been working eastward. We know their next stop."

I looked to Sinead. "And you, good Doctor Holland, will need to help me with the next step." I smiled at Freeman. "In fact, so will you."

I had hoped there were only a few witches. Maybe half a dozen.

So, of course, with my luck, there were eighteen of them.

From my research of murders across the country, at least six of them were super-powered.

The witches came at night. They walked into the Nassau County morgue with little problem. This was, in part, my fault. I had the security guard take the night off. He seemed to think that we had more than work on our minds. As long as he got the heck out of the line of fire, I was happy to let him think whatever he wanted.

The Nassau County morgue was special for several reasons. The main one being how big it was. Given its proximity to JFK Airport, the capacity was meant to hold the combined victims from two fully-loaded 747 airplanes.

The second thing that made it special was an incident that had happened back in January, when the bokor had raised every corpse and body part in the entire morgue, causing it to look like a zombie movie. It had been Sinead's introduction to the wonderful world of Saint Tommy, NYPD.

The first one to enter the main room with all of the drawers was one Tanya Grant. She was medium-sized and athletic, with dark hair, olive skin, and a heart-shaped face. She scouted each part of the building before waving the rest of her crew in.

The next one into the main morgue was Sonja Black. She was Hispanic, with lips that Angelina Jolie would have envied.

The third one was Zoe Kull. Imagine Alyssa Milano, only if she hadn't aged well. (Personally, I want JK Simmons to play me in the movie.)

The next fifteen piled in and ... I presumed they were all female, but it was hard to tell. They all had long hair, but their features were various stages of distorted.

Tanya Grant looked around the morgue as everyone piled in. She frowned the entire time she was in the room. She didn't seem to like the smell of it, or the way the floor was covered in a thick, sticky substance that resembled Vaseline.

"Did someone have an accident?" Grant asked aloud.

The other witches paid her no mind. She looked at the barren morgue. There were no gurneys. No chemicals. No chairs. No furniture. The tile beneath the sticky substance was charred and blackened from a previous fire (we had to cover up the first zombie attack somehow).

Grant's head snapped to, and she shot ramrod straight. She waved her hands in the air and screamed, "There's no power here! And the room's been cleared out! It's a—"

I presume the next word out of her mouth was supposed to be *trap*, but it was too late. We signaled an old pager connected to a pile of magnesium flash powder in the corner of the room. The pager ignited the flash powder. It burned white-hot for just a second. But that second was more than enough to ignite the jelled substance that covered the floor.

The jell was made of pounds of Styrofoam melted into gallons of gasoline.

The jell is commonly referred to as homemade napalm.

I had had eight hours to prepare and an all-access pass to a hardware store—this made me very dangerous.

The morgue floor turned into an inferno. A cry rose up from the witches inside. Three panicked and fled for the door. Sinead had locked it right behind them. I added a chain to make sure no one could telekinetically kick the door open.

I didn't pay much attention to what happened inside once the inferno started. One of them had made the mistake of Stop, Drop, and Roll—which didn't help when rolling around in what put them on fire.

After twenty seconds of this, some of the witches *really* ignited. The flames turned blue, and the flames came from inside them. Their own power now added to the blaze and consumed them entirely…

But there was one corner of the room where there were witches, but no blue flame. Eight of them stood amidst the flames, unscorched and unscathed. Well, maybe they were a *little* scathed. Their clothes had burned away, revealing some model-perfect naked bodies. Three of them were the first into the room—Grant, Black and Kull. The others were some of the disfigured … who I noticed were some of the least disfigured.

They have A-class bodies and D-class faces and are impervious to fire. They've been sharing the power, but not with everybody. The remaining are the witches with all the power-ups.

I grabbed my shotgun off the floor and handed Sinead's to her. "Run."

We were only a few feet away when the doors blew off the hinges.

"I think they're pissed," I muttered.

We got to the end of the hall. I took a step, pivoted, and dropped to one knee. I raised the shotgun at the ready.

The first witch stepped out—Tanya Grant. Her dark eyes locked onto me … and she smirked. She didn't fear the shotgun any more than she feared the flames. She raised a finger at me and opened her mouth. Probably to curse me.

Before she spoke, I fired the shotgun three times.

With the first impact, Grant stopped smiling. She probably noted that the first blast was holy salt.

The next shell was full of buckshot. It blasted her full in the chest. She staggered, her eyes wide. The buckshot had left holes in her skin. She bled, though not as much as she should have with a kill shot.

Crap. The salt didn't make as much of a dent in her as I thought it would.

The third shell was filled with dragon's breath incendiary shells. She caught fire. One snap of her fingers and the blaze went out.

Grant and Kull stepped out of the room behind Black, and the trifecta looked annoyed.

"Now!" I barked.

Father Freeman wheeled around the corner, his paintball gun raised high. Freeman fired down range, pelting each witch with pellets. Only instead of paint, the pellets contained holy water.

Tanya Grant reached into the morgue, grabbed one of her compatriots, and dragged her out into the hallway, and into the line of fire. The woman was splashed with seven balls of holy water and a blast of holy salt before I fired the buckshot and dragon's breath into her. She went down like a normal person.

The other witches fell back, preferring the fire they were invulnerable to rather than face projectile holy objects.

A continuation of the back-and-forth exchange would only serve to make the outcome uncertain. And while we had two chances to stop the coven, that assumed we would survive the first round. They had to win only once.

I was happy to get while the getting was good.

"Fall back," I snapped at Freeman.

It was a good thing we did. Tiles from the floor ripped up and shot out at us like razors. They turned the wall behind us into something like my playing cards into a piece of fruit.

We were out of the building in less than thirty seconds after that.

Yeah, I know. It wasn't the bravest move ever, but we weren't going to risk a straight-up entanglement. Because, while I wasn't a mathematician, in a match where we squared off against more than half-a-dozen witches, we were so dead in so many different ways.

"At least it's not about Tommy," Sinead said once I could hear myself think over the beating of my own heart.

My breathing still hadn't settled. "Yeah. Great. Just a bunch of murderers who made themselves invulnerable before making themselves pretty again. Yay."

Freeman nodded. "Noticed that did you?"

I smirked. "I'm surprised you did," I teased.

"I'm chaste. Not blind," he calmly retorted.

"Now what?" Sinead asked, ignoring our banter. "We took our shot, and we failed."

I shook my head. "They didn't increase their power any. That's good. And we can hurt them. We may have even killed one of the powered-up."

Sinead frowned and nodded, reluctantly admitting I had a point. While I had mixed the chemicals, Father Freeman had blessed the entire building when we first got here, ridding the area of any power for the witches to tap into.

"More importantly," Freeman noted. "We know where they'll go next."

I grimaced. "But I don't want to go back to King's Point."

Sinead looked at me in the rear-view mirror. "Oh, stop it, Alex. It's your job."

I rolled my eyes. "Technically, it's the SWAT team's job."

"You know what I mean."

I sighed. I really wanted to just turn this over to a special team. SWAT. Maybe the Fighting 69th or the 82nd Airborne. Vatican Ninjas would have been nice.

But it was unlikely. There was no one we could approach for help without ending up in the loony bin. Tommy was friends with criminals and gangs … okay, Tommy's friend was really a businessman who pretended to be a "gangsta," but he had enough guns to declare war on the mob. However, I didn't have the man's phone number, and he probably wouldn't pick up if I called. Tommy had told me about some sort of special Fed who seemed to know some of what was going on, but the Fed hadn't even left a name, to heck with a number.

What I *wanted* was an air strike.

What I had to work with meant that I had to get close to the witches, and confront them directly, and hope they let me do the one thing I was really good at…

Talking people to death.

My partner and I had killed the previous owners of the house in King's Point… to be technical, we had merely cleared out the death cult that had owned the house. Then they got up and tried to kill us again. They were extra-special dead once we were done with them.

A few months after that, we needed a place to have a shootout with the forces of darkness. An empty Hell house was perfect for it. The resulting conflagration had reduced the house to a massive hole in the ground.

And yet all that didn't make a dent in the property values at King's Point.

To say that King's Point is the nice part of Long Island doesn't quite capture it. To start with, you have to find it first. There's a little white-letters-on-green-background sign that meekly says "King's Point," as a way of guiding people who know what they're looking for.

If you're driving by King's Point, along Community Drive, there are plenty of tall, lush trees, covering the very existence of the area. It was the same level of flora that concealed the highway from neighborhoods they went through and vice versa. There is only the barest occasional hint that there is something behind the trees. At the right angle during the winter, when the trees are bare, you can catch glimpses of fine six-bedroom homes and wide arcing driveways, the occasional brownstone or bay window.

To turn into King's Point is to enter the land of *The Great Gatsby*—Great Neck (instead of "Big Egg"). The homes were closer to old-fashioned mansions than the McMansions that arose in the late nineties. Some had extra pieces of land that made for one heck of a front yard. Some had tennis courts and swimming pools that were jealously guarded by a chain-link fence (no barbed wire). At a wrong turn, one could unknowingly drive up someone's driveway, mistaking it for a street. Some homes were cut off from the others by an additional bodyguard of trees, isolating themselves from their neighbors. If one stuck to the outer perimeter of King's Point, one would find that every cul-de-sac oversaw the water. Many of the homes at the end of the cul-de-sac had docks and boats in their backyards.

The gardeners made more than I did.

King's Point at night remained idyllic. In areas where the street lamps might be insufficient, the external lights of all the homes lit the streets and the walkways, welcoming any and all in the streets to town.

In short, it looked nice. Some homes were more obviously wealthy than others, but most were subdued, and remained low key, unpretentious and not flashy. For the most part, it was what small business owners aspired to—nice home, nice neighborhood, a place to raise the kids without a problem.

The property we, and the witches, wanted was in one cul-de-sac that backed into the water.

The witches were in the back yard, and not in the hole. It made sense, since all of the necromantic activity had happened there, including the human sacrifices. I had hoped it had all gone away with the destruction of the Moloch statue we'd thrown into its own fire pit, but apparently not.

We had made it there late for good reason, but that still meant the coven arrived first. This time, they had set up their accouterments. I kid you not—they had a cauldron and a roaring fire going. They were still bare naked in the middle of a moonlit night.

However, they also had one of the neighborhood kids strapped down at the foot of where the Moloch statue used to be. He wasn't bound and gagged, but he didn't struggle. He barely breathed.

I remembered back to Ben telling me how one of the witches had mesmerized him. Apparently, they weren't content to wait on the ketamine … or worse, they were so powerful, they didn't need to rely on drugs anymore. Two of the disfigured witches had leaned over the boy's body, ready to cut.

Time to move.

I didn't have any guns aside from a handgun in my holster. I wasn't going to try to approach them with the shotgun out and ready. That was an invitation to have them throw fireballs first and never ask questions. Unfortunately, it was possible they would do that anyway. Thankfully, I was already dripping wet, thanks to Father Freeman pouring a bucket of water on me.

I cleared my throat loudly. "Evening, everyone."

Everyone turned to me. Some of them grabbed their special knives. Some grabbed chicken bones. None of them looked particularly concerned about my arrival.

Tanya Grant didn't have anything in her hands. This made me even more nervous. She didn't think she needed a weapon.

"You again," she stated flatly in an accent that may have been Latin American. I idly wondered if she should be a witch or a *bruja*. Either way, I figured I knew who had killed the inmate in Rikers. "Who are you?"

I smiled. I would have reached for my wallet and badge, but I figured the less movement, the less provocation. "Detective Alex Packard, NYPD. You're standing in my handiwork."

Grant looked more interested all of a sudden. "Really?"

I shrugged. I figured a little exaggeration wouldn't hurt. "I was here both times. Once for the shootout. Once for the fireball."

Grant's look became … *hungry* was the best way to describe it. It was one of the reasons I wanted to talk. They had gone out of their way to kidnap Ben, because he had destroyed the zombies at that murder site. They had killed an inmate who had been possessed during the riot. The security guard we had cleared out of the morgue had been in the building (on a different floor) during the great zombie shootout. They wanted people who had been present during the initial incident they hoped to channel.

I casually walked past Grant, and she was happy to let me. That meant that I was surrounded by them. I leaned over the cauldron and took a whiff. I tried not to vomit.

I patted the cauldron with both hands and made a show of looking like I had burned my left hand. They didn't notice that my right hand had lingered, leaving a little package behind.

"That's hot," I proclaimed. I turned to Grant as I calmly reached into my jacket. With one hand, I slid out a pack of cards, hiding by a pack of cigarettes. "So, I'm curious." I casually slid a cigarette into my mouth.

Grant leaned forward and snapped her fingers. A small flame appeared at the end of her index finger. "Yes?"

I leaned forward and lit up. "Thanks." I straightened and blew smoke away from us, over the pot. "What happens if you ladies *don't* conclude this little ceremony of yours? You don't collect all of the bodies you need for your endeavor?"

Grant shrugged. "Those of us who haven't already paid our debts will have everything taken from them as payment."

I visibly cringed. "Ouch. Well, that sucks. Sorry about that." I looked around. "I guess that the women who don't look like Hollywood actresses are the ones who need to pay off their debts, huh?"

Black and Kull closed in behind me. I heard their steps on the ground. *Time to act.*

I held up the box for playing cards and shook it. "Let me show you a bit of my own magic first."

I sidestepped from the cauldron and faced all three of them. Black and Kull had athames. The moonlight glinted off the blades.

I slid the cards out of the box and shuffled. I hoped they didn't hear the slide of metal on metal.

I fanned out the cards before Kull and smiled. They were all focused on the cards and not on my hands.

With a flick of my right hand, I hurled the metal prayer card into Black's throat.

With a flick of my right hand, the metal prayer card, blessed by Father Freeman on our way to King's Point, slid into Black's throat just as if it had been a playing card into an orange.

Black fell back and grabbed at her neck, gagging and choking on her own blood. The blessing had allowed it to slide right through her black magic defenses. The metal had made it punch through her veins, arteries, and neck muscles.

When I say I have a card up my sleeve, I mean it.

It worked! I thought briefly as I flicked cards at Kull and Grant. Grant threw her arms up, so the card bit into the flesh of her forearm. Kull twisted and the card stabbed her in the breast.

Jig's up! I split the deck in two and threw them at both witches before I dove for the dropped athame, the nearest weapon. I grabbed the knife by the handle and log-rolled, pushing myself to my feet with a creak, my body protesting.

I had the knife up and ready in my right hand. My right foot was forward like I was fencing.

Three of the disfigured had turned their attention away from the sacrifice and also pulled out their knives. The last one babysat the sacrifice.

Five witches, one knife. Yay.

Grant, Kull, and the other three made fists. As one, they flicked their fingers open. Balls of fire appeared in all of their hands.

I'm toast.

They all threw their fireballs at once. I dropped down to one knee and covered my head with my arms.

The air around me went up twenty degrees in a flash as all of the fireballs dissipated against my clothing. Father Freeman had not doused me in a bucket of water, *per se*—he had doused me in holy water.

I put my arms down and smiled at them. I pulled one more drag on my cigarette so the tip glowed nice and hot. "My turn."

I grabbed my cigarette with my free left hand and flicked it between Kull and Grant.

It landed on the package of homemade thermite I had attached to the cauldron.

Before anyone knew what was happening, the thermite burned, bright and red, right through the cauldron. The contents poured out like water through a hull breach, dousing the roaring fire.

The disfigured women screamed. Their bodies seized and contorted as they fell. Some of their facial features cleared up, as though they had been disfigured by their use of magic. All of their bodies ripped and shifted. Not only were they going through torturous pain, but their bodies lost all glamorous aspects. Some had scars appear. Some became fat. For all of them, their hair grew wiry and changed colors. They were universally some shade of blue or purple.

Kull and Grant looked around in horror as their compatriots reverted back to their original forms, before any magic had touched them.

Kull looked at me, screamed in rage, and rushed me, her athame held high.

I pushed to my feet, throwing myself into her. My left arm was up over my head in a block. My forearm met her wrist, intercepting the blow.

I drove Black's athame right into Kull's stomach without a problem.

Kull stopped. Her face looked more like she had been gut punched than stabbed. She blinked and looked down at the point of impact. With her left hand, she weakly grabbed the knife handle sticking out of her stomach. She tottered back, away from me. She twisted away as she fell. She started with the same convulsions as the others, but it was interrupted by a death rattle.

This left Grant and me all alone on the field of carnage. She looked around at her dead, then fixed me with a look fit to kill. Her mouth bunched up as she focused.

I smiled at her. "Does it help that I'm covered in holy water and I'm wearing a rosary?"

Grant's eyes widened a second. Then she smiled. *I may have just pressed my luck.*

Grant shot in and smacked me across the face. The blow sent me sprawling on my stomach. She kicked me onto my back and straddled me. Normally, I wouldn't have minded a hot naked woman on top of me. But she wrapped her hands around my throat and shook me like a rat.

"Did you forget how strong we are?" she said tightly as the fingers slowly closed. "I could rip your head off right now and be done with it. But no. You're not going to be allowed to die fast. I'm going to take my time with you."

I buckled my hips, but she tightened her legs around my chest. My ribs creaked. My vision narrowed and became blurry at the edges. I grabbed for her thumbs to get a little breathing space, but they wouldn't budge.

If I didn't do something in the next few seconds, I was dead.

With a flick of my fingers, I snapped another holy card from up my sleeve and drove it into Grant's face. Her grip faded a little, but it wasn't enough to keep me alive. It had had the same effect as before—it took away her invulnerability.

Which is why my other hand shoved another package of thermite into her mouth. I drove it in so hard, she choked on it a little. She swatted my hands away…

Which allowed me to breathe.

I slid the prayer card between my fingers and punched her in the throat. She gagged, the package of thermite still jammed in her mouth.

I grabbed my cigarette lighter, flicked it to life, and touched it to the thermite before I shoved her off me. I rolled away as the thermite ignited.

This time, the reaction was immediate. The power in her body exploded with blue flame. The concussion wave shoved me further, slamming me into the bushes at the edge of the back yard.

The flames receded, leaving Grant a pile of ashes.

"And that…" I panted, "is why … they *burn* witches… *bitch.*"

I sagged back and let my head loll to one side. The kid taken for sacrifice was already gone. Smart kid.

I so don't want to do the paperwork on this one.

Ten minutes later, Freeman and Sinead came and got me. We had figured I was going to either be triumphant or dead by then.

Sinead bent down next to me and checked me over. "Are you okay?"

"I'll live." I looked to the field of carnage. "More than them."

Freeman nodded as he stared at the bodies. "What happened?"

I sat up and groaned. "They failed to pay their exorcist bill. They got repossessed."

Freeman and Sinead helped me to my feet. After a minute of searching, we found a pile of clothing on the ground. Everything had been neatly folded. And all of their wallets were there. It was how I knew all of their names.

The priest and the doctor helped me back to the car, and I started considering the story I could file that would fit all of the facts.

Instead, I fell asleep in my car, exhausted.

Unlike my partner, I wasn't a saint. I would never be canonized. I would most likely be cannon fodder. But I did have a card or two up my sleeve.

"I can see our building has put quite the spell on you. Some residents have said they've never felt so free as they do here at home…though, of course, they keep any excess behind closed doors. The smoke detectors have all been recently replaced, and one of your possible neighbors here does the most impressive tricks. It's almost as though he can truly make things disappear."

* * * * *

Happy Birthday
by Steve Diamond

Happy birthday to me.

As I buried the blade of my shovel into the neck of a ghoul, the clock tower in my graveyard *gonged* out its tired refrain. Like myself, I think the old timepiece was going through the motions. It does what it does. Just like I do.

Black blood sprayed upward, making my white t-shirt look like a bad Jackson Pollack painting. Not that there are good ones… but the point stands. It was a new shirt, too.

The ghoul gargled once, and reached up to me, almost pleading. I twisted the shovel, popping its head off. It wouldn't be going after grieving families or stupid teenagers anymore. I pulled the shovel free and held the blade up in the moonlight. I could already see the undead's fluids trying to solidify. I'd either have to kill another ghoul to get more fresh blood on it or clean the iron spade soon.

I looked around. No other ghouls among the tombstones.

With a sigh, I tossed the shovel to the ground, grabbed the headless corpse by its filthy arms, and pulled it back to the hole where it had crawled from. A little lighter fluid and a match turned it into a bonfire.

Ghouls burn *hot*. All undead do. Way hotter than regular wood. Holding my shovel over the flames, I burnt off most of the ghoul blood, watching in fascination as it flared incandescent blue for just a moment before winking out. I've killed hundreds of ghouls and supernatural things. To say I'm tired of it would be the understatement of the century. But the way their blood burns? The sapphire brilliance of it? Never gets old.

The small clock tower finished sounding off the twelfth strike.

I'd been dreading this day all year.

Friday the Thirteenth.

My twenty-first birthday.

As I took my normal route out of the cemetery proper—toward the east entrance, past my parents' graves—icy fingers of dread clutched at the inside of my chest, and my heartbeat sped up, almost fluttering with a panicked anxiety. I'm no stranger to fear… but this felt different.

Before my parents died—which is the nicest way I can describe the end they both met—they let me in on the family secret. The family *business*. Besides telling me about all the *things* I'd end up having to kill, they also told me to beware and prepare.

"*Your twenty-first birthday will mark a change in your life, sweetheart,*" my dad told me. He never called me by my name, Friday. I don't know why. Only my mom did. So when he used my name, I knew he was serious. "*Don't roll your eyes at me, Friday Black. I'm serious. All the things we hunt down? All the monsters? Those are warm-ups. Once you turn twenty-one, your* soul *is fair-game. And there will be plenty of threats out there looking to take someone as special as you. The devil and his demons will be forever on your heels. Be ready.*"

I didn't believe him. How could I?

But after mom and dad died, life took on a new light. A darker, more hopeless light. And my dad's words haunted me ever since.

My twenty-first birthday.

Today.

An involuntary shudder crawled up my spine, and I felt the difference in the cemetery. I'd lived on the property all my life, and I could feel the slightest change in its temperature. Not its physical temperature, but it psychic one. Its supernatural barometer. And now… a pressure built in my skull, driving me to one knee. Sound faded.

I looked up to see the full moon staring back down at me. It seemed to tremble in the night sky. In fear? With laughter? Whatever the cause, and however real, my body shivered like I was stuck in the arctic wearing a windbreaker. What I took for dread became a very real feeling of suffocation as the air froze in my lungs.

I've been around all sorts of creatures. Ghouls, ghosts, the odd vampire or werewolf. But this… I'd never experienced this before. The force of this new pressure pushed me down until I lay face down in the grass. In my tunneling vision, I caught a glimpse of a tombstone. My mother's.

I reached out, forcing my hand over the earth, using my fingers to crawl the appendage forward. I stretched my shaking fingers, and their tips brushed the marble at the headstone's base.

Instantly the pressure vanished, and I sucked in a deep breath.

I pulled myself to the chunk of marble, resting my back against it.

"Thanks, Mom," I whispered. I didn't know what had happened, but my habit of walking by the final resting places of my parents might have just saved me. My dad hadn't been joking. Something big was happening today.

I leaned my head back against the stone. The moon above didn't shake like it had before. It was just the moon.

Letting my eyes close, I sucked in a few deep breaths to steady my nerves. "It's okay," I told myself. "It's all okay." A lie. Nothing was okay. The debilitating pressure might be gone, but not the change in the cemetery. I still felt it. Some disturbance, just below the surface of perception.

When I opened my eyes, a woman in a white dress stood over me.

A scream tried ripping its way out of my throat. I grabbed the shovel I'd dropped when I'd collapsed a few moments earlier and held it up in front of me, futilely warding off the new apparition. But the woman didn't move to attack me. In fact, she didn't even look at me. She stared straight ahead, her attention locked beyond me, mouth moving wordlessly. I shook my head, wondering if my ears were still plugged from the pressure.

"Hello?" My words sounded hollow, but I heard them. The figure didn't respond. "Can you hear me?"

Nothing. I reached out and prodded her leg with the point of my shovel. The woman's image flared bright where the iron touched her. The tell-tale sign of a ghost. She didn't react in the slightest… which struck me as a little strange. Usually they didn't like iron touching them. This one didn't seem to care, if it noticed at all.

What was she saying? Her mouth moved, and her eyes looked engaged with the missing other side of a conversation. Her expression was… pleading. I'd never been good at reading lips, a skill I suppose I should have trained up on. But I picked out a word here-and-there. "Please" mostly.

But "please" what?

She didn't behave like a normal ghost. No angry wailing. No attempted possession—never a fun experience. No flickering between the appearance of a corpse and their previously unspoiled self. She didn't scream in pain as the iron passed through parts of her form. She ignored it, and continued talking at someone, likely in the last moments of the life she was replying.

For a ghost to appear to me as this one did couldn't be a coincidence. The natural questions came to mind. Who was she? Why the appearance now? How did she die, and what was I meant to do about it, if anything?

I took in the details of the ghost as quickly as I could. I never knew how long I had to study the visitor. Apparitions could stick around for minutes, or only moments. Her white dress looked like an old nightgown. No one had ever accused me of being up-to-date on style. That gown could have been from the eighteen-hundreds, or something pulled off the rack at the local mall the day before. I didn't know these sorts of things. I had other stuff to worry about. Like not dying at the hands of various undead creatures.

The gown looked new, though. The white of it had a crispness one could only find in newness, though the hem was stained brown from dirt or mud. She didn't wear any other clothing I could see. Dark smudges of dirt marred her bare feet.

The ghostly form wore no jewelry except for a silver chain looped though a simple ring of the same color. A wedding band, maybe?

Her blond hair looked almost white in the moonlight, a perfect complement to the dress. Something in her hairstyle gave me the impression she'd been killed recently. I couldn't say what, exactly. A gut feeling, I suppose. It looked… modern. And on top of all that, no wrinkles of age stood out on her face, which meant she had been young at the time of her death.

Please. Please.

Those were the only words she seemed to say. But to who? And why?

One of my earlier questions received a partial answer.

The image flickered, and the ghost's hands flew to her neck, pressing at it. Red blood spilled down her neck, staining the prefect white skin and gown. Her life flowing down her chest stood out more vividly than it would have in the flesh. Blood never gleamed so red. A trick of the phantasmal form made the cause of death show more brightly.

One hand still grasping at the line in her throat, the other reached out in vain. She seemed so close to me, but I knew I could do nothing. She was doomed to her fate, no matter how real she looked standing before me.

Even still, I got to my feet and reached out, fingers brushing her outstretched ones. Where my flesh touched the apparition, I felt searing cold. But I didn't jerk my hand away like I knew others would. Could she feel my touch? I don't know. But whatever the religion or philosophy, she deserved to not be alone. So I let her coldness seep into the bones of my fingers, and I maintained contact until her bright blood had turned the entire front of her white gown crimson.

The ghost's eyelids fluttered, and then for a brief instant, her eyes met my own. Sadness filled them… and I swore they tried telling me something.

Then she winked away.

I slowly lowered my hand.

Happy birthday to me, indeed.

After walking out of the cemetery to the family home outside the gates, I went upstairs and took a hot shower to get all the ghoul blood off me. The black splashes of it already had the skin underneath itching. I scrubbed hard, then let the near-scalding water loosen and relax my muscles. Sleep should have come easy, but when I went to my room and flopped down on the bed, all I could do was stare at the ceiling.

The memory of that ghost haunted me clear through until sunrise, scaring off any hint of rest I desperately needed. Fighting ghouls and their ilk had a way of draining a person, regardless of how easy it all seemed. I think it's the way the mind deals with and compartmentalizes itself from the action of putting down something that should have already been dead. Something that shouldn't possibly be mobile and trying to gorge itself on living flesh.

I've thought about it a lot over the years, and when I—or anyone who ends up in a bad situation like I'm frequently in—kill a creature of supernatural origin, there is a psychic release of power. Like leg day for the psychically attuned mind.

All of this is to say I could have used a few hours of sleep.

I've seen more ghosts than the average thousand people put together over their combined lifetimes. Maybe the average ten-thousand people. A hundred-thousand? Who knows? I… don't get out much. As much as I hate dealing with monsters, I hate people just as much. Maybe more.

After my parents became lunch to a swarm of ghouls, no one helped me. No one threw any real sympathy my way. I often debated the "who is the real monster" question with what few friends I have.

The girl in the white gown. Was she a monster? Doubtful. The person who had sliced her throat open? Very likely. No matter how much my mind ran from the memory of her ghostly visage, she always caught up.

By seven that morning, I knew I needed to do a little research.

I briefly considered staying inside all day. Most girls on their twenty-first birthdays would spend the day shopping, or partying, or whatever people did these days. None of those were really my scene. If I wasn't out and about hunting down the supernatural mysteries of the world, I was either looking up *how* to hunt down said mysteries or taking care of cemetery business.

But today… I don't know. Maybe my dad's words had their hooks in me. I just needed the day to be over with, and I could get back to business as usual. A birthday, and a Friday the Thirteenth all rolled up into one. In October, no less.

My desire to block the doors and cover the windows couldn't have been stronger. But I couldn't dispel what I'd seen. That girl had looked so scared, and to see her killed like that… well, I felt like I owed it to her to figure out who she was, and when she'd died.

I showered again, then went downstairs and flipped open my laptop. One of my few friends, Rick Cammon, had hacked me into the systems of the local sheriff and police departments. I've been suitably impressed at the time—and still felt that way—but Rick had laughed away my praise. *"State and local agencies? That's child's play, Friday."* I remembered him giving me an almost pitying shake of his head.

"But I'll tell you what, you can thank me by cooking me some that barbeque you know I love. Plus... I know this'll help you help other people... like you did for me."

I still owed him that cookout. Maybe once my birthday was firmly in the rearview, and I hopefully wasn't dead.

Starting with the last week, I looked at all the homicides in state. My search didn't take long. We didn't have that many murders in Utah. I expanded outward to include suicides or undetermined deaths. Still no blondes in white nightgowns. Even when I increased the scope to the last month, then last three months, I still found nothing.

Most crime scene photos didn't bother me anymore. When you've come across a ghoul or zombie trying to suck the eyeball from the skull of a still-living victim, a picture of a gunshot wound doesn't have the same impact... no pun intended. However, a feeling of deep sadness did settle over me this time. So many victims, and many of them were so young. I closed my queries into deaths and brought up missing person's reports.

These always hit me harder than the actual deaths, though most of the time the missing hit the death reports later on. The unknown made them worse, both for me and definitely for those waiting for answers.

Adults. Children. Male and female. It didn't matter. All their potential just... vanished.

I filtered my research on females only. Ages eighteen to twenty-five. I doubted the ghost's previous corporeal owner had been outside that range.

And yet, nothing.

Plenty of blondes. But none that looked like the ghost that'd appeared to me.

I closed my laptop and checked my watch. 10:00am. This day just wouldn't speed by, would it? But so far, the only real weird thing had been right after midnight. Maybe today wouldn't be too bad.

I didn't have many other normal ways of searching for clues about my mystery phantom, but I did still have a regular business to run. As much as the loose end of my mystery ghost nagged at me, I couldn't just let the cemetery linger. Between new residents, some gravesite sealings to perform, and running off the usual teens and homeless, my daytimes tended to get filled up rather quickly.

Pulling the curtain to the kitchen window aside, I looked out to see the weather. A tapestry of dark clouds covered the sky above, but not in the normal grey I expected. The clouds themselves looked ill. Sick and infected with some angry contagion that made their centers yellow with linings of putrid green. Neither of those colors were normal.

"Wait a minute," I muttered to myself, and pulled out my phone. On the display screen it showed the current weather.

Seventy-five degrees.

Clear skies.

"No way that's a good sign."

I called up my only other friend, Audrey. She picked up on the first ring, *"Girl, I was just about to call you. Happy birthday! What are we doing today?"*

As much as I hated people, she loved everyone. She usually made a good counterpoint to my grimness, but today I just wasn't feeling it.

"Trying not to die," I answered her question. I cut off her answering laughter, saying, "No, seriously. Twenty-first birthday, Aud. I've told you the warning my dad gave me. It's already happening. And now I'm looking at some wicked cloud cover. Something worse is coming down the supernatural pipeline."

"What are you talking about, Friday? It's a perfect day. Clear blue."

I pulled the phone away from my ear and stared at it for a second. "What am *I* talking about? What are *you* talking about?" Eldritch, green lightning cracked among the clouds, striking down into the center of my graveyard. The power went out. "Aud, I just had green lightning strike somewhere in the middle of my cemetery. Nothing 'clear blue' about it."

"I'm on my way," she said, cutting off the call before I could warn her away. I didn't want her anywhere near this. Whatever *this* was.

Opening the cabinet next to the exit, I surveyed my quick-access gear. The bedroom adjoining my own upstairs had a full complement of material, but I always kept this repurposed armoire filled. Salt for ghosts. Holy water for anything demonic. Silver for what you'd expect. Body armor. And of course, lots and lots of guns and ammo. I pulled a vest covered in pockets free from a hanger and slipped it on, then began loading the pockets with shotgun shells. Rock salt, silver, iron bearings, iron powder. Some were consecrated. I just didn't know what I would be facing out there. And now my best friend was driving over in her pink Mini Cooper. I hated that car.

My mom's trusty Sig P226 went into a holster at my waist, and I shoved some extra magazines in the ammo pouches pre-threaded through my gun-belt. I thumbed shells into the Remington 1100, then walked to the door and yanked it open to go outside…

…only to be thrown backwards across the room by the banshee scream of my mystery ghost.

My back hit the opposite wall hard, drywall giving way under the impact. Air *whooshed* out of my lungs.

The ghost looked much like she had in the earliest hour of the day. Pale hair over more pale skin. The front of her dress a ruin of bright, red blood. The slash in her throat still leaked her life, but slower now. And still her eyes didn't meet mine. The ghost continued to stare ahead, focused on something directly in front of her that only she could see. Her killer, no doubt. Both hands now reached out, begging for help, or maybe pleading for the answer to why she'd just been killed.

Please. Please.

Those words. I couldn't hear them. Not exactly. Her now bloodless lips mouthed them soundlessly. But her death and her new form magnified their power in a way life never could. Waves of anger and fear radiated off her, pressing me against the wall, holding me there. She likely didn't even intend to hurt me. I doubted she knew I was there. It didn't matter. People with my gift are lodestones for all this. Every ghost, ghoul, and supernatural creature was somehow drawn our way, or we to them.

I strained against the sound pressure and lifted the shotgun I still miraculously held and pulled the trigger. The iron bearings in the shell shredded the ghostly form in brilliant flashes of blue, expelling her temporarily. Without her power holding me, I dropped to the floor.

"Great. Juuuussst great." I levered my way back to standing and looked at the Friday Black sized dent in my wall. I hated fixing drywall. With a snarl, I shouldered the Remington and went outside.

The strong scent of ozone assaulted by nose, and every hair on my head tried to stand on its end. Everything in my cemetery felt wrong.

The Tombstone Estates—I wasn't keen on the name, but my parents had always gotten a kick out of it—was hallowed ground. This didn't mean that bad things couldn't cross into my territory, just that they were weakened here, and that those who were buried on the premises were generally guaranteed to have their eternal slumber undisturbed. The cemetery usually held a quiet solemnity. A peacefulness so strong even those unsensitive to the supernatural world could feel. An emotional warmth on even the most somber day… of which there were many, here.

But not now. Static dread filled the air. Another green lightning bolt streaked down, again hitting the center of the property. It made no sense. Nothing of any importance sat there. Nothing and no one.

I took a step forward, then heard the beep of a car horn at the cemetery gates to my left. When I turned, I saw Audrey's pink Mini.

"Impossible." A quick check of my watch showed only a couple minutes had passed since her call. Unless she'd been in the neighborhood, she couldn't have arrived so fast. I jogged over to the gate and pulled it open for her.

As she drove in, I glimpsed a flicker of putrid yellow in the air around her car. Once her car was all the way in, Audrey got out, eyes wide.

"Friday, I swear to you the sky didn't look like this from outside the gates."

"Are you telling me it was all blue skies until you got on my property?"

Audrey nodded, eyes big as saucers as she stared up at the clouds.

"How long ago did you leave?"

"What?" Her eyes hadn't moved from the roiling masses in the sky. "Right after you called."

I grabbed her wrist and compared her watch to mine. Hers showed twenty minutes later than mine. My hunch hadn't let me down. Time passed differently in my cemetery right now.

"No offense, Friday," Audrey said, shaking her head slowly, "but I think this is above my paygrade. I'm just going to get in your way here."

She was right, and we both knew it. As much as I'd like to have my best friend here with me, she didn't have the training or abilities to handle something of this magnitude. I pointed back out the open gate. "Why don't you get out of here? This situation is probably about to get out of hand."

Audrey blew out a long shaky breath, set her car in reverse, and backed up toward the exit.

Then her car just… stopped.

"Aud, what are you doing? Get out of here while you can."

"Friday, my car just died."

This whole situation was getting worse by the moment, and I had a feeling it was going to keep on that downward slide.

"Leave the car and walk," I said, pulling open her door. Inside the Mini, all the digital panels were as dead as the residents of Tombstone Estates.

Audrey jumped out of the car and quick-walked to the open gate. For some reason I knew she wouldn't be able to leave, but I needed to see my suspicion confirmed with my own eyes. Sure enough, when she tried to cross the property threshold, she bounced off it like an invisible wall had been erected in the two minutes since she'd entered.

She was stuck inside. Which meant I was stuck, just like her.

"Friday, what's going on?"

"I don't know. Something big is coming. I've seen green lightning strike in the center of the property a few times now."

"The same spot?"

"Maybe. I was about to go check when you arrived."

"Well, I'm not letting you go by yourself. I've seen enough horror movies to know splitting up is what gets girls like you and me dead *real* quick."

I didn't have a good response to that. And I'm being honest, I didn't fancy being alone. I pulled off a belt of ammo pouches holding shotgun shells and walked to her side and handed her the belt and boomstick. "Alright. But you're carrying this.

You remember our lessons?" She nodded once, face white as a ghost's. "Good. Let's see where the lightning is striking, shall we?"

My graveyard seemed a lot larger than it should have. We walked for nearly ten minutes, and still hadn't arrived where the green lightning bolts struck every couple of minutes. What looked like a short walk seemed more like a mile, then two.

"There is some seriously bad juju going on here, Friday."

I nodded my agreement. "You know, when my dad first told me my twenty-first birthday would be rough, I thought he was overselling it to make a point. Now, I'm thinking he didn't warn me hard enough. I'm sorry you're stuck in here."

She opened her mouth to reply, then froze. She cocked her head to the side, listening, then looked back the way we came. I followed suit, and saw the cemetery gate a few hundred yards behind us. Forward or backward, I bet the supernatural manipulation of distance was equal. We were stuck in this bizarre sort of purgatory where neither time nor perception followed the rules of nature. At least... not *our* nature.

"What is it, Aud?"

"I swear I heard someone." She pointed to the property's entrance where her Mini sat. "Friday, we didn't close the gate. You don't think... It isn't possible that... "

"That someone else came in, and is now stuck? I hope not. I should have closed the gate. If anyone else came in, they're stuck too."

We walked for another ten minutes, inching ever closer to our goal. This time I heard the sound of chatter from multiple voices from behind us. When I turned to look back, three people walked out from between two mausoleums.

"Finally!" A college kid holding a large DSLR camera led the group. He waved at us then ran our way, the other two members of his group in tow. Five minutes crawled by as they trudged the visually short space between our groups.

Directly experiencing the perception manipulation was one thing, but to watch it happen to another group hurt my brain. They didn't move in slow motion, and they appeared to take full steps. But despite the walking, they barely moved forward. I closed my eyes and rubbed at a building headache. Sound traveled right, but not the physical form. This would have made for an interesting conversation with my parents. I could have used their support—just their *presence*—right then.

"What is going *on*?" the guy asked when he finally reached us. "I've been walking forever, but it was like... I don't know. Like I was on a treadmill or something."

"Yeah, sorry about that," I replied. "Things are a little messed up at the moment. First things first. Who are you, and what are you doing here?"

"I'm Pete Propin. A filmmaker. I sent you an email about a week ago? You said I could come by and do some recording for an indie film I'm making."

I stared at him blankly for a few moments, then vaguely remembered the email. Something about a ghost story. In the madness of the days leading up to my birthday, I'd forgotten all about it.

"We walked through the open front gate and saw all… *this*." Pete waved a hand at the sky. "The girls wanted to bail, but… "

"But you couldn't," I finished for him. "Yeah. Like I said, things aren't exactly normal right now. You may want to… "I trailed off, staring at the two women from the filmmaker's group. They wore matching dresses.

White dresses that looked more like nightgowns.

One of the girls had short hair, dark as midnight. On any other day I'd have been impressed by her looks and may have even complimented her on the hairdo.

Not today.

The other girl pulled all my attention.

Hair so light it almost looked silver. It settled on her pale skin like silken threads. Threads I knew would soon be covered in blood. Around her neck, she wore a single silver chain upon which was looped a ring. The girl pushed a lock of hair behind her ear and gave Audrey and me a nervous smile before her eyes were drawn to the green and yellow clouds above.

Not a ghost then. The real article.

Now I knew why I hadn't been able to find my ghost. She wasn't missing. She wasn't dead. Not yet. But she *would* die, and soon. How had her ghost gone *backwards* in time to visit me?

"Friday," Audrey asked. "You alright?"

"Yeah," I said. "I'll fill you in later."

"What is going on?" The soon-to-be-ghost stepped up by Pete and pointed skyward. "Those clouds weren't there until we entered the cemetery. And there was an *invisible wall* over the entrance when we tried to leave." Her tone grew more shrill with each passing word.

I knew I should care more about their fear. Normal people just weren't equipped to deal with reality being manipulated by supernatural forces. Psychiatric care facilities were filled with people whose minds broke from being exposed to events milder than the one currently happening in my graveyard.

But I didn't care. My mind fixated on the impossibility of this girl's future ghost appearing to me in the past. I'd have to work out the "how" later. For now I'd focus on the "why." Why had she appeared to me?

More green lightning struck, this time in a flurry of vivid green bolts. Dozens, one after the other in rapid succession, charging the air with latent electricity.

"What is happening?" Pete asked again. "This… this isn't natural."

"You just figuring that out?" I asked. "Look, I'm sorry. For all of you. You're caught up in something you'd consider 'supernatural.' You don't have to believe me. Frankly, I don't care if you do or don't."

"Are we safe?" the dark-haired one asked. She practically vibrated from trembling so hard.

"No," I replied. "Not a chance."

My answer caught them off guard. Maybe they expected me to lie to them, telling them everything would be alright. That they'd all be home by dinner, or they'd all wake up and this would all have been a bizarre dream. I wished I *could* give them those types of reassurances. But I knew better. And from the expression on Audrey's face, she knew better as well.

Poor Audrey. She'd been exposed to the world of undead, ghosts, and supernatural monsters just a few years ago. Her normally cheerful exterior eroded in the paranormal environment. No matter what she did, she always wound up involved in the horrors that found their way to me. I didn't want this for her. Audrey didn't want it for herself, obviously. But she always had my back, and for that, she had my spoken and unspoken gratitude.

"What do we do?" Pete asked. "Do you have a way for us to get out of here? A place for me—*us*—too hide?"

"I suppose you could go back to my house," I said, pointing back the way they came.

"I don't think so, Friday," Audrey said. "We don't know what is happening here. Sending them back that way could put them in more danger than if they just stayed with us."

"I'd rather stay with you, if it's all the same," the blonde said. I shouldn't have been surprised, but her words felt like fate punching me in the gut. The brunette edged closer to her friend and nodded her agreement.

Pete looked at the two girls in white and sighed. "I guess we're staying with you, Ms. Black."

"Call me Friday," I said.

"That's a strange name," blondie said.

"She was born on a Friday," Audrey said. "Today's her birthday."

"Some birthday," Pete said. He waved at the brunette. "This is Sariah."

"And I'm Mercy," my future ghostly visitor said.

Mercy. Great. Even if I didn't know she would get killed today, her name alone would have been a bad omen. "Alright. Well, we need to get moving. I don't know how long we have, or what exactly is going on yet. But we do know distance is messed up now. Sooner we start walking, the sooner we can try and figure this out."

"Where are we headed?" Mercy asked.

I pointed toward the center of the cemetery. Everyone's faces fell. Everyone except Audrey's. She already knew the destination and seemed to have accepted our fate. "That lightning is striking something."

"Friday," Audrey whispered to me, "I don't remember a creepy cage in your cemetery. Am I going crazy?"

In the center of the Tombstone Estates, headstones made a large circle, all outward facing. Silent, granite sentries, they stood guard around a plot in the center of a circular clearing. But not a normal plot. No, I suppose that would have been too simple for a day like today. An iron cage looked to be staked into the ground, covering the site. From where we stood, fifty yards away, the iron looked to be covered in rust. Weeds and brambles poked out between the bars, looking like crooked fingers trying to find a way free.

No other grave markers dotted the ground between the headstones and the cage. Only dead grass filled that circle, running right up to the encircling border.

Most importantly, none of this had existed in my cemetery yesterday.

"You're not going crazy… well, at least not from this. These graves don't exist in Tombstone Estates."

Pete had edged closer to us and overheard the exchange. "That doesn't make any sense. How can graves just *show up* in a cemetery?"

I almost ignored him, but the other two girls stood at his back, the same question obvious in their eyes. Normally, I kept explanations about my world to a minimum if I said anything at all. Scaring normies always left a bad taste in my mouth. But I also knew holding back too much information would put them all at risk. And if I had to protect them—even though at least one of them wasn't making it out alive—that also put me and Audrey at risk.

"Short version goes like this," I said. "All gravesites are connected. Big ones, anyway. Not single shallow ones out in the middle of fields." They all looked at me like I was crazy. I almost laughed. Here we stood, in the middle of a changing cemetery, with obviously supernatural lightning striking every few moments. The flow of time wasn't normal. They hadn't been able to leave because of an invisible barrier.

And yet my pronouncement had *me* looking insane.

A tired sigh escaped me. "Look. You don't have to believe me for it to be the truth. Fact is, all cemeteries around the world are connected through a land of the dead. Creatures travel those roads to get where they want to go. Wherever death calls them. People like me put them down when they show up in our neck of the woods."

"How does that explain… this?" Sariah pointed at the caged grave.

"Sometimes, if powerful enough, more than just a monster slips though," I answered. "Whoever—or *what*ever—is in that cage is definitely bad news. That's why it's caged in iron." I held up a hand to interrupt the next obvious question. "Iron is poison to undead. There are a lot of reasons why, but we don't have time to get into it."

"What do you think it is?" Audrey asked.

I tucked a rogue strand of hair behind my ear. "No idea. But I suspect we won't have to wait long to see. The frequency of the lightning is picking up."

As if summoned by my words, a green bolt splintered down from the sky, striking the iron cage and casting a shower of sparks into the air. I had to blink to clear away the afterimage searing into my retinas, and when I could finally see again, I discovered the cage blown apart. Pieces of it lay scattered around the circular clearing. Before I had a chance to recover and ask the others if they were okay, more lightning rained down, hitting each of the headstones in turn, blowing them into pieces. Granite shrapnel pelted me, cutting into my skin. Gravestone dust and chunks settled to the earth around me, almost like cremation ash.

A wave of energy rolled over me, knocking me to the ground. It left me feeling sick. Oily. Like my soul had been violated by something evil.

From the smoking ruin of the once-caged grave, a wail arose, piercing my brain. I covered my ears, but the horrid sound ripped through them; an unstoppable phantasm of pain. Through the agony, I looked up to see the air ripple above the grave. Something rose out of the prison. Formless at first. Ethereal. But whatever this new threat—however intangible—the hate rippling off it was nearly strong enough to touch. It nearly made me throw up what little I had in my stomach. To my left, the others couldn't hold down their revulsion, and they heaved into the grass.

My dad had said I would be tested. Intellectually, I understood the concept. But what could I do against this?

When all else fails, I default to bullets.

I drew my Sig, hand shaking, and put a few rounds through the hazy form. They'd been dipped in holy water, not that that did much to ghosts. Witches and demons, sure. But pray-and-spray seemed like the only viable strategy.

The rounds passed through the ghostly shape—now more tangible than before. Where the lead entered the incorporeal form, it slowed, and looked like bullets going through water. I was sure I'd just wasted a few good shots, but the wailing cut off, and whatever had been solidifying over the grave vanished completely.

It took me a moment to get back to my feet. My legs shook, and my breath came in ragged gasps. The others looked to be in worse shape, which didn't surprise me. I'd grown up with this stuff. Even Audrey, who'd only been exposed to a little of it recovered a little quicker than the rest.

"Is it over?" Audrey asked.

"I don't think so," I replied. I nodded up at the clouds. "They haven't dissipated. If anything, they are getting darker."

My friend took a step closer my way and leaned in, voice lowered. "You get the feeling those headstones and the cage were keeping something in?"

I nodded but didn't say anything. Pete and Mercy were locked in a hug, the latter sobbing into the former's shoulder. Perfectly normal. Normal reactions to non-normal circumstances.

But Sariah didn't look *normal.*

Her eyes stared blankly ahead. No. Not ahead. Straight at the grave.

I followed the direction of her gaze, and saw the air stir again above the smoldering ruins of the iron cage. Before I could say anything, or shout a warning, the formless entity streaked across the distance. Unbound by the same, strange, time-movement issues as us, the thing crossed the ground in an instant and slammed into Sariah. The force lifted the girl from her feet but didn't throw her backwards. Instead, she floated in mid-air, caught there, limbs flung wide like a fly in an invisible web.

"Friday?" Audrey said. I waved her off.

Pete and Mercy stared up at their friend, faces frozen in horror.

Sariah looked down at us, eyes solid white. They hadn't rolled back, the irises had just vanished. She smiled, the look cruel on her lips.

"This body is unsuitable." When Sariah's lips moved, an alien voice escaped from them. Sariah's soft tones were gone, replaced by the dry, cracked voice of an old man. If a corpse could talk, I imagined it would sound like whatever had hitchhiked in Sariah's body. Sariah looked down at Pete. "You were instructed to bring a vessel. This one does not meet my needs. But it will help grant me a modicum of strength."

Before I could really register the meaning of what the possessed girl in white had said, her back arched, spine audibly snapping. The skin on her exposed legs darkened until it looked maroon, then bulged outward, like the something beneath the surface was attempting to escape.

Her arms followed suit, then her face and neck. Her dress stretched and tightened as her torso warped under the fabric.

Sariah screamed, and the sound tore through my soul, making me want to rip out my eyes and eardrums at the same time. I'd never heard such an awful sound. The shriek didn't belong to the dusty corpse, but to the girl. Her head twisted my way, and I saw her consciousness had returned for the worst moment of her life. Her eyes pled for help. They pled for death. For anything to remove her from the obvious pain tearing through her ravaged body.

She convulsed once, and her screams cut off like her throat had been ripped out.

With a wet grinding, her body twisted in on itself, then bulged out one final time. Sariah exploded.

Blood, flesh, and bone rained down on us. She left behind nothing bigger than a piece of stew meat.

In the spot where Sariah had floated, a cloud of blood hovered. In small globules, it reminded me of all the videos of the astronauts everyone grows up watching, showing what liquid does in zero-gravity. In the middle of those floating droplets of blood, the hazy phantom hovered, drawing in what remained of Sariah. The crimson liquid vanished, one glob at a time.

When I tore my eyes away from the sight, I saw Pete standing behind a terrified Mercy. With a white-knuckled grip, Pete held Mercy in place. I should have been upset. Sad. Scared, even. Instead, a tired sigh escaped my lips. All that worry. All the fear. My worry how it related back to me, and my test.

It all came down to one person using another for personal gain.

It may sound simplistic, but what other reason could there be? People generally don't offer up others as sacrifices to an evil entity out of the goodness of their own heart.

I don't know what I expected, but with those questions answered in a way I wish they hadn't been, my mind turned to the ones remaining. Why had the ghost appeared to me? Was it a warning? A way to help me through my "test?"

Somehow, through the explosion of blood and flesh, Mercy and Pete had both remained unblemished by the torrent. I had bits of Sariah in my hair, and I knew from experience how long it would take to get stuff like that out. Blood and dripping bits clung to my clothes. I didn't look behind me, but I assumed Audrey couldn't be much cleaner than myself.

The *thing* hovered in mid-air, seemingly spinning slowly around. I couldn't be certain, but I got the impression it "looked" from Pete and Mercy to me and Audrey. Like it *considered* which of us to take first. I lifted the gun again, not sure if it had made any real difference before. But I wouldn't let it take Audrey. Her boyfriend would never forgive me.

I'd never forgive me.

The formless apparition darted at Mercy, slamming into her.

I should have been horrified, but instead relief flooded me that Audrey and I had temporarily been spared. I had a little more time to come up with a solution. Not that one came readily to mind. I still didn't know exactly what I was even dealing with.

Mercy didn't float, which might have been a good sign, or perhaps an omen that things were about to get much worse. Pete jerked his hands away, flinching in pain, fingertips turning blue. His breath misted out in front of him as he gasped.

Most people who think they are evil, when presented with the face of true malevolence, end up thinking better of their choices. Pete was no different. Maybe he made an actual choice, or maybe he acted in instinct, but the change wrote itself all over his face. Pain and shock from the unexpected cold surrounding the phantasm's new host. Then fear and dread from what I imagined to be the sudden realization that this wasn't something to make good on whatever it had promised Pete.

Pete pulled a knife. How distracted had I been that I hadn't noticed him carrying it to begin with? He plunged down at Mercy's neck with it, but I knew it wouldn't work. No stab wounds had been visible on her ghost in the times it appeared.

Blade inches from burying itself in Mercy's flesh, the point stopped, frozen in place. Pete's eyes went wide. He strained against the invisible force holding him, but to no avail.

"Going back on our bargain are we, Peter?" The desiccated voice again, this time from Mercy's lips. "That won't do at all. After all the effort I put in getting you to this point. Bringing me a vessel. I simply can't have you ruining all those plans now. Do you have any idea how exhausting it is entering people's dreams in my state? No, I don't suppose an ingrate like you would."

Mercy lifted a single finger, lips curling into a devilish smile at the gesture.

"No… no wait…" Pete pled for his life, but I knew it was already too late for him. The knife inexorably turned, point moving to point at his own face as the evil spirit used its power to twist Pete's wrist. The bones snapped under the pressure, but that didn't stop it from continuing its deadly journey.

I couldn't move. Audrey gripped my hand, and I felt hers trembling.

"Don't look," I whispered. No sense in her being traumatized more than she already was.

Blood poured down Pete's wrist from torn veins and flesh. The point of his knife now pushed toward his left eye. I lifted my gun, ready to take a shot. If she was going to die anyway, then better to put a bullet in her than to allow the thing inside Mercy to kill yet another person, regardless of the type of guy Pete seemed to be.

Mercy's other hand twitched, and the same power about to kill Pete arrested my movements. She turned her white-eyed gaze to me.

"I think not," Mercy said. "I'll deal with you and your little friend there once I've had my fun."

In the end, I had to watch as Pete's knife sunk millimeter-by-millimeter into his own eye. Oh, how he screamed. The pain must have been tremendous. The slowness of the process as it slid through his eye, and into his brain drew out his agony. I'd thought Sariah's earlier death throes were bad, but on further review, they were *nothing* compared to Pete's. Finally, his screams stopped, and Mercy let his corpse fall to the ground.

She turned to face me and Audrey, not a drop of Pete's blood on her.

I blinked, and in that space between moments, Mercy appeared directly in front of me. She put a hand on my shoulder and pushed me effortlessly to my knees.

"You will be the first to worship me." Not-Mercy looked around the graveyard and sniffed the air. "Is this your domain? Yes. Yes, it must be. I can *smell* your connection to it. And… and what's this? Oh… oh how sweet the fragrance of your youth fleeing. I see now why I was drawn here to this place. To this time. Days marking the day of birth from one such as you hold power… though not necessarily for you."

As she pushed me down harder, forcing me to prostrate myself before her, I dug my hands into the grass, willing my body to fight against the thing possessing Mercy.

"You fight," Mercy said, her laughter not her own, and sounding like a sandstorm in a desert. "Good. There is power in you. Once I've drank this body of sustenance, perhaps I will take yours. I will make you watch helplessly as I take your friend here as another sacrifice. As I take dozens of sacrifices. Hundreds. Thousands with no end."

Rocks and powder bit into the palm of my hands as I clenched them.

And I smiled, forcing my head up to look Mercy in her dead eyes.

"You shouldn't have gotten so close," I said.

I reached out, not knowing if my last-ditch gamble would pay off. A new look crossed Mercy's stolen face. Confusion. I grabbed her bare foot, pressing the dust and chunks in my grip into her pale flesh. Debris from the shattered headstones that had helped guard the phantom's resting place.

Mercy's ride-along shrieked, and the force of it felt like it would tear my head clean off my shoulders.

But the force trying to push me down vanished.

I stood, opened my other hand, and blew more of the dust into Mercy's face. When she took a breath to keep on wailing, she breathed in the powder.

Mercy coughed. Blinked. The white eyes cleared.

"Please," Mercy said, stretching a hand out to me. "Please."

Now I knew.

I knew.

I didn't want to do this. If this was indeed the real test, then it was going too far.

"Please. Please."

"Aud. I need your knife."

After a moment, I felt it pressed into my hand. Was it irony that this was the very knife I'd given her as a present last year? After her last supernatural encounter, she'd wanted protection, so I'd given her this blade.

I flicked it open.

"Please," Mercy continued, voice more urgent. "Please."

I nodded once. I hated this moment. But I knew if I didn't do this, the thing inside her—whatever it was and whoever it had once been—would get free.

I took a single, steadying breath, then lashed out with the knife, just like Mom and Dad had once taught me.

The stroke took Mercy in the throat.

Just like the ghost had shown me, blood slid down her neck, marring her once beautiful skin, and staining her white gown crimson.

Mercy fell to the ground, life leaking away to feed the hungry graveyard soil. She didn't even grab at the wound in her neck like most people would. She knew the score. I knelt at her side and pulled a handful of shotgun shells from the pouches on my vest.

"Aud, I need your help. Right-damn-now."

My best friend dropped to the ground beside me, no hesitation. "What do you need?"

"As I cut these shells open, if it's iron shavings and powder, dump it on the neck wound. All of it. Cake it on there. The iron should seal the ghost inside the corpse so it can't get out and get one of us."

I didn't wait for a reply, cutting into the first shell. I made quick work of the few dozen I carried. Salt and silver spilled out of many. Iron bearings out of a few more. When I found iron dust, I handed them to Audrey, who dumped them on Mercy's wound.

When I opened the last shell—thankfully more iron powder—I dumped it on the gash in Mercy's neck. Then I grabbed more headstone powder and pressed it on top of the coagulating iron, jerking my hand back when a small spark of green electricity sizzled over the cut I'd made. It fizzled out.

Mercy's last look up at me was a smile of gratitude that made me want to cry my eyes out.

"Let's get her to the grave in the clearing."

"Is this gonna work?" Audrey grabbed Mercy's feet.

I pointed up at the sky, where the clouds were fading. "It already is. We just need to get her in the ground."

With the supernatural power holding my cemetery hostage beginning to fade, the time slowing effect evaporated with it. We crossed the open ground to the grave like we normally would have and dropped Mercy into the hole. She vanished into the black void inside.

Audrey didn't drink. She hadn't in years, apparently. Even the mess we'd just gone through wouldn't get her to break her sobriety. I followed her example and pulled out two bottles of Mexican Coke. She downed half of hers in a single pull.

"Friday, what just happened?"

Outside, the skies were blue. The sun would set in a couple hours. We'd gone out into the graveyard in the morning, and the strange passage of time made the day pass by faster than it should have.

After throwing Mercy into the grave, Tombstone Estates had returned to its regular form in the blink of an eye. Like a magician's trick, that dark world vanished. Not permanently. No. Never permanently. I doubted I'd seen the last of it, or the last of that evil spirit.

"Apparently, that was the test my parents warned me was coming my way."

"Doesn't seem like a fair test."

"No. No it doesn't."

Silence stretched for a few minutes as we sipped at the Cokes. Audrey looked shaken, and I couldn't blame her. After everything, my biggest fear at that moment was her walking out the door, and never coming back. I didn't have many friends, so I knew the value of the few I'd managed to gather over the years. Audrey was my best friend. The sister I chose since all my blood relatives were dead.

Maybe she read my mind, or maybe she just knew me better than anyone else, because she looked up from her drink and smiled.

"Hey. I'm gonna be alright."

"You sure?" I asked.

"No doubt. Can I ask you a weird question, though?"

"Of course. Anything."

"Do you think I was supposed to be here?"

"Huh. You know… I'm not sure. Maybe. Why?"

"I never really believed in *fate*, or whatever before." She nearly spat the word out. It was the only time I'd ever heard her speak with any measure of vitriol.

I shook my head. "I don't think it's fate. I don't put any stock in that sort of thing."

"What then? I came by? Just happened to have the knife you gave me? Seems like—"

"No." I cut her off by waggling the Coke bottle at her. "No, don't go there."

"Then what am I supposed to believe?"

"What do you want to believe?"

Audrey leaned back in her chair, a pensive look creeping onto her face. She suddenly stood, knocking her chair over backwards. "Hold on."

She ran outside, only to return with a package in hand.

A present.

"I got you this," she said, handing it to me. "I didn't think much of it, and it's a simple thing. Just… just open it. Happy Birthday. And happy Friday the Thirteenth, I guess?"

I let out a short laugh and took the gift. When I tore the paper away, I revealed a picture frame underneath holding a small canvas print of me with my parents. Smiles all around, we stood in front of the entry gate to the cemetery. One of my favorite pictures of us all, and one of our last times together before their deaths.

"It's perfect." I'm not normally the sappy sort, but a rogue tear escaped to run down my cheek. "Thanks, Aud. This is awesome."

"Maybe that's why I'm here," she said quietly. "Maybe they reached out in their own way and pushed me here. At least… well… that's what I'm gonna believe."

"Good enough for me."

"The view of the cemetery is impeccable from this floor. Such quiet neighbors, and so peaceful in the sunlight. This story's residents are all dedicated to celebrating each other's milestones. A community, truly."

* * * * *

A Farewell from the Apartment Manager

"*Which of the floors has been your favorite? Surely one felt exactly right to your needs. Each story has so very much to offer. Oh no, I can't possibly take you back down the stairs, they only work in one direction, and unfortunately the elevator has recently gone out of service. I suppose you must stay…or, in the end, there is one other way down. It does involve a rather sudden stop to a long drop, but you'll have a quiet moment to reflect on our time together. Either way, I'm sure I'll see you quite soon. As I said before, our residents truly do seem to stay forever…*"

*****

Contributing Authors

Dan Bridgwater

Dan grew up watching Star Trek and Godzilla movies. This love of monster movies and Science Fiction led to his reading every bit of SciFi and fantasy he could get his hands on, from Asimov to Zelazny with Pratchett and McCaffrey sprinkled in as well. Eventually, all those stories in his head reached some sort of critical mass and now he's starting to create his own. An Army Brat and a Marine Veteran, Dan has lived on both coasts, the Midwest, Korea and Kuwait. He now lives with his wife and daughters in Colorado, where he supports training for the US Military.

D.J. Butler

D.J. (Dave) Butler has been a lawyer, a consultant, an editor, a corporate trainer, and a registered investment banking representative, and he is now a Consulting Editor for Baen Books. His novels published by Baen Books include the Witchy War series (Witchy Eye, Witchy Winter, Witchy Kingdom, and Serpent Daughter), In the Palace of Shadow and Joy, Between Princesses and Other Jobs, and Abbott in Darkness, as well as The Cunning Man and The Jupiter Knife, co-written with Aaron Michael Ritchey, and Time Trials, co-written with M.A. Rothman. He also writes for children: the steampunk fantasy adventure tales The Kidnap Plot, the Giant's Seat, and The Library Machine are published by Knopf. Other novels include City of the Saints from WordFire Press and The Wilding Probate from Immortal Works. His novels have won the Whitney Award, the Association for Mormon Letters Award for Novel, and the Dragon Award.

Dave also organizes writing retreats and anarcho-libertarian writers' events and travels the country to sell books. He tells many stories as a gamemaster with a gaming group some of whom he's been playing with since sixth grade. He plays guitar and banjo whenever he can and likes to hang out in Utah with his wife, their children, and the family dog. https://davidjohnbutler.com/

Steve Diamond

Steve Diamond is a Horror, Fantasy, Thriller, and Science Fiction author for Baen, Gallant Knight Games, and numerous other small publications. His most recent works are a collection of short fiction, *What Hellhounds Dream*, a Dark Fantasy/Horror novel co-written with Larry Correia, *Servants Of War*, and the Supernatural Thriller novel *Residue*. He is also the co-host of the writing advice podcast, The WriterDojo.

Kacey Ezell

Kacey Ezell is a helicopter pilot with 3000+ hours in the UH-1N Huey, Mi-171, and EC130

helicopters. When not beating the air into submission, she writes scifi/fantasy/horror/noir/ alternate history fiction. She is a two-time Dragon Award Finalist for Best Alternate History and won the 2018 Year's Best Military and Adventure Science Fiction Readers' Choice Award. She has written multiple bestselling novels published with Chris Kennedy Publishing, Baen Books, and Blackstone Publishing. She is married with two daughters. You can find out more and join her mailing list at www.kaceyezell.net

Declan Finn

As penance for his sins, Declan Finn spent over 40 years in New York City, but has since made his escape to Texas. He is the author of books ranging from thrillers to urban fantasy to SciFi, including the Dragon Award Nominated Novel for Best horror in 2016, Honor at Stake, and the 2017 follow-up, Live and Let Bite, now published by Three Ravens Press. His story, "They Burn Witches, Don't They?" is set in his world of Saint Tommy, NYPD, from Tuscany Bay Books. Finn is known for being annoyingly Catholic, his action sequences, and writing faster than most readers can keep up with. In less than a decade, he has written over 30 novels, and is waiting for all of them to be published. He's been part of multiple anthologies and will write for anyone.

H.Y. Gregor

H.Y. Gregor was born in Portland, Oregon, but will always call the mountains of Colorado home. She has a bachelor's in political science but managed to narrowly avoid law school and now happily uses her background to create intricate, colorful backdrops for her favorite work writing speculative fiction of all flavors.

Her debut novel Stonewhisper released from Eldros Legacy Press in June 2023, and her short fiction has appeared in Particular Passages: South Wing, Phoenix Initiative: First Missions, and Standing Free: Stories from the Last Brigade Universe, with more exciting projects in the works.

For free short stories and updates find her at hygregor.com

Facebook at H.Y. Gregor –Author

Twitter and Instagram @toviahy.

Rob Howell

Rob Howell is the publisher of New Mythology Press, including his work as editor of the Libri Valoris anthologies of heroic fantasy. He's the creator of the Firehall Sagas and an author in the Four Horsemen Universe. He writes epic fantasy, space opera, military science fiction, alternate history, and whatever else seems fun.

He's a reformed medieval academic, a former IT professional, and a retired soda jerk.

His parents discovered quickly books were the only way to keep Rob quiet. He latched onto the Hardy Boys series first and then anything he could reach. Without books, it's unlikely all three would have survived.

You can find him here:

Website: robhowell.org

His Blog: robhowell.org/blog

Firehall Sagas: firehallsagas.com

Amazon: amazon.com/-/e/B00X95LBB0

Twitter: @Rhodri2112

Rob's Riddles: patreon.com/rhodri2112, a collection of riddles he wrote and snippets from both his own works in progress and those of New Mythology Press.

Kevin Ikenberry

Kevin Ikenberry is a life-long space geek and retired Army officer. As an adult, he managed the U.S. Space Camp program and served in space operations before Space Force was a thing. He's an international bestselling science fiction author and renowned writing instructor which is pretty cool because he never imagined being either one of those – he still wants to be an astronaut. Kevin's debut novel, *Sleeper Protocol*, was hailed by *Publishers Weekly* as "an emotionally powerful debut." His twenty-five novels science fiction novels include *The Crossing*, *Vendetta Protocol*, *Eminence Protocol*, *Runs In The Family*, *Peacemaker*, *Honor The Threat*, *Stand or Fall*, *Fields of Fire*, and *Harbinger*. He is core author of the mega-bestselling Four Horsemen Universe, with more than a dozen novels spawned by *Peacemaker*. Kevin is an Active Member of the International Association of Science Fiction and Fantasy Authors, International Thriller Writers, and SIGMA – the science fiction think tank. Kevin continues to work with space every day and lives in Colorado with his family.

Matt Novotny

A lover of Science Fiction, Fantasy, and Horror, Matt Novotny has been an avid reader since childhood. Still firmly convinced that the worlds between the pages are more interesting than the one he lives in, Matt began writing in 2020 in order to escape the voices in his head, or at least quiet them down.

When not writing he spends time gaming, antiquing, or wandering in the mountains, A Colorado native, he lives in Littleton, Colorado, surrounded by ever-increasing piles of books, Lovecraft collectables, and unfinished home and garden projects.

Connect with Matt at:

Website: www.mattnovotny.net

Facebook: www.facebook.com/MattNovotnyWrites

Nick Steverson and Melissa Olthoff AKA The Evil Twins

Allegedly separated at birth, Nick and Melissa are rumored to share a single brain cell. Nobody is entirely sure if they each use half the cell all the time, or if they pass it back and forth like some sort of weird timeshare. Regardless, they always seem to be thinking the same thing at the same time despite Nick living in the alligator, snake, and tourist infested sweaty armpit of North-West Florida, and Melissa residing in the post-apocalyptic Mad-Max wasteland of West Tennessee. When not splitting the use of their one brain cell, Nick drives a liquor truck and Melissa is a systems accountant for Uncle Sam.

Each evil twin has written works in the Salvage Title Universe, The Four Horsemen Universe, This Fallen World, and The Last Brigade Universe.

Both are also Imadjinn Award winners. Nick is the 2023 Imadjinn Winner for Best Science Fiction Novel, and Melissa is the Imadjinn Award Winner for Best Short Story. Melissa was also a finalist in the 2023 BAEN fantasy contest and ultimately took 2nd place.

You can find them at:

Website: www.nicksteverson.com / www.melissaolthoff.net

Facebook: www.facebook.com/nick.steverson.56 / www.facebook.com/melissa.moroney.5

Amazon: www.amazon.com/stores/Nick-Steverson/author/B08B2XNNXX / www.amazon.com/stores/Melissa-Olthoff/author/B0887TC95H

Mark Wandrey

International bestselling author of military sci-fi, space opera, and zombie apocalypse, Mark Wandrey is also the only 4 time DragonCon Dragon Award finalist!

Newest Release - Blood in the Water - Book 5 in the 4HU Frontiers series, set in the Four Horsemen mil-sf universe.

Living the full time RV lifestyle as a modern day nomad, Mark Wandrey has been writing science fiction since he was in grade school. He launched his professional career in 2004 with the release of Earth Song - Overture. Now, 15 years later, he has more than 25 books out, including many bestsellers.

Sign up for his mailing list at http://www.worldmaker.us/news-flash-sign-up-page/ check out his Patreon page for free stuff at https://www.patreon.com/MarkHWandrey or shop on Amazon at amazon.com/author/www.worldmaker.us.

Marie Whittaker

Marie Whittaker enjoys teaching about publishing and project management for writers. She works as Associate Publisher at WordFire Press and Director at Superstars Writing Seminars. She also puts in time as personal assistant to Kevin J. Anderson. In 2021, she co-founded the epic fantasy world of Eldros Legacy. Marie is an award-winning essayist and author of horror, fantasy, children's books and supernatural thrillers. She is the creator of The Adventures of Lola Hopscotch, is published in *Weird Tales*, and habitually adopts rescue animals. Find out more about her at www.mariewhittaker.com.

Marisa Wolf

Joelle Marisa Wolf is a second-generation nerd who started writing genre stories at six. At least one was good enough to be laminated, and she's been chasing that high ever since. Over the years she's taught middle school, been headbutted by an alligator, earned a black belt in Tae Kwon Do, and finally decided to finish all the half-started stories in her head.

She writes SFF throughout multiple corners of the genre, including military science fiction and space opera as a core author in the bestselling Four Horseman Universe, urban fantasy in Hit World, and video and table-top gaming in tie-in stories. Her debut solo novel, *Beyond Enemies*, will be out from Baen in February of 2024.

Marisa is currently based in Texas, though she lives in an RV with her husband and their two absurd rescue dogs, so it's anyone's guess where in the country she is. More at www.marisawolf.net

Christopher Woods

Writer of fiction, teller of tales, and professional liar was born way too long ago to be talking about it and has spent the majority of his life with a book in hand. He is known for his popular Soulguard series and creating the shared universes in The Fallen World series and the B.E.NT. series. He has also written the Legend series in the Four Horsemen Universe, several works in the Salvage system universe, and working in the Car Warriors Universe. With books ranging from fantasy to post-apocalyptic and military science fiction, there should be something for everyone. He lives in Woodbury, TN with his wife Wendy. As a former carpenter of thirty years, he spends his time between various building projects and writing new books. To contact him, go to www.theprofessionalliar.com and send him a message. https://theprofessionalliar.com/

Take a look at some of our other award-winning series at
https://threeravenspublishing.com/series-universes/

Visit us at https://www.threeravenspublishing.com and sign up for our
newsletter for the latest and greatest news on upcoming titles and events.

Other series and titles you might enjoy.

DECLAN FINN
DECLAN FINN
DECLAN FINN
DECLAN FINN
Demons Are Forever
Honor At Stake
Live & Let Bite
Good to the Last Drop
The Dragon Award Nominated Series
FREE on Kindle Unlimited!

AVAILABLE ON
AMAZON
JOINT TASK FORCE
13
HOLDING THE LINE
BETWEEN HEAVEN AND HELL

MYSTERY,
MAGIC &
MAYHEM
WITH A TWIST
OF ROMANCE
J.F. POSTHUMUS
FIND ME on AMAZON

B.E.N.T.
BIOLOGIC   ENHANCED   NASCENT   TALENT

THE RAVEN
AND
THE CROW
MICHAEL K. FALCIANI
FIND ME
ON AMAZON

STARFLIGHT

IT CAME FROM THE
TRAILER PARK

3R
Three Ravens
Publishing
Are you looking for fun, new fiction?
The FEATHER and the LAMP
CROSSWAYS
THE WAYMAN CHRONICLES
MICHAEL J ALLEN
DARK STORM RISING
LEGENDS
STAFF OF CHAOS
The Written Word Will Never Be The Same…
https://www.threeravenspublishing.com
Veteran Owned and Operated

You can also keep up to date with our latest release announcements on Scifi.radio and get some of the best fandom programing on the planet.

Scifi for your Wifi

Spare Parts Emporium
and Towing
est. Henry's Garage ™
For all of your Rare
& Spare Parts Needs

SILLY LADY
PEPPER
COMPANY

FELLHAVEN
Restaurant & Tavern